THE CHRONICLES OF LUX VERITAS

Master of Destiny

CHRISTOPHER DIGNAN

THE CHRONICLES OF LUX VERITAS
MASTER OF DESTINY

This is a work of fiction. All of the characters, names, incidents, organizations, and dialogue in this novel are either the products of the author's imagination or are used fictitiously.

iUniverse books may be ordered through booksellers or by contacting:

iUniverse
1663 Liberty Drive
Bloomington, IN 47403
www.iuniverse.com
1-800-Authors (1-800-288-4677)

Because of the dynamic nature of the Internet, any web addresses or links contained in this book may have changed since publication and may no longer be valid. The views expressed in this work are solely those of the author and do not necessarily reflect the views of the publisher, and the publisher hereby disclaims any responsibility for them.

Any people depicted in stock imagery provided by Thinkstock are models, and such images are being used for illustrative purposes only. Certain stock imagery © Thinkstock.

ISBN: 978-1-4917-4637-0 (sc)
ISBN: 978-1-4917-4636-3 (e)

Library of Congress Control Number: 2014916407

Printed in the United States of America.

iUniverse rev. date: 10/01/2014

Also by Christopher Dignan:

THE CHRONICLES OF LUX VERITAS
(PART ONE) – EVIL AT THE GATES

For my lovely wife Aygul and my wonderful son Eric,
for your unconditional love and your infinite patience,

and,

In memory of Jeanine, Raymond and Jean-Marie,
now resting well beyond the Crystal Gates...

"Je me souviens"

Contents

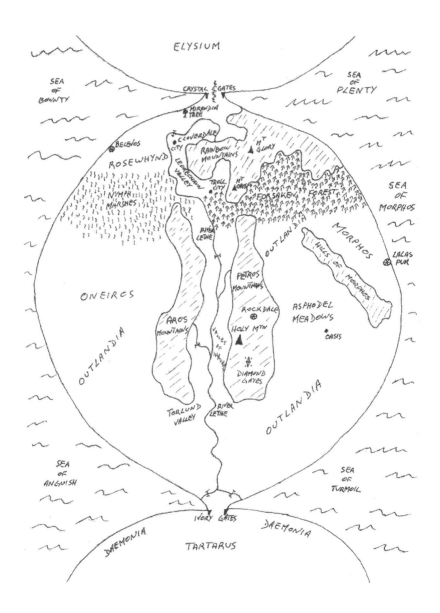

PROLOGUE

In the beginning, legend tells us, there was nothing ... nothing but the Lord Creator. When at last he woke up from the deepest slumber, he said, *"I am"*—for he was. This was the truth.

And he was the truth. And he was the light. And he was good.

Following the awakening, a little voice within asked, *"Am I?"* This was the doubt.

And the doubt was the lie. And the lie was evil. And evil was chaos.

Thus was born the eternal struggle between the Lord Creator and Chaos, the light and the shadow, the truth and the lie ...

LUX VERITAS AND THE EVIL ETERNAL

Chapter I

The Stealth Demon

"The universe is made mostly of dark matter and dark energy, and we don't know what either of them is."
—Saul Perlmutter, astrophysicist.

I

The silent meteor came shooting across the celestial aether with a vengeance. Like a guided missile, the translucent nether-ball crashed down deep in the cornfields of Sherbrooke County.

The sphere of evil released its messenger.

The Stealth Demon had landed.

No one saw it. No one heard it. No one was any the wiser ... except, of course, for the ever intuitive Solas Gambit.

What the hell was that? he thought as his eyes sprung open.

He adjusted his optic to the early morning light. The start of a bright and hot summer day greeted him. Indeed, summer had arrived in Sherbrooke. Birds were chirping. Trees were now in full bloom and the delicate fragrance of jasmine, lilac and wild flowers softly drifted inside the bedroom, through the draught of the open window. But today, something was unusual. The birds seemed agitated and the distinct odor of smoke and incense filled the air too.

What could Orenda be up to on the old Iroquois lands so early on a summer morning?

In disbelief and confused by his senses, Solas shook his head.

Not again ... I think I'm having flashbacks.

Solas rested his hands behind his head and remained motionless in bed for a little while longer, staring at the shifting images forming on the textured ceiling as he pondered the significance of his latest premonition.

Suddenly, heart racing and gripped by an overwhelming feeling of discomfort, Solas flung the bed sheets to the ground and jumped out of bed. He came to a frightening conclusion.

He's here. I don't know how, but he's here.

Solas fidgeted nervously as he threw on his shorts and slipped on an A-shirt with a logo crested onto it: 'Property of Central High'. He velcroed tight his sandals and tussled his sun-bleached blonde hair back into shape.

Possessed by some inexplicable paranoia, Solas carefully made his way to the bedroom door – which he had left opened a crack – and glanced into the hallway. He stared down the length of the corridor. Nothing. After a short moment, he lifted his eyes, regained his composure and smiled.

Come on, get real. Let's go get some breakfast already.

Reassured, Solas pulled on the door handle and swung open the bedroom door. Suddenly, like a flash from an old nightmare, the Stealth Demon appeared around the far wall. The beast was tall, dark as the night, and slick as a reptile. Its front limbs were short and thin, its hands bearing bony stretched fingers with sharp curvy claws. Its hind limbs were sturdy. The beast stood positioned like a kangaroo, the end of its feet equipped with three outstretched toes and long sharp talons at the heels. A long tail supported its frame and helped balance its movements. The demon swayed it back and forth in rhythm as it flaunted its vicious spaded tail. Its chest looked impregnable; its upper body muscular and ripped with tendon tissues. Its face was slender but defined, with pointed elf-like ears, protruding stubby horns set high on his brow, a slimy goatee, thin drooling lips, sharp cutter teeth, a slithery tongue, and set deep into its sockets the hollow incandescent eyes of a mad killer.

Shocked, Solas froze on the spot. Their eyes locked together. The beast gazed at him – at once with glee and contempt – while uttering an array of fizzled and gurgled sounds. Panic struck Solas. He suddenly worried about Grandma Jeanie still sleeping in the adjacent bedroom, unaware. He looked back inside his sleeping quarters and aimed his sights on the open window at the far end of his room as a means of escape.

"Over this way," he whispered to the demon, signalling to him with his index finger to approach. The demon's delight continued. As Solas backed up into his room, he snatched his hockey stick and jumped over his workstation and computer chair before reaching his escape route. The Stealth Demon followed as ordered and now stood in the bedroom doorway. It hissed again.

"What do you want? I have nothing." Solas explained.

The Stealth Demon seemed to understand and made an effort to communicate with Solas, addressing him in a slow, broken and slurry voice.

"The sword." the beast demanded.

"Well, sorry buddy. As you can see for yourself, I don't have it anymore," Solas answered. "Would you settle for a piece of my shiny new hockey stick instead?"

Following Solas's taunt, the Stealth Demon hissed and growled.

"You die," the beast replied in a quivering voice.

Solas never lifted his eyes from the beast. He positioned himself on the ledge of the windowsill and prepared to leap out the short distance to the front lawn of the house.

Solas delayed his jump until the very last moment, but the Stealth Demon stalled when suddenly Grandma Jeanie's bedroom door opened. The whipping tail motion of the beast had awakened her.

"What's all that banging noise, Solas?" she asked, before her eyes met up with the beast standing only feet away from her.

Grandma Jeanie went straight into shock, unable to move, breathe or think. As the beast looked over his shoulder and snarled at the easy prey that presented itself, Solas yelled out to the demon.

"I have Lux Veritas. Follow me if you can, slimeball."

And Solas exited out the window and began to run through the front yard toward the street curb. The Stealth Demon momentarily lost sight of his prize and, fearing losing track of Solas completely, rushed to the window's edge, sharp as a whip. The beast watched its treasure getting away.

2

In a flash, Solas reached his road bike, tied up to the front fence of the property. The demon jumped out the window and kept its eyes fixed on the boy. After a light struggle loosening his bike – which felt like an eternity to Solas – he saddled his ride and began to pedal fast down the road, following the descent of the steep hill. The beast followed, speeding up in hot pursuit.

None of the city folks took notice of the strange event occurring on their street so early on a Saturday morning. This middle-class community was usually quiet at this hour of the day. The district took pride in its civil compliance and otherwise exemplified the ideal of the all-American neighbourhood. Not a soul could be found stirring at six o'clock in the morning, except for rare exceptions.

Solas sped up as he rounded the corner of the next intersection and met up, quite by circumstance, on a group of young revellers – the exception to the rule in Sherbrooke – who were killing off the remnants of a few bottles of booze as they returned home from a hot night of partying.

Solas skidded to a halt in front of them, kicking up some dust and gravel as he stopped. The teenagers reacted by stepping aside in order to avoid Solas whom they imagined about to crash into them. One of the tallest fellows of the group, which was made up of about six young adults – flashy Harley-type rockers clad in dangling metals and chains – approached the reckless bicycle rider and objected to his cockiness.

"Hey watch it, man! Where ya flying so fast? You seen a ghost or what?" the chubby Afro-American said, as he puffed out his chest and swayed a half-consumed bottle of rye in his hand.

"Listen guys, I really don't have time to explain, but there is a freak in a Halloween costume following me. Stall him for me, will ya? I owe you one. And tell him I went the other way."

Solas pointed in the opposite direction. Upon those words and without hesitation, Solas handed off his bike to the startled stranger standing before him, slapping him on the shoulder to thank him, and ran full speed between the two nearest houses, two-stepping over a six-foot wooden fence leading to the back yard of a private property.

"Whaddaya mean a Halloween freak?" yelled the puzzled leader of the group. "What's going on?"

Solas disappeared out of sight.

"Wow bro … That's a hell of a bike man," slurred one of his comrades-in-arms, a beer smelling scrawny redhead with a stand-up Mohawk haircut, a bull-ring pierced through the nose, a missing front tooth, and a tattooed crown of thorns around his neck. "Say, your fat ass won't fit on that thing, bro. Why don't ya let me have it?" He smiled at his buddy as he grabbed a hold of the handlebars.

"I'll let you have it all right. Now get your filthy hands off my wheels man," he replied, jerking loose the bicycle.

Just as the rest of the boys gathered around the bicycle, jiving and jeering their good buddy about his new windfall, the angered demon rounded the bend. The beast slowed down as it came into visual contact with the group, but kept a steady pace, walking straight toward the young men. Recognizing the bike, it grumbled and looked around the area trying to locate the fugitive.

"Holy shit!" said one of the revellers. "Would you check out this guy's costume?"

The group kept quiet, staring, sensing something haywire with the creature approaching. Its appearance looked surreal. As the Stealth Demon neared and stood only feet away, the group began to step back, using the bike as a makeshift barrier. The creature stopped in front of them and breathed heavily, wheezing as it did so. It spewed slobber from its mouth and its piercing eyes studied each individual in the group.

No one dared to move.

For a brief moment, it was silence. A canine began to bark in a nearby yard; a guard dog yelping at a scurrying Solas. The demon turned its head and tweaked its ears toward the source of the noise. It winced and grimaced at the thought of Solas getting away.

"What are you doing in this friggin' costume, man?" asked the drunken redhead, the brashest soul among the lot. "That's one wicked looking outfit. Love the eye effects ... looks so friggin' real," he sputtered. The partier let out a chuckle before guzzling back the rest of his beer and crushing the aluminum can with his hand.

"Here ... have a beer and chill out!" said Willy, the pack leader. He offered a cold one to the curious being standing only feet away from him on the opposite side of the bicycle. The beast continued to breathe heavily, slobbering gobs of drool onto the street pavement. It briefly considered the silver can and hissed as it whacked the object out of the donor's hands.

Willy yelled to the heavens as he pulled back his bleeding hand. The beast had sliced right through the flesh with three of its razor sharp claws. The scream startled Solas who stopped running, looking back in the distance and imagining the events that were developing. All the while, the guard dog kept barking and growling in the adjacent yard. It wouldn't be long before the neighbours would wake up. Now that he had cleared the last residences standing in his way, Solas resumed course, his eyes fixed at the top of the hill. Up there stood the old Iroquois reserve, the home of shaman Orenda who was once the trusted guardian of the mighty Sword of Genesis, Lux Veritas. If anyone could help at a time like this, Orenda could.

Blood began to flow from Willy's hand, soaking up his clothes as he bent down and applied pressure on the wound by keeping it tight against his body. The cursing started up and the tattooed redhead was first to toss his crushed aluminum can at the demon, bouncing it off his chest with a ping. Two other boys pulled out their jackknives while another wrapped a spike-clad set of brass knuckles around his fist.

"Come here you freak. We're gonna bust you up now!" one of the boys said. He picked up the bike and threw it at the beast.

Using only its left arm, the demon batted the bicycle away with impressive force. The beast then rushed its assailants and, with one vicious swipe of its tail, brought three of the boys down like bowling pins. The demon screeched and spewed gunk from its mouth as it tensed up its body muscles like a Mister Universe bodybuilder in a show of strength. The drunken redhead deftly snuck up from behind and swung his knife at the beast, only to see it cling off its back.

The Stealth Demon whipped around and seized the impetuous young man with one hand, grabbing him by the throat, and lifting him up at arm's length, clear two feet off the ground. The tattooed punk with the Mohawk hairdo thrashed about and choked up, struggling to fight for air. The beast, gargling a mumbo jumbo of sounds between its clenched teeth, swung the boy around to face his companions. The frantic young man's eyes began to roll up to the heavens as he appeared to lose consciousness from the pressure exerted on his carotid arteries. The beast's claws began to dig deeper into the neck of the dangling victim, carving the skin and drawing blood.

Just as the punk's body went limp, the beast tossed him effortlessly to the wayside, right smack into the middle of the three young men still sprawled out on the ground. Witnessing this brute show of strength, the boys, now convinced that the freak standing before them was no ordinary mortal disguised in a Halloween costume, began to hyperventilate and froze with panic. The Stealth Demon licked the traces of human blood clean off its fingers and claws with its outstretched, snake-like, slithering tongue.

The frightened young men quickly sobered up, scrambled to their feet and bolted away from the beast, leaving their wounded and unconscious drinking buddy behind.

The demon now turned its attention toward the barking animal, and like a first class bloodhound, picked up the scent of the runaway. The Stealth Demon scooted away and without a noise disappeared like a shadow behind the walls and bushes of the closest residence.

3

Solas continued his brisk pace, climbing up steadfast to the Iroquois belvedere, cutting through the natural hedge of cedar woods at the foot of the hill to reach the clearing. He struggled to keep his footing as he slipped on the slick morning dew covering the blades of grass that overgrew the open fields. He tired as he pushed on, and prayed that Orenda was home.

The Stealth Demon followed the walkway and surged into the backyard of the posh residence where the watchdog stood guard; an aroused, slick and nimble jet-black Doberman intent on getting some long-awaited action. The demon never batted an eye and paid no heed to the silent canine now rushing toward it. Instead, the hell-sent gazed up behind the properties into the distant slopes with hawk-like precision and grinned as he honed in once again on his moving target scampering up the hill. The

Doberman growled as it lunged for the intruder, and with a cat-like reflex, the demon stopped suddenly and straight-armed the snarling animal, discharging such a heinous dosage of willpower that it crippled the canine instantly into submission, sending it yelping into a cowering crouch.

This unwelcomed distraction angered the demon. The beast took a moment to approach the turtling Doberman, leaning over it, hissing, and sending such telepathic waves of loathsome fear into the canine that the guard dog began to convulse. The Stealth Demon soon turned away and hurried to resume its course, swiftly jumping up and over the last fence barrier before disappearing through the trees, and charging up the incline toward the Iroquois sacred lands.

As Solas reached the crest, he began to yell out Orenda's name. The modern clubhouse and the open Mongolian yurt structure, which was often used for ritual potlatches and which housed a cenotaph for funerals, appeared vacant. The stern expression of the proud eagle head figure dominating the Totem pole seemed to convey a silent and ominous message to the young visitor. The smell of fresh burning incense still pervaded the area. Solas, still catching his breath, looked away, cupped his hands around his mouth and yelled out Orenda's name at the top of his lungs. The sound echoed between the buildings. Just then, the old shaman appeared from the rear of the clubhouse.

"Orenda!" said Solas, relieved to see the high priest.

The shaman approached dressed in full ritual gear, worn only for special occasions or for urgent prayer convocations.

"Solas!" answered the shaman, his voice quivering with concern. He lifted his head and hands skyward to thank providence. "You are a Godsend! I have important news."

"Just wait a second, Orenda," said Solas, "I need your help. It's urgent!"

The two began to babble over each other's voices, each one trying to monopolize the conversation. Solas tried to explain how he needed to find Lux Veritas; and Orenda, that there was more trouble in Purgator. Suddenly, the shaman overheard a few telling words from his young friend Solas.

"What did you say?' he asked, begging Solas to repeat.

"I said there is a demon chasing me," repeated Solas. "He's right here in Sherbrooke. I'm not sure how he got here. All I know is that I lost him down this hill. He's come here looking for Lux Veritas! He's mean and nasty. I have never seen his kind before. Help!"

Orenda stood speechless for a brief moment, as though he had just seen a ghost. Solas studied the old Iroquois's gaze, expecting a response. He grabbed the shaman by the shoulders and shook him slightly, hoping for a reaction.

"Well ... did you hear what I just said?" asked Solas.

"Is your demon tall as the bear and dark as the raven?" Orenda asked calmly.

"Yes, that's him ... that's him!"

"Is he muscular like the puma with hollow eyes like the witch-owl?"

Solas, perplexed at Orenda's words, stood straight up and froze.

"Yes ... I think so," he answered with some hesitation.

"Well then, it seems that the quintessence of evil has now reached the sacred grounds of the elders," said Orenda.

Solas slowly turned around and saw the beast standing only 50 feet away. They stared at each other. The Stealth Demon seeming to cherish his moment, drooling and hissing with perverted delight at seeing his next victims without recourse.

"I need Lux Veritas," Solas whispered to Orenda.

"Well, luck is on our side. I have it in my care, Solas. Shaman Chepi sent it down through the Wheel of Souls at first dawn," replied Orenda softly, never lifting his eyes off the beast for one moment. "That's what I wanted to tell you. Chepi also told me to warn you about the Stealth Demon."

"Stealth Demon?" repeated Solas.

"Yes," confirmed Orenda, "he has special powers and he is clever like the fox."

"Ugly as a goat too," added Solas. "Where is the sword now?"

"Same place," replied the shaman.

The Stealth Demon began to stir and advanced in a slow deliberate manner toward his two stranded targets, studying them. Solas threw a quick glance toward the open cenotaph lying under the ceremonial yurt structure. He casually began to make his way toward the monument, all the while keeping his eyes focused on his foe.

"Go. I'll keep him busy," said Orenda. The old seer began to chant, lifting his head and his arms up and down toward the heavens, shaking them, and then stomping his feet in rhythm, entering into a native spiritual dance ritual. The decoy worked, and for a short moment the hell-sent seemed oddly entertained by the oracle's colorful display.

Solas profited of the few seconds offered him by the diversion to edge his way toward the cenotaph. But the Stealth Demon suddenly froze, perplexed, as it noticed Solas's evasive manoeuvre. The beast now ignored shaman Orenda's gimmick and its full attention returned to the boy. It snapped, growled and hissed, showing certain displeasure at the idea of being duped yet again. Solas froze too. Orenda redoubled his trance, chanting louder, jumping higher. The demon turned to Solas and began to pick up the pace, now charging towards him. On a whim and a prayer, Solas turned and ran to the cenotaph hoping to find, like he had a few months earlier, his trustworthy weapon Lux Veritas laying inside the vault of the open sepulchre.

The beast caught up fast to the scrambling teenager, but at the nick of time Solas managed to reach the crypt where, as Orenda had hinted, the mighty Lux Veritas rested, shining like a timeless and priceless jewel. Solas quickly seized the sword and turned to face the charging threat. The weapon activated and lit up like glinting silver, a crackling white charge running up and down the blade. The Stealth Demon came to a sliding halt and came face to face with its nemesis. Not daring to strike Solas and face a certain death, the wily demon hissed and then proceeded to let out a shriek of rage so loud that its message of frustration likely echoed all the way to the deepest nether regions of Tartarus, abode to his master and Lord of Darkness, Chaos.

Orenda had stopped chanting now and observed the situation with bated breath. Solas flaunted the weapon and brandished the sword before the beast, forcing it to back off one careful step at a time. The beast continued hissing, while quivering and foaming at the mouth. At last, the two stopped and squared off in a staring duel, separated only by the blade of Lux Veritas.

"You're a smart boy, huh?" said Solas, "You know about the power of the sword, don't you?"

The demon growled.

"Come on then … take it!" Solas implored the beast. "Come on you overgrown chicken. Take it. That's what you came for, ain't it?"

The beast's anger seemed to diminish for a moment. It reached out its right hand and began to address Solas again in a broken, jittery voice, but trying a soothing tone.

"Master wants his weapon … Give."

"*His* weapon! That's fresh," replied Solas. "Just like that, huh?"

"Master is eternal, foolish boy … what Master wants, Master gets," the drooling beast articulated, with an odd expression of assurance and contentment.

"Well, that's not how I remember it," retorted Solas. "You should double-check your facts."

The demon began to lose its temper once again and it clenched its teeth just before setting a rendezvous with Solas.

"I go now, Outlander," it said, snickering. "But we shall meet again at the Crossing."

Solas frowned, confused by what seemed like a bunch of aimless words.

"What … what crossing? Purgator?" asked Solas.

The Stealth Demon grinned and revealed a round object somewhat smaller than a baseball, which it held in the hollow of its right hand. The curio resembled a crystal ball of a dark obsidian color, active with flashy swirls of deep green shades and blood-red hues. Attached on top of the object was a loop, akin to a pin, through which the beast proceeded to insert its index finger, producing a resonant and harmonious chime. Then, as Solas and Orenda looked on, the beast lifted the object high above its head. The Stealth Demon then mumbled a series of phrases in a language that seemed perfectly natural to the beast, but sounded like it might originate, one could only guess, from the land of the damned. The object grew and transformed into a transparent ball which enveloped the Stealth Demon, forming a cocoon. Slowly, the ball darkened into a swirling mass, spinning faster and faster, until the demon with the stern gaze vanished behind the murky haze. After a short delay, the object lifted and, in utter silence and without warning, streaked out of sight beyond the blue yonder, past the line of the firmament where the nether-ball ignited into a bright flash of light as it exited the ozone layer into the upper mesosphere.

4

Solas and Orenda, shaken but relieved, remained fixated upon the abnormal event they just witnessed long after the object had disappeared beyond the skyline. Lux Veritas deactivated. Solas, perplexed, slowly lowered his weapon, still clutching the hilt with both hands as the tip of the blade came down and softly kissed the ground.

Solas sat down on the lower step of the cenotaph, resting his forehead on the sword's crossguard while staring at Orenda with a look of utmost disbelief. The shaman, standing motionless, stared right back, incredulous. *How could the Stealth Demon, this most vile and unspeakable taboo, dare trample on our most revered Iroquois grounds and desecrate the spirit of our elders … not to mention scaring the bejesus out of me?*

"Wow, that was a close call," the shaman finally uttered.

"Tell me, what in the hell was that demon doing here in Sherbrooke, Orenda?" asked Solas.

"I don't know … he wants the sword I guess," answered Orenda. "I didn't invite him, you know."

Solas stood up.

"Yeah, but why does it want it so bad? Something's going on. Did you not communicate with Chepi in Purgator? Did he not tell you? What's going on? Why is Lux Veritas in my hands again?"

"Calm down my good boy," replied Orenda, as he approached Solas to reassure him. "Everything will be all right. Are you not happy to see your trustworthy old sword? It seems to me she just bailed you out again, no?"

Solas looked at Lux Veritas and admired her for a brief second.

"Yes," he replied, "but what am I to do with her now?"

Orenda sighed.

"Well, it's true. I did speak with Chepi only a few hours ago, just before the dawn," he replied. "His spirit was tormented. He said Purgator was in trouble again. Only this time, it was more serious. He also warned about the Stealth Demon. It was searching for Lux Veritas. But that's not really surprising, is it? So, Chepi hurried to send the sword down to me. *For the boy Solas*, he said."

Solas paused a moment to take in those words, to try to make sense of them.

"That's it?"

"Oh," replied Orenda, "and he gave me this." The shaman pulled out an odd and familiar looking object from the pocket of his ceremonial garb. "For you also," the shaman added.

Solas carefully accepted the object and had a closer look at it.

"It looks like that same object the Stealth Demon had in his hands just before it transformed itself into a cocoon and went ballistic," said Solas. "But this one is white," he added.

"Yes," said Orenda, "and look again. It also has a pin and it's active."

"You're right," said Solas, "swirls of light blues and yellows. It reminds me of the Sylph-aura that Amy received from Zoe and Ariel, the Sylph faeries who were living deep in the Forsaken Forest of Purgator. It kind of reminds me of that."

The two studied the curious object for a moment longer.

"Well, what am I to do with it?" asked Solas.

"You can ask Chepi yourself when you see him," answered Orenda.

A look of concern and a sense of disbelief suddenly came over Solas.

"What do you mean ask Chepi yourself when I see him?"

"Well, I would say you need to go back to Purgator. You heard the demon. Didn't you?" replied Orenda.

"You are out of your mind old man if you think I am going to go back in there and do it all over again. Not a snow ball's chance in Hell, I tell you," said Solas, chuckling nervously.

Orenda stared at him in complete silence and observed until the boy reached the understanding on his own. Solas walked a few steps over to the adjacent clubhouse to put down the mysterious object on the window's ledge. He turned around, still clutching Lux Veritas and spent a good minute admiring her, pondering. A series of mixed emotions overcame the boy, those brought back from the fond memories he shared with the divine weapon as well as the nightmarish ones too. As Solas reflected on the situation, a warm breeze began to lift again bringing with it the scent of wild flowers, mixing together with the worship incense already about the air, all of it invading his senses. The field larks added their playful melodies to this sensory mix and awakened the boy's spirits. This was a bittersweet moment, rekindled by the not-so-distant memories of Asphodel Meadows – Solas's point of entry into Purgator. And thoughts of everlasting peace quickly fleeted away and scurried out of mind.

While still clutching the sword in his right hand, Solas sprawled down flat on the grass, his arms and legs outstretched like a snow angel, in utter surrender. He looked straight up into the bright blue sky above, watching a few passing clouds change shapes as they rolled away. His head began to spin. After filling his lungs with a huge gulp of fresh oxygen, he let out a scream of frustration, rivalling that of the Stealth Demon's earlier, and poignant enough to wake the Iroquois ancients from the dead. Suddenly, he saw a figure towering above him, looking down. Orenda put out his hand. Solas winced. He sighed and slapped his left hand into the shaman's, who quickly yanked him up to his feet.

"Why me, Orenda? Why?" he asked.

"Why us, do you mean," replied the elder shaman with the squinty eyes and the distinct crow's feet. Orenda smiled, tripling the old man's facial lines.

"Yeah ... I guess you're right," said Solas, after further consideration. "I just don't understand," he continued, "the Stealth Demon mentioned a crossing. What crossing is he talking about? I can only remember the crossings over the River Lethe. And we burnt or destroyed those!"

Orenda frowned in puzzlement and rolled his eyes looking for an answer.

"Unless they have rebuilt, I have not the foggiest idea, my dear boy," he answered, "but there must be another crossing somewhere in Purgator, another bridge or passageway to some other land perhaps. You will need to find it, I presume."

"And do what?" asked Solas. "Can you at least tell me what I must do there?"

Orenda laughed a hearty laugh, to the puzzlement of Solas this time.

"Well, I may be a shaman, Solas, and it's true that I may talk to the spirits in the night, but I am still just earthly old man. And

I certainly do not hold all the answers," he replied. "Once you get to the afterlife, find Chepi. Perhaps he knows the way."

"What makes you believe I need to go back to Purgator anyway?" asked Solas. "I have the sword. Nothing's going to happen now. The demon's gone. We are safe."

"You would let Purgator fall to the forces of evil after all you have already done for the Lord Creator? He has entrusted you with his almighty weapon, Lux Veritas. You know her better than anyone does. The Stealth Demon is on a mission. He tried to intercept Lux Veritas. You saw it. And he will not so easily rest. Now you have your mission too. Follow the beast and restore the peace once more. Purgator needs you, not to mention the Lord Creator."

"And how do you suppose I get back to Purgator now? Can you tell me how I will find my next ride on the Wheel of Souls, huh? And who will go with me … you?"

"Solas, you know my place is here," replied the shaman, "however, I am quite sure a few of your friends would be interested in joining you. Go speak to them. And tonight, come back to see me. You are all invited to my séance. Under the circumstances, we will need to communicate with Chepi again. He is expecting my call. And candid as he is, I am sure he will be eager to tell you all you need to know about this new predicament."

"That would be great," replied Solas, "I would love to ask Chepi a few questions. But right now, I need to go home to check on Grandma. Then I will give Dorian and Amy a call, for sure. What a shock this is going to be."

"Go then," said Orenda, "I will get things in order for tonight. Come at the midnight hour."

"All right, then," replied Solas, as he turned away to fetch the mysterious object he had left sitting on the clubhouse's windowsill. He carefully stuffed it away in the front pocket of his cut-offs. "See you tonight," he said to Orenda before walking away in the direction of his home without wasting another second.

As Solas hurried heading down the east slope of the hillcrest toward home, Orenda called out his name before the boy could clear entirely out of sight.

"Solas!" he yelled at the top of his lungs.

The fleet-footed boy, as much as fifty yards downhill by now, stopped and turned around while holding Lux Veritas at present-arms over his left shoulder.

"Be prepared," the shaman shouted.

Solas hesitated a few seconds as he pondered this simple command. Then he lifted Lux Veritas straight up high above his head, thus acknowledging the implicit message sent by the old Iroquois priest to come ready for all possibilities or eventualities.

5

Many thoughts now raced through Solas's mind. The descent back home felt like déjà-vu. The only striking difference was the change of seasons – the snow had long melted away – and of course, that weird object tossed in his pocket. The boy whizzed by the fateful bush, place of his first encounter with the powers of Lux Veritas. The mature broom shrub was none the worse for wear, having survived the rapid meltdown, and its yellow flower blossoms burst to life as though they had now found special favor in the heart of the mighty Goddess Flora.

Finally, he reached the bottom, crossed the street, jumped over the property's red picket gate, sprinted down the stone walkway and burst through the front door of his home, just as he had in much similar circumstances only a few months earlier.

"Grandma!" he yelled.

This time, Grandma Jeanie was awake, pacing impatiently back and forth in the kitchen and praying for Solas's safe return. She startled and jumped upon hearing his voice.

"Dear Lord! Dear Lord!" she repeated, as she scuttled around the corner to greet him. "Solas my boy, my treasure, I was so scared."

Solas embraced her as she collapsed into his open arms. They hugged and comforted each other for a short heartfelt moment. They collected their thoughts and caught their breath, before parting.

"You're alright," said Solas. "Thank God."

"Whatever happened?" she asked, dismayed, and noticing Lux Veritas. "You have the sword again?"

Solas quickly glanced at his weapon.

"Yes, that's her," replied Solas. "Isn't she great?" he added, trying to diffuse the stress of the situation.

"Where is that demon creature? Is it gone?"

"Yes, yes, it's gone Grandma. Don't worry," he answered, as he rubbed her shoulder with his right hand to reassure her.

"What was it doing here? What did it want? Did you kill it?" she continued.

"Hold on Grandma! Calm down!" Solas replied. "No, I didn't kill it. It went away. It sort of vanished. That's all that matters. But I have to call Dorian and Amy right now," he continued, as he walked down the corridor to his bedroom to fetch his cell phone.

"Why do you still have the sword then, Solas?" she asked, knowing full well that the answer she was seeking would likely not be the one that she would receive.

"Well, Grandma," answered Solas, as he snatched his phone from his desktop and began dialling, "I have another job to do … but don't ask me what, I am still a little fuzzy about that."

"Oh my good Lord!" she said. "I better sit down."

Solas paced around waiting for Dorian to pick up his phone. Suddenly, Dorian arrived on his bike, which he promptly dumped against the side fencing before swinging the front gate and reaching the open front door of the residence. The friends' eyes connected. Solas put away his phone.

"What's going on?" said Dorian approaching. "Did all Hell break loose again?"

"Dorian, man, you are not going to believe this. There was a demon right here in my home. He chased me. Look, I have Lux Veritas!"

"Holy crap!" said Dorian, "how did all this happen?"

"Just tell me first, where's Amy?" asked Solas.

"Don't worry, I called her," replied Dorian, "she's on her way. So is Jiji."

"I called all your friends, Solas," said Grandma, "I left them all a message. I was worried. I warned them, you know."

Just as Grandma finished her sentence, a cab pulled up to the front of the house. Amy jumped out of the vehicle and the waiting trio greeted her on the front porch. Solas was relieved to see his girlfriend arrive so quickly. The boy advanced a few steps along the walkway. Amy had her hair brushed back and bundled into a ponytail and the look of concern on her face quickly switched to a look of surprise and apprehension the instant she laid her eyes on Lux Veritas. She stopped a few feet short of Solas and gazed into his eyes in disbelief. Solas lightly bobbed his head.

"Yeah," he whispered; and that said it all.

Amy finally reached for him, kissed and hugged him as tight as ever. The group did not exchange another word and retreated into the home to the comfort of the living room. A couple of hours passed. Solas explained the events of the early morning, and showed his friends the mysterious white object. The group attempted to make sense of it all and looked forward to Orenda's evening séance up on the Iroquois reserve. The spirits would surely shed a new light on the matter. And the séance itself, especially one so tangible, had to be worth the price of admission. Shaman Orenda was a gifted medium; this, the friends knew all too well. In the meantime, Jiji had made her way to join the group and added her pearls of wisdom to the conversation. After all, she had spent the longest time in Purgator and her help regarding all things concerning the afterlife and its environment was indeed invaluable. They decided to turn on the news at noon to see if perhaps somebody somewhere had seen or heard something about the sudden arrival of the unwanted visitor.

"...in local news, police were called to an early morning incident in the quiet Rosemont neighbourhood of Sherbrooke. A young man was found lying unconscious and bleeding from an apparent vicious beating. The victim sustained cuts to the side of his face and neck from an apparent knife attack. Police would not confirm that the assault was gang related, only that this was an isolated incident. KPQS news' Lori Dunham was on the scene and reports that the victim did regain consciousness and claimed to have been assaulted by a 'superhuman-like creature from Hell.' Police confirmed that the youth was known to police and that he suffered from shock, was incoherent and was still under the influence of alcohol. The young man is now resting in hospital and is recovering from his injuries."

"Wow," said Dorian, "this punk never had a chance. Now he's made a fool of himself too with his talk."

"There were several guys in the group," said Solas, "I guess they took off once they saw what they were dealing with. I doubt they will say anything at all."

"Yeah, well, there is your proof. Who would believe them anyway?" added Amy.

"I had heard rumours of odd creatures and demons that would sometimes come up to the surface from the lower regions of Purgator, from the maze of paths deep beneath Mount Glory," said Jiji, pensive, in a sober tone. "Legend has it that they appeared from another dimension. There is some sort of a connecting grid there. But no one in Lalas Pur was ever brave enough to go down there to find out. It is such a trek, and a dangerous one. I suspect the Stealth Demon may come from there."

"A connecting grid to another dimension you said, Jiji?" asked Solas.

"Yes," she answered, "if I recall well. I overheard customers at Valhalla tavern talk about it, usually out-of-towners. But even they were not sure. It made for colorful conversation over a few pints of beer, I guess. Spooked a few folks too, me included!"

The newscast continued.

"*...in other news, the scientific community is puzzled and alarmed this morning over a hole forming in the ozone layer which seems to have appeared overnight in the Appalachian mountain region in the state of Maine. NASA's ultra-sensitive instruments on the International Space Station recorded a burst of light over Mount Katahdin just before dawn and scientists speculate the hole was created when a meteorite passed through the stratosphere otherwise undetected and entered the troposphere. They are now trying to locate the remains of the foreign object and are asking for the public's help...*"

"And there's your point of entry," said Solas.

"The bastard," added Dorian, "punching holes in our fragile little blue planet like that!"

Before the group could add any other comments, a loud series of knocks interrupted the conversation. They looked around at each other, somewhat perplexed.

"Who can that be?" asked Solas.

Amy quickly checked through the side window to see who was there.

"It's the police!" she whispered.

"What the heck do they want?" asked Solas, in rhetorical fashion. "Hold on to Lux Veritas, Dorian, and stay out of sight. I will be right back."

Amy accompanied Solas. Standing at the door were three local police officers from the Rosemont detachment.

"Hello officers," said Solas. "Can I help you?"

"Are you Mr. Gambit?" asked the first officer. The policeman was the tall and robust army type with a square jaw. He wore his badge and regiment's cap with pride, tilted on an angle over his head.

"Yes, I am."

"Does this bicycle here belong to you, Sir?" he asked, as the second officer, a chubby older fellow, presented the bike. "It has an identity tag. We traced it back to you."

"Yes it is," answered Solas, "thank you very much. Where was it?"

"We found it discarded in the middle of the road only a few blocks away from here," explained the officer.

"What ... somebody stole it?" Solas asked with a hint of surprise in his voice.

"Do you not keep it under lock at night, Sir?"

"Yeah, I do," replied Solas. "I guess I must have forgotten this time."

The policeman forced a smile and stared straight at Solas, not believing the boy.

"Were you out anywhere with your bike earlier this morning?"

"No," answered Solas, frowning, "why?"

"Would you happen to know an individual by the name of Colby Holston, would you?"

The third officer moved closer and tucked his thumbs inside the front of his belt, perhaps expecting some sort of sudden admission from the boy. Solas's eyes travelled back and forth between the two sheriffs.

"Pfff," Solas vented, "never heard of the guy."

"Are you sure?" he insisted.

"Yeah, I'm pretty sure," Solas replied.

"He was assaulted earlier this morning, just a few blocks away from here. He claims a young man came down the hill riding your bike, abandoned it, and then ran off behind some houses. Apparently, some individual disguised in a demon costume was chasing him. And this person ended up assaulting him. Do you know anything about that at all?"

Amy's eyes went round as melons as she heard those details, and the two officers standing by took notice.

"Wow, that's terrible officer," replied Solas. "Sorry, I wish I could help you. I was sleeping tight. I only woke up about an hour ago. You can ask my Grandma if you like."

"That's fine," said the officer, "make sure you keep your bike under lock or inside your house from now on."

"Shall do," replied Solas.

The officers turned around and went away. As they got back to their cruiser, the second officer shared his thoughts with his colleagues.

"That kid knows something. The girl seemed nervous too."

"Yeah well, I guess we'll just have to follow the other leads to get to the bottom of it," replied the chief officer. "I wonder what the canine unit managed to dig up following that report from the old man who saw that same costumed freak jump over his back yard fence."

"Yeah, Bob and Oscar are the best man-dog team in the state. I get the feeling we'll be back to see this boy here before long," added the third officer.

Solas closed and bolted the front door behind him and went back into the living room, keeping an eye on the officers as they got back into their vehicle.

"What did they want, Solas?" asked Grandma Jeanie.

"Nothing; they were returning my bike and asked a few questions," answered Solas. "I am not sure we have seen the last of them though. They didn't believe me."

"What do you mean?" asked Dorian.

"I could tell. Besides, they didn't need to bring three officers to return a bike, did they? They know more about this morning's events than they would let me know," answered Solas. "The last thing we need is these guys probing into our affairs. I need to fix this problem and bring back Lux Veritas to Purgator ASAP. I never want to see the Stealth Demon around here again … or the cops."

6

Grandma Jeanie and the four teenagers discussed the situation until mid-afternoon and tried to find an adequate solution to the problem. Jiji and Amy flicked the channels on the tube and checked the internet looking for any sort of relevant information available about the inopportune visit of the Stealth Demon earlier that morning. At least, Solas's mind was set: he was going back to

Purgator. The question was how, but he trusted the answer would come, perhaps tonight at the séance. He had only one other true concern.

"Dorian," he said.

"Yeah?" his buddy replied.

"So ... are you in or out?" he asked after making full eye contact with him.

"In or out of what?" asked Dorian.

Suddenly, all was quiet in the home, save for the dull background voice of the TV news anchor. A sense of anticipation set in and the girls turned right around and now stood at full attention. The boys kept staring into each other's eyes for a moment longer. Dorian got the message.

"Oh, I see," he replied, his spirits now lifting despite better common sense. Raising his voice, he continued. "Well of course I'm in. What did you think? Besides, we are guaranteed a hell of a good time. Aren't we?"

Solas smiled. Dorian approached his buddy and embraced him, slapping him on the back.

"Small request ... do hang on to your sword this time, will you?" he whispered in his ear.

Solas chuckled.

"And if I don't, what are going to do about it, big guy?"

The boys smiled, both recalling the many times Dorian bailed out Solas out of dire predicaments in the afterlife, out in the land of demons, deceit, doldrums and despair.

Now, Solas stared straight at Amy.

She closed her eyes, took a deep breath, and reopened them upon exhaling. She took a few confident steps toward Solas, wrapped her arms around his neck and slightly up on her tippy-toes gave him a soft kiss on the lips, her eyes sparkling all the while; and this, so naturally, in lieu of saying yes. She posed her head on his chest, finding comfort near his heartbeat. Solas caressed her hair, as he often loved to do.

All eyes were now on Xiao Ren, or Jiji as her friends loved to call her.

Jiji stepped up and joined Dorian. She grabbed his arm, leaning her head against his shoulder, smiling. Thoughts of the green hills and flowering fields of Morphos flashed through her mind, vivid memories of the endless blue skies stretching over the horizon above the Sea of Plenty, the buzz of the market in the heart of the agora of her beloved city Lalas Pur and of course the cozy warmth of Valhalla tavern. But she rejoiced most at the idea of seeing her best friend Linoa again, her elkin soul sister. Serene as the white lotus, she prayed quietly for her, as her earthly friends awaited her response.

"I would love to see Lalas Pur again," she said in her soft voice. "It was my home for so long. When do we leave, Solas?"

Not that Solas ever had any doubt about his friends' courage or loyalties. Still he composed himself to make a little speech, before answering this most pressing question.

"Thank you my friends. I feel more at ease now. Deep down, I just knew you would follow me back to Purgator or to God-knows-where the Lord Creator is sending us. My morale was down; I just needed to hear it from you. From the moment I saw that friggin' demon, I knew it was game on again … even if I didn't want to believe it. I don't know how we are going to catch up to that demon." He hesitated and thought about it for a moment. "I don't even know how we are going to find the passage back to the afterlife or what other challenges we will face once we get there. And I am not really sure when we will be leaving either, Jiji, to be exact. But we better be ready, because tonight may be the night." Then, Solas pulled out the strange object out of his pocket for another look. "And we may well need to use this thing … whatever it is."

"Do you know how to use it?" asked Dorian.

"Orenda will probably have the answers," replied quick-witted Amy.

"I wouldn't be so sure about that," said Solas.

Just then, the phone rang. The group paused, startled by yet another unsolicited interruption.

"I'll get it," said Grandma. She picked up the phone with a nervous hand and a concerned look, and answered the call in a jittery voice. "Hello."

The person at the other end began to speak and without adding another word, Grandma Jeanie stretched her arm out toward Solas and offered him the handset.

"Solas here," he announced with purpose.

"Solas … This is Orenda. You better leave your house right now and come up here quick."

"What's the emergency?" asked Solas, already fearing the return of the beast.

"No time to explain," replied Orenda. "Just come and be fast." And he hung up.

Solas put down the phone and looked at his friends.

"We need to get up to the Iroquois reserve and now," he said. "You guys ready?"

"Hang on, Solas," said Dorian. "Tell us what's happening."

"Orenda didn't say. But we need to act fast. I get the feeling the time has for us come," replied Solas. "Let's go!"

"Wait!" said Amy. "Maybe I should go get my jeans and put on better shoes. Do we not have a little time?"

"You know what, Prissy," replied Dorian, "if we have to catch another ride on the Wheel of Souls, it won't really matter what you wear. Remember the last time? We landed butt naked in the middle of cow pastures."

"And what if we need to take a ride on that thingamajig, like the beast did, huh?" retorted Amy, "should we not be better prepared this time?"

"We will worry about that later," said Solas, "we've got to get going."

"Oh, my good boy," said Grandma Jeanie, her emotions rising to the fore. "Do be careful. I don't like that dreadful beast at all."

"Don't you worry Grandma," replied Solas, as he reached to hug her, "I have Lux Veritas. What can happen? Besides, I will be back in no time!"

"I love you, Solas."

"I love you too, Grandma."

Upon these words and after a warm embrace, the pair parted.

7

Grandma Jeanie smiled and felt reassured. Solas had this effect on her. And it was true; as days went by in Purgator, meanwhile time stood still on Earth ... or almost. And Solas would be back in a flash. Before leaving the house, Solas emptied his hockey bag of all his equipment and managed to hide the long sword inside, with only parts of the hilt and pommel showing. No way did he want anyone spotting him walking around with Lux Veritas in broad daylight. The supernatural weapon was much too precious, and she would draw too much attention should any earthling catch even the slightest glimpse of her. The front door slammed behind the quartet and like a group of reluctant renegades, the conspicuous foursome exited the front yard of the house, crossed over to the other side of the street and reached the slope of the hill leading up to the Iroquois reserve. Jiji took one last look behind her to verify that the coast was indeed clear of any suspicious or vagrant eyes. After all, these native grounds were fenced and clearly labelled private property. Trespassers were strictly forbidden to enter and citizens of the neighbourhood did not hesitate to call the police whenever they noticed any abnormal activity in the area, especially from a bunch of teenagers. There already had been enough trouble up there in the past.

"Solas," said Xiao Ren, "stop! I think there is some weird guy parked in a white car about three doors down from your house. He's laying low inside the vehicle. And he's kind of looking this way."

The teenagers stopped and identified the vehicle.

"Good call, Jiji," said Solas, "that's an unmarked police car right there. They're watching us."

"Why?" asked Amy, "we didn't do anything."

"Well I don't know, but something is definitely rotten in the state of Denmark, as Shakespeare would say," Solas replied.

"What do we do now?" asked Dorian. "He's seen us."

"We keep going, what else?" answered Solas. "Let's move."

And up the hill they went, not spending much time worrying about the police. After all, if Solas and company could only get back to Purgator fast enough, their problems would surely disappear upon their return – that being only a few minutes away in real Earth time. As for the rest, it could certainly be explained away. The real concern was the emergency in the afterlife and the real possibility that the Stealth Demon would show up in Sherbrooke again at any given moment. As they reached the top, standing by the ceremonial yurt structure housing the cenotaph, was shaman Orenda, still dressed in full ceremonial attire, awaiting their arrival. The smell of burning incense was stronger than ever.

"Hurry, hurry," he cried out loud as soon as the group was within hearing distance, "there is no time to waste."

"He sure gets excited," said Dorian.

"Come on guys," said Solas, urging his friends, "one last push."

Just as the foursome arrived, Orenda rushed headlong into a briefing.

"I have been called to perform a last rite sacrament for departing Nokomis, an elderly woman from the Ojibwa tribe about 10 miles from here. This is your opportunity to catch the Wheel of Souls back into Purgator."

"All right then, let's go!" said Solas, as he tried to catch his breath. "What about the séance with Chepi?"

"Do not worry. I have already prepared the lines of communication with Chepi in the afterlife. He is awaiting our contact. You can speak with him and ask your questions. But we must do it now. Come over this way," he said as he turned and led them away, "to my private tipi, right behind the clubhouse."

The group headed down the dirt pathway separating the ceremonial yurt from the clubhouse. They quickly reached Orenda's tipi, a sanctum which had been for years untold the lieu of many an Iroquois shaman's séance with the afterlife, of all healings and mystic connections with the spirits of the elders, and now the transcendental gateway to Purgator and to great shaman Chepi. The tipi was wide, tall and circular, made of stretched animal hides tightly sewed together and attached to wooden poles moored into the ground in a hexagon formation. Large tattooed depictions of wild animals adorned the tanned skin walls of the tipi, presumably to ward off evil spirits.

Orenda entered the shelter first, followed by Solas and his friends. Inside, three six-foot-tall raven head sceptres positioned in a triangle held flaming torches. Their light cast undulating waves of eerie shadows and odd figures against the skin walls. Mixed with strings of smoke given off by the smouldering incense, the interior of the tent took on a rather turbid, austere and mysterious aura. The five sat inside the triangle's perimeter on thick wolf, bear and beaver pelts neatly arranged in a circle, with each of the victims' heads still attached and facing outward of the ring. Their glazed eyes seemed fixed into the void. But their spirits no doubt guarded the proceedings. Their mouths were set wide open with their razor sharp teeth showing. So, these pelts were laid down on the ground around a waxed hardwood table carved with native inscriptions on which was placed a lone translucent crystal ball. Burning sticks of incense and a couple of thick, wooden trays completed the rudimentary yet esoteric necessities required for the séance.

Beneath this table was a long tomahawk peace pipe, which Orenda now stuffed with tobacco leaves. He crumbled them methodically under the watchful eyes of his guests and lit up the pipe with the fire of one of the waxed honey candlesticks.

"We are several," he told his young friends. "But we must bond, so that our spirits can be as one."

They followed Orenda's example and each inhaled a heavy toke of the leaf mixture. Solas and Dorian enjoyed the proceedings while Amy and Jiji frowned and winced doing their best to withhold the fumes.

"I will now summon Chepi," said Orenda, as he faced the crystal ball.

The four friends looked at each other and held hands as they sat in a semi-circle right behind Orenda.

"But before we begin," Orenda continued, "we must all consume the peyote."

"Consume what?" asked Solas.

"We must all eat the peyote," repeated Orenda, as he grabbed one of the wooden trays on the table containing a mixture of dried slices of peyote, a cactus indigenous to the southwest United States well known for its narcotic properties. "We must be free like the eagle to be in tune with the great spirits."

Orenda chose five choice morsels and distributed them to each member of the group. He ate the first piece.

"Is this really necessary?" asked Dorian.

"It will help your soul journey," explained the shaman.

"Well, what is this exactly?" asked Amy.

"Just a piece of cactus," answered Orenda.

"Cactus doesn't grow in Sherbrooke," said Solas who was holding Lux Veritas across his lap. "Where did you get it?"

"Walmart," replied Orenda. "They have a nice selection in the plant section."

The four hesitated before Solas finally took the first bite, like the good sport that he was.

"How is it?" asked Jiji.

"Yeah, it's okay" he answered, merrily chomping on his piece. "Try some."

Jiji and Amy both bit into a tender piece of the blue-green cactus at the same time, chewing it in synchronicity.

"Dorian," said Orenda, noticing that the boy was still stalling, "are you going to eat some or not?"

"No thanks," he replied and he handed the slice back to Orenda who proceeded to swallow it right away without giving it as much as a second thought.

"Fine," said the shaman, "perhaps you would prefer some *fly* caps." The shaman grabbed the second tray off the table and offered the yellow-orange fungus to Dorian. "Join us on our flight, won't you?"

"Mushrooms? No friggin' way!" exclaimed Dorian, "never again! I had enough of that experience in Purgator the last time. Give me back some cactus then."

"Sorry young man," said Orenda, "that was the last piece. There are only mushroom caps left. But don't you worry; the *fly* has amazing soaring abilities too."

Since ages long past, the local Amerindians had become natural experts with all matters concerning the usage of toadstools, in particular the one magical fungus called *Amanita Muscaria*, better known as the *fly* for its hallucinogenic properties.

"Are you serious?" said Dorian as he looked over at Amy, anticipating her reaction.

Of course, Amy found this moment rather amusing since she could remember quite well the mushroom induced psychedelic episode that Dorian had to endure back at the oasis of Asphodel meadows in Purgator. And Dorian was not keen to ever try eating another piece of fungus again.

"Come on Dorian," urged Solas, "let's go already."

Dorian shook his head in disbelief, grabbed a piece with some reluctance and popped it in his mouth without looking at it.

"There," he said, sticking his tongue out to show the mushroom had disappeared down his gullet. "Let's get on with the show now, shall we?"

Orenda asked for silence and stretched out his arms above his head. He remained inert with his head hung low. For a couple of minutes, no one heard a noise or made a move. The peyote and the *fly* cap began to take effect. Orenda stared into the crystal ball and entered into a trance, shaking as the four other participants observed. The room began to swirl and their spirits began to lift. The shaman then reached under the table and grabbed a powwow drum, which he began to strike in a slow steady beat with a rattling drumstick. Then he sped up, humming and singing to the beat of the drum. His chant got louder and louder. The smoke of the incense continued to rise above the table and gathered like a cloud above the crystal ball. Although still indistinct, images started to appear on the face of the magic ball. These were images of creatures, places and troubles in Purgator and beyond, though incomprehensible they were. These mixed visions projected upward into the funnelling haze above them. Orenda stopped drumming. That is when the most singular event occurred; Orenda became possessed by a foreign spirit. It spoke.

8

"The sky is crying," the deep voice uttered. Orenda's head tilted upward toward the hut's narrow skylight opening above. One could see only the white of his eyes fluttering and his long flowing tresses now dangled to the ground. "Come Solas … quick, to dry the tears of the wretched. Purgator needs you once more."

By now, the foursome was already engrossed in this surreal spectacle. Their intuitions were tweaked to the max and their minds receptive to the higher understanding.

"Who is speaking?" asked Solas, who was feeling rather out of sort asking Orenda this question when he was sitting just a foot away. But he needed to be sure.

"It is I, Chepi," answered the voice. The murky smoke of the incense formed a gradual and fleeting image of the drawn out face of the old shaman speaking. It lasted mere seconds, but was enough to make out. "The vessel has been provided to make your journey across on the Wheel of Souls. Nokomis will lead the way."

"Yes, but tell me what the problem is, Chepi," Solas asked with some urgency, "so that I know what to expect. And where shall I go once I reach Purgator?"

"The evil comes from beyond Purgator, Solas," answered Chepi. As he spoke, snapshots of trouble areas and of Lord Chaos's minions appeared in the form of crackling flashes in the suspended fumes above the glossy and opaque crystal ball. "It comes from another world, Solas."

"What are you talking about from another world, Chepi?" interjected Dorian, in true dorianesque fashion. "You mean the Hell we know as Tartarus. Is this what you mean?"

There was a sudden lull. All was quiet. Orenda began to convulse a little more as he attempted to regain the lost lines of communication with the afterlife. He groaned for a moment as his concentration drained his psyche. Then, he recomposed.

"There is a breach from beyond Purgator," the voice continued. "You must stop the Stealth Demon. He will open the floodgates and all will be lost. But there is no time, we must hurry."

"And what about this thing right here?" asked Solas, waving his newfound object while sensing that the window of opportunity to ask questions was closing fast. "What do I do with it?"

"Bring it with you. The beast must not find it," he informed the group. "It will help you reach the other dimensions. Meet me at Fidem's hideout. I await you there … and beware the Stealth Demon."

And with this last effort, the mystic vanished and Orenda collapsed into the arms of Amy sitting in a lotus position behind him.

"Ha!" she screamed.

Xiao Ren rushed to his help and patted the shaman's cheeks in an attempt to bring him back to consciousness. The Iroquois priest's eyes rolled and refocused. After a few seconds, he regained his faculties.

"Wow," he said, "that was intense … well then?" he asked as he stood up with the help of his friends.

But before they could provide the medium with any sort of answers – as well as ask him a whole pile more questions – the sound of a dog whimpering and barking on the premises interrupted their concentration. The group, now flying higher than a kite, stepped out of the tent into the bright daylight. A little more than 100 feet away were a couple of police officers advancing up the trail in front of the Iroquois clubhouse with the help of a tracking German Sheppard. The dog, spotting the group coming out of the hut, immediately began to bark, pulling hard on the leash.

"The cops," said Dorian, with a delayed reaction.

"Get back inside," said Orenda.

The quartet backed up into the refuge, trying to avoid detection. But the dog master noticed the stir. Orenda calmly waved at the officers and advanced to meet them.

"Over this way, Stan," said the dog handler to his colleague. The canine's yelping intensified and the officer ordered the German Sheppard to stand down. But the restless dog continued to whimper and growl and appeared much agitated.

"What's with Oscar today, Bob?" Stan asked the dog master.

"I don't know. He's never like this," he answered. "Anyway, I just saw a few people enter that hut over there."

"Well, let's go check it out," replied Officer Stan. "And catch a load of this guy, would you? Another fellow in a costume all dressed up in this heat … What is he, some kind of chief?"

As they met up with Orenda, the shaman raised his arm and greeted them in formal Iroquois fashion, for effect.

"Hao!"

"Hello Sir," the officers replied. "I am officer Stanley Hurst and this is officer Robert Downes and his dog Oscar from the K-9 unit of the Sherbrooke police department."

"I am shaman Orenda. What business brings the white man's police to the sacred grounds of the Iroquois nation?"

"We're looking for an individual you may have seen in the area earlier this morning. He was wearing some sort of a black demon costume … a Halloween costume of some kind. It looked pretty real. Would you happen to have seen someone resembling this description pass through here?" asked Officer Hurst.

"What has he done?"

"He assaulted someone with a weapon. He may be armed and dangerous. Oscar picked up his trail and it led us up here. Would you know anything about this individual?"

Orenda was starting to feel the full effect of the peyote. His head was spinning, he had double vision and the officer's words came out in slow motion at first, and then sped up like a bullet. The shaman's mouth stayed half-opened and his eyelids drooped over his eyes.

"Nope … afraid not," he answered.

The officers looked at each other not certain whether to believe the old man.

"Well he came up here for sure," replied Officer Hurst. "Oscar never gets it wrong. He is the best-trained dog in the county. This individual may be hiding around here somewhere. We are going to keep looking around if you don't mind."

The restless canine kept whimpering all the while. Officer Downes tried hard to motivate his dog to continue following the scent. Oscar fought back and refused to do so, until he made a straight line for Orenda's tipi.

"You are wasting your time," Orenda said aloud. "I doubt very much you will find him here."

Inside, the group listened to the sound of the dog and the two officers approaching. Solas quickly hid Lux Veritas under a bearskin and the group sat around the séance table pretending to be enthralled in some out-worldly native ritual. The dog started barking wildly outside the tent.

"Good boy Oscar, good boy," said Officer Downes, as he petted his dog to thank him for his good work. "Be careful, the individual may be inside this tipi," he said to his partner Stan.

"Is there anyone in there?" Officer Hurst asked Orenda.

"I was in the middle of séance with a group of young people," he replied.

"I'll go take a look," Stan told his colleague.

Officer Hurst slapped the hanging skin door open and carefully entered the tipi. The smoke of the incense overwhelmed him. He squinted, adjusting for the lack of natural light, and saw the quartet sitting peacefully around the séance table. Solas and Dorian turned around and made eye contact with the sherrif.

"Hi there!" he said. "This is Officer Hurst of the Sherbrooke police department. Do you folks mind stepping out of the tent for a minute? I have a few questions to ask you."

"What is it Sir?" asked Solas.

"Step out, please!" ordered the officer.

The four friends stood up and exited the tipi, with Solas in the lead.

9

Oscar started to bark furiously once again, growling, showing his teeth and pulling hard on his master's leash.

"Down!" ordered his master. The dog responded, but remained agitated.

"Do you have any I.D. on you?" Officer Hurst asked the group, coming to the immediate conclusion by Oscar's latest reaction that Solas had no doubt some connection to the morning's events.

Soon the two officers' suspicions would be confirmed once and for all. For the second time in less than twelve hours, the Stealth Demon appeared out of nowhere, sneaking up like a ghost right behind shaman Orenda and picking him up right off the ground with the strength of a single arm. The beast seemed utterly unconcerned with anyone else, at least for the moment.

"The luret?" he asked in his habitual slur and only two inches away from the shaman's face.

Were it not for the effect of the double dose of peyote, Orenda would have panicked. The rest of the group, however, almost jumped out of their skins by the shock of this most unwelcomed surprise. Oscar now growled at the beast and the two startled officers scrambled fast to draw their guns, standard 13 round Glock 23 models.

"Release the individual, get down on the ground and don't move!" yelled Officer Hurst. "Do it now!"

The demon rotated its head a quarter turn to view the screaming human and the barking dog. Behind Oscar and the two officers, the group of friends slowly backed up. Amy and Jiji held each other.

"Holy crap!" said Dorian, at the sight of the beast.

The beast pressed on with the matter at hand. It stared down Orenda once more and continued holding him up in the air with one hand while applying pressure to the shaman's throat with the other hand.

"The lu-ret," the demon repeated in slower, clearer syllables.

Orenda struggled and choked from the pressure exerted on his trachea. Officer Downes, hesitant to fire the first bullets, decided to release his German Sheppard Oscar to subdue the assailant. The canine charged the beast full speed. The demon, sensing the threat, stopped the dog in its tracks with one straight-arm gesture aimed toward the animal, leaving Orenda dangling by the neck.

"Good boy," said the demon. "Come to me…"

The dog's ears flapped straight back into a submissive role and its tail began wagging as Oscar panted, whimpered and crawled on its stomach trying to reach the beast. In one movement, the demon had tamed the dog. The officers were stunned. Nonchalant, Solas eyed the tipi and continued to back up slowly.

The demon caressed Oscar with his long scrawny fingers and sharp claws. The dog licked his hand, turned around and began growling at the two policemen.

"Release the citizen," yelled a stupefied Officer Downes, noticing Orenda fighting for his life.

He fired a warning shot to the left of the beast, hoping to scare the demon into letting go his captive. The plan worked. The Stealth Demon tossed Orenda to the ground like a rag doll, but now marched, hissing, toward the officers. At the same instant,

Oscar charged at his old master following the demon's command. Shaman Orenda got back to his feet. Solas turned and rushed inside the tent to retrieve Lux Veritas from under the bearskin. Dorian, Amy and Jiji continued to back away.

"Stop and lay down flat on the ground!" ordered Officer Hurst, himself backing up a few steps. "Stop right there or I'll shoot!" he yelled as a last order.

As Oscar latched on to his old master's arm despite all of Officer Downes' efforts to regain the canine's confidence, the beast continued its path forward. Officer Hurst aimed and shot at the demon, hitting the beast in the leg, to no effect. Then he fired a second shot and like the first one, the bullet pinged off the leg, leaving barely a spark at the point of impact. Now with the beast only a few feet away, the officer shot yet again, and this time hit the demon square in the chest. The bullet clinked off the beast's mysterious, impregnable armor, deflected and found a target in shaman Orenda, striking the helpless spectator flush in the upper chest just below the throat. The old man let out a groan and dropped on the spot. Jiji and Amy screamed. The beast turned its head in time to witness Orenda's fate and began laughing heartily, mocking the unfortunate officer, who then fired another shot. The growling stopped. This time, it was Oscar the German Sheppard. A shaken Officer Downes had pulled the trigger on his old canine companion. Thus, the officer avoided having his arm shredded off by the possessed and enraged animal trying to lunge for his throat.

Solas reappeared out of the tent with his mighty weapon and stood square beside the Stealth Demon.

"Is this what you are looking for?" Solas yelled, brandishing his glinting weapon and flashing the small, round mystical object.

The beast stopped, turned and hissed at Solas while tensing its muscles. Now everyone, including the two mesmerized officers, stood watching. Jiji and Amy ran to attend to shaman Orenda's wound.

"Well, why don't you come and get it?" asked Solas.

The beast seemed to calm its nerves and stood straight up, its tail slithering back and forth behind him like a snake. It snarled and spat at Solas in disgust. Then, it turned and walked away from it all as though nothing mattered and, with a sudden burst of speed, vanished once more, this time behind the Iroquois ceremonial yurt building.

Solas and Dorian then joined Amy and Jiji by shaman Orenda's side.

"He's dying," said Amy in a quivering voice.

"Oh no!" said Solas.

The officers approached behind them and offered to help.

"I'll call an ambulance," said Officer Hurst, still rattled by the incomprehensible events he witnessed.

"It's too late," said a despondent Amy. "He won't make it."

Shaman Orenda gurgled, drowning in his own blood. As a last sign of respect, Dorian and Solas picked up the old shaman and carried him inside the open yurt, where they laid him down on the marbled cenotaph where Solas had found Lux Veritas on two separate occasions. Then, by coincidence or by design – which only the Lord Creator could know with certainty – the Wheel of Souls appeared above the dying man.

"Look," said Amy, "the Wheel of Souls!"

The four friends glanced at each other.

"Let's ride into the vortex," said Solas.

The officers, awed once again and overwhelmed with mixed emotions, stood back and observed the show like little kids watching a magician's tricks for the first time.

"What is that?" asked a stunned Officer Downes, still clutching his wounded arm.

Solas looked at them and attempted to explain.

"It's called the Wheel of Souls. It will take us to the afterlife," he said.

"The afterlife," repeated a perplexed Officer Hurst.

The vortex intensified. A swirling wind picked up and shaman Orenda's soul began to lift and depart into the tunnel.

"Hang on!" yelled Jiji, as the whooshing sound of the vacuum intensified.

The four friends joined hands in a circle above Orenda's body. Amy and Solas held on tight to the active, glinting Lux Veritas; hand over hand on the hilt. Solas slipped the ring of his mysterious round gift onto his index finger and held it like a baseball in the palm of his other hand. The passage through to the afterlife was rocky, this he knew, and keeping the object in his pocket was not a good idea, to be sure. Solas then turned to Stanley and Robert one last time and made a sign of silence with the index finger bearing the cryptic object. The befuddled officers nodded and repeated the gesture … "Hush."

The departing soul of shaman Orenda and its transparent ghostly outline continued to ascend softly into the vortex. The foursome followed behind, rising together into the whirling tunnel now spinning like a dust devil, and entered the Wheel of Souls.

Officers Hurst and Downes watched this strange phenomenon when suddenly, out of nowhere, the Stealth Demon returned with a lightning burst of speed. The beast brushed aside the two onlookers and jumped above the sepulchre, diving into the vortex in the nick of time to join the teenage quartet, unawares, and steal a most opportune ride to the afterlife … destination: Purgator.

Chapter II

The Will-master's Luret

"For destiny never swerves, nor yields to men the helm."
—Ralph Waldo Emerson (1830 – 1882)

I

The group was soon engulfed in the spinning vortex of the Wheel of Souls. This was a second experience for Solas, Dorian and Amy – they had been through this passage only a few short months ago – but despite all of their efforts, hanging on to one another proved fruitless. The centrifugal force and the flipping end over end inside the tunnel pulled apart the four friends and scattered them far and wide so that, before long, they were no longer in contact with each other or even within sight of one another. The spirit of Orenda had all but vanished without a trace, in true shamanic fashion. And no one in the group was yet aware that an intruder was following close behind. Forthwith, the four travelers were stripped of their nonessential garments and the grueling physical changes in the life sustaining ether of the vortex were soon underway. Resisting them only made the process that much more difficult to bear. Solas held on as long as possible but was forced to let go his grip on Lux Veritas. Like torture, he watched his beloved weapon separate from him and float away out of arm's reach. He kept an eye on her as best he could, each time he switched in and out of consciousness. The rapid jolting physical changes were painful to endure, but Solas now knew that the end result – a cut and fit body strong enough to rival that of any epic Greek hero – was well worth the straining and the agony.

Thus, it was on the last flash awakening that Solas became conscious, as he searched for a visual of his weapon, that the Stealth Demon was present. There it was, only a short distance away. With the same intense grin on its face, the beast flipped just like Solas did, end over end, powerless and out of control. A sense of shock zapped Solas and he began to panic. *What is the beast doing here? And where is Lux Veritas?* Not that Solas worried about defending himself. That was one thing. But he worried most about the Stealth Demon getting its hands on Lux Veritas first. Solas could not let this happen. And so he fought not to sway in and out of consciousness in spite of all the brutal metamorphosis exerted on his body at each and every moment. His lungs were immersed and burning from the life sustaining gel-like substance in which he floated and tumbled. He glanced round in all directions, in this enclosed tornado-like environment of flashing electrical bursts. At last, he caught a glimpse of Lux Veritas.

Solas attempted to reach his precious weapon through sheer willpower, stretching his arms and wriggling, motioning his body to follow the given direction. And horror of horrors, the beast was nearer yet. After what seemed like a long struggle, Solas, sword and demon came within mere feet of each other. Eyes of man and beast met, all with the same pressing purpose in mind. The flashing changes continued and at a precise moment, with one simple glance, Solas noticed something rather singular and shocking about the Stealth Demon. It was changing too. Not a lot, but enough to show that beneath this mantle of steel and evil lay a sentient being, at one time perhaps a human being. It smiled and it had a heart, a soul. Or so it appeared. Solas attempted to refocus and not to fall into deception or some other vile trick from the demon. And it happened again; only this time clearer. Solas, drunk from the exertion, could not believe his eyes. *Was I looking at the image of someone I know? Who was that?*

A quick glimpse at the stark image unveiled by the demon was enough to sober up Solas. *Could the Stealth Demon be someone I know?* But time was of the essence and getting to Lux Veritas first was the only objective that mattered. Yet, it was the beast that edged closer and was about to snatch the weapon. As they both came within near reach of the mighty Sword of Genesis, their eyes met one final time. Under the pressure and the tumult of the moment, Solas saw it ... the face beneath the mask, for just a split second. Under sudden shock, Solas pulled his hand away by fear and by instinct. Lux Veritas was now within easy grasp of the beast. And, as the Stealth Demon made one last valiant attempt to seize the weapon with his sharp and crooked fingertips, the vortex of the Wheel of Souls sped up with one violent jolt and pulled the threesome apart for good.

The tunnel narrowed and began to spin faster and faster. The metamorphosis became unbearable and Solas lost consciousness for good, in much the same manner he had the first time he went through the vortex prior to landing in Purgator.

Solas crashed down hard. He was back in Asphodel Meadows, a vast plain of grass and pastures extending for miles around, right in the heart of Purgator. That's where the fun began for all humans who exited the Wheel of Souls and finally reached the afterlife. As usual, the sun was shining on this heavenly postcard landscape of colors and flowers and filled with the subtle scents of summer. For a moment Solas might have believed that he was back home, somewhere in the open fields of Sherbrooke county. Except that when he came to, he was as butt naked as the day he was born. He coughed up the mucus still stuck in his mouth and throat before taking his first breath and slowly opening his eyes.

I don't remember it hurting this bad, he thought as he turned himself over onto his back.

The daylight blinded him as he stared up into the big blue sky, but he wasted little precious time getting up to his feet. He wobbled as he stood up.

"Damn, my ribs!" he mumbled, putting a hand on his aching chest.

Perhaps he had broken something. He crouched and coughed up some more before noticing he was back in his new body; this borrowed temple of flesh gifted him by the higher power that was. This cheered him up somewhat. The pain went away.

I've got to find Amy, Dorian and Jiji. I hope they're alright.

Solas knew full well that danger roamed the four corners of the land, and that without any protection they were all at the mercy of any wild creature that might take a fancy to them. And God forbid if any units of Daemonia should find them first. This very thought made Solas quite uneasy.

Where is my sword, and my ring thingy? And, with some urgency, Solas began to search for his mighty weapon, looking around the green grass for any glinting reflection from the sun.

2

Lux Veritas he did not see, but behold Solas was not alone; another being appeared in the distance.

Damn! thought Solas. There was no mistaking it; it was the Stealth Demon.

Solas paid no heed to the beast anymore than he should. There was little else he could do anyhow. He scrambled back and forth like a desperate soul fearing the worst trying to locate Lux Veritas in the tall grass.

Come on baby, where are you?

Solas glanced up sporadically to see if the Stealth Demon had taken notice of his presence. He rushed and prayed, he rushed and prayed and on his last check, Solas noticed the beast making a beeline for him with a hard, sturdy gait. Solas kept about his business, scouring the surrounding area hoping to find his beloved Lux Veritas. The Stealth Demon was just 60 yards away when Solas calmed himself and relied on his faith.

If the Lord Creator believes in me, who can be against me? Indeed, he had remembered the most valuable lesson that master Senex had taught him on his first journey to the land of Purgator: unconditional trust. And so it was at that very moment that Solas was blinded by the glint of the sword, as it rested half-way out on the path of the oncoming beast. Solas did not hesitate and rushed full speed ahead in his newfound body like an Olympic athlete on a 40 yard dash to reach Lux Veritas in time. The startled demon, on the other hand, stopped his advance to ponder the apparent foolishness of Solas's act. That is when the beast understood and caught a glimpse of the sword laying in the grass. The Stealth Demon snarled and hissed in surprise as much as in anger and rushed toward the weapon.

The demon was lightning quick and recovered lost ground. The crunch for time was so critical that the entire event seemed to occur in slow motion. Solas dove to reach the sword, rolling like a gymnast and picking up the weapon by the hilt on the fly. Lux Veritas lit up instantly. In the motion, the sword slashed the leg of the charging beast and cut the demon at the base of the shin. The beast stumbled but quickly sprung back up. The Stealth Demon stared back at Solas and let out a blood chilling scream of pain and anger. The sound reached into the distance of the flatlands of Asphodel Meadows and warned the three wandering Outlanders, Dorian, Amy and Xiao Ren, that something was abnormal. Solas's three companions also separated during their voyage through the vortex and landed in different parts of the open fields of Asphodel. *Solas!* they thought. As per instinct, the trio shared an idea. They would follow the source of the sound. Perhaps, with a bit of luck, they could find each other again.

As Solas stood back up, he held his charged weapon upright before him. A trace of the purplish blood that ran through the Stealth Demon's veins now began to trickle down its ankle. Solas noticed it and found this rather peculiar. But he was glad to know that the beast's seemingly impregnable armor was vulnerable after all, or at least it was so against the mighty Lux Veritas. The two foes huffed and puffed while staring each other down. Solas brandished his live weapon and flashed its sharp metal edge against the sunlight coaxing the beast to make another move if it dared. As he did so, quite unexpectedly, Solas noticed posited before him the ringed object which he had lost during his travels through the whirling vortex. He had hardly had the time to realize it was missing. But there it was, lodged like a magnet at the upper edge of the blade; melded as it appeared onto the base of the crossguard of Lux Veritas.

This was yet another puzzle for Solas. But before he could consider the object or the meaning of its odd emplacement, Solas needed to keep a steady eye on the Stealth Demon's every move. The injured beast was angered beyond all get-out, and its calm outward demeanor only betrayed its explosive nature. Beyond the fathomless depth of its hollow gaze, the crimson red of its empty soul simmered the thousand hell fires of contempt. Neither foe would commit. The demon understood the essence of the mighty Lux Veritas. And with Solas in his upright state of mind, challenging him for the weapon was pure suicide. The boy, on the other hand, could not strike first. The sword of Genesis would not allow it; she was the atoner, not the beast. Neither beast nor man would flinch in this battle of will. But the apparent stalemate was to be short lived.

3

As fate would have it, Amy arrived next on the scene. Solas lifted his eyes and glanced over the shoulder of the Stealth Demon into the distance – a mere hundred yards away or so – to discern the nature of the being approaching. He suddenly became edgy and a single look into his dilating eyes was enough to clue in the beast. The demon turned its head to see the girl closing in. Solas became increasingly agitated, fidgeting with his weapon and pondering what to do next. The beast – unabashed and gleeful at the blatant opportunity that just presented itself – stared back at the boy and grinned scornfully.

With an explosive burst of speed and no apparent ill effect from the wound, the beast turned and ran toward Amy to intercept the girl.

"Nooooo," screamed a helpless Solas, in a desperate attempt to warn his love.

Amy recognized his voice. She stopped suddenly and a cold chill ran through her veins. Her heart began to race at the thought of seeing the Stealth Demon rushing towards her. She stood frozen like a clay statue in the middle of the green expanse. She mumbled a prayer to sweet Mary Mother of God. And with nowhere to go and no place to run, she braced herself for the inevitable. The beast shifted gears and slowed down a few feet shy of his target. The demon walked up to Amy and grabbed by her left arm, raising her up onto her tippy toes. She screamed and struggled to keep her balance. The driveling demon, still trickling a light stream of bluish blood onto its soaked left foot, turned Amy around abruptly to face Solas who was trailing only a few seconds behind.

"Let her go," warned Solas.

Lux Veritas still stood on guard, just as true as Solas still stood naked before the world. Amy paid no attention to this detail. A "Help Solas!" was all she could muster up. The beast continued to snarl as it taunted Solas by flaunting its catch.

"Let her go," repeated Solas, who was left with little more than a prayer himself. The beast grinned and breathed heavily through its flaring nostrils, but did not say a word. It squeezed Amy's arm that much harder, raising her up yet an inch higher.

"Aaaaah … Solas please," she begged.

Solas thought hard and fast about how to trick the demon and break the deadlock. Amy was still alive. This much was good because the beast could have ended her life in a snap. But it had not, at least not yet. How he wished Fidem Aenas had still been around. A sharpshooting elkin archer might have been enough to fix the problem; just maybe. How he wished his mighty weapon Lux Veritas could bend the rules for once and act rather than react to the situation. A thousand thoughts raced through his mind. Yet, as delicate as the moment was, Solas was again awe struck by Amy's natural beauty. He looked at her newly fashioned body and wondered how much the Lord Creator had lavished upon her the flawless grace of the angels! She was a beauty unequalled on Heaven or Earth to be sure, and most certainly in this hell they called Purgator. Her flowing blonde locks covered her fragile facial features chiseled in rose alabaster. Her sparkling blue eyes denuded his soul; her smile gave meaning to life; her voice was the symphony of rapture; and her curves the dream vessel of the muses.

"Let go of Amy," Solas implored. "I am sure we can work out some kind of a deal."

The beast chuckled softly behind a gurgling sound.

"You … know," said the beast in its jittery voice.

"Don't you give it to him Solas," yelled Amy. "Don't!"

Amy's words of defiance angered the beast some more and it proceeded to twist Amy's arm and raise her higher yet, so that her toes now hardly touched the ground. She moaned and writhed in pain, feeling as though her arm was about to be ripped out of its socket. Now the beast seized Amy by the throat with its free hand, choking her and directing her face toward Solas so that he could have a clearer look at her. Solas remained resolute.

"Now give the sword," the beast continued, "or she dies."

Amy went quiet and struggled to breathe. Her throat was cut and drops of blood began to drip. Solas hesitated. The demon gradually applied more pressure until it appeared as though Amy would lose consciousness.

"If she dies," yelled Solas, "you will never get your filthy hands on Lux Veritas. I will hunt you down and I will rip your heart out with my own bare hands."

The beast chuckled some more at Solas's threat. It was Solas who was getting his heart ripped apart at the moment. Nothing was more obvious. The demon held Amy's face only inches away from his and considered what to do next with the natural beauty. Her eyes began to roll back and her limbs went limp. Solas, nervous and distraught, fought back a whole range of emotions. He was about to give in out of a combination of pure agony and sheer madness. He thought about charging at the beast in an act of absolute desperation. But then turning to Solas, the demon spoke.

"She comes with me," the beast uttered, cool as the void. Its odd stutter suddenly vanished and Chaos's first lieutenant spoke ever clearer now. "She comes to my world," the demon continued, "beyond the Diamond Crossing. That is where you will find us." And further provoking Solas, it grinned and added: "Come boy if you dare to the demon haunted world … your love will await you there."

Solas took in all this confusing information trying to make sense of it all. Amy was now unconscious. The beast released the pressure on her throat and held her dangling body at arm's length with stunning ease. The Stealth Demon now pulled out that mysterious dark swirling object from some hidden pocket beneath its cloaked armor. The beast held the arcane item above its head, uttered more gibberish and following the playing of some alluring musical chime, the unit reactivated and enveloped in a translucent cocoon both the beauty and the beast. All the while, Amy remained oblivious to the events surrounding her.

The protective capsule lifted up and like a silent bullet shot up into the great blue sky at breakneck speed leaving behind it only a trail of flittering sparkles. And just like that, Amy was gone. Solas dropped to his knees in despair. In the stillness of the open plains of Asphodel Meadows and under the hammering heat of the afternoon sun, only the sobbing cries of a vanquished Solas could be heard drifting away into yonder fields on the hardy wings of the warm whispering breeze.

4

It was without a doubt this mix of screams, flashes and whimpers that eventually led Dorian and Xiao Ren straight to Solas's location.

"Solas!" yelled Dorian the moment he recognized his friend curled up face down on the grass.

Solas lifted his head to witness his friends arriving, who were also kind enough to bring with them a small dose of consolation.

"Are you alright?" asked Dorian.

Solas stood up to welcome his friends. They hugged. Although he found it hard at first to speak any words at all, he eventually found his voice.

"It sure is nice to see you guys alive and well. I can see you haven't changed at all. You're back in your Purgator bodies again."

"You too, Solas!" replied Xiao Ren. "You even have your scar back."

"I do?" said Solas.

He put a hand over his face and tried to feel the evidence of the wound he suffered against the blade of Daemonia while saving Amy from danger on his first tour of duty in Purgator.

"You landed here together?" continued Solas.

"No, but we met up by chance a little ways back," answered Dorian.

When the heartfelt greetings were over, Solas showed his friends how the object had melded onto the upper blade of Lux Veritas and explained in full details the events of the Stealth Demon in the vortex, as well as the unfortunate set of circumstances that led to the kidnapping of their beloved friend Amy.

"I may never see her again," said Solas.

"Don't say that," said Xiao Ren. "Amy is strong. You need to have faith."

"Even so," added Solas, "the good Lord only knows what the Stealth Demon and his minions will do to her over there. That very thought is killing me."

"Come on Solas," said his friend Dorian, "think positive. But for now, I hate to remind you but we best get moving out of here and fast. Remember, on our last trip to Purgator we were attacked by a slew of freaks, dwarves and demons. We need to find Fidem's oasis right now and meet up with Chepi. He will have the answers, I am sure."

Solas nodded in agreement.

"Only, which way do we go now Jiji?" asked Dorian.

"Follow me, it's that way," she replied pointing to the direction. "Fidem would often tell us stories about his hunting prowess and other exploits around the oasis. Besides, I have been to Asphodel Meadows on several occasions in the past – you know, back in the days when life was more peaceful. I think we should have no trouble finding it from here. Although I must admit I have never been to his hideout."

"Well, we have," said Solas. "Just get us there, Jiji. And let's hope shaman Chepi will be at the rendezvous like he told us. I really don't look forward to the prospect of making another trip to the Forsaken Forest in order to find him."

"Lord no," said Dorian. "That would mean going through troll country again. I hate trolls."

The trio began to walk in the direction indicated by Xiao Ren, hoping that before too long and most certainly before nightfall, they would come upon the oasis for shelter. The heat of the late afternoon sun began to take a toll on the travelers, and in particular Jiji.

"I usually do not feel overly self-conscious," added Jiji, "but it's getting really hot out here. I'm getting sunburns all over. I could really use some clothes and a comfy pair of moccasins too."

"And weapons," added Dorian.

"All the more reason we need to push ahead and find the oasis," replied Solas. "Fidem used to keep a good number of reserves and supplies in his den."

"Yeah but his shelter must be abandoned now, ever since he died," added Dorian.

"Well, we shall see," answered Solas.

"Speaking of seeing … what is that I see coming straight our way?" asked Jiji.

"Better not be Daemonia or those pesky Torlund dwarves already," said Dorian.

"I don't think so," replied Solas who stopped to have a better look. "For some reason, the units of Daemonia do not seem to be as numerous this time around. This is just a solitary individual. It looks human too."

"You're right Solas," said Jiji. "He appears to be naked like we are."

"All right," Dorian cheered, "this is good news … more humans."

As they approached the newcomer, he stopped advancing and attempted to hide in the tall grass in order to avoid detection. On the horizon, the skies grumbled. Huge clouds rolled in bringing with them thunder, lightning and heavy summer rains.

"Look," said Jiji, "he's trying to hide. That's so cute."

"What a wily old fox," added Dorian. "It's like he knows what to expect already. He's not taking any chances."

"Well, he should thank his lucky star," said Solas. "We could have been demons."

"Or Torlund dwarves," added Dorian.

"Yes but newcomers don't know that," said Jiji. "This is a really strange reaction."

Suddenly, with the trio only 20 yards away, the earthling sprung up from the turf.

"By Hahgwehdiyu," he proclaimed, raising both arms in the air, "it is you!"

This statement surprised them. Lux Veritas stayed inactive and Solas addressed the stranger first.

"Who are you my friend? Do we know you?"

"Solas ... Dorian ... Xiao Ren," the cheerful human replied, to their complete amazement. "Do you not recognize me?"

The puzzled threesome exchanged blank looks at each other. Finally, the young man revealed his name.

"I am shaman Orenda."

"Orenda?" they repeated.

"It is I, in the flesh."

Xiao Ren was first to greet him. She was not afraid to welcome him even though Orenda looked nothing like the old shaman she knew. Of course, she understood this was the norm in Purgator. Upon entering the afterlife, humans took on the rejuvenated form that most convened with their own ideals, mindset or just deserves and this gift was ultimately bestowed upon them as a reward (or punishment in the case opposite) by the bountiful graciousness of the Lord Creator. And shaman Orenda looked like a fine young man in his brand spanking new vessel. He was fit, strong, sturdy, as well as handsome one could say. Dorian checked out the new version of the old man, smiled and slapped Orenda a double high-five. Solas only had words for the young shaman.

"Welcome to the afterlife, Orenda," he said. "If your new body is any indication, you must have been one fine fellow in your youth. But tell me, how did you know it was us? We look as different in this land as you do."

"I was not sure at first, so I tried to hide. And that's easier said than done in this open grassland," he explained. "You did look different from far away in these new bodies and all, it's true. But there is only one Lux Veritas."

"Of course," said Solas, "Lux Veritas."

"I was never happier to see her," added Orenda.

"Forgive us, Orenda," said Solas. "We knew you had passed away. We were there. We saw it happen. And thanks to you, we were able to enter the Wheel of Souls. You led the way, Orenda. But for some silly reason, we just never expected to find you here in Purgator with us. Truth is ... we would have much preferred that you had passed through the Crystal Gates straight to Elysium. The Lord only knows you deserve it."

After those words by Solas, Orenda appeared downcast and he went entirely speechless.

"What's the matter, Orenda?" asked Solas. "Come on, cheer up. You are with us now."

"It's just that ... I died," said he. "You will return home when your mission is over, but I shall never see my home again. I must stay here, you see. My work is not finished I suppose, just like shaman Chepi. No Elysium for me."

Now the first drops of rain began to fall and a cooler breeze picked up. The heavens above rumbled some more and flashes of lightning lit up the skies above Asphodel Meadows.

"Chepi," said Solas. "I am glad you mentioned his name. Where were you headed just now Orenda? Do you know the way to the oasis per chance?"

Orenda raised his voice to compensate for the change of weather, the blowing wind and the driving rain.

"The oasis?" he repeated. "Chepi lives on the edge of the Forsaken Forest, in troll country as I remember. Children, I believe you are going the wrong way."

"No Orenda," replied Solas. "Do you not remember the instructions that shaman Chepi gave us during the séance in your tipi? He told us to meet him at Fidem's hideout at the oasis."

"Oh," replied Orenda. "I did not know that. I was in a trance, I guess. I wouldn't remember a single event or a single word."

"Okay, well we need to get to the oasis," explained Solas. "And the oasis is in the opposite direction you were going ... according to Jiji anyways."

"Yes," said Orenda. "I think she is right. I saw a small wooded area back there near where I landed. Maybe that was it."

"By God, Orenda," said Solas with a smile. "You were there already my friend. Let's go."

The southerly winds grew stronger yet and the pouring rain beat down in droves on the quartet. All were drenched now. The four friends helped each other along by wrapping their arms around each other's waists and forging ahead against the wind. Despite the increased efforts required to reach their destination, the idea of being so close to the oasis boosted their spirits and even spurred Dorian to hum along a little ditty and sing the verses to one of his all-time favorite tune *'Couldn't Stand the Weather.'*

5

Without any sort of protection, the rain drops stung their bodies like pin needles and the four travelers were forced to turn their faces away from the blowing gusts. The skies darkened fast and it felt as though the day had shortened and dusk was upon them hours early. For a moment, they also feared the worst: the gale would soon turn into a full raging twister. They were not in Kansas at all, nor in the Land of Oz, but no one at this juncture could have told the difference. And it was with mixed emotions that the foursome finally reached the coveted shelter of the thick wooded grove. Indeed, as they looked up, it wasn't the wicked witch of the West they saw – for she would have been no trouble at all – but none other than a murder of gargoyles, Daemonia's pestiferous beasts of reconnaissance, which had taken refuge beneath the boughs of the first line of trees. Perhaps they were six or seven in number. In any event, the entrance was blocked.

"Do you see what I see?" asked Dorian who was first to notice the danger ahead.

"Gargoyles!" said Solas. "Crouch down low!" he ordered.

"They haven't seen us yet," said Xiao Ren.

"Yes, that's because they have all curled up under their wings like bats. They are waiting for the storm to pass," explained Solas.

"What do we do now?" asked Orenda. "We can't turn back."

Suddenly, a huge thunder roll rumbled overhead and several sporadic flashes of lightning blazed up the sky and brought daylight upon the area, exposing the foursome. And a couple of the hell-birds did take notice. Lux Veritas tended to shine bright when reflecting light, especially in the heart of darkness. Solas did not possess its sheath and hiding the weapon under such circumstances proved rather troublesome. The creatures deployed their wings and screeched until all of the gargoyles had awakened. Four of them took to the air and turned away over the oasis. They flew upwind, forcing against the strengthening gale with great difficulty and being tossed about hither and thither, up and down, and across and over by the capricious whims of the storm. Still they tried, and like the fine scouts they were, went off to warn the powers that be and seek the help needed. As for the three remaining dark angels, they waited and kept watch over the entrance, eyes aglow and not budging an inch. They seemed to implore 'Come if you dare!'

'We barge right through. That's what we do," said Solas. "These overgrown chickens are no match for Lux Veritas."

"I pray you are right Solas," replied Orenda. "These beasts look nasty."

"Do not fear. They are nothing like the Stealth Demon," said Solas, now screaming over the tempest in order to be heard a mere five feet away. "Form a line behind me and follow me close. We must get to the shelter before Daemonia returns in force!"

"Sounds like a plan," yelled Dorian.

As the quartet approached the entrance, the three hell-birds became restless. Finally, as the rain stopped, one of the flying demons spread its wings and rose vertically ten feet in the air. Partially sheltered by the tall oaks and helms, the struggling beast managed to hold its position and hovered straight above Solas and company. Now, the howling wind increased across the plains, the thunder rumbled steady and the flashes of lightning became more frequent. The oasis was in the eye of the storm and the crown of its trees rustled in every direction. Leaves, branches and shrubs broke off and were tossed into the blast. Solas held his mighty weapon just above his head for protection from beast and storm. Suddenly, the flying demon screeched a deafening high pitch and shot a burst of flames at Solas and company. At the same moment, the two standing gargoyles lunged at Solas with their long sharp claws and talons drawn, and flapping their long powerful wings in an attempt to knock him off balance.

Lux Veritas countered the assault by erecting an immediate shield right above the foursome, which deflected the stream of fire toward the charging hell-birds. The two gargoyles fell to the ground and nearly burnt to a crisp as they caught on fire. When the fire starter finally stopped to catch its breath, a thunderbolt met the end of Lux Veritas's blade. The lightning strike impaled the fire breathing demon on its way through and sent two additional rods of lightning through the gargoyle corpses lying on the ground, putting an official end to their writhing agony. The thunderbolt recoiled as quick as it appeared and the flying demon crashed to the ground to join its partners. In a matter of seconds, the ordeal was over and the entranceway to the oasis was freed.

Solas stepped around the vanquished enemy's smoldering pile of soot colored bones and entered the oasis with a certain amount of prudence. More enemies could have taken shelter inside and could be lurking in the shadows. His three deprived friends followed closely behind him and acted as extra pairs of eyes. Beneath the shelter's canopy, the darkness was even more intense and before long the guiding light of Lux Veritas went out. The danger had passed and the group took comfort in knowing that they had reached their destination at last. Somewhere inside this refuge, shaman Chepi awaited them. He would supply them with clothes, equip them with weapons and all necessities required for survival in this land of madness, and provide them with all the answers they sought … or so Solas hoped. The four members were shivering now and they still needed to locate Fidem's old hideout. The wind died down and the friends could better communicate once again. Here and there, flashes of light from the dying storm pierced through the canopy and allowed for a glimpse of their surroundings. They followed the main path until they reached the heart of the oasis. There, they rested on a felled log – wet though it was – set beside the remnants of Fidem Aenas's old campfire, where on many occasions past during their first voyage to Purgator, Solas and Dorian had shared tasty treats with their now departed elkin colleague.

"Wow, I'm bushed," said Dorian, as he tried to find a comfortable position. "This place brings back memories, doesn't it?"

"Yes," replied Solas, the only other person present who could relate to that statement. "It sure does. And if I remember well, Fidem's den should be just over that way, about 20 yards down the path leading behind the old oak tree where we first met Fidem."

The clouds started to dissipate faster and allowed the late afternoon sunrays to peek through the canopy. Dorian was able to pinpoint the tree in question, which was standing only a short ways across the drenched fire pit.

"Yes, you're right," he said, pointing to it. "That's it right there. Let's go find Chepi now and be done with it."

"What if there are more gargoyles in this forest, Solas," said Orenda, still shaken from his first close-up encounter with members of Daemonia, "what shall we do then? They could burn down the shelter, the whole oasis even."

"Actually, that fire demon was not a gargoyle, even if it looked like one," said Xiao Ren, still quivering from the effects of the rain on her skin. "It was a spitfire ... the same kind that burnt down our sails on the Sea of Morphos during our getaway from Daemonia. The village of Lalas Pur burnt down and we ended up drifting at sea until we landed on the shores of the Forsaken Forest. Remember? We told you the story."

"Well, these spitfires are a whole lot nastier than I had imagined," replied Orenda.

"I don't know," said Solas as he knelt down to examine the remaining cinders of the fire pit. "I doubt spitfires and gargoyles would venture too far inside a forest. But their partners might, if these foot prints here are any indication."

Solas had just discovered tracks of foot-demons, dwarves and other beasts about the pit.

"Good God," said Orenda.

"Let's move," ordered Solas, "before they come back. We're almost there."

6

After this short rest, the group hurried on and attempted to locate the whereabouts of Fidem's hideout. Before long, Solas came upon an area of interest, one that seemed familiar to him. He walked around in circles until he heard a creak under his feet.

"There it is!" he said.

He bent down and cleared away loose ferns, dead leaves, twigs and moss which covered the wooden trapped door to Fidem's den. He knocked three times and the group waited eager for an answer. Dorian, Jiji and Orenda scoped the surroundings like thieves on the prowl to make sure Daemonia was not present anywhere about the place.

"Chepi!" said Solas, careful not to speak too loud. "It's me … Solas. Are you there? Open up."

An object like the eye of a submarine protruded out of the ground ten feet away from the trap door right behind the visitors. The foursome never took notice of it. Instead, they were preoccupied and worried that perhaps shaman Chepi might not have made it to the rendezvous. But he had. Through the eye lens of his examining tool, Chepi recognized three of the foreigners and hurried to unlatch the door. The unlocking noise startled them and the group stood back. The door swung open.

"Come on in, fast," whispered the shaman, as he glanced around the area quickly, more concerned about a potential threat than by the presence of his friends. "And be quiet!"

Xiao Ren, Dorian and Orenda climbed down the birch ladder leading to the hidden chamber, followed last by Solas. Chepi could hardly be mistaken for someone else. He wore thick moccasins, tanned suede pants with frills and a white cotton shirt with embroidered Indian motifs. His long black hair was split down the middle and arranged in tresses which hung half way down his chest, and around his neck he wore a collar with an array of dangling animal claws and teeth. He made sure to lock the swivel door behind him. Nothing much had changed since the last time Solas and Dorian had visited these quarters; the wooden table and the four chairs were still there, as was the straw bedding in the corner with plenty of blankets to keep warm for the cool summer nights. Large torches planted in the hard clay stone supplied sufficient light to the underground lodging. Hanging off the ceiling were Fidem's old hunting traps and suspended beside them were tasty leucurus jerky – better known to humans as prairie dog – and other dried meats. But most important, the four friends noticed the pile of stacked clothing and the neatly laid down weapons awaiting them on the table top.

"Greetings my young friends," said Chepi in a deep voice as he welcomed them to his humble abode … or rather, Fidem's. He hugged each returning member to Purgator, beginning with Xiao Ren. "What a pleasure it is to see you again! I was truly worried. Old Nokomis passed away and made the trip to the afterlife, but you did not come along. I was expecting you and there was no sign of you. I wondered what could have happened. Perhaps you had missed the rendezvous, but I kept the faith. I knew you would find a way."

And before completing his last embrace, his eyes locked with Orenda's. Hoping to be identified, the Iroquois shaman from Sherbrooke allowed himself a tepid smile, despite his naked state.

"Do I know you young man?" Chepi asked.

Orenda offered no answer. He just kept smiling. Then, by natural intuition, it dawned on the old shaman of Purgator.

"Orenda," he said, "my friend."

"It is I."

Chepi paused for a moment.

"I suppose I should be glad to see you, Orenda," he said. "What happened?"

"The Stealth Demon," answered Orenda.

"The Stealth Demon," repeated Chepi.

"Yes."

"I see. And where is our lovely angel Amy?"

Solas sighed and the mood of the group turned somber. Chepi invited his friends to sit at the table to tell him all about it. He cleared up the clutter and removed a few items from the table, including the weapons. He distributed the respective moccasins and clothing he had set aside for his friends. Only Amy's remained untouched. As for Orenda, he was rather lucky; Chepi befitted him with some of his personal attire he kept as spare. The foursome was quite grateful. The youngsters' spirits lifted somewhat as they donned the clothes given them and offered many thanks to their host Chepi for his generosity and for all of his troubles. Much of the apparel had been brought in from the city of Lalas Pur and was of superior quality to the sort one may expect to find in the rest of the land of Purgator. Solas and Dorian wore black cotton capris tied with laces below the knees and a leather belt around the waist while Jiji's outfit was caramel brown. Each was also given a loose v-neck white cotton tunic top. Dorian's had carefully needled motifs representing various guardian spirits. Jiji's was cerise red and longer. She tied her belt around it at the waist. Chepi brought out some wooden cups and plates. In quiet, he offered his guests a drink of homemade wine he kept stored in the lodging as well as a few jerky sticks to fill their stomachs. But the handing out of the weapons would wait just a little longer.

The hungry lot enjoyed their snacks. Solas and Orenda went on to explain the events following the coming of the Stealth Demon to Sherbrooke County and the circumstances that led to the unfortunate demise of Orenda and to the kidnapping of Amy upon their arrival to Asphodel Meadows.

"Well, I did try to warn you about the Stealth Demon," said Chepi.

"There was not much we could do," replied Solas. "He knows about the power of Lux Veritas. He is smart and patient, not impulsive at all like the other beasts. He is quick, nimble and strong and has a hard shell to protect him."

"Where does he come from and what does he want anyway?" asked Dorian.

"Well, he wants Lux Veritas of course. The struggle between Good and Evil is as old as time. Lux Veritas is Chaos's Achilles heel, his ultimate nemesis. His pursuit is relentless and he will never stop until he possesses her. And now this latest insurgence into Purgator comes from beyond the Diamond Crossing."

"The Diamond Crossing," repeated Solas. "I don't understand. What is that? Why have I never heard of it? Only the Stealth Demon mentioned it to me once."

"It is a mysterious gate," answered Chepi, gesturing with his hands. "It is a sort of mystic portal to other worlds and other dimensions. I do not know enough about it I'm afraid."

"And that's where the Stealth Demon comes from?" asked Dorian.

"Yes," replied Chepi, his dark eyes rounding like saucers.

"What do you mean when you say other worlds and other dimensions, Chepi?" asked Solas.

Chepi casually poured some more wine to fill his friends' cups while he pondered how to provide the most accurate answer.

"Few souls ever get to travel beyond the Diamond Crossing, my young friends," he explained. "The gate can lay dormant for ages. Those who have ventured beyond – if we are to believe them – tell us of other Purgators, other Earths, and other beings from other times, different realities, different dimensions and other universes. It would seem that the Lord Creator is a whole lot greater than we could have ever imagined. We humans may not be so unique after all. Our world, our reality may be nothing more than the proverbial drop in the ocean."

"You mean … there are more Earths and more Purgators?" asked Dorian.

"That's what they say."

"And what does this Diamond Crossing do?" Solas continued.

"Every dimension has its Diamond Crossing," answered Chepi. "But it would appear that it is the exact same Diamond Crossing; the one and only … the unique center piece that keeps everything interconnected."

"Kind of like a doorway through the center of the universe," concluded Dorian.

"And perhaps more than that," added Chepi.

"And where is this … Diamond Crossing?" asked Solas.

"Look," explained Chepi, "you must understand that I cannot pledge for the accuracy of the stories I have recounted. The Diamond Crossing is somewhere in the gut of Purgator, deep below the surface. So I have been told. But I have never seen it."

"And who told you this?" Solas continued.

"The leprechauns."

"The leprechauns?" repeated Solas, Dorian and Xiao Ren in perfect harmony.

"Yes … the leprechauns."

"You mean those annoying money-hungry gold-hording contemptuous ignorant lying little creatures that live on the edge of the Rainbow Mountains by the foot of Mount Glory … those leprechauns?"

"Yes, those ones."

"And why would they know anything about the Diamond Crossing?"

"They are expert miners," replied the shaman. "They know every cave, every grotto, and every in and out of the intricate maze of underground tunnels beneath Purgator. They have been there. They have seen it. That's why."

"And why should we believe them?"

"They know the Stealth Demon," Chepi explained. "They have seen him enter and exit through the Diamond Crossing with the help of the mystic gadget they like to call the Will-master's luret."

7

Solas was stunned by these revelations from old shaman Chepi. He imagined the possibilities of traveling through space and time to other lands and to other eras. He believed again. His confidence grew. He would find Amy now. Solas got up from the table and grabbed Lux Veritas which was leaning upright against the wall. She now looked mightier and more beautiful than ever.

"Is this the Will-master's luret you speak of?" he asked as he spun the blade of the weapon to expose the mystic object melded onto it. "You did send it to me after all."

"Yes it is," exclaimed a surprised Chepi. "The Stealth Demon has the other one. But what is it doing stuck to your weapon?"

"I was hoping you could tell me, to tell you the truth," replied Solas. "You wouldn't happen to know how to pry it off the blade by any chance?"

"No I don't, I'm afraid," he answered. "They do fit quite well together, don't they?"

"How did you come into possession of it Chepi, and why would you send it to me anyway?" asked Solas.

Chepi took a deep breath, and as he began to speak he topped up his guests' wine goblets with more of his fine vintage. Solas covered his cup with the palm of his hand.

"It all started when I had gone to the market in Troll City on the edge of the Forsaken Forest to find some ingredients for my potions, my medicines and for my séances too … you know, herbs, toadstools and such. As it turned out, the leprechauns were looking for me; and one individual in particular."

"Was his name Fergus?" Solas asked.

"Yes. Yes it was," Chepi confirmed. "How did you know?"

"I had a feeling. We've had some dealings in the past."

"Well, he was real eager to pawn off his item, this Will-master's luret here as I've told you. I had already heard a lot of rumors about the object and its abilities. And I knew it didn't belong to the leprechauns. This Fergus is a genuine con artist and I figured he must have come about it through some shady dealings. But I suspected that he had stolen it. And he tried to extort a pretty penny from me too. He imagined that I would be interested in this occult object, being a shaman and all. And I was curious about it, of course. But it was the first time that I had laid my eyes on it. I remembered when Master Senex and I shared conversations about the Will-master's luret, the Diamond Crossing and what was to be discovered beyond … perhaps a way back home. It was all speculation of course. We did not know enough about it, what it was called or what it looked like. And there was that cheat Fergus, who had it in his hands … unmistakable, as you can well see."

"What sort of payment did he want for it?" Solas asked.

"Can you believe that he demanded Lux Veritas in exchange? I said a rock must have fallen on your head, my little green fellow. What makes you think I have Lux Veritas?"

"But you did have Lux Veritas," said Dorian.

"Sure I did – I became its keeper after the restoration of Purgator as you know – but I wasn't going to tell him that," replied Chepi, who suddenly seemed quite fond of the grape as he guzzled down the rest of his cup. "So, this leprechaun Fergus began to sell me the virtues of the Will-master's luret, that it would lead me beyond the doors of destiny and to endless riches. He mentioned that he saw me on more than one occasion with old Master Senex at the troll market. Therefore, this jokey hobgoblin concluded that I had to know the whereabouts of Lux Veritas and how to reach her. I told him that I did not and that as far as I knew, she was home in Elysium, in the temple of the Lord Creator."

"So what did you give him in exchange instead?" asked Dorian.

"I didn't. He left."

"What do you mean he left?" asked Jiji.

"How did you manage to get the luret then?" added Solas.

"Well, you see, he didn't believe me and he didn't want anything else in exchange. He was convinced that I knew where Lux Veritas was. So he simply told me that he would be back with something much more interesting, a gift I could not refuse. And he did come back to see me a few days later. He asked a couple of my troll connections to show him the way to my hut in the Forsaken Forest. But this time, he was in a real panic to get rid of the item. So much so that he just handed it over to me for nothing and told me I should make it disappear and fast. The Stealth Demon was hot on his trail. It was the first time that I had heard of this beast. You see, that creepy leprechaun confessed to me that he had used the Will-master's luret to get on through to the other side of the Diamond Crossing. He didn't go into great details, but he did tell me that he raided gold and precious stones from rich unsuspecting souls who lived there. The trouble was he got caught red-handed by the Stealth Demon. In order to save his pitiful life, the leprechaun showed him the white luret he used to get through the crossing. But that wasn't enough for the beast, so he tricked the Stealth Demon into believing that he knew where to find Lux Veritas. Together they returned to Purgator through the Diamond Crossing. Fergus knew the old mines well and he took the demon down through the maze of pathways running beneath Mount Glory and the Rainbow Mountains. And that's where he managed to escape. The wily old elf ran and ran all the way straight to me, and arrived altogether livid and exhausted from the chase. He begged me for help, crying and crying, saying only Lux Veritas could save us."

"Save us?" said Solas. "But you had nothing to do with all of this."

"Of course not," replied the shaman, "but now I was guilty by association. That foolish leprechaun got me into a real pickle; the beast was on its way, and by the great Manitou I was not going to let the Stealth Demon get its hands on Lux Veritas if it could smell her."

"Why did you not tell Fergus to get lost, to fly away on his luret?" asked the practical Dorian.

"I did … sort of. I told him to go fly a kite instead," responded Chepi, "but Fergus told me it was no use. The Stealth Demon would find him sooner or later. Lux Veritas was the only answer and he was not about to leave. I decided I had little choice but to hide my friend the stubborn leprechaun and I attempted to contact my fellow Orenda here and summon the Wheel of Souls."

"Yes," said Orenda, who had so far been rather intrigued by the story, "I remember our initial contact. I didn't quite understand what was happening, but I knew there was a whole lot of trouble up here."

"Yes indeed," added Chepi. "I saw the fear in the leprechaun's eyes and I knew there was reason to worry. Things had been peaceful in Purgator for some time and now it appeared as though Hell was breaking loose again. How many more minions could follow behind the Stealth Demon? How many more beasts would burst through the Diamond Crossing and come looking for Lux Veritas and me, if that wretched soul Fergus could do it? So, after a stiff drink of my homemade elixir you are now enjoying and once the exhausted leprechaun fell asleep for a nap, I sent Lux Veritas and the Will-master's luret through the portal of the Wheel of Souls back to Earth to be put in the care of my brother, shaman Orenda. Fergus never saw a thing. From there, I had no doubt Orenda would contact you."

"Yes, but that is not quite how it happened, Chepi," said Solas. "The Stealth Demon found me before Orenda could."

"That's because that cursed Fergus had told him all about you, my dear Solas," replied Chepi. "After all, you were the hero who once wielded Lux Veritas and freed Purgator. And that Stealth Demon is like a bloodhound once he gets on a lead."

"That's for sure," added Solas.

"That's also why I decided to leave the Forsaken Forest behind and head for Fidem's hideout at the oasis, where we are now. And I asked you to meet me here. I was not about to wait for the Stealth Demon to show up."

At last, Solas and his friends began to make more sense of it all. It often happens this way that understanding the events of the past can help find a solution in the future. For now, they needed to find the Stealth Demon and his dark luret, and close down the apparent breach in the Diamond Crossing that could allow a whole influx of demons and beasts from other dimensions and alien worlds to break through and reach Purgator. The question was how.

8

Dorian was rather a restless spirit and his attention diverted to the clutter of weapons that Chepi had set aside in the corner of the room before the shaman brought out the food, the drinks and the story telling.

"This looks like a mighty fine arsenal you keep here, Chepi," he said. "I'm curious to know how you managed to bring all these weapons here from such a long distance as the Forsaken Forest all by your lonesome self."

"Well, I did get a little help," replied the shaman, as he got up from the table to fetch the weapons. "You see, I first went to Troll City and secured a donkey from a troll friend. Then I made a side trip to Lalas Pur to pick up supplies and this sword here to prepare you for your quest, my dear Dorian. I hope you like it."

He placed the weapon on the table in front of Dorian, who immediately picked it and examined it.

"And here is the sheath that goes with it," Chepi added.

"Thanks a lot Chepi. She's a beauty," said Dorian. "This brings back a lot of memories. Tell me, did you get this samurai sword from blacksmith Voshar by any chance?"

"I sure did," replied Chepi.

"That figures. She's very similar to the one I had before. The blade is the same; only the carvings on the handle are different," added Dorian.

"And this is Amy's," Chepi said as he presented the weapon to Solas. "I guess I will just keep it here until our angel returns."

Solas nodded in agreement.

"Tell me, Chepi," said Jiji, as she pointed at the weapon waiting for her, "is this mine?"

"Yes," answered the shaman, "this short bow is the best I could find in all of Lalas Pur."

"Wonderful. Thank you Chepi," an exuberant Xiao Ren replied.

Jiji inspected the bow with the same intensity as the craftsman who made it, feeling every bend, every groove and every curve with the delicate touch of her fingers, and testing each strap and knot with the savvy of the expert marksman she was. On Earth, she still practiced archery with the dedication and passion of an Olympian. And in Purgator, many years she had spent in the company of her beloved mentor – the wise and elder Master Senex – perfecting her shooting skills out in the fields surrounding her home city of Lalas Pur and in the nearby hills of Morphos. With a quickened heartbeat, every memory came flooding back to her now.

"I had your good friend Linoa help me choose it. You like it?"

"Oh my God, Linoa," said Jiji cheering up as she grabbed a quiver full of arrows from Chepi's hands. "What I wouldn't give to see her again."

The old shaman smiled and retreated to the far corner of the room.

"And I believe this is yours Solas," he said.

The old shaman presented Solas with Lux Veritas' very own sheath, the one given him by Master Senex during his first voyage to Purgator. Its leather case was lined in a gold and silver alloy.

"Wow!" said Solas, "where did you find it? I had always imagined that it had vanished for good."

"Well, my young Solas, you are indeed lucky," replied Chepi, "I bought it from a leprechaun trader at the Troll city bazaar. I recognized it right away. God only knows how the green goblin managed to get his dirty hands on it."

"I hope she didn't cost you too much."

"Well, I just had to have her you know," the shaman replied with a smile.

"Thanks again."

Solas secured the sheath on his back and slotted his weapon home. Then his thoughts turned to a more pressing matter.

"Well I think I'm ready now," he said. "But tell me Chepi, this Diamond gate, how do you travel through it? I mean, how do you cross to the other side?"

"I wish I could tell you," answered Chepi. "The only being who knows for sure is Fergus the leprechaun. And I abandoned him to fend for himself in the Forsaken Forest. It would be ill advised to go back there and ask him; that I can tell you."

"Well, I agree but I don't know that we have another choice," replied Solas. "And we should hope that the scoundrel is still alive. I do remember hearing the Stealth Demon utter some sort of a code before the luret activated. Then a cocoon formed around the beast and it was gone."

"So what we really need is that code then," said Dorian.

Now everyone's attention was focused on shaman Chepi who was very pensive. After a few seconds, he snapped out of it.

"I think there is another solution."

"And what is that?" asked Solas.

"Rumor has it that the Will-master's luret belongs to a guru who lives on the far side of the Petros Mountain range at the very summit of Holy Mountain, just before one reaches the descent into the Valley of Shadows where the tireless River Lethe runs its course toward Tartarus. He will know the code."

"You mean to say that we have to go to the top of a mountain to find a guru who may give us the code. And that is, if he exists and if we can find him," said Solas.

"That's right," said Chepi. "It's worth a shot, isn't it?"

"You're kidding, right," said Dorian. "Why not the bottom of the ocean while we're at it?" he added with a slight touch of sarcasm.

"Don't despair, my young Dorian," replied Chepi. "Be patient, there is a reason for everything under the sun."

Solas sighed. "All right," he said. "And where exactly is this Holy Mountain, and how do we get there?"

"When you leave the oasis, go in the direction opposite Morphos and Lalas Pur. Head for the mountains you see in the distance at the end of the flatlands of Asphodel Meadows. There, you must find a small village called Rockdale. There are several Sherpa guides there who know the way to the top of Holy Mountain and understand the network of underground galleries beneath the Petros Mountains. Seek their service."

"And why would they want to help us?" asked Solas.

"Show them Lux Veritas and the melded luret. They will show you the way to the guru."

"And what shall we tell the guru once we get there?" asked Solas.

"You must convince the guru to give you the code. He must be aware of the situation by now and he will be glad to see that you have found the Will-master's luret. Remember: you must close the breach at the Diamond Crossing. This means you must find the Stealth Demon and destroy the dark luret or he will open the floodgates to Purgator and all will be lost."

"I must find Amy too," said Solas. "I am not leaving without her."

"Yes of course," replied Chepi. "Wherever the Stealth Demon is, she will be also. But you must be most careful in your dealings with the beast if you ever hope to get her back alive."

"I understand. And he will want Lux Veritas," said Solas.

"Trust your instincts. Lux Veritas will guide you. She helped you vanquish the mighty Cerberus once, and the Lord Chaos himself. Trust and you will be successful. This is what Master Senex would tell you," replied the old shaman. "Now let's get some rest. You have a long journey ahead of you tomorrow."

It was now getting late in the evening and the party needed a good night's sleep more than anything else in the world. Orenda was already resting his head on the table top, his eyes struggling to stay open. The day's travels and its series of rushed events – from repeated Stealth Demon encounters to battling winged beasts in storming winds, and enduring wicked corporal changes in the Wheel of Souls to losing Amy in an instant of misfortune – these had all been very taxing on the young travelers' bodies and souls. Even a little pile of straw in the most remote corner of the universe would surely bring much needed relief. They all lay down and made their spots as comfortable as they could. Chepi handed out the knitted blankets. Before wishing his friends good night, he put out all of the torches but one and made sure the cleverly hidden vents were opened up to let in the cool night air so vital for rejuvenating the youngsters' spirits.

Chapter III

Holy Mountain High

"Chasing angels or fleeing demons, go to the mountains."
—Jeffrey Rasley, mountain trekker.

I

In the early morning hours, just about dawn, the most peculiar noise woke shaman Chepi. Of the five humans huddled up in the hole, he was the lightest sleeper. The rustling of leaves, the cracking of twigs, the heavy breathing and off-hand snorting, added to the light commotions and the stifled voices – in all, the presence of beings not of the friendly kind – stirred above the old elkin abode. The shaman rose to his feet and stood just beneath the trap door, lending a careful ear to the restless stirrings. But it was the slight creaking of the swivel-door timber, cleverly camouflaged under some spongy moss, which finally got Solas's attention – that, and the silverish foreshadowing glint of the mighty Lux Veritas.

The boy stood up sword in hand, minding not to bother the other three sleepers, and light-footed his way to join Chepi who held his index finger tight over his pouting lips. Indeed the old shaman needed not say a word at all. The gesture did that well enough. Above ground, alerted by the flying gargoyles of yesternight, Chaos's minions were on the prowl in an attempt to locate the four human renegades. Solas looked over at his friends and by some mysterious telepathy their eyes opened in sync with the innate awareness of the present ongoing outside their boxed confines. At last, the bustle faded away and the nervous lot returned to its normal self.

Orenda, Dorian and Xiao Ren rose out of bed and stared up at the ceiling trying to catch a listen of the moving about above ground, and imagining all the sorts of beastly ghouls which had come to flush them out.

"How many are there?" asked Dorian in a barely audible whisper.

Chepi answered him through a series of semi-intelligible gestures and Dorian concluded that the enemy had likely come in vast numbers. In any case, for the moment, quiet was in order. And it was in this silent atmosphere that the group spent the next quarter of an hour at least, listening, sitting about and pondering their present situation if not their entire fate.

"You must be going now," Chepi said out loud. "New beasts and demons are surfacing all over the land it appears, and more are sure to come. Daemonia is once more an impending threat and the quicker you act, my good Solas, the better your chances are of success."

Solas remained quiet and the group pensive. Chepi went about the room gathering the necessities and preparing the young trekkers for their departure.

"You must head for the mountains now. No doubt that vermin Fergus stole the luret. I can't see that the guru should wish to part with it; certainly not for some mongering leprechaun. The yogi will be please to see you. Here are your things then, and may the spirit of the great Manitou be with you."

Solas gathered as best he could his scattered thoughts and found a few simple words to say.

"Thank you Chepi. Should we succeed, where will we find you?"

"I will be in Lalas Pur," the shaman answered, "or so I hope. I can no longer go home to my tipi in the Forsaken Forest. And this hole here has served its purpose. Lalas Pur is the safest place for me. The city has a moat and ramparts, and it still boasts a formidable defense, even for the most resilient foe. The lamentar and loathar soldier-guards are fierce warriors and the citizens are well trained in archery. Lalas Pur is where you will find me upon your return."

"But how will you reach the city alone, Chepi?" asked a concerned Solas. "The units of Daemonia are scouring the land again. How will you ever fight them off?"

Old Chepi smiled.

"I have a few tricks up my sleeves," he replied, "and a small pouch of Mirandia crystals; not much, but enough to get me there I suppose."

"You have Mirandia crystals?" asked Dorian.

"Yes," answered Chepi. "I kept a little of Master Senex's old magic in reserve, just in case. And a bag full of other herbs, potions and tricks too. You need not worry about me."

Orenda spoke up after reflecting on the situation.

"I would like to accompany you, brother Chepi," said he, "I have much to learn from you and I think my time will be better spent with you than by being a hindrance on our three young braves here. This is a foreign land to me and I know nothing about fighting demons. Let me come along with you, Chepi. We can share knowledge and learn from each other."

This request seemed reasonable to all parties and it was decided that shaman Orenda would indeed stay with shaman Chepi, together like brothers-in-arms.

Before Solas, Dorian and Xiao Ren prepared to exit the underground den, shaman Chepi offered Dorian a sentimental gift for the journey ahead, a good luck charm. He detached his collar – a leather string from which hung an interspersed array of animal claws and teeth.

"Here warrior Dorian," said Chepi. "Accept this modest necklace. The spirits of the land will protect you in your travels."

"No claws of Cerberus this time?"

Dorian remembered oh too well the last gift he had received from the old shaman. On that occasion, he had been told to return the claw to the mighty Cerberus, the monstrous three-headed gatekeeper to the abode of Lord Chaos in hellish Tartarus.

Chepi chuckled softly as he fastened the charm around Dorian's neck.

"Sorry, I only had one of those," he answered. "And you did well with it, and I trust you will do well again. But these teeth and claws come from the spirits of the wolverine, the eagle and the bear. Let them bring you strength and courage."

"Well, thank you Chepi," said Dorian.

Chepi knew his young friends needed to seize the day and take advantage of every opportunity. And this early morning break was such an opportunity; Solas, Dorian and Xiao Ren's chance to make a run for the mountains before the relentless units of Daemonia returned. Chepi hurried and probed the area above the hideout with the help of a rudimentary tool, his self-made periscope. Once assured that the coast was clear, he swung open the trap door and the three youngsters, equipped with their weapons, stepped out into the crisp fresh air of the emerald oasis.

"Godspeed shaman Chepi and Orenda," said Solas in a lower tone of voice. "Thanks again for all your help. Do be careful on your way to Lalas Pur. We will see you there soon enough."

"Yes. Bye for now my young braves. Remember, keep a straight line and Godspeed to you too," replied Chepi with a wink.

And upon these words, the old shaman quickly shut the door and latched it up tight.

2

Solas took a moment to look around the immediate area to make certain the coast was clear of any unwanted presence. It was, but he did notice the ravages done by the storm. Branches were torn off and strewn all over the grounds; plants and ferns were battered down every which way. The trio rejoined the trail leading back to the fire pit located in the middle of the oasis and continued straight through until they exited out the west side of the woods. Now stretching before them was the vast expanse of Asphodel Meadows. On the plains, the grass was still wet but the sky was clear. A hot summer day awaited them. In the distance, the Petros Mountains were visible with their majestic snow covered peaks. Solas observed them studiously.

"That's Holy Mountain right there," said Solas as he pointed to it. "We'll just make a beeline straight to it."

"Yes, I see it," said Dorian. "But that's quite the walk from here. It's going to take us all day."

"Let's not waste time then," answered Solas.

The nervous trio stepped out of the shelter of the oasis into the wide open plains; nervous because out here in the fields there was nowhere to hide and the threesome would be within easy sight of any demon-bird out flying in reconnaissance. Staying low-key would therefore be the greater challenge and making good time essential to their success. This meant trotting along at a good pace toward their destination.

The friends set on their quest and for several hours they wandered about the open plains of Asphodel Meadows in the given direction and kept busy making small talk – mostly about Amy – while their eyes were fixated upon the four horizons on the lookout for the new face of the dreaded enemy. As their thirst began to grow under the heat of the rising morning sun, they came upon a clear water stream which merrily sinuated across the land. The three fortunate souls stopped to refresh, to clean up, and to enjoy for a short while this peaceful paradise setting. The soft mountain breeze descending from the hills of Petros fluttered their hair and caressed their senses while the carpet of white daisies, yellow buttercups and blue violets danced in sync to the beat of the wind. Dorian profited of the occasion to create a tiny colorful bouquet which he presented to Jiji. She accepted the flowers with a smile and placed them gently behind her right ear, tucking them securely in her long silky raven hair. Solas however remained stoic. He sat down on the grass, chewed on a straw and reflected upon their situation while he listened to the soothing chirping sounds of the robins and the larks ... until a growing thumping noise disrupted this melodic surrounding.

Indeed downstream the enemy reared its ugly head and a number of demons riding on mounted beasts approached at a steady gallop. Never had Solas witnessed such creatures before. One thing for certain, they were not from Purgator. Five enraged demons arrived straddling the back of broad and stocky hyena-like creatures. These animals foamed at the mouth and ran like a lion but were the size of a buffalo. They huffed and puffed as they stampeded toward their target. In a split second, Xiao Ren nocked her bow and prepared to fire at the enemy.

"Hold your fire," ordered Solas. "Save your arrows and get behind me."

Jiji and Dorian did exactly as they were told. Solas brandished his glinting weapon and waited for the assailant to make the first move. As the enemy approached, a slew of rounded spikes the size of fastballs flew toward the trio. Lux Veritas deflected the missiles away from harm as they zapped or pinged off its invisible shield. Three of the galloping riders swerved off the straight path and attempted to reach the threesome from the rear. The other two reckless imps charged headlong at Solas. Imps they were, for they appeared at first glance to be smaller in stature, a hideous gremlin-like demon, kaki green in color, with oversized eyes and ears.

"Get down," Solas yelled at his friends behind him.

Just as Jiji and Dorian did so, Lux Veritas stun-froze the rushing imps and trounced with one circular swing the heads clean off the alien daredevils. As the imps were chucked off their saddles, their beastly mounts skidded on and crashed to a halt, full stop, full dead.

Solas then turned his attention toward the three trampling beasts coming up from the rear. Xiao Ren, perhaps worried or antsy to get in on the act, fired her weapon and powered an arrow clean through the chest of one of the imps. The other two little imps pulled hard on the reins, stopping their ride. They dismounted and approached the trio at a very leisurely pace, as though they were studying their foes. Then, without further warning, they charged at Solas and Dorian with a five-blade glaive in hand. Solas dismissed instantly his foolhardy opponent while Dorian rediscovered a touch of the old samurai mastery by sidestepping and skewering the impetuous imp with one thrust of his katana. Its death was not immediate though, and the imp spewed a mix of vomit and traces of blue blood as the fires of hate in its eyes extinguished.

3

The trio looked over the carnage they had inflicted and observed the three remaining beasts peacefully quenching their thirst by the side of the stream. To Solas, this appeared to be very odd behavior coming from such aggressive brutes. In reality, these were mindless animals, carefree and unconcerned that their caretakers were no more. Half hyena, half buffalo or half whatever they were, these corpulent, muscular and imposing beasts were as docile as common horses. They had no mane or hair to speak of and their large roundish faces resembled that of the sloth, but they possessed a square and powerful jaw full of long overlapping canines and razor sharp teeth. Set above the mouth were huge nostrils acting as air intakes to power with oxygen these rabid machines. Xiao Ren prepared another arrow.

"Don't shoot," said Solas, as he stepped in front of Jiji and slotted his weapon back into its sheath. "Lux Veritas has stopped glinting. There is no more danger here."

"Then let's go," said Dorian, "before more of these freaks show up."

"No," replied Solas. "I have an idea. Maybe we can ride these animals."

"You're kidding me, right?"

"Well, we need to make time and these things can help us do that."

"But we don't know how to ride these things," objected Dorian.

"We'll learn then," replied Solas. "It can't be that difficult if these pint-sized demons could do it."

Solas walked slowly toward the beasts along with Dorian, who still had his katana in hand, and Xiao Ren in tow. The animals were already harnessed, saddled and prepped for action and Solas did not want to miss the opportunity, there for the taking, to catch a fast ride into town. Solas spoke with a soothing voice to the animals hoping to coax the beasts into confidence. After getting their fill of water, the beasts vegetated by the side of the stream and let the rays of sunshine dull their spirits into further quiescence. These animals moaned sweet little. The first beast turned its head as a prudent Solas neared from the side.

"Addaboy," said Solas as he tapped the beast on its shoulder. "What's your name, huh?"

The hairless beasts had legs solid as tree trunks and large paws with a full set of claws. Solas, Dorian and Xiao Ren exchanged a few glances and shared a few smiles as they seemed to establish a trust with the animal. Solas then grabbed the horn of the seat and set his left foot on the stirrup in an attempt to mount the beast. The animal offered no resistance and soon Solas was sitting high on the saddle. Dorian and Jiji backed up as Solas tried an initial maneuver. He pulled on the reins and the animal responded well, turning gently to the left.

"You see," said Solas, "there ain't nothing to it at all. The animals are tame. Get on your horses, guys."

Before long, Dorian and Xiao Ren had triplicated the feat.

"That's one tiny saddle," Dorian complained. "I can barely fit."

"This is so cool," said Jiji, who was by nature always game for a new challenge.

The happy trio directed the beasts over the gulley of the narrow and shallow stream and resumed course toward the mountains of Petros.

"I would have never guessed that these absolute beasts were so easy to handle," said Dorian. "It's not even a hard ride."

"We should give them a name," suggested Jiji.

"Good idea," said Solas.

After giving it some thought, the group agreed to name the beasts after some of the most famous thoroughbred horses in American racing history.

"I will call mine Eclipse, the greatest sire of all time," decided Solas.

"Mine will be Man o' War … seems only appropriate," said Dorian.

Jiji was stumped for a moment. But then she remembered the visiting guest jockey at Central High who spoke about the greatest horses of all time and who had named a filly as perhaps the greatest one of all.

"I will call mine Ruffian."

The trio continued their trip across the plains, worry free and grateful that they did not need to endure this great distance all on foot.

4

They became accustomed to the animals and vice versa, and the beasts did not seem to them like beasts at all anymore, except in appearance. It was midday now. The riders' conversations carried on for a while until Solas grew jaded and wished to test the animals to see 'what they had in the tank' and have a little fun. They would save travel time too.

"Why don't we pick up the pace and see what these animals can do?" said he. "You know, race them."

"No fair," said Dorian. "Jiji will win. She's a lightweight."

"What, you're making excuses already?"

"I'm just saying," replied Dorian. "Come on then, let's go champ," he urged.

The fun was about to begin but each member had his or her concerns: Solas's was how to get the animal up and running to full gallop, Dorian's was how to stay on without falling off on such a powerful beast while riding on such a tiny saddle, and Jiji's was how to put the brakes on the animal altogether and stop. Controlling the beasts would require strength. This would be their first lesson. Solas started the countdown.

"Are you guys ready?" he asked as his two friends nodded half-heartedly.

They got into position.

"3-2-1, go."

The trio yelled and screamed and jumped and kicked the creatures with the heels of their feet for some get-up-and-go and the next thing you know, they were off like a sling shot. They reached mid-speed with little effort from the animals, yet it took a whole lot of effort from each rider just to keep on the saddle. There was little talk now, much concentration and a few giddy smiles from Dorian who found the experience rather exhilarating. The beasts did not seem to tire one bit. They kept on and on and on. They were by all accounts marathon runners, but could they sprint at all? This, the trio was about to find out, but not in the manner they had intended.

"Solas," screamed Jiji, as she managed to pull Ruffian closer to Eclipse. "Solas!"

A smiling Solas looked at her, with both hands still on the reins.

"Wahoo," he yelled.

But the excitement on his face was short lived when he saw Xiao Ren load up her shortbow in mid-stride and fire an arrow straight into the open sky behind her. He looked back and noticed a handful of hellbirds – gryphons and spitfires – closing in from the rear. No sooner did the birds of Tartarus begin to nose-dive at the riders in an attempt to scoop them or otherwise knock them off their mounts. Solas, Dorian and Xiao Ren resorted to evasive maneuvers which consisted in swerving and zigzagging about the fields, using the uncanny agility of Eclipse, Man o' War and Ruffian to their advantage. Solas reached for Lux Veritas and drew the weapon out of its sheath. Her blade was already white hot. A plunging spitfire caught up to Dorian and fired a steady blaze of flames at him. By instinct, Man o' War veered off in the nick of time, but nonetheless felt the sting of the dancing flames. The animal moaned like some enraged hippo and suddenly found a higher gear. In a wild burst of acceleration, the animal went from a mere canter to a full gallop in a split nanosecond and pulled away from the group and its airborne assailants. Dorian could only tuck his head down low and hang on with all his might.

This kneejerk reaction caused Eclipse and Ruffian to follow suit. Solas and Xiao Ren now could only brace themselves. The task was rendered all the more difficult for Solas who also held on tight to his lifeline Lux Veritas. The unorthodox gallop of the creatures was nothing like the horse. It was as though the trio was riding on the back of frightened gorillas, the tireless animals' paws pounding like fists of fury onto the turf. Their speed was also considerably faster than a thoroughbred, to say the least, and their weaving nimbler than the gazelle's, and as a result the hellbirds' pursuit was all the more troublesome and exhausting. So the gryphons and spitfires chose the economical route and followed the alien creatures and their riders by gliding high up overhead, and waited like vultures for the mad stampede to fizzle down. But the creatures never let up for one moment. They jumped over potholes and puddles, climbed up and down knolls, and negotiated trees, bushes and other obstacles in stride and with relative ease.

Instead, it was the hitch-riders who were now tired and could barely hang on. The miles kept rolling on. The mountains kept getting nearer. Solas attempted to regain control of Eclipse, but nothing doing. And as a flinching Xiao Ren depleted her last ounce of energy and was about to forego her grip, Ruffian came to a steep halt. Behold another waterhole! The creature was thirsty. So were Eclipse and Man o' War. And drank they did, gulping down whole drafts of liquid by the bucketful. They exhaled like mad bulls and never lifted their heads. The trio dismounted and collapsed on the grass. Dorian was sprawled on his stomach, Jiji too. Only Solas laid on his back, spreading out all four limbs like a starfish, weapon still in hand. He tilted his head to the side when he noticed Lux Veritas glinting again.

Solas brought the sword around as he scrambled to his feet. At this exact moment, a wall of flames hit Lux Veritas' shield and parted around it like the Red Sea. As the flying culprit swooshed past overhead, Xiao Ren fired an arrow at the passing hellbird and hit it flush in the wing, bringing it down in screeching pain a little further downfield. Alarmed, the creatures drinking at the pond went into frenzy mode. Man o' War and Ruffian turned on the two landed gryphons while the other two hellbirds circled above. Eclipse chased down the spitfire in the fields like a bloodhound retrieves a fowl shot by his master. The wounded demon-bird had barely completed his fall from grace that Solas's gentle creature pounced on it like a mad ape and pounded on it with all four limbs, crushing the spitfire under its weight and then tearing it apart like a rabid hyena. The sight was gruesome. The trio turned away from the savage display in utter disbelief and now watched ever closer the battle ready to unfold between the two creatures and the two gryphons.

Man o' War and Ruffian approached the gryphons with more caution. For one, the gryphons were a much bigger foe than the spitfire, and they could inflict some serious damage through powerful strikes. The gryphons were like giant eagles but had the body of a lion with long dorsal wings, sturdy legs and clawed talons. The gryphons were not at all interested in the alien creatures that stood between them and their goal. But the creatures from beyond Purgator felt threatened and were provoked by all the relentless pursuing, the dive bombing attacks and the fire spitting. An inevitable skirmish ensued. The hellbirds struck first. They batted their massive wings with strength and vigour. Witnessing the mega-frenzy the gryphons created was akin to seeing a rooster fight for the first time but on a grander scale. They knocked over the two creatures. The gryphons' claws cut open Man o' War and the creature now bore a thick 18-inch gash on its chest. In the commotion, Ruffian managed to bite the wingtip of its aggressor and began to spin the gryphon round and round like a canine tugs on a rope. Xiao Ren, who would not just stand idle and watch the spectacle, fired an arrow at the bitten hellbird and struck it in the hind leg, which caused the beast to lose its balance and collapse. A bloodied Eclipse now rejoined the group and leaped on the downed gryphon, and just as it did with the spitfire, started to batter the stupefied hellbird. This act caused the other gryphon to back up and take flight once again – albeit with some difficulty – and join up with its two already airborne partners hovering above the lot. Ruffian kept a good chunk of wing tip and feathers as a souvenir for its troubles. The three remaining hellbirds circled over the area once or twice more and left, heading away from the mountains and south toward Tartarus.

Eclipse, Man o' War and Ruffian stopped their ruthless assault once they realized that the last gryphon had seized to fight back. The battle did take its toll on the three creatures however and Man o' War was gushing a fair amount of blood now. As for Eclipse, it had suffered a few burns from the spitfire and had lost a few clumps of flesh from the desperate bites of the tenacious gryphon. Ruffian did suffer a few knocks and bruises of its own and had lost a front tooth as well, but as a whole was the better of the three.

5

After all the intense action, the group took a moment to refresh and clean up near the waterhole. The creatures did not hesitate to make a splash and jumped right in the shallows. They washed up and waddled around the pool of water like a bunch of happy hippos. When the animals stepped out, Xiao Ren was waiting for Man o' War and gently applied a coating of mud onto its wound in order to stop it from bleeding and to help it heal. The creature enjoyed the care and attention and never budged an inch.

It was mid-afternoon now and the sun beat down on the plains with increased vigor. At least, the hot rays did serve one purpose well: they fully dried the beasts and the leather tack which was still harnessed to them. The sunbath also rejuvenated the animals and restored their energy. The creatures were like natural solar panels. Solas concluded that they were warm blooded to be sure, and were not at all like those green blooded flying lizards. In other words, in some odd way, the alien creatures had a whole lot more in common with humans than with demons. Soon, Solas, Dorian and Jiji were back on their rides and were quietly moving toward the mountain side now just a short mile away.

There was much to converse about, many matters to discuss and many questions to ponder. In Purgator, events occurred at bullet speed. Expect the unexpected; that was the rule. For now, the subject carried on about the creatures.

"You see these animals right here, the ones we're riding on?" asked Dorian in rhetorical fashion. Solas and Xiao Ren raised their eyebrows and said yes. Being curious, they turned their heads and listened to the rest of their friend's forthcoming wisdom. "Well they have a split personality, that's what. They need a shrink. I mean, one minute they are gentle as a bunny rabbit, the next they go ape-shit. What is that all about?"

"At least they didn't take their frustration out on us," a grateful Jiji replied, putting a hand over her chest.

"Well, they kind of remind me of a buddy of mine when he plays hockey," said Solas with a chuckle.

"Oh that's real funny," retorted Dorian without missing a beat.

"You must admit," added Solas, "they may be full of surprises but so far they have been most helpful, wouldn't you say? Me, I kind of like the little critters."

"They're unpredictable is what I'm saying," replied Dorian. "That was one tough piece of rough riding back there I tell you. I was hanging on for dear life. If I had fallen off, the hellbirds would have made a meal of me in no time, and I don't think your critters would have stopped to save me."

"Yes Solas, why do you think these creatures are helping us?" asked Jiji.

"I am not really sure," he answered, "I guess they trust us better than their last owners."

"Perhaps they are lost like we are," added Jiji.

"Perhaps they want to go home like we do," said Dorian.

"Yes," agreed Solas, "and perhaps they can show us the way there too."

Now, the trio stood in the shadows of the Petros Mountains. There was still much daylight to be had but the sun had disappeared behind the colossal towering peaks which were now looming over them grim and tall. The temperature dropped a few notches by the skirts of the mountains and there was an added chill in the gentle breeze. The foothills and mountain slopes were covered in the lush green of pine wood which extended almost as high as the eyes could see. Above, the white snow blanketed the mountain top and formed a shifting plume over the open sky.

"Is this the Holy Mountain?" asked Jiji as she kinked her neck round to admire the natural monument.

"I believe so," replied Solas.

"Wow!"

"There is a trail around here somewhere leading us up over that spur. We need to locate it. Chepi said this is where we will find the city of Rockdale and the expert Sherpa who will lead us to the great guru."

"So we hope," added Dorian.

A trail along the mountain side there was, and the trio kept following it in search of the passage that would lead them up and beyond the great cliff wall. Soon, they came upon it and they began their gradual climb up the rocky slope. The dirt trail was compact and became narrower the higher they climbed so that the threesome was forced at last to form a single file. Solas led the way. The climb became more arduous and the creatures focused their energy on each and every step they took. The trio was now sandwiched between an imposing green forest on one side and a great steep cliff on the other. At times, the trail wound ever closer to a ravine which made the group rather nervous.

"My head is spinning," said Xiao Ren, "I think I have vertigo."

"Don't look down," said Solas, "just keep looking up."

"Thank God we have these animals to ride on," reckoned Dorian. "Otherwise we would be all but exhausted by now."

"Well, how do you like them critters now, huh?" said a proud Solas.

The trio kept climbing in relative silence. Only the sound of dislodging rocks and tumbling pebbles disturbed the peace as well as the occasional crowing from a handful of scavenging blackbirds and grackles, those gloomy specters of doom. The air was fresher now and below, the radiant sundrenched valley of Asphodel Meadows extended endlessly out of sight. The trail eventually leveled off and grew larger. The creatures reached the edge of a plateau and stopped advancing. Blocking their path were two watchmen.

6

The parties stood 20 yards apart. They exchanged a few looks and without saying a word, Solas dismounted Eclipse as a gesture of goodwill and friendship and advanced toward the two men while holding his ride by the bridle.

"Hello there," said Solas to break the ice. "Perhaps you could help us. We are a little lost, you see. We are looking for the city of Rockdale. Do you know where it is by any chance?"

The two sentries – one of them a loathar – remained quiet and would not utter a single word. Their attention seemed wholly focused on the alien creatures.

"Stop," they said, brandishing their spears at arm's length. "Identify yourselves."

"My name is Solas," he answered as he stopped ten yards away. "These are my friends Dorian and Xiao Ren. We come in peace."

Dorian rolled his eyes and thought: *Not that answer again!* That trademark declaration '*We come in peace*' was a surefire way of landing them in trouble. At least, it had in the past. Sensing the possibility of a misunderstanding brewing, he and Jiji followed Solas's lead and got off their rides.

"You are not from this land," replied one of the guards, judging by the creatures accompanying the trio. "You are now on the eastern edge of Rockdale. Where are you from? And state the true nature of your business."

The group felt immediate relief at hearing that they had reached the city of Rockdale at long last. Now, what they needed were friends.

"We are humans from Earth, as you can see," answered Solas. "We need the help of a Sherpa to help us find our way through the mountains. Can you help us find one?"

"You may appear human, and you may come from Earth," the watchman replied, "but the beasts are not from Earth. And they are not from Purgator either. Where are you really from and what are doing in these parts?"

Solas sensed the tension increasing. So he came up with an idea. Instead of engaging into a long winded explanation to try and win over the confidence of the two sentries, he would show them the luret. After all, a picture is worth a thousand words. Isn't it?

"Here," said Solas, "let me show you why we are here."

Upon those words, he gently drew out Lux Veritas. But before he had the weapon half way out of its sheath, the spokesperson of the two guards – a human – raised its spear into launching position and sent a stern warning to the newcomer.

"Pull out that sword and you're dead," he yelled.

Solas froze on the spot while the other sentry prepared his bow and arrow.

"Hang on a second," said Solas, "it's not what you think. I have an item here of interest that I need to show you. It will explain everything."

Just then, Lux Veritas began to glint and the two sentries were able to catch the top of the blade shining bright. The guards were taken aback.

"What … what is that?" stuttered the javelin wielding human guard.

"This is my sword," answered Solas. "She is called Lux Veritas."

"Lux Veritas!" he repeated. "Isn't that the legendary sword of Genesis, the mighty sword of the Lord Creator?"

"That's her," replied a relieved Solas with a smile.

"Why do you have it?"

"That's a long story. Can I pull her out now? I have something else to show you."

Somehow, the presence of Lux Veritas seemed to put the two guardsmen at ease and they lowered their weapons. Lux Veritas stopped glinting at once and Solas showed them the sword, still from a certain distance. He turned the blade around to present the Will-master's luret melded onto the upper end of the blade.

"The stolen luret," gasped the guards in unison.

"Yes, the luret," said Solas. "I just want you to know that I did not steal it. I just want to return it to its owner. Do you know who that person is and where I could find him?"

The two guards gave each other a puzzled look and after a brief hesitation came to a nonverbal agreement.

"We have agreed to accompany you to Rockdale. There, you will find your answers."

"Thank you," said a grateful Solas as Dorian and Xiao Ren let out a sigh of relief.

The human guard approached Solas and shook his hand in friendship, as did his loathar companion. The two guardsmen had a pleasant appearance dressed in their simple tanned cotton tunic, leather pants and knee high laced-up sandals. Their handshakes were firm however, a testimony to their strong and upright character.

"My name is Richard," said the human guard, "and this is Bomor."

Solas proceeded to introduce his friends Dorian and Xiao Ren, and even the strange creatures on which they were riding, to wit Eclipse, Man o' War and Ruffian. It took much walking and much explaining to set the story straight with the two sentries. Richard was most curious about the origins of the newcomers, about the life in the city of Sherbrooke and how things had changed on Earth. As the group rounded the mountain side, reaching ever closer to the city of Rockdale, the story now became clearer and their spirits lightened up.

"You know," said a more cheerful Richard with a certain measure of pride, "I come from the windy city ... Chicago, Illinois that is." It was not often Richard had the chance to share his story with a group of humans, and he did not fail to seize the opportunity. "I have been here for so long. I think I have lost track of time." he continued. "I miss home, my family. I had it good back then. I would change so many things if the Lord Creator would just grant me that wish."

"What would you change exactly?" asked a somber Xiao Ren as the curious group listened on.

"I am not quite sure," he replied. "Some say that our fate is sealed. There is not much point to fret about it, I guess. But

I would surely live each day like it was my last. *Carpe diem* as they say."

"Right, seize the day," uttered a dreamy Dorian, kicking up a few loose stones as he chugged along the rocky road.

"Ten times a day or more, I would tell my family just how I much I loved them all. I would make peace with my dad, and my sister too. If only I could be forgiven. I never thought about all of this trouble when I was alive. But now that I am the living dead, I think about it all the time. I guess that's why I am still here stuck in Purgator, a lonely wretched soul simmering in personal misery." Complete silence fell upon the group. No doubt each member was by now fully engrossed in his or her own thoughts, pondering all too carefully the weighty words of the remorseful Richard. He finished his discourse on the following tone. "I can't imagine how things must be in the stifling confines of Tartarus. Purgator is Hell enough as it is. And it is said that we have it good here in Rockdale."

It also has been said that curiosity killed the cat, and the tactless Dorian had done it more than his fair share.

"What about you Bomor … are you from the good old U.S. of A. too?"

Bomor turned his head, clenched his fists, foamed at the mouth, and grumbled at Dorian.

"I'm sorry," intervened Xiao Ren on behalf of her man, "Dorian means no harm. He is just so absentminded sometimes." She stared at Dorian and threw darts at him with her eyes. And then Dorian remembered the order of life and death in Purgator. When a human dies here, if he has not yet earned the right to enter Elysium or been cursed and sent down to Tartarus, he returns, first as an elkin and then as a lamentar or a loathar, just like Bomor, the memory of his past lives cleaned out for good. And so Bomor surely could not remember anything at all, which upset him. Lamentars and loathars as such were not a happy lot. Dorian waved at Bomor in lieu of an apology and before long the tension dissipated.

It was at this moment that the group left the shadows of the towering cliffs behind and stepped back into the sunlight. Richard suddenly stopped walking, halting the convoy in the process. He stared into the distance over the immensity of the flatlands just as he had done a thousand times before, and took a second or two to recharge his batteries.

7

The view over the valleys of Asphodel Meadows was breathtaking from such heights and Solas took a moment in his explanations to point out the oasis, which was now all in all just a speck on the map.

"That's quite the distance to travel in half a day," said Richard quite surprised at this feat. "Can your alien creatures fly too?"

"Not quite," replied Solas, "but they can sure run like hell."

"And run like hell we needed to," added Dorian, "with a pack of gryphons and spitfires honing down on us."

"Are you sure they were gryphons?" asked Richard. "They never leave Tartarus unless they are on a mission."

"Well, Lux Veritas is mission enough, isn't it?" replied Solas.

"I suppose. We did see some odd looking beasts and demons pass by and fly around at the foot of the mountain earlier today. But we couldn't tell for sure. It was rather unusual," explained Richard.

Just as he finished his sentence, Xiao Ren gasped in surprise. "Oh my God," she said.

At last, the group had reached Rockdale. The hidden city was built straight onto the side of the western rock face on an incline at the foot of the mountain. There, the slopes leveled off and below, the green fields and pastures began. The village cattle consisting mostly of goats and sheep would graze there and roam at will. The housing quarters were single units round or oval shaped, white in color, standing adjacent to one another, touching side by side, row upon row. In the distance, the sun was now setting over the Sea of Bounty on the western edge of Outlandia beyond the flatlands of Oneiros. The last rays cast by the flamboyant star descending over the horizon and the red glow from the oil lamps hanging on wooden posts set before the Rockdalian homes gave the tranquil city a surreal pinkish gleam, a sight to behold.

"This is home," said Richard, "Rockdale."

"Wow, it's beautiful," said Xiao Ren.

"Such an ideal location," said Solas, "no one ever bothers you here, I imagine."

"Oh, we've had our share of troubles," answered Richard, "like that time during Daemonia's last insurgency, for example. You might recall."

"Do we ever," replied Dorian. "This is why we must prevent it from happening again, if it isn't already too late."

"Come with me, I will introduce you to the village chief. You can explain the situation to him."

"What about Eclipse, Man o' War and Ruffian?" asked Dorian. "What shall we do with them?"

"Don't worry, we will look after them," answered Richard, who immediately ordered his loathar partner Bomor to take the creatures away to the communal grange to be given water and food.

As the group followed the main trail into the village, Richard met up with the two sentries dispatched to replace him on his watch. They exchanged formalities and the new guards indicated that Chief Larsen was indeed in his dwellings. The group continued on, greeting the occasional citizen on the way, most of them lamentars and loathars although a few elkins and humans were seen here and there. Before long, they stood on the door step of the chief's residence. The clay walls of his modest home were overrun with climbing ivies and several drooping vines covered the wooden arched doorway. Bouquets of scented wildflowers grew all about the chief's lodgings, adding a colorful and florid display to the rustic surroundings. The sweet fragrance of this delicate potpourri reminded Solas very much of Grandma Jeanie's prize winning garden back home in Sherbrooke. *Ah, home sweet home!* he thought. His heart skipped a beat as his thoughts were on Amy too. He took a deep breath and closed his eyes. *Please be strong my love, I'll be with you soon,* and dared not imagine the worst otherwise.

Knock, knock, knock ...
Through the crack of the open window, the group could hear mumblings inside the home. The front door swung open with hardly a screech.

"Richard," said the chief quite by surprise, "why are you back from your watch so soon?"

Chief Larsen was a short stout man standing no more than five feet tall. He was probably as round as he was high but he had about him an air of confidence and authority. His bushy grey moustache, cheeky jowls and series of dark circles under his eyes betrayed his age. His long peppered hair was weaved into a single fishtail braid and a large white bandana wrapped around his head held the top together.

"Hello Chief," replied Richard, "I came back early. And I brought here these travelers: Solas, Dorian and Jiji." He hesitated on Xiao Ren's name preferring to call her by her nickname. "Is that right?" he whispered as he looked at her.

"Yes," she answered with a smile, "Jiji's fine."

"There is an important matter that these travelers wish to discuss with you Chief Larsen. They have come from far. Could you spare a moment for them?" he asked.

Chief Larsen took an instant to inspect the desolate lot standing before him.

"Why sure! Come on in," he said before turning and throwing his voice to the lady of the house, "Lenora ... Lenora please put on the tea. We have guests."

8

Solas, Dorian and Xiao Ren entered the humble home making sure to thank the village chief for his spur of the moment hospitality. The group and their host squatted on mats set around a low standing red cedarwood table. Always vigilant, Solas kept Lux Veritas by his side. The chief's better-half Lenora greeted the young visitors and promptly brought about some green tea to drink, sweet honey, and an assortment of grain biscuits to lift the hunger. They consumed the snacks and shared pleasantries – for Chief Larsen, who once hailed from Copenhagen, Denmark as it turned out, was a jolly old fellow when given the opportunity to entertain guests. Solas explained in details the circumstances that brought them to Rockdale, the purpose of the mission, all that was at stake in the land and what's all the more relevant, the personal loss of his sweetheart Amy. Chief Larsen was all ears during the account and once the telling was done, he ordered Richard the sentry to go and find the Sherpa guide that the trio would require in order to continue on their journey to the top of the mountain and beyond into the heart of Purgator.

"Let me show you Lux Veritas," said the intuitive Solas, now sensing he could trust the chief, "and the luret in question that is melded onto its blade. Perhaps you might know a way to separate them."

Solas pulled out the mighty weapon from its sheath and held it out with both hands, laying it flat before him at eye level.

"Magnificent," exclaimed the chief. "May I?"

Solas offered a polite nod and urged Chief Larsen to take the sword. His reaction was typical of the select few individuals who in the past had been fortunate enough to get this close to Lux Veritas. He inspected the weapon from every angle, surprised by the lightness and flawlessness of the metal.

"Very odd," he said at last.

"What do you mean odd?" asked Solas.

"Well," the chief replied, "it would seem that the sword and the luret are made of the same metal, whatever it is, and is not from

Purgator or from Earth, to be sure." The group remained silent as the chief continued. "No, I can't," he added with a perplexed look on his face.

"You can't what?" Solas asked, looking for a bit more precision.

"I can't pry them apart," he answered, "but I have the feeling Guru Roshni will know what to do."

"Tell me more about this guru," pressed Solas, jumping to the matter.

"Well," replied the chief, as he handed back the sword to its caretaker, "he doesn't come down from the mountain top very often. He is very much a recluse and if you want to see him, you must go there yourself, which is easier said than done. The way to the summit of Holy Mountain can be treacherous, at best. Your steps must be sure. Otherwise, what can be said of the Guru? ... He meditates a lot."

"What," said Dorian, "the guy lives on the summit of a mountain just like that. He must freeze to death sitting around there in that awkward position all day."

Chief Larsen let out a roaring belly laugh at Dorian's naïve remark before continuing.

"No, no, no, it's not like that at all," he replied, "the Guru has a shelter inside the mountain, a monastery if you will. And he is not alone; he has followers who practice the same as he does."

"Practice what?" asked Dorian.

"Yoga," the chief replied, "quiet contemplation through meditation. You've heard of it."

Dorian raised his eyebrows and gently shook his head wondering what sort of good this practice could serve anyone in the land of Purgator.

"How well does he know this luret?" asked Solas.

"The luret used to be in his care until it went missing a little while back," the chief answered. "We searched over, under, and across every mountain in the region hoping to recover the stolen item. But there was nothing doing, there was just no trace of the luret at all. The guilty leprechaun simply vanished into thin air.

And now, here you are showing it to me with it stuck at the top of your blade ... the blade of the mighty Lux Veritas no less."

Solas went on to explain how he came into possession of the object; first retelling the story of leprechaun Fergus's escapade beyond the Diamond Gate, how the luret reached shaman Chepi who then sent it through the Wheel of Souls down to Earth to be put in shaman Orenda's care, who finally handed it over to Solas, only to find it melded onto the end of the Lux Veritas upon re-entering the afterlife. Chief Larsen was quite impressed by the story and was left frowning and pondering the meaning of it all.

"Well," he said in a convincing tone, "Guru Roshni will have the answers for you. I am sure of it. After all that's his job, isn't it?"

And upon these words, the portly village chief seemed quite relieved to see his sentry Richard return in the company of the Sherpa guide whose presence he had requested.

9

Outside, the great expanse of the twilight was now sprinkled with a myriad of the early evening stars. Richard preceded the Sherpa through the open door of the chief's residence which had been left yawning to allow for the cooler evening air to enter.

"Found him," said Richard as he introduced the mountain guide.

"Ang-Norbu," exclaimed Chief Larsen, "how nice of you to come so quickly. I hope we did not call you away from some pressing business."

"I was only feeding Rajah his evening rations," replied the mountain guide.

"I would like you to meet these fine young people here: Solas, Dorian and Xiao Ren," said the chief. "They have come to us seeking help and I would like you to provide it for them."

"I'm flattered, Chief," replied the Sherpa. "How can I be of service?"

"Come sit with us and have a drink, and we will explain everything."

Ang-Norbu accepted the invitation and dropped his rather large knapsack and overflowing canvass bag on the ground before joining the table. The group shared yet more tea with Richard and the Sherpa as they entered into lengthy discussions about the present conundrum facing the travelers, as well as the general state of affairs in Rockdale and Purgator. Ang-Norbu was presented Lux Veritas and to his utter astonishment discovered the missing luret. With every passing moment, the old chief livened up a notch from the sheer exhilaration at the prospect of the glamorous mission ahead in which he and his village could play a key role, and before long, he cracked open a bottle or two of his finest reserves to celebrate the occasion.

"So what will it be, my fine Ang-Norbu?" said Chief Larsen. "Are you in or out?"

"It will be a great honor," the Sherpa replied, as he glanced over at Solas sitting across from him.

"That's my boy," exclaimed the cheerful chief before proposing a toast and raising his goblet high over the center of the table. "Here is to mission success."

"To mission success," repeated the members of the newly formed posse.

Silence reigned briefly while the group drank bottoms-up. Dorian was first to finish and slammed his cup back down on the table before wiping his lips with the upper sleeve of his garment.

"Rajah and I will take you as far as we can," said Ang-Norbu. "We will do our best."

"Rajah?" asked Solas.

"Yes, Rajah! He is my lantern. Even a guide needs a guide sometimes. And there are none better in this land than Rajah."

"Well, we will be more than glad to make his acquaintance and shake his hand," said Solas.

Richard smiled and Chief Larsen started to laugh. "You mean his paw."

Ang-Norbu went on to explain.

"You see, Rajah is a snow leopard," he said. "He goes trekking with me everywhere I go, from the highest summit to the deepest cavern."

"Oh, I see," said Solas. "All the same, we will shake a paw then. He does take well to strangers, doesn't he?"

The Sherpa smiled.

"You bet. He is a bright animal. He knows me well. My friends are his friends," he replied, before continuing. "We should retreat for the night now. We will need to leave early in the morning. It is a long arduous climb to the top after all. With any luck at all and if the weather holds, we will reach Guru Roshni's monastery before nightfall. If not, we will need to stop over at the base camp of Alta-Mir."

"Great," said Solas, "sounds like a plan."

"What about Eclipse, Man o' War and Ruffian?" asked Xiao Ren. "They will be able to come with us, won't they?"

"Who are they?" asked the surprised Sherpa.

"Our rides," answered Xiao Ren. "They have been quite helpful so far."

"Oh yes, I remember now," replied Ang-Norbu, "Richard told me all about your creatures on our walk down here. I am afraid they cannot come. Getting to the top of Holy Mountain is one thing, but getting through the steep and narrow hollows beneath her is an entirely different matter altogether. They cannot pass. It is best that they remain here. I hope you understand."

"But they came to Purgator through the Diamond Gate. They made it though the caves once already," objected Jiji. "They may know the way. They could be a great help to us."

"I do not doubt it," replied the Sherpa, "but the way I propose is not the way through which these creatures reached Purgator, I can assure you."

Xiao Ren, Dorian and Solas seemed rather saddened but resigned themselves to reason and agreed to leave the creatures behind.

"Before I go, I wanted you to have these items of clothing and also a good sturdy pair of mountain shoes," added Ang-Norbu, "and these spiked plates too. You will need to slip them on for the icy terrain."

The Sherpa untied his large canvass bag to reveal an array of items ranging from wool socks and hats, tough skin jackets and tall fur-lined mountain boots with double thick leather souls.

"Well, you do think of everything Ang-Norbu," exclaimed Chief Larsen.

"I come prepared. The mountain is unforgiving, as you well know," replied the Sherpa. "When Richard briefed me on what to expect, I got ready."

As Ang-Norbu handed out the pieces of clothing to each of his new travel mates, he offered a piece of advice.

"I will come back at sunrise. Do make sure you are wearing these clothes. You see, Rockdale is situated on the first tier of the mountain slope. It gets cold quickly once we reach higher up the mountain. And the weather can turn. You won't be able to change then, at least not until we reach the second base camp."

"The second base camp," uttered Dorian.

"Yes, Alta-Mir," replied the Sherpa.

"Roger!" said Solas, "and thanks for everything. We'll be ready."

Richard the sentry and Sherpa Ang-Norbu stepped out of the house, but not before wishing the newcomers and Chief Larsen a good night's rest. The morning would come soon enough. As the door closed behind them, the chief's better-half Lenora led the young trio to their sleeping pad; one they would share in close quarters, resting on fur mats, blankets and pillows set on the ground as makeshift beds. Solas, Dorian and Xiao Ren thanked their most gracious host and lay down for the night, making comfortable in whatever way they could. At last, as Solas's tired eyes began to close in the still darkness, he clutched Lux Veritas over his chest. His thoughts of Amy suddenly turned to dreams as a silent tear rolled down his cheek to the edge of his lips, following the crease of the scar he had gained for her, not so long ago, on the plains of Asphodel Meadows.

As Solas slipped into a dream, somewhere out in the far depth of a foreign realm, Amy struggled with her detainer.
"Eat your food, princess!" said the demon.
Amy spat into the bowl of stewed cockroaches.
"You wait!" she screamed. "Solas will come and skin you alive, snake!"
The beast snickered and walked away.

10

The village cockerel was first up for Ang-Norbu's rendezvous and its shrilling cock-a-doodle-doo announced the arrival of a brand new dawn. The sleeping trio woke up at once under the grumbling objections of Dorian who swore to make a fine coq-au-vin of the responsible rooster for dinner. Solas was up and changed into his new outfit in no time flat. Dorian and Xiao Ren were slower out of bed but followed Solas' example and slipped their new garb overtop their old one.

"Not a bad fit," said Dorian as he strapped on his katana blade. "It's better to roast alive than to freeze to death, I guess."

Just as they finished their preparations, Ang-Norbu came knocking at the door. Lenora greeted the Sherpa who chose to stay put on the door step in wait of Solas and company.

"Good morning Ang-Norbu," said Solas as he exited the bedroom with Dorian and Xiao Ren following close behind. "Wow, you really are ready," he added.

"I am always ready," replied Ang-Norbu.

Ang-Norbu really did look the part of a Sherpa, and not only because of his level of preparedness, dressed as he was in full climbing attire with ropes and picks firmly attached to his back, but because of his obvious physical features. He was tall, tanned and skinny. He spoke with an Indian accent. Back on Earth, he hailed from the region of Lucknow in Uttar Pradesh. When he was young, his father would often take him to the mountains, the mighty Himalayas in bordering Nepal, which he adored. He was a natural and a devotee of the hills. In Purgator, the mountains were calling to him, and he answered his calling by being a Sherpa.

Behind Ang-Norbu, Solas noticed another presence. It was Richard the sentry, who had decided to join the expedition.

"Richard," said Solas, "will you be coming with us?"

"You bet," he answered. "I did not want to miss this opportunity. I figured you could always use an extra hand."

"Super ... welcome aboard Richard," said Dorian.

The group bid farewell to the chief and his wife, exited the dwellings and stepped out into the fresh morning air. And there waited Rajah, the snow leopard. The animal was corpulent and robust in its thick and spotted white coat, and was easily twice the size of common lion, which of course seemed quite unnatural to Solas and friends.

"Goodness gracious," exclaimed a surprised Xiao Ren.

Noticing the uneasiness of the trio, Ang-Norbu put their worries to rest.

"This is Rajah," he said, "my companion and my best friend. He is as docile as he is indispensable. Right Rajah?" he continued as he head-locked and caressed the animal.

"Nice to meet you Rajah," said Solas as he approached the beast which did not seem to mind one bit.

Rajah was ready for action – that being the mountain of course – and was harnessed much like a horse, with bags of supplies strapped to his back and hanging off his sides.

"Rajah carries provisions, a tent and a few emergency items, just in case," explained Ang-Norbu. "Let's go now. We must leave and make good time."

Thus the group left the dormant city of Rockdale behind and negotiated its first ascent up the green slopes of the lower mountain in direction of the base camp of Alta-Mir, a snow covered refuge for climbers and travelers alike anchored year round in permafrost.

The group followed a trail which angled its way back and forth up the slopes. After about an hour, they slowed down and tired a little needing to catch their breath. Then, the cooler gusts of wind which the Sherpa had foretold picked up and the temperature made a sudden drop. If this did not chill their spirits at all, the words of Richard sure did.

"I do not sincerely wish to alarm the lot of you, but I think you should be made aware of this," began the sentry. "Late last night, a couple of our traders who were returning home from the eastern edge of Asphodel Meadows informed my lookout partner Bomor that they had heard yesterday the distant droning sounds of the horns of Lalas Pur."

There was a short pause before Xiao Ren spoke up.

"Oh my God," she said, the first to realize its meaning. "The citizens sounded the alarm."

"That means the city is under siege," added Solas.

"The Stealth Demon must have sent the forces of Daemonia to Lalas Pur," concluded Dorian. "He thinks that's where we went."

"We must hurry," said Solas, whose complexion began to turn white as the snow. "Soon the whole of Purgator will be crawling with freaks and demons from Tartarus looking for us, not to mention other creatures from beyond the Diamond Gate."

"I hope Chepi and Orenda are okay," whispered an anxious Xiao Ren, "they were headed to Lalas Pur for safety."

"Perhaps the Stealth Demon has succeeded in increasing the flow of traffic through the Diamond Crossing," said an agitated Dorian.

"If that's the case, we're in big trouble already," added Solas.

"Keep calm," said Ang-Norbu, acting as the voice of reason. "Stay focused on your mission. You will be safe here in the mountains."

But before the group could regain full composure, it was now the trumpets of Rockdale that could be heard sounding the alarm.

There was yet another short pause before Xiao Ren spoke up once again.

"Oh my God!" she said. "Is that Rockdale under siege too?"

It was now Richard and Ang-Norbu's turn to unnerve.

"Let's go, we must hurry," said the Sherpa, "before Daemonia catches up to us."

"Shouldn't we go back and help?" asked Richard. "We must go back and help," he insisted.

"Not a chance," replied Ang-Norbu. "Chief Larsen would want us to push on. Besides, I have faith in the fighting forces of Rockdale. Let's keep moving."

The group scampered higher and higher up the mountain side at a steady pace and with renewed energy. The climb grew steeper and before long storm clouds gathered – as they often tend to do at higher altitudes – and the first tiny flakes of snow began to twirl in the cold blowing wind. Up ahead in the distance, a glacier stood before them and they needed to go through it in order to reach the last narrow path leading to the Alta-Mir base camp. Below, the clinging sounds of clashing metal could be heard, and for well over a long while. The faint yells of war and screams of agony echoed up the hills to haunt the fleeing mavericks. There was no turning back however, and it only took a quick glimpse over the shoulders to see a cloud of smoke now rising high above the city of Rockdale.

Dorian was trailing the lot when he noticed from a distance something unusual rushing up the hill behind them. He stopped and drew his katana which alarmed the other members of the group who were following each other in a single file.

"We have company," he yelled.

Solas turned and prepared Lux Veritas in anticipation of an imminent battle, although the sword did not gleam yet. Xiao Ren kneeled down and prepared her bow, ready to fire. So did

Richard and Ang-Norbu. Rajah roared. As the unknown beings approached, Solas was able to make them out.

"Hold your fire!" he yelled to the archers. "It's Eclipse, Man o' War and Ruffian," he said, at once surprised and relieved to see the animals rush to rejoin them.

"And Bomor," added Richard.

Indeed, Bomor, who had been left in charge of the creatures, was riding Eclipse and had managed to escape the assault on Rockdale. The animals slowed down and Bomor the loathar, winded and shook up as he was, dismounted his ride and began to recount the story.

"Richard," he called out, "they came by the hundreds and began to slash and burn everything in sight."

"Who Bomor, who?" asked Richard, urging him to calm down.

"Daemonia," he answered, "and also Imps and other strange beasts like I have never seen before, some riding on creatures just like these ones. The guards were quick to raise the alarm before the enemy arrived and the citizens had just enough time to prepare for battle."

"And how are our troops doing now? Did you see Chief Larsen?" asked Ang-Norbu.

"We fought bravely with Chief Larsen at the helm, but still we suffered many casualties. When I left, the battle was still raging. It's too soon to tell if we were able to foil the invader."

"You deserted?" asked Richard in a heavy tone of voice.

"That was not my intent," replied the loathar, "But the grange caught fire, and I was forced to free the animals. I jumped on the back of Eclipse to charge into battle but the creature took off for the hills and headed straight for your position. The animal would not respond to my command."

"Did anyone follow you? Did anyone see you come this way?" asked Solas.

Bomor shook his head.

"I couldn't tell," he replied.

"Well somebody did," said Dorian. "Who might this be then?" he asked as he pointed to a cluster of rampaging beasts charging up the hill.

12

A dozen hell-riders from Daemonia were fast on their way. The archers readied their bows once more; Bomor, Dorian and Solas stood on guard sword in hand. And Lux Veritas glinted this time, a sure testament to the true nature of the beasts headed towards them. When the demons could be heard growling and were within striking distance, Xiao Ren, Richard and Ang-Norbu let fly their arrows, two of them finding their targets and falling the foes. The enemy fired back, narrowly missing the group, with two arrowheads slamming into the sacks of provisions carried by the feline and angering Rajah to the brink of unrestraint.

"There are still more beasts coming up behind them," yelled Xiao Ren.

"Let's ride," ordered Ang-Norbu as he jumped on Rajah's back.

The other members of the group were taken by surprise but soon followed suit, with Bomor and Richard sharing Ruffian, Dorian and Xiao Ren Man o' War and Solas the lone ranger on Eclipse.

"Quick to the snowpack," said the Sherpa guide. "We will lose them going over the ice bowl. Follow me."

Rajah and the three creatures took off up the incline like thoroughbreds out of the starting gates amidst a volley of projectiles launched by the enemy now a mere 50 paces behind them. All the rough riders could do now was to hang on and to keep from falling off. The group began to create a bigger gap with Daemonia. Rajah was first to jump onto the edge of the glacier and under the direction of his savvy master Ang-Norbu zigzagged back and forth over the slippery terrain. The three mounted creatures followed behind with relative ease. Their stamina was never in question and their huge paws afforded them good traction on the snow covered ice. Daemonia's warriors continued their pursuit and took the easiest route toward their target by rushing ahead in a straight line. This foray proved to be a costly mistake as the terrain would not allow for such a direct approach and most of the imps, demons and their rides began to stall, fighting to stay on their feet or to stop regressing downhill.

Now the group began to slow down and observed the struggles of Daemonia from afar. The enemies made up one single group now and numbered perhaps two dozen units. They rode on the back of beasts altogether different from anything any members of the group had ever seen before. Because of the dire circumstances, Solas and company had not really paid much attention to such petty details, but now that they were at a safe distance, they could all reflect upon it at ease.

"What are these things anyway?" asked Richard.

"You mean those mutant things?" added Dorian.

"They look like a cross between a bear and a Komodo dragon," said Xiao Ren. "Disgusting!"

"They do move pretty fast though," said Bomor.

"Yeah but they're dumb, just like their masters," added Ang-Norbu.

Solas was more contemplative and concluded that more drastic measures were in order and they needed to finish the job that Daemonia had started.

"We must finish them," he said. "They will inform the others of our whereabouts if we don't."

"You are not suggesting we should go back, are you?" asked Dorian.

"This will not be necessary," said Ang-Norbu. "Leave it to me, I know what to do."

"Which is…" continued Dorian.

"We will set them a trap," explained the Sherpa.

The howling wind picked up once again bringing with it stinging little pellets of ice crystals and a bone chilling cold. Now more than ever, the trio was grateful for the extra gear they had put on just before leaving Chief Larsen's home. They climbed higher and higher up the side of the hanging glacier making sure to give Daemonia a chance to keep pace, but from a safe and tolerable distance. Rajah's coat began to clump into icicles which bothered him little. As for the coatless creatures, they huffed and puffed in quick sporadic spurts to keep their blood flowing fast and keep warm. The rest of the travelers tucked their heads under their bomber hats and turned their faces away from the wind. At last, they reached the top of the glacier and its majestic rocky headwall. The group needed to get behind and around it, using the narrow pathway which appeared to the left, leading up to the base camp of Alta-Mir, the last stop before the final climb to the summit of Holy Mountain.

"Here is the way up to Alta-Mir," yelled Ang-Norbu as he pointed to it, his voice muffled by the wind draft. "If all goes well, we should be there in a couple of hours. But now has come the time to rid ourselves of our pestering foe."

"What's your plan?" screamed Solas.

"Follow me, and do as I do," ordered the Sherpa, repeating the command until each of the leading riders thumbed up.

Ang-Norbu led Rajah over the top crest of the glacier where an accumulation of fresh snow had fallen and covered the top layer of the snowpack. He ordered his feline to pounce up and down, thumping as it landed on the loose snow. The cat did a marvelous job and led by example. The other three creatures followed behind in a single file and, after a little coaxing from the riders, began to imitate Rajah. Not to be outdone, Eclipse, Man o' War and Ruffian relished the exercise, trampling and pounding down on the white carpet as only they could. Down below, Daemonia was still braving the rough ground conditions and the capricious weather but stopped their marginal advance just long enough to take a peek up at the faint commotion they could hear and the strange behavior they saw.

Suddenly, the sound of a loud crack resonated throughout the bowl. A huge slab of ice broke away from the main cirque and tumbled down like an avalanche toward the hapless Daemonian units. Up above, Rajah and the three creatures lost their balance for a brief moment but managed to keep their footing. Down below, Daemonia was left scarce time to react or to brace for impact before being engulfed by the avalanche and swept away half a mile down slope before being buried under a gigantic column of ice and debris.

"Yes!" yelled an exuberant Dorian. "That's one cool ending for the poor bastards," he added. "Hell just froze over all in one swoop."

"Well, let's not get too exited," warned Ang-Norbu, "We still have a ways to go to reach Alta-Mir and the weather is not cooperating, which means we could be the next to freeze over if we don't hurry."

Despite the warning, the victorious members congratulated each other, high-fiving as they turned around before beginning their rocky climb up the trail leading around and over the high cliff wall.

13

The winding path up to the second tier of Holy Mountain was indeed long, narrow and treacherous. Snow began to accumulate in spots along the ledge and loose rocks made the ground unsteady. On the positive, the wind was now pushing from the rear, helping the convoy along and urging the group to keep on moving. Only Bomor and Richard, who closed out the procession riding on the back of poor Ruffian, suffered the brunt of the icy tempest. No one uttered a single word; there was no use in trying as the whistling tailwind yowled on without reprieve, and all that the members could do was to spend their precious energy trying to stay covered and catch their breath. The effect of the cold was more worrisome now and it began seeping right through their clothes, stinging like pin needles any exposed extremity; fingers, ears and nose most of all.

When man and beast had endured all that their willpower could manage, the group rounded the corner. *At last, Alta-Mir,* thought Solas. Relief appeared in the form of a sturdy log house partially sheltered under an overhanging rock wall. In the flats, the wind and snow were now swirling in every direction. Led by Ang-Norbu, the group completed the last 100 yards to the refuge and entered the home through the rear of the adjacent storage shed.

"Oh my God," said Xiao Ren as she dismounted Man o' War. "My feet are numb, and I can't feel my nose anymore."

"My ass is frozen solid," added Dorian.

Little else was said or added. Dorian's last statement conveyed the overall feeling of every member. The shed was large but obscure. The only rays of light entering the lodging were through the lone frosted window facing the open daylight. Each member of the group spent the next little while shaking off the clinging icicles from their mountain gear, before finally removing coats and boots. The animals were left to rest in the shed and the group entered the house through the connecting doorway.

Inside, the space was large and much better lit. For one, there were several more windows; and for two, there was a fireplace. And the hearth was still smoldering with the remnants of logs consumed the previous night by passing travelers. Xiao Ren rushed to the side of the dwindling fire and sat next to the heat to expose her frigid and tender toes. The dwelling was equipped with all the basic necessities required for comfort over a short stay. Couch, tables, chairs, pantries and two beds – all these made of wood – furnished the cabin. The group found an array of fur skins and blankets, a full set of iron pots and pans, steel cutlery and even a few extra weapons hanging on the walls. Solas found the whole set-up rather surprising; it was a lot more than he had expected. Richard quickly went about rekindling the fireplace with some of the dry wood which was kept in reserve in the shed. Ang-Norbu appeared rather at ease in this half-way home. He sorted out the provisions he brought up from Rockdale, stopping at a bottle of wine which he opened at once in order to warm up his companions' spirits. He poured some of the grape mixture into wooden goblets and passed them around to his friends.

"How long has this log cabin been here in Alta-Mir?" asked Solas.

"It has always been here," answered the Sherpa, straight as an arrow.

"What do you mean always been here?" Solas continued.

"It's been here as long as I can remember," replied Ang-Norbu. "The folks in Rockdale have been using it for ages. God only knows."

"And who keeps it going? I mean, who takes care of it … you?"

"Not just me," answered Ang-Norbu, "everyone. The general rule is that anyone passing through is to bring along something with him. That usually means wood, whenever possible, or provisions for man and animal. When the weather is bad, like it is now, you could be stranded for days. You can never be too prepared."

"How many times have you been here?" Dorian asked.

"Too many times to count," the Sherpa replied. "That is for sure."

"Whatever brought you to the mountains in the first place?" asked Solas. "When I first landed here, the last place I wanted to be was in the mountains."

"Not so for me," replied Ang-Norbu. "As a kid, I spent many years in the Himalayas. The mountain is like home for me. When I saw them the first time, I smiled. Heaven I thought. It was an easy choice."

These answers seemed to satisfy Solas's curiosity. But Ang-Norbu's was just beginning.

"Do you really think you can stop the new incursion by the forces of Chaos?" he asked. "They have joined together and are gaining in power. It is chilling to imagine how many other worlds, how many other Purgators exist. What will you do once you reach the Diamond Crossing? You have but one sword, mighty as she is, and you cannot be everywhere."

This questioning got everyone's attention, especially Dorian's and Xiao Ren's.

"I wish I had a ready-made answer for you, Ang-Norbu," answered Solas. "It is true. I have just one sword. But an old wise man who went by the name of Senex once told me that the more you prune a plant, the more vigorously it grows. The more you rectify evils, the more they accumulate. Find the root of the evil and cut it off. The Stealth Demon is the root. I must destroy him and his luret."

"And how will you ever find him?"

"Senex also told me to trust, have faith, and never waver for that is all I need. The answers will come and the Lord Creator will guide me. So in God and Lux Veritas I trust, and in the advice of Master Senex too. And how I wish he was still of this world."

The group spent the rest of the evening considering solutions and pondering the future of the party, of Purgator and of the universe. Richard and Ang-Norbu were much concerned about the fate of their beloved friends and fellow citizens in Rockdale. But their resolve was to see Solas reach his destination and complete his mission. That was all they could do. It was late afternoon now and the group was not to venture any further. The weather had not let up, and a good night's rest was needed. After a good hearty supper of soup, bread, and meat jerky, the group laid down for the night. The warmth and soothing sound of the crackling fire filled the lodging and soon the group fell fast asleep.

Chapter IV

Black n' Blue

"There is darkness in light, there is pain in joy, and there are thorns on the rose."
— Cate Tiernan, American author.

I

In the morning, the weather had cleared. The mountain was calling once again and Ang-Norbu was first to respond. He banged a spoon on the metal cauldron he used to make the soup the previous evening and made such a racket that even Rajah and the creatures in the shed were startled.

"Up and at it everyone," he hollered. "The sun has risen and they are waiting for us."

"Why are you banging on that pan?" asked a grouchy Dorian, his squinty eyes peeking out over the blanket. "Did we eat the darned rooster last night? Is that it?"

"Who's waiting for us?" asked an always pragmatic Solas, quite to the point.

"The guards of the monastery, of course. They watch over the entrance to the underground tunnels. They will greet us there and escort us the rest of the way."

"Oh!" exclaimed a surprised Xiao Ren. "Does this mean we have finished our climb?"

"No, not really," answered Ang-Norbu. "We still have one last ascent to undertake. This is why I want to get moving while the mountain beckons and the weather gods are smiling upon us. And for this last leg, you will all need to slip on your spiked plates and secure them to your boots, just in case."

The industrious loathar Bomor was up at first cling and was already attending to the animals, strapping on their tack for the final trek. Meanwhile, Richard was rummaging through the canvas bag of provisions searching for breakfast and tossing dried jerky sticks to each member as he found them.

"Thanks Rich," said Dorian still lying down, as his piece of grub landed inches from his face. "Chicken I hope … rooster maybe."

Each member of the group hurried and munched on their food while putting on their clothes. Jiji was happy to see that her gear was nice and warm after it had been set to dry overnight by the fireplace along with the rest of her traveling mates' clothes. After one final check, the group was ready to brave the elements once again. Outside, the air was crisp and the sky was clear. There was not a single cloud to be seen around and hardly a soft breeze to be felt. But you could cut the breath with a knife. They mounted the animals and rounded the corner to discover the stunning beauty of the summit of Holy Mountain towering high above them, something they were not able to see the day before because of the blowing ice storm. Ang-Norbu pointed out to Solas the rock face they would need to reach before finding the next shelter inside its gallery of tunnels. All that was required now was one last effort.

"Let's do it guys," said Solas, as he looked up at the blinding fresh snow blanket glistening on the steep hill.

"Damn, I should have brought my sunglasses," said a squinting Dorian jokingly.

"Sunglasses," repeated Ang-Norbu, smiling. "Yes, I remember now. That's a luxury we don't have here. But it would be so, so nice indeed."

Under the guidance of the Sherpa, the group made sure to stay the course and followed the trail along the edge of the rock side while keeping off the treacherous snow as much as possible. Trees were a thing of the past here. Even eagles didn't dare. This meant no hellbirds, a blessing of sort since the atmosphere was too thin here and the effort needed to fly was forbidding. The four animals climbed ever slower, carefully gripping the ground and lunging for every step like mountain rams in order to make any progress. The effect of the altitude and the lack of oxygen began to take its toll on the group. Solas, Dorian and Xiao Ren panted worst of all, and the uphill rodeo took up much of their energy. After a while, they veered off and followed a snowy crest along a ridge and then stopped as they came face to face with a new obstacle.

"What is it?" asked Solas.

"A crevasse," answered the Sherpa. "We must cross it."

"And how do you plan to do that?" asked Dorian.

"We will jump over it," answered Ang-Norbu, "at its narrowest point."

The group set out to find a slender passage across. After spending considerable time searching, Ang-Norbu settled on an agreeable spot to make the traverse, a minor chasm of only 10 feet in length. As a precaution, the Sherpa tied a long rope through and around the harness of each animal. Should any of them slip during the attempt, the others would be there to stop them from falling into the icy grave.

"Rajah and I will go first," he said.

The feline ran up to the fissure and pounced over it, landing square on the other side without dislodging any of the unstable snow.

"Piece of cake." yelled Dorian.

Solas was next. He followed Ang-Norbu's example hoping Eclipse would do the same.

The creature lunged over the gap at first try and made it look all too easy.

"All right," Dorian yelled this time.

Now it was Bomor and Richard's turn on the back of Ruffian. This was a much more difficult leap as Ruffian carried two riders, and Bomor the loathar was as beefy as loathars get. At first go, success. This exercise seemed no great challenge at all for the husky creatures, even when laden with a load well in excess of 400 pounds. And now there remained only Man o' War, carrying Dorian and Xiao Ren.

But this time, at the exact moment when the creature sprang off the edge of the precipice, a block of ice broke off under its legs. Man o' War lost its balance, wobbled and managed just enough lift to stretch its front paws clampering onto the opposite ledge. Caught by surprise, Ruffian, Eclipse and Rajah were forced into immediate action to uphold the full weight of Man o' War. At the same time, the wonky leap jolted Dorian and Xiao Ren off their ride. The couple only avoided falling straight into the cold abyss by the sheer strength and determination of Dorian who was still clinging tight to the pommel of the saddle with both hands. Jiji struggled to keep her arms firmly wrapped around Dorian's waist, but she soon began slipping. Solas, Richard and Bomor rushed to the edge of the crevasse and attempted to reach their two fallen friends. Ang-Norbu guided Rajah, screaming at him orders and urging the feline along, but the snow and ice were too unsteady for the animals and the great weight of Man o' War began to drag them all back slowly toward the precipice. Soon, the hapless creature dangled horribly over the crevasse. Dorian was out of reach. He winced and clenched his teeth using every last ounce of energy to hold on. Suddenly, Xiao Ren screamed as she let go of Dorian's legs. Her friends, stupefied, could only watch her fall. Her body struck the side wall and slid down, coming to a rest on a narrow ice shelf jutting out inside the icy cavity.

2

The girl was knocked unconscious, but by some miraculous intervention had avoided free falling to the very bottom of the pit. Dorian gasped in despair as Solas screamed at him to hang on. But the animals kept slipping and now Ruffian came dangerously close to the edge. Ang-Norbu pulled out his khukri, raised his arm and prepared to cut the rope.

"Noooo!" screamed Solas as he blocked the Sherpa's attempt in extremis, grabbing his wrist in full swing. "Are you crazy?"

"We have no time," answered Ang-Norbu, "the animals will die."

"But Dorian is still alive," yelled Solas as he pushed the Sherpa flat on his back into the snow.

Now his attention was back to Dorian. Flat on his stomach, his desolate face peeking over the crevasse, Solas made eye contact with his childhood buddy.

"Cut the rope Solas," yelled Dorian with his last bit of energy. "Cut it!"

Now Bomor had pulled his blade too and awaited Solas's order. Ang-Norbu and Richard looked on. Man o' War moaned as Ruffian, Eclipse and Rajah struggled fighting a losing battle. The two friends' eyes locked once again, then Dorian let go.

Dorian plunged as Xiao Ren did before him, losing his gear before bouncing off the cave wall and landing perilously on the ice shelf below only feet away from his beloved Jiji. Dorian struck his head and the force of the impact caused him to continue tumbling on over the narrow ledge, but the spiked plates on his boots helped grip the ice and slow him down. Dorian quickly pulled out his katana and planted the blade flush into the hard ice, just enough to halt his slide. He pulled himself up and rested his body beside his belle. Blood was pouring from the back of his head. His glossy eyes looked up a good 60 feet at the crack of clear blue sky above him, and at the still moaning, dangling Man o' War. As his eyelids fluttered, he reached out to hold Jiji's hand and slipped into unconsciousness to join her.

Solas witnessed the whole event and called out to Dorian, but to no avail. Bomor was about to cut the rope when Ang-Norbu noticed the animals begin to steady their grip and reverse direction, regaining ground. The simple effect of Dorian letting go, thereby shedding his modest 200 pounds, had been just enough to switch the balance of power. And now there was hope. Bomor and the three humans rushed to join the creatures and helped pull on the rope as hard as possible, as though in a vital tug o' war contest. After much effort, Man o' War scrambled to safety and climbed out of the crevasse. All parties were safe now, but physically spent and mentally exhausted.

"Dorian ... Dorian," Solas yelled time and again over the edge of the precipice.

Ang-Norbu and Richard approached him and raised him to his feet offering words of consolation.

"Give me the rope," ordered Solas. "I'll go down to save them."

"It's too risky," answered the Sherpa. "You could fall. It's much too difficult and the ice could break again."

"We can't just leave them down there like that," objected Solas, agitated beyond reason.

"But we are not," replied Ang-Norbu. "We will go get help from the monks instead. We are not far now and they have all the tools necessary. It will be much safer this way."

"Fine," agreed Solas after a brief reflection. "Go; I will stay."

"This is not a good idea," replied the Sherpa. "The enemy could return, as could the snowstorm. Come with us. We need to act fast."

Solas remained unmoved.

"I will stand guard until you come back," he replied.

"Your friends are safe where they are now. Can you not see that? And the storms cannot reach them either," said Ang-Norbu. "Come; we have wasted enough time as it is."

"It's true," added Richard.

Solas thought over the situation for what seemed like a long while, staring down into the heart of the cold abyss at his fallen friends. He imagined what advice Amy, Xiao Ren and Dorian would offer at such an hour. Surely, he concluded, they would ask him to carry on, and to remember the primary objective of the mission to slay that dastard Stealth Demon, close the breach and restore the Diamond Crossing. And after all, it was his unselfish friend Dorian who begged him to cut the rope. Solas knew his buddy well and Dorian would be the first to kick his butt into gear. Solas smiled at the thought, and then turned around to face his perplexed travel companions Ang-Norbu the Sherpa, Bomor the loathar and Richard the sentry, and uttered a meek *"let's go."*

3

The foursome mounted the creatures once again and required still more effort from them. Riding Eclipse, Solas looked back over his shoulder with a mix of hope and remorse as the group led by Ang-Norbu pressed on toward the rock face and the entryway to the tunnels of the monastery.

The last push seemed the longest of all for Solas but after two more hours of snow trekking, the group did at last reach its destination.

"Here we are," indicated Ang-Norbu proud to point at the entrance to the caves, 100 feet up the cliff side.

And indeed, way up high, one could clearly notice an opening in the rock face.

"Yes, I see it," said a cheery Solas. "And if my eyes don't deceive me, it looks like someone is up there too."

"Those are the monk guards I told you about," replied Ang-Norbu. "They have probably been watching us arrive."

"And how do we get up there exactly?" asked Solas.

"Follow me," said Ang-Norbu. "I will show you."

The Sherpa led the group to a long stairway at the foot of the cliff. Its steps were chiseled straight into the hard stone and were covered by a slight dusting of fresh snow. The narrow pathway – just wide enough for the large creatures to pass through – wound up the rock side and led to the entranceway. As the group reached the opening, the ground leveled off and Solas noticed that inside the passage, the cavern was wide and warm and lit by many torches. The group dismounted and was greeted by several of the monk guards, a handful of them bearing weapons. No doubt the unknown creatures intrigued them.

"Namaste Ang-Norbu," said Tenzin, the eldest of the monks. He placed his palms together in reverence, raising them to his eyebrows before tilting his head to salute. "You brought company today."

Ang-Norbu politely returned the formal greetings and answered the thin bald monk clad in a dark robe.

"We are in desperate need of your help Tenzin," admitted the Sherpa. "There are four of us here before you, but earlier we were six. Two of our companions have fallen into a crevasse on our way up here. They are lying unconscious on a ledge inside the precipice. Please help us, we must act quickly."

Ang-Norbu rushed through presentations, introducing Solas and explaining that there was nothing to fear of the strange creatures. Rather, he insisted on the gravity of the predicament which Dorian and Xiao Ren – now being stranded, injured, unconscious and risking hypothermia – were facing. Sensing the urgency in his old friend's voice, Tenzin acted quickly by dispatching eight of his men to lead the rescue. Equipped with plenty of ropes and ladders, spikes and ice picks, the designated monks joined Bomor, Richard and the three creatures back to the scene of the unfortunate mishap. Solas and Ang-Norbu remained with Tenzin who, along with three of his men, escorted them down the underground tunnels to the temple of the monastery. Meanwhile at the entrance of the caves, Rajah remained and stood watch along with a handful of the remaining monk guards.

4

Solas followed the torch bearer Tenzin down the rock tunnels. The pathways were at times high and wide or long and narrow, but always damp and dripping with ground water. Where the passages split every now and then, a series of well placed torches lit the way. On each occasion, Tenzin chose the high path to the monastery.

"Now I understand why the creatures can't come," said Solas.

"In truth," replied Tenzin who was a monk with a most assured and patient step, "the animals could come. But they would need to take the long way around. It would take time and effort, and even if they did manage to find their way through the maze of tunnels, plunderers and looters would probably get to them first."

Solas was quite taken aback.

"What do you mean plunderers?"

"Up here there is little to fear, Solas," explained the elder monk. "Relax. We sit on top of the food chain, so to speak. But beneath us, in the entrails of Holy Mountain, reside the most gruesome and ruthless beings you can imagine. I should warn you."

Solas exchanged a look with his guide Ang-Norbu whose facial expression seem to confirm the old monk's words.

"And why do these plunderers not bother you?" asked Solas. "Do they not know the way up here?"

"They do," answered Tenzin most calmly. "We just have nothing for them of value."

"The monks are fierce fighters too," added Ang-Norbu, as he made a quiet cut-throat gesture to Solas.

"I see. But what about Fergus the leprechaun?" continued Solas. "He stole the luret from you, did he not?"

Upon those words, Tenzin stopped walking. He glanced over his shoulder.

"Yes," he answered. "But this was a long while ago. Still, one must know how to use the luret."

"Yeah, I get that," replied Solas. "I wish I knew too. But Fergus was able to figure it out. He's the one who led the Stealth Demon to us after all."

Tenzin resumed walking, calm and serene, and chose not to partake in this conversation any longer.

"We have almost reached the temple of Kashi," he said, "and the home of Guru Roshni."

And as they completed their walk down the last corridor, a great cave opened up and before Solas stood the pillars and gates of an ancient stone temple.

Back at the crevasse, Dorian had awoken from his knock. His head was spinning and the light reflecting off the ice walls blinded his eyes. After a moment, he realized where he was and remembered what had happened. He looked up far above and saw no one. His head hurt and he moaned in pain. He leaned to his side as he tried to move his body and rested his weight on his arm as he faced Xiao Ren still lying beside him unconscious. He also noticed the frozen pool of blood. He patted the back of his head and flinched. It was numb, but the blood had stopped dripping. The ice had helped seal the wound.

"Jiji," he said, "Jiji."

Dorian repeated his girlfriend's name and shook her slightly as he waited for a response. At last, she began to stir.

"Dorian?" she asked in surprise.

He smiled.

"Yes, it's me," he answered. "Are you okay?"

She screamed as she tried to sit up.

"My leg," she said, managing to prop herself up, "it hurts."

Dorian attended to her wound and examined her limb.

"It's broken, Jiji," he concluded.

"Now what?" she asked. "How did we get down here anyway?"

"We fell," answered Dorian, "first you, then me. Don't you remember?"

"Look at all that blood," she said, gasping.

"Don't worry, it's mine," replied Dorian as he showed her the back of his head.

"Oh my god!" she said. "We need to get you some help. Your scalp is split wide open. I can see your skull."

"Well, good luck with that," he replied. "I get the feeling we are all alone now."

"This can't be," said Xiao Ren, now recalling the events leading to their circumstance. "Solas would never abandon us."

"Yeah," agreed Dorian, "something must have happened up there."

Dorian ripped a piece of loose clothing from his garment and handed it to Jiji who carefully wrapped it around his head to protect and conceal the wound. All the while, the couple kept screaming for help. None seemed forthcoming until at last a multitude of heads leaned over the edge of the crevasse.

5

Solas followed Tenzin up a half dozen broad stone steps leading to the lofty gates of the temple of Kashi. There, a small group of monks were tending the doors and proceeded to swing them open to allow Tenzin and his company to enter. Solas's senses were immediately overwhelmed by the smell of burning incense and the steady humming sounds of praying monks, although he could not see them just yet. Inside the wide entrance hall, torches were affixed to center columns and wide burning dishes set on pedestals were disposed here and there to brighten the foyer all the way up its high ceilings. Conspicuously absent, however, were furnishings of any sort. Tenzin led Solas and Ang-Norbu straight beyond the anteroom to a large, round, open chamber reminiscent of a durbar where Indian princes would welcome and entertain visitors to their palaces. The noticeable difference was the missing nobility and the lack of ritzy opulence. Three dozen chanting monks occupied the humble room, resting lotus position on the cold slabs of stone. They formed an even circle around Guru Roshni who was sitting on a meditation cushion, dressed only in white cotton pants and wearing no top.

"Namaste Guru Roshni," Tenzin said out loud as he interrupted the proceedings.

The humming stopped, yet no one moved. Guru Roshni took a deep breath and snapped out of his semi-trance. After opening his eyes and observing the newcomer that Tenzin had brought with him, he greeted the group with a silent salute. Tenzin did not add another word but gestured to Ang-Norbu to speak. An edgy Solas stood by and watched.

"Namaste great Guru," began the Sherpa. "I am afraid it is my duty to be the bearer of bad news. There is trouble in the land once again. The great evil has returned. Only yesterday, the forces of Daemonia besieged our beloved city of Rockdale and inflicted great damage. They tried to follow us to the temple but we managed to lose them by the glacier. I must warn you great Guru; Daemonia may not be far behind and may soon be knocking at the gates of the temple."

"I am aware," replied the bald Guru with the shaggy grayish beard. He stared right at Solas as he spoke. "I sensed it. We all sensed it. That is why we have joined in prayer today to repel the negative karma. I will however have my men ready, just in case. Thank you Ang-Norbu."

"I have brought with me a friend," continued Ang-Norbu, putting his hand on Solas's shoulder. "He is the legendary hero who delivered Purgator during the last uprising. He has returned to quash the enemy."

Growing impatient, the jittery Solas opted to barge straight into the middle of the conversation and introduce himself.

"My name is Solas Gambit," he said quite loud. "I have come here seeking your help, but we must act fast. Look!"

Solas reached for Lux Veritas and drew the weapon out of its sheath, which alarmed the deft and fleet-footed temple guards who approached Solas with their bows tensed. Lux Veritas began gleaming. Unruffled, Solas continued while all eyes were now fixed on the mystical sword.

"Do not be afraid," said Solas, "I come in peace. This is Lux Veritas, the mighty sword of the Lord Creator which he has entrusted to me."

Tenzin quickly ordered the elite guards to lower their weapons. The wide circle of sitting monks – made up of an odd mix of humans, elkins, loathars and lamentars, of both genders – remained intrigued and fixated on Solas and his weapon. Perhaps what was most fascinating about the sword was the object attached to it just below the crossguard and Guru Roshni wasted no time pointing it out.

"I see that you have found the Will-master's luret," he said, "and it seems to be quite fond of Lux Veritas. However did you find it?"

To answer this question, Guru Roshni invited Solas to have a seat by his side and to retell the circumstances that led to finding the Will-master's luret. Solas did just that and then some, begging the great Guru to pry the object off Lux Veritas and to give him the secret code that would allow him to travel beyond the Diamond Crossing and find the Stealth Demon again.

6

Back at the crevasse, Dorian and Xiao Ren rejoiced at the thought of being rescued from their dire predicament. But hope soon turned to fear when the couple realized that it was the enemy that had reared its ugly head. Indeed, Hell's minions had arrived on the scene. And arrive in numbers they did.

"Oh my God!" said Xiao Ren. "We're doomed this time."

"The rotten weasels," said Dorian, "they must have followed our tracks. Let's hope Solas and the boys are okay up there."

The worried couple scrambled closer to the ice walls trying to keep out of sight. Jiji bit her lip as she winced in pain from her broken ankle. But soon, Daemonia's archers spotted them and sent arrows whizzing past them. Before long, Chaos's demons deployed rope ladders to climb down into the crevasse. When the first hell-sent had reached halfway down, Xiao Ren prepared her bow and from a lying position fired an arrow straight through the beast. The demon came crashing down onto the ledge, narrowly missing Jiji. Dorian took no chances and completed the kill by slicing its head clean off and rolling the body over into the void. More demons were fast on the way however and while Jiji kept firing at the enemy, Dorian noticed that one of the ghouls right above them carried on its back an extra bundle of ropes.

"Jiji, look!" he said, pointing at the demon in question. "Bring down that freak. He's got ropes we can use."

Xiao Ren took a fraction of a second to clue in to Dorian's idea, and happily honed in on the target. With meticulous accuracy, she hit the bull's eye and watched the corpse free fall onto their small platform. Solas rushed to detach the rope package from the slain ghoul, and after dumping the deadweight over the edge, he anchored the ladder onto the icy ledge by its metal prongs and unrolled it farther down into the heart of the abyss.

"Let's go now!" ordered Dorian. "Can you manage?"

"I think so," answered Jiji. She felt rejuvenated in light of this new escape route presenting itself.

"I'll go first," said Dorian. "It looks pretty dark below."

With an added burst of adrenalin, Xiao Ren overcame the pain in her leg and reached out to the ladder to follow Dorian. With her injured limb dangling, and relying mostly on the strength in her arms, she hopped down the wobbly rope ladder one step at a time. Several minutes passed before a trio of minions landed onto the ledge where Dorian and Jiji had been. They looked down and saw little through the darkness but fired a couple of arrows to try their luck, before continuing on down the rope.

Just as the fired missiles whistled by the couple, Dorian reached the last rung of the ladder.

"This is it," he said.

"What do you mean?" asked Jiji.

"We've reached the end of the rope," he explained, "but the good news is that I can see the floor now. I think we can make it, but we will have to jump."

"Jump? I can't jump," objected Xiao Ren. "How far down is it?"

"I don't know," Dorian hesitated, "no more than 15 feet I guess."

"Oh my God!" said Jiji.

Dorian lowered himself as far as he could until he was left hanging by both hands on the last wooden bar of the ladder. In the lower depth of the crevasse, the natural light of day was at its dimmest and visibility was limited.

"I will jump down now," he informed Jiji. "Then it will be your turn. I will catch you. Got it?"

Hearing the unrelenting rumblings of Daemonia above and seeing the descending shadows of the enemy, Xiao Ren felt devoid of any viable option and agreed with the plan.

"Got it!" she replied in a jittery voice.

Dorian let go, hit the ice floor and tumbled. He got up and dusted himself off; he was fine. Above him, he could better see Jiji now.

"Come on Jiji!" he said. "It's not so bad. I will catch you. Trust me."

Xiao Ren mustered up some courage and since her arms were growing weak from holding up her weight, she let go and dropped the rest of the way, praying for the best. Dorian caught her, breaking her fall. Jiji knocked Dorian to the ground as she let out a cry of pain. As they got up, they could see the trio of demons following close behind.

"Come on," said Dorian. "Let's keep moving. Hop on my back!"

But before she could do so, the three demons landed beside them, snarling and hissing. And more were on the way. Dorian drew his katana and protected Xiao Ren by sheltering her behind him. She slowly backed away as Dorian faced the approaching danger. The first demon lunged at him with a morning star – a spiked club – which Dorian avoided before slicing his opponent clean through the bowels. The second foe followed right behind the first and swung at him with a chained spiked ball. Dorian reacted just in time to block the weapon with his katana. The chained ball wrapped around the sword twice with the demon still hanging on to its weapon. Dorian pulled his katana back, thus drawing his enemy forward before thrusting forth his sword and skewering his foe right through mid-chest. With Dorian's weapon tied up, the third demon profited of the opportunity and was already swinging his sword at Dorian's back when an arrow struck the unsuspecting ghoul through the back of the skull.

"Well done Jiji!" said Dorian as he jerked his weapon loose from the carcass of his vanquished enemy. Then, he noticed several demons carrying torches right above him. "Aim for a demon with a torch!" he ordered Xiao Ren.

Jiji complied, bringing down yet another foe to the bottom of the ice pit. Now the couple possessed a much needed torch to light the way. Dorian lifted the injured Xiao Ren and carried her on his back while she brandished the torch on high. The duo wasted no time fleeing the area and followed the long crevasse corridors extending before them into the distance. A scant minute behind them, more relentless torch bearers touched ground and were hot on their tail. The burning flame assisted the couple in getting away faster, but in this cold, narrow and obscure abyss, it also betrayed their whereabouts to the enemy. They kept their fingers crossed hoping for an exit. Soon their prayers were answered when they came upon an escape route, a tunnel of sort dug straight into the mountain rock. One look behind convinced the couple to choose the outlet. And so Dorian hurried and hopped along down the dark tunnel with Xiao Ren clinging to his back on a mysterious path toward the unknown.

7

At the temple of Kashi, Guru Roshni seemed rather impressed with the telling of Solas's long eventful journey that brought him from Sherbrooke to the top of Holy Mountain.

"Well, it is all beginning to make sense now," said the wrinkly old man. "But I'm afraid that with all your expectations of me, I will be a great disappointment to you instead."

"How so?" asked a surprised Solas, now frowning.

"Well, it happens that I cannot separate the Will-master's luret from Lux Veritas," he explained. "Nor can I give you its magic code, the one which would allow you to cross the Diamond Gates."

"Why not?" objected Solas, his voice intensifying.

"It's just that I do not know how to pry the objects apart," answered Guru Roshni quite calmly. "And what's more, I do not know any codes either."

"I don't understand," said Solas, "Chief Larsen said that you did. Shaman Chepi said so as well. You were the keeper of the luret for years. This cannot be."

"They were hoping I knew, more than anything else," admitted the Guru.

"You mean to say that I came all the way up here for nothing!" cried Solas.

"That is not true, my good boy," replied the great Guru. "There is a reason for all things. Why don't you meditate on it with us? You are in good company here. The answers will come."

"This is a joke," replied Solas, looking at Ang-Norbu with fire in his eyes. "I have risked my life to get here. I have left my good friends Dorian and Xiao Ren behind. How will I ever find Amy now … and that cheat the Stealth Demon?"

"Your spirit seems a little lost and confused, my good Solas," said Guru Roshni. "Come, sit, rest, and find your inner peace … which is the path to the answers you seek."

"Well, I may be confused alright, and it is true that I don't know the way to the Diamond Gates," said an irritated Solas, "but let me give you a little advice of my own: the path to *your* salvation is in a place called Elysium, just north of here. The way to Paradise passes through the Crystal Gates. This much is crystal clear. I can show you the way if you like. Why not meditate on that?"

"Vanquish the bitterness that has invaded your spirit Solas," said the Guru, "and this right soon. If all of us souls present here in this house of worship were meant to be on the good side of the Crystal Gates, we would be there already. But do tell me my dear Solas, and please enlighten me, to what ultimate end do the good people of the city of Lalas Pur strive so hard?"

"They dream of redemption … and to enter through the Crystal Gates to reach the Promised Land of our Lord Creator: Elysium," answered Solas.

"Good. And what of the people of the city of Belenos, or of the people who inhabit the various lands throughout Outlandia, be they human or elkin, lamentar or loathar, troll or Torlund, or any other kind of creature?"

"The same," answered Solas, "Elysium! What of it?"

"You see, we are no different here," explained Guru Roshni. "There is more than one path to Elysium Solas, perhaps as many as they are individuals willing to find it. We all deal with it in our own way. Here, Brahman Hindus and the Buddhists of Nirvana have joined forces together. We all strive to improve, the best way we know how."

After these words, Solas began to settle down somewhat as he reckoned the old Guru was right. His thoughts wandered though, and in his heart of hearts, he worried most about Amy.

"And do not worry about Amy," advised the sentient Guru. "She is doing fine."

Solas figured the old man must have had a sixth sense. He could almost read your mind. At the very least, he could sense your emotions, and feel your intentions, a little like the mighty Lux Veritas.

"What would you know about Amy anyway?" asked Solas, testing the Guru.

"She is a strong spirit, to be sure," answered Guru Roshni. He closed his eyes and began to drift into a meditative state, perhaps to render a service to Solas or to help him put his troubles at ease;

maybe restore his confidence and his resolve too. "She has faith in you. Her love for you is boundless. She believes. This I sense."

"It's nice to hear you say that," said Solas. "I have been worried sick, ever since the evil one crept up and slipped away with her … Tell me, can you see her? Where is she now?" Solas continued, excited by the prospect of some absolute, magical answer.

"Of this I cannot be sure," said the Guru. "She is being held captive in a safe place, not in Tartarus or amongst members of Daemonia. The Stealth Demon would not take such chances. Amy has too much collateral value. He has her living a semi-normal life, I feel, in some other world, which is now yours to find I suppose. Indeed, she has left Purgator and is now somewhere beyond the Diamond Crossing. This is all I know."

"How can I ever hope to find her then?" asked Solas, dejected. "No one here can help me. I have no code. This is impossible."

"Follow your intuition," replied the Guru, his eyes opening once more to look into the deep of Solas's soul. "Have faith in yourself like Amy has faith in you, and you will discover once again that truth alone triumphs."

8

"*Truth alone triumphs … Truth alone triumphs.*" Solas played these words back in his mind, wondering what sort of use they could have.

"Words are cheap, great Guru," concluded Solas. "What I need is the code."

"Do you?" asked Guru Roshni.

"What do you mean, do I?" retorted Solas. "Of course I do. The Stealth Demon had one. Twice I've heard him mumble it before vanishing."

"How do you know it was a code, Solas?" asked the Guru.

"Let's not get technical here," replied Solas. "He definitely used some kind of gibberish to activate the luret."

"And why do you need to separate the Will-master's luret from Lux Veritas?" continued the old Guru. "It seems quite at home where it is, and quite safe I might add."

Solas had no reply. Clear answers were still eluding him, but the strange wisdom of the old Guru was starting to shine through. Solas began to realize that perhaps he had been looking for answers in all the wrong places. He had been looking for answers to questions that didn't really exist. Perhaps he already held the key to the puzzle.

"You seem rather pensive. Ready to meditate on it now?" asked the Guru.

Solas chuckled.

"Maybe I should," he answered. "Tell me, great Guru, how did you come to be the keeper of the Will-master's luret?"

"The luret has been residing in the temple of Kashi since time immemorial, my good Solas," answered the Guru. "No one knows for sure. But the Will-master's luret has always been a source of inspiration for the monks. We are thrilled to see that it is now in your care alongside the legendary Lux Veritas. The Lord Creator knows best."

"I will return the Will-master's luret when my mission is complete," said Solas. "Rest assured."

"I do not doubt," replied the Guru, smiling.

"One more thing though … if truths alone triumphs, as you say, then tell me why this temple is protected by so many guards?"

Now it was the Guru's turn to chuckle.

"Truth triumphs from within, Solas," replied Guru Roshni, "alas, it does not dwell within the enemy. And after all, there is only one Lux Veritas. We have the right to protect what is ours too."

"How could you lose the Will-master's luret then?" asked Solas. "Did you not realize that Fergus was not a friend?"

"When Fergus came to us, I did have my doubts about him," explained Guru Roshni. "He was confused, to be sure, but he was neither a bad soul nor a mean one. In the end, he was only seeking salvation, just like the rest of us try to do in this wretched land of Purgator. We just go about it in different ways, but we share a common goal: salvation and Elysium. I sensed it. So, I trusted him. The monk brotherhood took him in. He visited us once in a while. He was curious about our way of life. We were complete opposites. He wanted riches; and we wanted none. He came with many questions and we tried to answer them all. Then, one day, the conversation turned to the Will-master's luret which we kept right over there, in that empty crystal urn sitting on that small marble pulpit. I explained to him the mysterious qualities of the object."

"Well, that was a big mistake," said Solas. "You should have known that he would try to acquire the luret, if not steal it."

"Leprechauns seek wealth and riches, my good Solas, not ways to travel to other dimensions," replied the Guru. "The object itself is rather small and has little monetary value. But I guess Fergus knew the location of the Diamond Crossing and no doubt he had heard countless stories about the endless sources of wealth that can be found beyond the Gates. Now that he could get his hands on the Will-master's luret, he could travel back and forth and become the richest being in the universe."

"And that is when all this trouble started," said Solas.

"Yes indeed," replied Guru Roshni, "Fergus went crooked."

"He always was crooked," added Solas.

"Perhaps! One regrettable evening, our little conniving leprechaun Fergus betrayed our trust and exploited our goodwill to snatch away the luret from its pedestal. It wasn't long before the guards sounded the alarm, but by then Fergus had disappeared like only leprechauns can down the maze of tunnels and mineshafts. We never saw him again."

"And how did he manage to pass through the Diamond Crossing? Are you sure you didn't give him a code or something?" asked Solas, hoping to trigger a memory from the guru or some sort of confession.

"What code?" replied the Guru, startled at the bizarre question. "There is no code. Do you really think that if a code existed at all I would reveal it to him? I just gave him the same sermon I gave you, as I do for anyone who is doing some real soul searching. That is all."

"You mean *have faith in yourself* and *truth alone triumphs*," said Solas.

"Good. I see you understand."

9

Solas wondered how in the world such an unscrupulous being like Fergus could have realized the unthinkable: cross over beyond the Diamond Gates. No matter how the leprechaun managed the feat, Solas gained confidence. He knew that if Fergus could do it, no doubt he could as well. And Solas already had in his possession the Will-master's luret. Now all he needed was to find the location of the Diamond Crossing.

"Great Guru, please tell me the way to the Diamond Gates," said Solas. "I will trust myself and have faith that the answers will come to me. But time is of the essence, and I must keep moving on."

"I have never seen the Gates, Solas," answered the Guru. "But I do believe that my good Sherpa Ang-Norbu knows the way."

Ang-Norbu had been up until now a passive participant but an avid listener to the conversation and now his expertise was needed.

"Yes," he replied. "I do know that the Diamond Gates are deep within the bowels of Holy Mountain. I have never seen the Crossing either, but Rajah and I will take you as far as we are able."

"Thank you again Ang-Norbu," said Solas. "I do admire your dedication and your courage, considering all that I have already put you through. Together then, as soon as Dorian and Xiao Ren rejoin us, we shall chase justice."

The word *justice* uttered by Solas brought yet another light chuckle from the Guru. For him, justice appeared to be an entirely foreign concept.

"Do not chase justice, Solas," said the Guru, "something which you cannot bring forth. In Purgator or in the mortal world, there is no justice at all, only corruption. Remember that justice belongs only to the Lord Creator. Within the walls of Temple Kashi, we refer to it as Karma … destiny, if you prefer. Go chase your own destiny then, if you must, but be true and keep a close eye always on your own salvation."

Solas chuckled in turn and was not in a most compliant or agreeable mood, and so he objected to this great infallible wisdom.

"I thank you for your priceless counsel, oh great Guru," replied Solas. "I will keep this advice to heart regarding my own affairs. But it seems to me that you have overlooked one important factor. Why is Tartarus such a permanent Karma, with no exit? Has destiny been sold?"

Guru Roshni kept quiet and before replying to this most pertinent question, he picked up a stick of agarwood incense. He lit it with calmness under the attentive eyes of Solas, Ang-Norbu and the monk following. He lifted the burning object toward the heavens liberating its inebriating scents while rubbing it between the palms of both hands and releasing the eternal essences of truth and wisdom into the air.

"You think that Hell lasts forever, do you?" he asked. "Not even Tartarus lasts forever. The Lord Creator knows all that is in your heart. If Lord Chaos would repent with purpose, the Lord Creator would forgive him too. And there would be no more Hell. For it is the essence of the Lord Creator to love, to understand and to forgive all and each of his creations. He cannot do otherwise. That would be against his very nature. You see, my young one, it is we who create our own Hell. It is our pride, our greed, our envy. Therefore, curb your selfish desires and be more like the Lord Creator; forgive all and forgive yourself most of all, and there will be no more Hell. In the end, all lies fritter away and all that remains is the truth, and *truth alone triumphs*."

10

Meanwhile, Dorian and Xiao Ren kept on running down the dark and damp tunnels beneath Holy Mountain to escape their demonic pursuer. They had been heading down the sloping passages for a good 20 minutes now. They turned to the right, and then turned to the left, and followed a series of corridors in a desperate attempt to shake off Daemonia. But with the weight of the injured Xiao Ren on his back, Dorian tired faster and the torchlight of the beasts chasing the couple could not be extinguished. To make matters worse, the pair soon faced an unexpected dilemma: there was yet another great light shining in front of them.

Dorian put Jiji down, if only for a moment, to catch his breath. "What do we do now?" asked a worried Xiao Ren, leaning up against the rock wall, her head pivoting back and forth between the two dangers. "We're trapped."

The rushing sound of Daemonia amplified as the demons rounded the far corner. Dorian was keeled over from exhaustion, huffing and puffing and ready to throw up.

"Think positive," he said, lifting his head, his wet and dirtied black locks hanging over his face. "There is always supposed to be a light at the end of every tunnel. Isn't there?"

"Right, well here is praying!" said Xiao Ren, as she one-hopped onto the back of her ironman again.

And with a last surge of willpower and a final burst of energy, Dorian sprinted ahead like a bat out of hell screaming like a deranged man toward the new light.

With Daemonia blazing along and running amok right behind him, Dorian reached pronto a great and bright cave-like opening. Arriving in utter desperation and with several projectiles now whipping by him from the rear, Dorian broke the threshold of the gapping hollow and, unaware, stepped onto a trapping mechanism which triggered the release of nettings. The couple was abruptly snapped up, caught in a tangled web of nets and left dangling right above the mouth of the tunnel.

At once, a bustle of little people came rushing to the fore to examine the catch of the day. Xiao Ren screamed in shock and in pain, eyes aghast. Dorian struggled to reach for his dagger and cut the cords while the curious beings approached. The diminutive folks, no more than three feet tall, armed their weapons. Dorian and Xiao Ren believed the end had finally come. They were left hanging on nothing but a prayer when the rampaging crew of Daemonia arrived, bursting through the mouth of the tunnel just beneath the suspended couple.

The flyspeck inhabitants of the cave opened fire on the intruders, peppering the unwelcomed demons, imps and accompanying freaks with a volley of tiny but venomous missiles. The units of Daemonia, whose fury could not be quenched so readily, poured out of the tunnel in numbers like frenzied termites out of an anthill, and were thrust into the thick of an unexpected battle. Dorian and Xiao Ren could only watch the surreal spectacle unfold. The invaders slashed, trampled and skewered as many of the little people as they could but the swarm of Lilliputians was overwhelming even for the great evil warmongers from Tartarus. Soon, despite having inflicted considerable damage, Daemonia's units were depleted and its few remaining leaders, still defiant, retreated back to the tunnels to live and fight another day.

I I

Following the carnage, the focus of the little people turned to the two humans responsible who were caught in their trap.

"Bring them down!" ordered a loud voice.

Several eager lutins lowered the nets and freed the live catch, while several others kept their tiny blowguns with poison darts aimed at the couple. Dorian helped Jiji stand up as she was still moaning in pain and struggling with her injury. The distressed couple tidied their clothes while under the watchful eyes of a small army of little beings. The most distinguished one of the lot, wearing a long pointy crimson hat, stepped forward waving his cane.

"Who are you and what brings you here?" he said in a harsh tone, his beady slanted eyes glowing with scorn. "Speak!"

Dorian raised his hands in the air to put the beings at ease.

"This is Jiji, and my name is Dorian. We are humans. We come in peace."

The couple glanced at each other. Xiao Ren was surprised to hear Dorian speak the exact same words Solas used in such situations, considering that this utterance of good intention seldom worked. Dorian shrugged his shoulders.

"You call this peace?" replied the leader, already short of patience. "I can well see that you are humans. Why is Daemonia chasing you? You almost had us all killed. What do you want from us? Speak!"

Dorian did his quick best to explain the series of unfortunate events which led him and Jiji down to the caves in such a manner.

"So you are on a mission, are you?" said the leader of the little people.

"Yes we are," insisted Dorian. "But we have been separated from the other two members of our group, Solas and Amy, like I said."

"I believe you," replied the leader, now much calmer and smiling too. "I believe you."

Dorian found his reaction and change of mood rather odd.

"Are you mocking us?" asked Dorian.

"Not at all," he answered. "You know too much about the Will-master's luret, the Stealth Demon and the mighty Lux Veritas for your story not to be true."

"Good!" said Dorian, exhaling a sigh of relief.

"My name is Kiltop and we are the Millikeen people," he said, showing off his entourage with pride. "This mountain is our home, and it has been so for ages now. Come with me," he continued. "This area has become unsafe, and I have something of interest to show you."

This announcement peaked Dorian and Xiao Ren's curiosity, besides putting them more at ease. And so Kiltop led the couple away to his village, and the Millikeen people – who were indeed small in stature, but appeared by any other means almost humanlike – carried Xiao Ren along on a stretcher and tended to her wound. They carried away their dead too, leaving no one behind. Dorian discovered that Kiltop and his people endured many violent encounters with Daemonia in the past and, much to his surprise, with the leprechauns too.

12

Back at the temple of Kashi, Solas did not entirely endorse Guru Roshni's vision of Hell. Solas wasn't the creator of his own hell; other people were hell. He did however agree that in the end *truth alone triumphs*. This seemed a reasonable philosophy to him, if not almost an inevitable one, considering that he held in his hands the mighty Lux Veritas and that, be it the duty that the Lord Creator bestowed upon him, he would make sure that truth triumphed in the end. Only it was left up to him, and him alone, to make this wishful credo come to pass. *So which came first, the chicken or the egg?* He thought. Should Solas have faith in the Guru's wisdom or the Guru in Solas's abilities? Solas did not wish to waste any more time on this conundrum, and concluded that the inherent message therein was to rely on his faith and in the truth, in order to meet with success. And indeed, the wisdom of this message could be of service to him. In the end, was the ultimate *truth* none other than the Lord Creator himself?

Richard, Bomor and the monks returned from the crevasse in a most flustered state of mind, and with good reason. They announced that Dorian and Xiao Ren were unreachable or altogether missing. Not only that, but Daemonia had arrived on the scene in great numbers. Richard and company had barely avoided detection before fast drawing back. Solas stood up frantic, demanding news from his friends and answers.

"What do you mean Dorian and Xiao Ren are missing! Did you not see them?"

"We could not," answered Richard. "We retreated before being spotted. We could do nothing else, other than sign our own death warrant or bring the wrath of Daemonia back with us to the temple of Kashi."

"Give me your men!" ordered Solas. "And we will go back to save them."

"What good will this do?" replied Guru Roshni. "If your friends have succumbed to the enemy, then it is already too late. If they have not, perhaps they have escaped or are hidden somewhere, in which case you will not find them. By going back, you will accomplish nothing but put our lives at risk."

"You speak of faith and courage, but you have none yourself," replied Solas, just a little miffed at the Guru's complacency. "I will go back alone then. I know Dorian. He is still alive. This I sense."

Without wasting another second, Solas turned away from Guru Roshni and his lot of sitting monks and made his way to the exit.

"Solas wait!" yelled Richard. "I will come with you."

"Me too," said Bomor.

"And I," added Ang-Norbu. "But I know a quicker way to the bottom of the crevasse. Best you should follow me."

Solas was caught by surprise but pleased to see that he could still count on a few good friends.

"Let's go," he said, as he grabbed Ang-Norbu on the fly. "Show me the way."

"What about Rajah and the creatures?" asked Richard.

"They won't pass," answered Ang-Norbu. "We must leave them behind."

The four hurried off, securing their weapons and loading up on ammunition, arrows mostly. Just as they were about to exit the temple south, Solas thought better to say farewell to Guru Roshni and thank him for all his help. As Ang-Norbu and company slowed down and waited, Solas locked eyes with the great Guru and brought his hands together to salute him, nodding and offering a simple "Thank you for everything." Guru Roshni returned the courtesy saying only "Oh, it was nothing." Solas smiled as though he found the reply humorous, but his smile soon faded away when he realized deep down that this 'nothing' was quite a lot. Indeed, the Guru did not give clear answers to any of the important questions; only he had eliminated them all. Now Solas had no more questions; for only he possessed all the answers, whatever they were, and no one else in the whole universe did.

Solas nodded again and saluted the Guru with a sincere look of appreciation this time. Guru Roshni saluted back and smiled.

13

After a long tortuous walk through an extensive network of tunnels, Dorian and Xiao Ren reached Millok at last, the underground home of the Millikeen people. The village was located in an ancient cavernous quarry which was now teeming with little folks going about their business from hut to hut. To Dorian's utter amazement, the town was inundated with natural light. Kiltop explained this simple phenomenon, pointing out that the village was on the far edge of a tall and abrupt rock face on the lower western side of Holy Mountain. The light entered through two great openings from which, standing at its edges and looking down, one could see far into the distance and down to the valley below. From its vintage point, Dorian and Xiao Ren were treated to yet another spectacular display of nature's beauty. The view extended beyond the flatlands of Oneiros, all the way to the Sea of Bounty on the western edge of Outlandia. Straight below, the River Lethe slithered its way through the valley of Shadows, forging ahead between the Petros Mountains on one side and the Aros Mountains on the other.

"That's one incredible view," said Dorian, "and an impossible location to reach up this side."

"You are right on both counts," agreed Kiltop. "But you must be hungry now. Why don't we go and enjoy a nice meal over a fine bottle of wine? I would love to hear more about the good friend you lost, Slodas and the mighty Lux Veritas."

"Solas!" said Dorian. "His name is Solas."

In the center of the village was an open communal fire pit around which banquets and gatherings were held, as well as debates and discussions of the most important kinds. Kiltop and his guests sat at the head table, joined by a great number of the townsmen at the others. Meanwhile, many of the Millikeen cooks and chefs prepared the food, the wine and served the tables for the pure enjoyment of their kinfolks. Dorian and Xiao Ren never felt more like giants in such company and under such circumstance.

"How is your leg doing, my dear lady?" asked Kiltop, seeing to the absolute comfort of everyone.

"It is feeling a lot better, a bit sore still, but a lot better. Thank you," she answered. "Most of the pain has gone away. I would love to know what's in that medicine. It works wonders."

"For that my dear, you would need to speak to Potrul, our village druid," replied Kiltop. "He creates the most amazing concoctions of poisons and cures from magical herbs. Soon you will be as good as new."

"Fantastic!" said Xiao Ren, ecstatic. "I never thought it possible to heal broken bones so fast."

"Yes. And thanks to you Kiltop," added Dorian, "the back of my head is all healed up too."

The food arrived. Meat, bread and vegetables were served, and Kiltop and his guests ate like true survivors.

"More leucurus?" asked Kiltop.

"Oh thank you," said Dorian. "I see that eating prairie dog is still in fashion in Purgator. By the way, forgive my curiosity but how do you get all this food up here?"

Kiltop laughed through a mouthful as he patted his chin with the end of the tablecloth.

"We usually trade for it," he said, "or we hunt and harvest it ourselves."

The humming of conversations from the merry lot of Millikeens amplified bit by bit and soon a strange and broken chorus of burps added tempo to this mellow drone. And by all accounts, Kiltop was a real pro at the craft of belching. Lady Xiao Ren did not participate of course, but Dorian sure outdid himself on this occasion.

"You were right," said Dorian. "This place really is spectacular and quite interesting. Thank you for receiving us so amicably after such a false start, and for fixing up Xiao Ren and me too."

"You're welcome," replied Kiltop. "But this is not the main reason I brought you here. Come, it is time that I show you."

14

Dorian and Xiao Ren – who was now walking on her own with only a small limp to bear – followed Kiltop to a more somber part of the village, way at the rear, where natural light does not reach anymore and artificial light now shows the way. The trio approached a guarded tunnel in form of a cul-de-sac. There were single rooms dug into the rock with solid metal bars and locked doors. This was the village jail. Dorian and Xiao Ren were rather perplexed and felt somewhat uncomfortable. But what a surprise they had when they came face to face with one of the prisoners.

"Fergus!" said Dorian.

The leprechaun looked up and could not believe his eyes. His prayers had been answered, he thought.

"Is that ye I see," said Fergus in his trademark accent, "Dorian the earthling back in Purgator again?" He squeezed the cell bars with both hands and pressed his face against them to have a better look at his visitors. "But what are ye doing here and where is that friend of yers, Solas … and his mighty sword, Lux Veritas?"

"We came alone," answered Dorian, not wishing to give away too much. "But he sure will be thrilled to see you when he gets here."

The leprechaun frowned, confused, while Dorian and Xiao Ren looked at each other and smiled. They both realized that Fergus was the answer to many of their problems. For one, he knew how to operate the Will-master's luret, and two; he knew the location of the Diamond Crossing, and where to find the Stealth Demon as well … and perhaps their good friend Amy.

Dorian turned to Kiltop and smiled, patting him on the shoulder for a job well done getting his hands on a most slippery customer.

"You're welcome," replied Kiltop.

"And what has Fergus done this time that you would throw him in prison like this?" asked Dorian.

"It's all a big misunderstanding," said Fergus, frazzled and desperate for his release. "Get me out of here, Dorian. I am innocent. I swear it."

"It's a long story," answered Kiltop, not minding the yappy little green fellow with the red hair who was really not much taller than he was. "He had it coming to him."

Kiltop gave Dorian the condensed version of the long history the Millikeen people shared with the leprechauns. It wasn't nice. For ages the leprechauns subdued the Millikeen people into forced labor digging the tunnels and mines under every mountain region of Purgator looking for treasures and gold. The leprechauns perceived the Millikeen people to be an obstacle to the greatest riches in the land, and so they raided their camps and took them away by force to put them to work, mostly beneath the majestic Rainbow Mountain range. These mountains were within easy reach of the Crystal Gates of Elysium where the leprechauns would lay down their hoarded wealth as offerings. Through these gifts, they hoped for redemption from the Lord Creator. During those dark days, the most notorious of all the leprechauns was one of their leaders, a ruthless slave-driving vermin by the name of Fergus.

Following the defeat of Lord Chaos and the restoration of Purgator, the Millikeen people were set free from the bondage of labor imposed by the leprechauns. The Millikeen people put a bounty on Fergus's head should he ever be foolish enough to venture near the tunnels and caves of Holy Mountain. He did, of course. The pickpocket had been up to his old tricks again and got caught trying to claim what wasn't his. And what a delight it was to capture the most wanted leprechaun of all. Now he lingers in a Millikeen jail, where he belongs, until he pays his dues.

"Oh, that's rubbish!" Fergus cried out.

Dorian and Xiao Ren were shocked by this revelation. Of course, they were well aware that the leprechauns were consummate scrooges, but they had always imagined them as devout workaholics too. The couple soon began to worry however, stating how important it was to find Solas. The hour was late and the situation urgent. Things would only get worse if nothing was done right soon about the new threat of Daemonia. Dorian seized the moment to strike a deal with Kiltop.

"Release Fergus and put him under my care," said Dorian. "The scoundrel has caused you enough grief already. And he will be a great help to us."

"Yes, yes," concurred Fergus. "That's an excellent idea."

Kiltop considered the request carefully and agreed to it on the condition that Fergus be returned to the Millikeen people as soon as the mission was completed. This way, the leprechaun would not cause them any more trouble and he could resume paying his debt.

"Of course," said Dorian, happy to have concluded this agreement. "I will bring him back myself if I must. And if I do not, he will be dead."

"Oh no!" said Fergus.

"This will not be necessary," replied Kiltop. "I would much rather give you five of my best men to accompany you in your travels until the job gets done. They are great guides and they will make sure to bring Fergus back to me in one piece."

"Even better!" said Dorian.

"Open the door!" Kiltop ordered the guards. "And keep the wily weasel's wrists shackled."

Fergus exited the cell wearing a grin of victory on his face. This was really a great day for everyone, not only Fergus. Kiltop dispatched five of his elite men as promised. On the outskirts of the village, the leader of the Millikeen people saw Dorian and Xiao Ren on their way.

"Farewell my friends," said Kiltop, "and may the Lord Creator see you through."

"Thanks for everything Kiltop," said Dorian. "The Millikeen people are the greatest."

"Oh please!" mumbled Fergus under his rusty beard.

Dorian then turned to the lead scout Artin, who was holding one of five torches.

"Please take us to the monastery of Guru Roshni," he said. "I hope to find my buddy Solas there."

"Yes Sir," replied Artin.

Artin, Dorian and Xiao Ren led the way into the tunnel. Behind them, the Millikeen guards pushed grumbling Fergus along promising to cut off his tongue if he did not keep quiet.

CHAPTER V

The Diamond Tesseract

*"Here you leave today and enter the world of
yesterday, tomorrow, and fantasy."*
—Walt Disney

I

Solas followed his Sherpa guide Ang-Norbu down the dark and
narrow passageways leading to the bottom of the crevasse with
Bomor the loathar and the ever-loyal sentry Richard. Solas's heart
was pumping faster now; his conscience guilt-ridden for leaving
the side of his fallen comrades. Every now and then, the quartet
would reach yet another fork at the end of a tunnel, and needed
to make quick decisions about which way to turn.

"I cannot understand how you do not lose your mind in this
crazy labyrinth," said Solas.

"Shhhhh," said Ang-Norbu. "We need to be quiet."

"Why, do you think Daemonia could hear us down here?"
asked Solas in a lower tone of voice.

"Yes, there is always that," answered Ang-Norbu. "But voices carry quite far in this maze of corridors and if we listen closely, they can often tell us the way."

"Or not the way," added Richard.

"That is correct," said Ang-Norbu. "We wouldn't want to run into a group of those nasty scavengers and plunderers that roam these tunnels in search of easy loot."

"What do you mean plunderers?" asked Solas. "Some creeps actually like crawling up and down these halls, do they?"

"Not so much up here," answered Ang-Norbu, "but in the lower caves, yes. You never know."

"Well, in this darkness, rest assured that Lux Veritas will warn us well before they show up," whispered Solas.

"It's this way," said Ang-Norbu. "There is a cave opening at the next junction. It's a major meeting point. So, we will need to take the second tunnel to our right, and we will be half-way there."

"Excellent," said Solas.

"In any case," continued the Sherpa, "be on your guard. Now that we are getting closer, Daemonia could always be lurking right around the next corner."

Further away, Dorian, Xiao Ren and the rest of the group kept moving along at a good pace following behind Kiltop's shrewd Millikeen guide Artin.

"Stop!" said Fergus, before dropping to his knees. "Ye're taking us the long way, ye are. I am exhausted."

Two of the guards grabbed the whiny leprechaun by the scruff of the neck while Artin turned back to see what the matter was.

"Get up!" ordered Artin, pointing his dagger at Fergus. "And keep quiet or do you want Daemonia to hear us, you miserable rat."

"Dae-mo-nia," he repeated whimpering, "Daemonia's here?"

"Yes, and they would love to get their hands on you," replied Artin. "But you will go from being a deadweight to being plain dead, long before I let this happen. Now get up you slimy rascal."

"Ye can't kill me," said Fergus, as the guards dragged him to his feet. "Ye heard yer boss, what he said. He wants me back in one piece."

"Yes, but he never mentioned dead or alive."

Fergus's eyes drooped again and he resigned himself to his fate. The group resumed its course and all appeared in order, for a good two minutes at least.

"There's a quicker way, ye know," said Fergus.

"Be quiet!" said one of the guards as he twisted Fergus's arm to send a message loud and clear to the leprechaun.

"Ahhh!' yelled Fergus.

Loud and clear it was. Following that yelp, Artin stopped dead in his tracks, as did the convoy.

"Shhhhh," said the frustrated guide. "You will have us killed, fool. Now listen; we will soon reach a junction, and we will need to take the fourth tunnel to our left. Get your weapons ready just in case we should meet with looters. This is one of their favorite spots. And with all this racket, they may well be rubbing their hands already."

2

Solas and his escorts reached the junction first. They paused for a moment just inside the mouth of the tunnel before deciding on when to enter the open area, already illuminated by the soft light of torches anchored into the rock walls.

"Did you hear that?" asked Solas.

"Sounds like someone met with the end of a blade," said Richard.

"That cry came from where we need to go," added Bomor.

"All right," said Ang-Norbu, "take a deep breath now, and let's keep moving."

In the centre of the cave was a huge drop. It was impossible to see to the bottom of it, but several ladders carved into the rock sides led down to the lower levels of the mountain. In the tunnel opposite Solas, Dorian's group had now reached the main junction too. Even so, Artin, who had drawn his dagger as a precaution, did not slow down. Dorian and his band proceeded behind him, staying as low-key as possible, and creeping along the walls of the cavernous area in complete silence. Soon, the group managed to reach the fourth tunnel; the one leading up to the monk monastery, and the same one Solas and company were on the verge of exiting.

That is precisely when Lux Veritas began to glow, alerting both groups of each other's presence. Expecting the worst and separated by only a few feet, both sides remained quiet and hesitated to move forward. In the open cave, Artin pointed to the light coming from the tunnel. Dorian acknowledged his signal and cut in front of the line, katana drawn, ready to strike. Fergus crouched in fear, Xiao Ren prepared her bow and the five Millikeen warriors readied their blowguns. Inside the tunnel, Solas darted in front of Ang-Norbu and gestured to the trio to back off.

Imagining thugs or beasts just around the corner, Dorian waited to trounce the first oblivious creature dull enough to venture before his blade. This creature, albeit astute, turned out to be Solas. Trusting his weapon, he jumped into the alleyway brandishing Lux Veritas. Dorian was about to strike when, at the nick of time, he caught a glimpse of Lux Veritas and recognized his best buddy Solas.

"Solas!"

But before Dorian had the chance to warn his partners, the Millikeen fired a handful of poison darts at Solas. The projectiles pinged off Lux Veritas's blade like bugs off a windshield.

"Hold your fire!" yelled Xiao Ren, waving her hand at the Millikeen warriors.

Artin and his partners were startled, but none more so than their captive Fergus. The leprechaun was in awe of Lux Veritas. The mighty weapon presented a way to redemption, he thought – not in view to gain mercy from the Lord Creator, as was the case the first time he saw it – but as a bargaining chip before the Stealth Demon, should the occasion occur. He smiled and relished the idea.

Dorian and Solas lowered their weapons and embraced like never before. Ang-Norbu, Richard and Bomor, although cautious, stepped into the light. Xiao Ren welcomed back her fellow travelers as Artin and the diminutive Millikeen guards looked on. Then she hugged Solas.

"I feared the worst," said Solas.

"So did I," replied Dorian as the others listened. "What happened up there?" he asked, referring to the events at the crevasse.

"We went to get some help," answered Solas. "We didn't have the tools. It was too risky. But when Ang-Norbu came back to get you, Daemonia's minions had arrived in full force."

"They really came at us Solas," explained Dorian. "We barely managed to escape by the tunnels below the crevasse, in spite of Jiji's injury. The Millikeen people saved us in the end."

Dorian turned around and pointed to the group of small warriors standing behind him.

"This is Artin by the way, our guide," he said, "and Broc, Dak, Sookan and Vodin. The Millikeen people are terrific. They healed our injuries too."

They saluted. Solas slotted his weapon back in its sheath and greeted the group with a simple *hi*, before thanking them and then noticing, to his utter shock, the leprechaun curled up against the wall.

3

Solas approached the humbled captive, now a mere shadow of his old self.

"Fergus?" he said. "Am I dreaming, *the* Fergus?"

"It is I," replied the leprechaun, feeling obliged to confirm the observation.

"Hallelujah!" cried Solas to the heavens before high-fiving his buddy Dorian. "This is amazing. How did you ever catch him?"

"Artin can tell you better than me," said Dorian. "Fergus is their prisoner after all."

"It is true," said Artin. "The leprechaun is nothing more than a petty thief. He has also committed crimes of the highest order against the Millikeen people and now he must purge his sentence. Our leader Kiltop has allowed mister Dorian to use the prisoner as he sees fit for the purpose of your mission. After completion, he must be returned to us to finish paying for his felonies."

"Felonies! This is rather serious," said Solas. "I knew him a con artist and a trickster, but a felon?"

Artin further explained the nature of the offenses that Fergus committed – citing the oppression of his people and racketeering among the most evil. But since the Millikeen guide's discourse about Fergus's acts appeared endless, Ang-Norbu intervened.

"Well," he said aloud, "truly, I am glad that we are reunited in fine health and in good spirits, but it is time to move along. We must still be mindful of the unseen dangers that lurk in these caves and tunnels."

"You are right Ang-Norbu," replied Solas, "however I do believe that from here on Fergus should lead the way to the Diamond Crossing. You do remember the way, don't you?"

"Me? Why would I?" answered the leprechaun. "What is a diamond crossing anyhoo?"

"Let me jog your memory," said Solas. He pulled out Lux Veritas from its sheath, turning the blade around to expose the Will-master's luret melded onto it. "You do remember what this is, don't you?"

The nervous leprechaun's eyes lit up at the sight of the object. His jaw dropped as he propped himself higher against the wall.

"Yes, yes, of course I remember," he answered, his mouth dryer than the ashes of Tartarus. "It's the mighty Lux Veritas, what else?"

"Exactly, Lux Veritas and what else?"

"Ye mean that shiny thing?" said Fergus.

"You should know, you stole it from the monks at the temple of Kashi," said Solas raising his voice, "and then used it to pass through the Diamond Crossing. Do you remember now?"

Fergus trembled some more, his eyes looking for a sympathising face in the crowd.

"Ye've got me mistaken with someone else, ye do," he replied. "I swear on me mother's grave."

Dorian chuckled.

"Oh come on, you never had a mother."

"Well then," said Solas, "since you cannot be of any help to us at all…" He paused and turned to address his childhood friend. "Dorian, on the count of three, could you please toss this no good onus into the void? No sense dragging along any extra loads."

Dorian executed his orders and picked up Fergus by the scruff of the neck, dragging him closer to the edge of the drop. Fergus mumbled, whimpered and begged for mercy.

"I got the anus in position," said Dorian. "We're ready for the count."

"Oh forget it, just toss him!" said Solas, nonchalant as can be.

Never was there a quicker come-to in the entire existence of Purgator.

"No, please! I'll speak, I'll speak. I'll tell ye everything," said Fergus in tears.

"How wise of you," said Dorian.

He pushed the leprechaun back onto the middle of the pathway as the group watched and waited for Fergus to gather up his wits.

4

The band was on the move again, with Fergus at the head of the file and Solas and Ang-Norbu following close behind. The leprechaun would spill his secrets soon enough, but standing out in the open cave was unwise and the group decided to keep moving on. No one in the ranks uttered a single word for a long while; all ears were loyally receptive to the slightest sounds emanating from the adjacent corridors. The cold dark pathways spiralled down toward the heart of the mountain. Deep in this gloomy anthill, time and space had no meaning, and none could tell whether it was day or night anymore. The maze of tunnels seemed endless and disorienting, and Solas began to wonder if the sly leprechaun was not leading the group on a wild goose chase.

"Are you sure you are taking us the right way?" asked Solas.

"I am," answered the leprechaun. "I know these tunnels quite well. Me people dug many of them over the ages and..."

"You mean the Millikeen people," corrected Solas hastily.

"No, not this particular one," replied Fergus, scratching his chin trying hard to remember. "That was the Orboz, I believe."

"The Orboz?" asked Solas before turning to his Sherpa Ang-Norbu and to Artin the Millikeen leader. "Have you two ever heard of these guys, the Orboz?"

"Yes," said Ang-Norbu. "They have a nasty reputation. And as far as I can tell, Fergus is taking us the right way, Solas."

"I have heard of them as well," said Artin. "The Orboz are marauders who roam the lower tunnels and caves of Holy Mountain. They are strong, terrifying brutes. My people have had a few encounters with these savages in the past."

"Savages!" repeated Solas. "You enslaved savages to do your dirty work Fergus?"

"Not me," answered Fergus, on the defensive. "That was long before me time. Leprechauns of days long past brought them here."

"Brought them here from where?"

"From some distant world," replied Fergus. "Does it matter? They live here now."

The answer Fergus provided triggered a myriad of fears and scenarios in the mind of Solas. It occurred to him that the present dilemma with the Will-master's luret and the breach in the Diamond Crossing was neither unique nor recent. Solas was determined to push on for answers.

"And why would the leprechauns bring the Orboz here from some distant world?" asked Solas. "How did they accomplish that?"

"There are plenty of hidden treasures right here within the mountains of Purgator. Me people needed good workers to extricate its wealth. So they brought in the Orboz from beyond the Diamond Crossing to do the job."

"Did they use the Will-master's luret to do it?" continued Solas.

"Of course," replied Fergus. "There is no other way."

"Is this how *you* managed to get across?" asked Solas.

"Guilty as charged!" laughed the leprechaun. "I cannot hide anything from ye, can I?"

"And you are going to tell me how to get across, aren't you Fergus?" said Solas, who did not appreciate being mocked by a natural sham; his guide and prisoner to boot. "What's the secret?"

Fergus grinned some more, as though he held some high power, a place of vital importance in the universe, and some indispensable knowledge. The group stood by, riveted more than ever by the words of the strange leprechaun.

"Well," he said, "I could tell ye, young soul, but I doubt it would be of any use to ye anyhoo."

"And why is that?"

"Do ye ever wonder why it is called the Will-master's luret?" asked Fergus.

"It has crossed my mind," replied Solas.

Fergus chuckled some more.

"Well, here's the secret," Fergus announced in a whisper. "There is no secret."

Right about then Solas lost his patience and grabbed the leprechaun by the lapel of his green garment.

"Stop playing games with me, Fergus, or I swear I'll smash your head against these walls and splatter your brains all over."

"No, no, no," said Fergus in a panic. "What I mean is that the secret to the Will-master's luret is in yer will power."

"What the hell are you taking about?" said Solas.

"It took me an awful long time to master the item, I admit, but with intense concentration, a clean conscience and a pure heart, ye can will the luret into action and ye will master it at last."

This unlikely response amused Dorian and the rest of the group.

"You ... a clean conscience and a pure heart?" said Solas as he applied more pressure on the leprechaun. "You must take me for a fool."

"No, no, no," replied Fergus, "I tell ye the truth. Only ye can master the luret. There is no key. There is no secret. Ye *are* the secret. The key is within ye."

Solas shook him up some more.

"I will take ye to the Diamond Crossing," continued Fergus. "Ye can try it and ye will see fer yerself."

The last words of advice from Guru Roshni flashed in Solas's mind: "*Truth alone triumphs.*" And so he gave Fergus the benefit of the doubt. Maybe there was something to his story after all, but it still did not explain how Fergus or the Stealth Demon could figure out a way to pass through the Diamond Crossing. After all, they were not the most saintly beings in the afterlife. Something was amiss.

"How could the Stealth Demon pass through the Diamond Gates then? I heard him utter a code or a phrase of some kind before blasting into the sky with the luret?" asked Solas.

"The evil one also possesses a luret, a dark one," answered Fergus. "I cannot say. But ye have the light one. It is different, is it not?"

Solas nodded and let go of the leprechaun.

"Perhaps," he answered. "We will soon find out. Now take us to the Diamond Crossing, and make it fast."

"Further below, there is another clearing," explained Fergus. "We must pass through it before reaching the Diamond Crossing."

"Let's go!" ordered Solas.

And upon this command, the band was on the move again, just as before, with Fergus at the head of the line and Solas, Ang-Norbu and the rest following close behind.

5

The journey continued down the damp and narrow corridors toward the lower tiers of Holy Mountain. All was quiet now. No one uttered a single word as all ears stayed at full attention. The heart of darkness made little sound too, save for the subtle plopping of water droplets into the numerous subterranean puddles or the travelers' footsteps splattering into the gentle and inexorable tinkling streams of fresh water conduits. To everyone's surprise, the enemy was absent. No threat or foe was seen or heard anywhere. Nonetheless, something soon interrupted the trekkers' advance. Sewer rats squeaked and scurried down the gullies of the corridor and a foul stench overwhelmed their senses. Covering their breathing passages, the group progressed with caution before stumbling upon a most sickening and worrisome sight: rotting corpses.

"Disgusting!" said Dorian as he shooed away the large rodents gnawing on the remains of the cadavers.

"Yuk, what is that?" asked Xiao Ren staring at the two decomposing cadavers lying by the side of the passageway.

"They are Torlund dwarves, they are," said Fergus. "Fresh kills!"

"Torlunds?" said Solas, surprised.

"Fergus is right," said Bomor. "Just take a closer look at their dress and armor … typical Torlund attire."

"No thanks," said Xiao Ren, leaning away against Dorian's shoulder.

"Yes," added Dorian, "I recognize those pants."

"Who did that to them?" asked Solas. "I always thought the Torlund dwarves were the undisputed kings of ruthless."

The group stayed quiet as they searched for a plausible culprit.

"The Orboz," replied Fergus in timid fashion, not wanting to stir up more anger at him or exhaust his speaking privileges. "The Orboz are cutthroats, ye see," he continued, pointing out the evidence with a flick of his head.

"Tell me Fergus, what business do the Torlunds have down here anyway?" asked Solas. "Aren't the leprechauns friends with the Torlunds as I recall?"

"We do trade with them. That is true," answered Fergus, feeling somewhat amused by the remark, "but we are not friends. Ye have us confused with Daemonia."

"Yes, of course," said Solas. "That would explain why the Torlunds are down here. We must be getting closer to the Diamond Crossing and the Stealth Demon."

"Great!" said Dorian. "And what about these Orboz freaks, Fergus? How many of them live down here anyhow?"

"There are fewer of them now," the leprechaun answered. "Remember, they are not from our Purgator. When they die, the Wheel of Souls carries them away ... home to their own Purgator, in one of the other dimensions."

"Other dimensions ... how many other dimensions are there anyway? Don't the Orboz need to pass through the Diamond Gates when they die?" asked Solas.

"To get here, yes, but not to return upon death," answered Fergus. "It's like a shortcut, so to speak. I mean if ye enjoy dying, that is." The leprechaun started to chuckle at the thought of choosing to die in order to get 'home' faster.

"That's messed up," said Dorian.

"Yes," agreed Solas. "That could also explain why they are so vicious. They are caught in no man's land with nothing to lose."

"Can we move along now?" asked Xiao Ren, overwhelmed by the smell of the festering corpses. "I am about to throw up."

"I agree," said Dorian. "Let's get to our destination already. I'm sick of crawling down these endless rat holes."

Solas nodded.

The group passed by the scene of the slaughter hugging the walls of the tunnel and stepping around the victims. Following another quiet walk in solitary contemplation trudging along still lower and lower down the stark confines of the mountain, a distinct commotion warranted the band's attention. The members of the group did not speak a word and progressed in silence down the hallways to investigate the source of the noise. As they approached another major cave opening deep in the heart of the mountain – the one Fergus had mentioned earlier – they stopped and observed from high on up a bustling army of beings hard at work.

6

Beneath in the clearing the group could witness a great number of slaves chained to one another, pickaxes or shovels in hand, filling trolleys with dirt, rocks and such or pulling carts on wheels out the exit tunnels. The overlords of the operation looked on, driving these hapless servants to labour, yelling at them commands and insults or whipping them into submission when necessary. Fergus whimpered and gasped at the sight.

"These ... these are me people, they are," he said with a stutter. "The Torlunds have turned on us."

"It is the Torlund dwarves!" said Solas. "What are they doing to the leprechauns?"

"How cruel!" cried Fergus. "We are rendered chained animals now, lowly slaves and nothing more."

"Oh the irony!" said Dorian.

"Now you can see for yourself what the Millikeen people endured for so many years at the hands of the leprechauns, Fergus," said Artin. "Poetic justice at last!"

"This is not the time to bicker," said Solas. "And let's keep our voices down. From what I can tell, Fergus told us the truth. Torlunds and leprechauns aren't friends at all. But what is the reason for this bondage, Fergus?"

"It's not me fault," cried Fergus. "It's not me fault, I swear."

"Why would it be your fault?" asked Solas. "Speak."

The leprechaun took a brief moment to recompose while the Torlund masters echoed their shouting orders straight off the cave ceiling and cracked their whips at the chained gangs.

"Ye see the tunnel to the far end of the cave," said Fergus, "the steep one going straight down?"

"Yes, I think so," replied Solas.

"That one is unfinished," he explained. "Today, I see that the rumours I heard are true. The Stealth Demon ordered me people enslaved to dig a tunnel to the walls of Tartarus. The Torlund dwarves were left in charge, that's all. I didn't want to believe it. But it's all because of me and that darned luret, it is." And he started sobering.

"Why dig a tunnel to Tartarus anyway?" asked Dorian.

"I don't really know," answered Fergus, "but it can't be good, can it?"

"It won't do him any good," said Solas. "Lord Chaos is surrounded by the first light of Genesis, '*the conscience of the Lord Creator.*' It is impenetrable."

"Oh!" replied Fergus, surprised by this account. "Now ye teach me something new, young one. Perhaps they want to break down the walls of Tartarus."

"That's pure madness," he said, before hurrying to the heart of the matter. "Now tell me Fergus, which tunnel is it to the Diamond Crossing?"

The shackled leprechaun pointed to it with his stiff, half-length rusty beard.

"That one," said he.

Fergus, Solas and a medley of heads leaned over the sidewall to peek at the passage.

"Well, how do we get to it from here, Fergus?" asked Solas.

"How do you think, great warrior?" replied the amused captive, now smiling from ear to ear.

"No, we have to find another way," said Solas. "This is crazy. There are just too many dwarves down here, and countless others waiting in the wings, I am sure … not to mention Daemonia."

"There are also a lot of leprechauns," said the cuffed bargain hunter. "Free me people Solas! And we will join yer quest and fight Daemonia together, as before."

Dorian and Xiao Ren chuckled at this absurdity while the Millikeen guards began to agitate at the prospect of Solas considering the proposition.

"Are you mad?" said Solas.

"And what's more," Fergus continued, addressing Artin in particular, "to show our goodwill, the leprechauns will make restitutions to the Millikeen people fer all their years of suffering. I give ye me word."

This declaration angered the Millikeen guards something fierce and had an equal adverse effect on Artin who pulled out his dagger and rushed at the leprechaun, holding up the blade flush against his throat before anyone could react.

"Do you mock us?" he said with clenched teeth. "The leprechaun's word isn't worth a copper leper, you weasel. I ought to toss your miserable carcass into this shady pit and let these Torlund jackals at it so you can get a taste of your own medicine for once."

Fergus gulped, frozen in fear, before Solas intervened.

"Calm down, Artin," said he. "We will do no such thing. Now let go of Fergus." And Solas rested a sympathetic hand on the Millikeen guard's shoulder. Artin stared deep into the leprechaun's eyes from only inches away, before backing off.

"Now there has to be some other way," said Solas.

"I do know of another way around," said Ang-Norbu.

"Yes," agreed Fergus, still visibly shaken up, "but it will take us much longer still."

"Well, how much longer are we talking about here?" asked Solas.

But before the Sherpa or the leprechaun could offer an answer, each member of the group's attention was diverted to the sudden glinting of the mighty Lux Veritas.

7

By reflex, Solas drew his weapon from its sheath. Dorian did the same and everyone stood on guard as each member of the expedition looked about the area trying to spot the imminent lurking danger. Soon enough, the threat manifested at the far end of the tunnel. It was the Orboz; a motley crew of beings bent on vengeance against one and all, an enraged brotherhood annoyed at lingering aimlessly in this foreign environment, this Hell not their own. Reputation told that they lived by one credo and one credo only: take no prisoners. There was hell to pay, and by Lord Chaos someone would pay for this ordeal. They surfaced from the shadows of the tunnel, approaching with a confident gait, weapons in hand, and facial expressions sick enough to rival those of Daemonia's minions.

"The Orboz!" said Fergus, struck with fear. He crouched into a ball behind his protectors.

Solas stood first in line and prepared to engage the savage raiders. The metallic glow of Lux Veritas was intense and shed a soft light halfway down the corridor. The five Millikeen guards armed their blowguns and awaited the firing signal. The aliens, although smaller than Neanderthals, exhibited most of the prehistoric men's natural features. They were robust woolly hominids, with long and wild hanging hair. As they neared, Solas felt a strange sense of empathy for them but noticed that reason was altogether absent from their empty gaze and the humanlike creatures appeared to function only on instinct, fuelled by anger and little else.

As far as Solas could tell, the Orboz numbered in the dozen. Perhaps more followed behind but he could not tell. One thing was certain: Solas and his cohorts were stuck somewhere between the proverbial rock and a hard place.

"We must shoot now," said Artin.

"Hold it," ordered Solas. "The Orboz seem mesmerized by Lux Veritas."

Indeed, the glint of the sword intrigued the apelike beings with the appearance of scaled-down Bigfoots. They paused, grinned curiously and then charged without warning, yelling and stampeding forward like mad beasts. The Millikeen warriors fired their tiny poison missiles at once. The stinging darts struck the alien creatures, immediately activating the lightning effect of the wicked venom, which spread across their skin like a bubbling virus, dropping the first line of beasts in an oozing heap of putrid, purulent pustules. The Orboz responded by throwing their own projectiles which Lux Veritas's shield countered with ease. Solas struck the hard ground with the blade of his weapon, creating a violent earthquake that rumbled down the tunnel knocking and felling the onrushing enemy. The loud tumult alarmed the Torlund dwarves who dispatched several units to investigate the commotion. Just as the Orboz got back to their feet, the ceilings and walls of the corridor started to collapse on top of them.

"Exit the tunnel," Solas shouted, "fast!"

Fully exposed, the group rushed out to the open cave and faced a more important threat: the entire Torlund dwarf garrison. Narrow walkways followed the inner walls of the cavernous quarry and spiralled down to the lower levels where the majority of the chained leprechauns laboured. The arrival of Solas and his crew granted the prisoners a much-needed relief as the Torlund dwarves now diverted their focus toward intercepting the intruders.

There was no turning back for Solas and company as the tunnel caved in behind them. The group kept moving and ran downhill toward the enemy hoping to reach the bottom of the pit where Solas could make a better stand against the warrior dwarves. A slew of arrows from the Torlund archers rained down on the group, narrowly missing the diminutive and agile

Millikeen guards escorting prisoner Fergus. Xiao Ren, Richard, Bomor and Ang-Norbu riposted by firing arrows of their own and reached their enemy targets with greater accuracy as the Torlund dwarves were gathering in large numbers of a hundred or more. As the burly dwarf soldiers came up the pathway, Solas countered with Lux Veritas, slashing and skewering his foes one after the other, then dispatching their corpses over the edge and sending them crashing to the flats below to the great delight of the chained leprechauns. The Millikeen guards picked up shields from the fallen enemy on the way through just in time to thwart yet another volley from the Torlund archers. Now the band had reached the bottom of the pit. Dorian, Bomor and Richard joined their swords to the battle while the feisty Millikeen sharpshooters inflicted considerable damage to the Torlund foe from short range with their deadly poisoned stingers. Before long, the overwhelmed Torlunds had depleted their troops and the remaining dozen dwarves or so beat back in retreat and fast disappeared out the nearest exit tunnels.

8

Richard, Bomor and Xiao Ren performed one quick inspection of the area to make sure that the last of the enemy had checked out. All was stun quiet now. Fergus raised his head from the midst of his Millikeen escorts.

"They are gone, they are gone," he shouted. "We won!" And he smiled from ear to ear and began to do a little trot on the spot, hopping from leg to leg while chirping a little leprechaun ditty.

His chained comrades – numbering in the hundreds and shackled to each other in a long line by steel chains – were in shock, not fully understanding the sequence of events that just unfolded before them. But soon upon seeing that the oppressor was vanquished, that provisional freedom was restored and that their kindred Fergus was doing his little song and dance, the lot of them joined him in his makeshift festivities, clapping and cheering at their good fortune. Artin seemed nervous and the

Millikeen guards were out of sorts with the new situation. Solas and the rest of the group watched on as the ruckus of joy grew and filled the cavernous void like never before.

Fergus climbed on top of two nearby corpses stacked on top of each other and from the height of his glory addressed his fellow leprechauns.

"Dear fellers," he shouted, "today is indeed a triumphant day fer us leprechauns. Thanks to me great friends here and to the mighty Lux Veritas, and by the grace of the Lord Creator, ye are now free!" And Fergus repeated this declaration again and again to the utter jubilation of the chain gang. "Free I tell ye... free ... free!"

Now Solas thought the better of it and stepped on the mound beside Fergus to steal his thunder. Seeing this, the crowd tapered down to a lull.

"My name is Solas Gambit and I am the keeper of the mighty sword Lux Veritas. Today, you witnessed first hand its divine power. You owe much to the Lord Creator. But the leprechaun nation also owes a great debt to the Millikeen people and in particular to Artin, Broc, Dak, Sookan and Vodin standing right here before you. These brave souls risked their lives to free you today. Yet, they were once your slaves. The Millikeen folks know too well how that feels and understand this injustice. They hold no grudge."

Artin and his partners looked at each other in confusion at hearing the words of Solas. He continued.

"You will be freed from bondage now. The Lord Creator needs you to get back home to Cloverdale City to make a stand against the forces of Daemonia that are overtaking Purgator once again. But your leader Fergus still has a larger debt to pay to the Lord Creator and he shall remain with us."

The leprechauns grumbled, muttered and murmured amongst themselves, but welcomed their release from confinement and relished their newfound liberty. When the moment had come, one individual screamed above the crowd to get everyone's attention and spoke on behalf of the leprechauns.

"My name is Ebed," said he, in an accent similar to that of Fergus. "Me people thank ye fer all yer help Solas, but which way out is best to avoid the enemy? We know these tunnels better than anyone does, and still we feel confused. What else, how do we fight Daemonia with no weapons?" The leprechaun fellowship roared its approval. "So we leprechauns have chosen to follow ye, yes?"

"No, you cannot join us," answered Solas in a heartbeat. "You are too many. And our mission will not allow it."

"Pick up the weapons from the fallen enemy and follow me!" blurted out Ang-Norbu, to everyone's surprise. "Many of you will be armed and I will lead you to the Valley of Shadows. From there, you can follow the River Lethe back home to Cloverdale."

The crowd rumbled once more.

"Are you sure about this, Ang-Norbu?" asked Solas. "You would do this?"

"I will, Solas," he answered, nodding his head. "You are nearer the Diamond Crossing now. Artin and Fergus know the rest of the way better than I do. Besides, you are right Solas; too many of us could hinder the rest of your mission. I can render better service by helping the leprechauns, and I am eager to get back home to the city of Alta-Mir and help my people too."

"I understand," said Solas.

"I will join you too, Ang-Norbu," said Richard, "that is if you don't mind Solas. Once you reach the Diamond Gates, what are we to do? The journey back out of the depths will be dangerous without you and Lux Veritas, perhaps impossible. Here, at least, we are in the hundreds and we can help some more."

Solas smiled.

"I choose to go with Richard," said Bomor. "We are partners."

"Well, who am I to hold you guys back?" replied Solas. "We will miss you, but the three of you have done plenty for us already. Dorian, Xiao Ren and I are grateful. Bring the leprechauns home now and we wish you Godspeed."

"And Godspeed to you Solas," said Ang-Norbu. "We await your safe and victorious return."

"Do take good care of Eclipse, Man o' War and Ruffian," said Xiao Ren to Bomor.

The loathar sentry smiled and nodded.

"I will."

The members of the group exchanged farewells. Listening in on the conversation, Artin did some thinking of his own.

"Sookan and Vodin will accompany you," he declared to Ang-Norbu, choosing to volunteer the services of his two guards. "They can avert confrontation with the Millikeen people and will better explain the situation to our leader Kiltop in person. They will give him a full report of our progress too. He will appreciate it."

"Fine," replied Ang-Norbu. "We can always use more help."

"That's a great idea," said Solas. "Imagine … two Millikeen guards leading the leprechaun troops … who would have believed it?"

"I just do not wish to see anymore bloodshed between the Millikeen people and the leprechauns," explained Artin. "We both face a much greater threat now, and we must do it together. There is no room for misunderstanding."

And now the remaining individuals on the fateful mission were down to a lucky seven: Solas, Dorian, Xiao Ren, Artin, Broc, Dak and of course the troublesome but indispensable Fergus. As Solas guided his newly formed band down toward the far tunnel leading to the Diamond Crossing, Fergus shouted out a few last words of encouragement to his fellowmen: *"Leprechauns forever!"* and *"Our day will come!"* The throng of little green men responded by chanting his name and pumping their fists high in the air.

"Fer-Gus … Fer-Gus … Fer-Gus!"

Fergus grinned with pride and looked back from the distance before disappearing into the waiting mouth of the tunnel.

"Some hero you are!" said Artin in a snarky tone. "Remember, your friends may be free but *you* are not off the hook, vermin!"

9

The group pushed on through the dark and damp passages near the heart of the mountain mindful that at every turn the enemy could surge. Indeed, on many occasions, intrepid souls of the kind never seen before on the surface of Purgator ambushed Solas and his convoy before Lux Veritas dispatched them summarily. For a while, this was routine; however, there was nary a sign of Daemonia. Many of the tunnels became steeper and steeper yet, and every step taken cautiously measured and steadied against a rock to prevent a slip or fall. This exercise was most tricky for the hand-tied leprechaun who continued to bemoan his fate and curse the apparent pitiless cruelty of his captors. Time crawled without end, and the limits of human endurance tested when, at last, to the weary group's delight, the ground levelled off. Fergus sighed and collapsed to the floor.

"We made it," he said.

To Solas, nothing much had changed except that he could now stand up straight and stretch his body parts, which had been kinked up far too long.

"We made it where, Fergus?" he groaned.

"No more descending," he answered, catching his breath. "We've reached the flats … the bottom ye know. I reckon we shall be at the Diamond Crossing before long."

"Which way is it then, Fergus?" asked Solas.

"Straight ahead," the leprechaun answered.

"Let's keep moving," said Solas, giving him a nudge. "No rest for the wicked!"

"Ye really are worse than the Torlunds, ye are."

The tunnels were bigger, easier to manage and better lit. Torches were at every turn and at every angle. As a result, it was getting warmer too.

"Who's responsible for all these lights anyway?" asked Dorian. "This is odd."

The band progressed at a slower pace, vigilant and well aware that, even in these depths, strange beings lived and roamed. And if the Stealth Demon had any success at all, an influx of demons and strange creatures could soon flow freely down these corridors on route to the surface to wreck havoc on Purgator.

But the travelers were in for another surprise when they saw beyond the end of the tunnel the silhouette of the most unusual being encountered yet. But as fortune would dictate, this one was not of the beastly sort. The members halted their advance and stood still, staring at the tall immobile figure standing before them blocking the way with impunity. Lux Veritas kept quiet.

"What is this now?" whispered Solas to Fergus.

"Not to worry," answered the leprechaun, "that is the Sage of the Grotto."

"The Sage of the Grotto?" repeated Solas.

"What the heck does he want?" asked Dorian, butting his way to the front. "He acts like he owns the place."

"He might as well," replied Fergus, chuckling. "He lives here after all."

"Who in his right mind wants to live down here?" said Dorian.

"A crazy old man, that's who," said Fergus. No one pays attention to him really. He talks a lot to say nothing."

"Well, he's just like you then," replied Solas, as Fergus rolled his eyes. "Since you already know him, let's go say hi. I am sure he will be a great help to us."

With Fergus at his side, Solas approached the mystery man at a casual pace. Dorian and the rest of the group followed close behind. As soon as the two were able to make eye contact, the tall man dressed in the dark, long, woollen greyish robe raised his arm straight forth with authority.

"Who goes there?" he asked in a firm but scratchy voice.

Solas stopped, and seeing that the old man was no threat at all, set to test his wits at once.

"This is mighty brave of you to ask since you are one and roaming about these parts are violent forsaken creatures even Tartarus would not accept."

"I do not fear such beasts," replied the man with the gaunt face, the deep-set eyes and the shredded white beard. "I am much more concerned about seeing lost wandering souls invading these parts led by a sly leprechaun named Fergus."

Solas, Dorian and Xiao Ren chuckled at this remark while the Millikeen guards were somewhat less amused.

"I see you already know each other," said Solas, smiling.

The old man remained unmoved.

"Do you have a name, young one?" he asked.

"My name is Solas Gambit … of Sherbrooke, Earth. And you are …?"

The old man approached the group with his arms crossed, head tilted and highbrow raised.

"Ha!" he said, "No one has bothered to ask me this question for ages. But since you ask, if it matters at all, my true name is Uffa, Lord Uffa. At least, that's what they used to call me back in my days on Earth. Nowadays, things have changed a little bit. Some call me plain Looney; others call me the Sage. It is a fine line, isn't it? Take your pick."

"I told ye," whispered Fergus to Solas.

Uffa was a giant, albeit a skinny one, and stood a good head clear above Solas. No sooner finished, he glanced over top Solas to see the rest of his company. Solas proceeded to present his friends Dorian and Xiao Ren and the remaining members of the Millikeen guards. Fergus needed no introduction.

10

Uffa gained Solas's confidence, especially after explaining that he knew the Diamond Crossing well. He had been keeping a watchful eye on it for ages. Dorian and Xiao Ren warmed up to the old sage as well. He invited the group to a safer area where plunderers were few and Daemonia seldom appeared. On the way, Uffa, a man with a long effortless stride, made a few astute observations and began to fire away a few questions.

"Solas Gambit you said your name was," he said, never lifting his eyes.

"Yes it is," replied Solas.

"Ha!" said Uffa, "you are different than I imagined. If it wasn't for you carrying Lux Veritas on your back, I might have believed you were just another looter."

"You know who I am," said Solas, perplexed by his comments. "You were expecting me?"

"Well of course," he answered. "These are unusual times indeed; it's been Hell around here if you haven't noticed: raiders, creatures from Lord-knows-where, and Daemonia too. I fully expected someone to come and put an end to this madness, by Lux Veritas! Strange things are happening to the Diamond Crossing, the kind I have never seen before. I reckoned the sword of Genesis would be summoned eventually. And to be honest, I had a hunch it would be you, Solas, after all the stories I heard told by the druids of Purgator at the last gathering."

"They know my name?" asked Solas.

"Do they!" replied Lord Uffa. "At the last convention, they spoke highly of you. The elders spent much time retelling the heroics of Master Senex and his protégé Solas Gambit and friends. The druids praised the powerful effects of his Mirandia crystals, and the prowess of the mighty sword Lux Veritas. Your exploits are legendary all over this land."

"Tell me, did you know Master Senex?" asked Solas, eager to hear more anecdotes about his old mentor and beloved grandfather.

"I had the honor to meet him a couple of times," answered Uffa. "He was a witty fellow, a wiz-master of the Mirandia crystals. He took pride in it. It was a well-kept secret of his. He didn't want the formula to fall into the wrong hands, you know. I witnessed on two occasions Master Senex demonstrating the awesome power of the crystals. I dared not look into this torture for very long; I was reminded what a pitiful soul I still am and how much further I must still strive, if I ever wish to reach the majestic Crystal Gates of Elysium. Good heavens!" The old lanky fellow halted his thoughts, but kept rushing ahead at a steady gait as he rounded the next corner. By now, the druid forced Fergus and the smaller Millikeen guards to hop and trot behind the group just to keep up the pace. "Master Senex was quite the accomplished archer too, I dare say," he added.

Xiao Ren smiled, remembering all the times she had spent with the Master honing her skills in archery on the sandy beaches of Lalas Pur out on the edge of the Sea of Morphos.

"What a lucky soul he is!" she said, reminiscing and sighing. "I know that he is now resting well beyond the Crystal Gates. I miss him. Only, it may be a very long time before I ever see his smiling eyes again."

"Ha!" uttered Uffa. "Do not underestimate what you may find beyond the Diamond Crossing, young one."

Uffa's remark shocked Solas, Dorian and Xiao Ren. Yet, just as the old sage finished his words, the group arrived at its destination.

"We're home," he said with a certain cheer.

They exited the tunnel and stood in an open but modest area where the ceiling reached three stories high. The cavern basked in the bright lights of many burning torches. Straight in front, the travelers faced a huge rock wall. To the right and to the left, more tunnels led on toward other regions of the underground.

"This is home?" asked Dorian.

"Well, don't be deceived by appearances," said Uffa. "Now watch carefully."

Lord Uffa stepped up closer to the rocky wall. He lowered his head and stretched out his arms. After a few seconds, a large stony slab of rock began to swivel, grinding its way slowly around before stopping. There was an opening beyond, showing the way to a concealed staircase. The members of the group were astonished at the magical transformation they had just witnessed. They could have never guessed some secret passage existed beyond the wall. They stood speechless; all except one.

"Nice! I like it," said Dorian.

11

Indeed, in lieu of a common door, a large swivel mechanism opened the hidden entrance to the sage's abode.

"Welcome to my grotto!" he said, gesturing his hand to point the way. "Won't you please come in?"

Curious and in dire need of a rest, Solas did not hesitate to accept the courtesy. The group followed Uffa up the stairway. As they stepped onto the fifth stone slab of the stairwell, the door closed automatically behind them. The slam sent a vibration echoing up the shaft of the stair tunnel. The Sage of the Grotto kept on climbing the many spiralling steps, perhaps 70 in total, when another swivel door, smaller in size than the first one, opened before them by some similar mechanism. They had arrived at Uffa's home.

The old man's residence was a small cozy affair, well appointed and befitting a household of one. In the centre of the room was his favorite rocking chair whose plush crimson cushions had assumed the outline of his body. The stale musky odor of his tobacco pipe lingered in the air. At the far end of the room, the old sage kept, sitting on a hand-carved, antique cherry bookcase, several esoteric items, druidic potions, rare herbs and a modest library made up of hand written notes and scrap books filled with occult recipes, secret locations, and a vade mecum of trickeries, illusions and magic spells. Further on was an alcove, an open terrace, which overlooked yet another cave on the opposite side of the grotto.

"Shall I get you a beverage?" he asked, positing a ready-made pitcher full of a refreshing infusion in the centre of the coffee table.

Solas, Dorian and Xiao Ren took off their gears and quickly occupied the few available resting spots about the room. Fergus and the Millikeen guards had retreated to a corner of the home where they sat on carpets laying overtop the cold stone floor. Uffa threw a quick glance at the leprechaun from the corner of his eyes.

"Ha! … My little runaway Fergus!" he said, squinting with one eye. "We meet again, you see. You may be able to outrun this old fox now and then, but you cannot outrun fate, can you?"

Fergus pouted and grumbled as he stirred before turning his head. Uffa had the attention of the whole party for everyone could sense that the reprimands of the wise were about to come down on the little leprechaun."

"You do realize that you are to blame for this whole mess," the sage continued, pointing and shaking his finger as to an unruly child. "You did not heed my warnings when I apprehended you. You were quite willing to upset the whole balance of the universe for the meagre gain of a few coins. Now your body is in shackles, the result of your past actions. But what of your soul; do you ever care about such things my poor Fergus?"

At once, the sulking leprechaun came to life.

"Do ye think the Stealth Demon is me friend, do ye? I was running fer me life. I had no choice. I only hoped to gather a little gold, a sample to show me friends, to spread a little cheer fer everyone. The Lord Creator would have been pleased with mine efforts. I was to become the most charitable being in the land. I swear it. But nobody hears me out; nobody understands me intentions."

Then Fergus turned his head away once more and resumed sulking.

Now, Uffa wished to address him on a more pressing matter, but not before sending him one clear warning.

"You were only playing with fire. And now you can see the consequences. On Earth, as I recall, there is a saying: *The road to Hell is paved with good intentions.* Do keep that in mind, Fergus!"

There was a period of pensive silence among the group before the old man continued.

"I understand you stole the Will-master's luret from my good friends the monks at the temple of Kashi. But however did you manage to activate the luret? This fascinates me. What is your secret?"

"There is that blasted word again … *secret*," replied the frustrated leprechaun. "As I told the young Outlander before, there is no secret. I tell ye the truth. There is no key. There is no secret. Ye *are* the secret. The key is within ye. Ye must master the luret from within, from a pure heart and good intentions. That is all."

Lord Uffa began to chuckle as did Dorian and the three Millikeen guards. Solas and Xiao Ren remained perplexed as they listened closely to Fergus while sipping their cold tea.

"You leprechauns are great entertainers. This much I grant you," said Uffa, tears of laughter swelling up around his bloodshot blue eyes. "The concept you speak of is clear enough, my dear Fergus. I just cannot reconcile the words *pure heart* and *good intentions* with the name leprechaun. Still, you did manage the feat. So then, who told you this?"

"The elders, that's who!" answered Fergus, faster than a blowgun's dart. "It's all part of an old legend I heard told long ago. It's ingrained in leprechaun folklore. And trust me, it works. When I saw the luret, I just could not resist its spell. I had to give it a try, but I was never really sure what to expect. I was as surprised as anyone. Ye saw it fer yerself, Uffa. And I tell ye this: the legend is true! Take me to the Diamond Crossing, and I will show ye how."

"For that, we will need the luret I'm afraid," Uffa replied, in his scratchy voice.

All eyes then turned to Solas.

12

Solas stood up and pulled out Lux Veritas from his gold trimmed leather sheath to show where the Will-master's luret had melded onto the sword of Genesis.

"I have the luret, Lord Uffa," said Solas, waving the blade of the sword back and forth in order to flash the various facets of the intricate item.

Uffa nearly tumbled over from shock when he saw the magical white luret appearing only inches away from him.

"My gracious!" he exclaimed while leaning on his trustworthy chair to hold his balance. "It must be true then; I am getting old," he said laughing. "My intuitive powers are shot to bits. I had not the slightest idea you had it in your possession all this time. Why did you not announce it sooner?"

"You wouldn't happen to know how to separate the two pieces, would you?" asked Solas stoically, and ignoring Uffa's question altogether.

The old Sage of the Grotto seemed truly enthralled by the joining of the two items and by the majestic purity that emanated from them.

"What a work of wonder!" he said, giggling and trembling all at once. "They make a fine couple, don't you think?"

"Well … can you separate them?" Solas insisted.

"May I?" asked Lord Uffa, his puffy eyes abegging the young sword master.

Solas saw no reason to object and handed the sword with the luret to the old sage, all the while hoping the old man could pull a rabbit out of his hat. Uffa stayed quiet and studied closely the marriage of the twin metals, following the creases of the objects with his fragile fingers and with the most subtle of touches.

"Ha! Mighty must be the man who can tear asunder what the Lord Creator has joined together," he cried out. "All the same, the luret is protected; it will not be hindered in the performance of its functions. Whatever forces joined these divine objects together will also pry them apart when the time comes."

Solas sighed.

"Downer!" said Dorian. "We sure came a long ways to find that out."

"Okay, so what do you know about the luret?" asked Solas. "And why are you here so deep down in the depth of Holy Mountain? What is your purpose here?"

Uffa started by chuckling in amusement once again, finding some kind of humor in Solas's boldness.

"These are great questions Solas, if not natural ones," he replied. "My role here is to be the keeper of the Diamond Gates. I am to watch after the strays coming in and out of the Diamond Crossing. I warn any would-be trespassers; and I warn the rest of Purgator of impending dangers. All in all, I am the beacon of the underground."

"That's quite a responsibility," said Dorian.

"To be honest, until recently, the job was quite easy," replied the old sage in a modest voice. "Now it has become impossible and I have been reduced to nothing more than a passive watchman. Now a trickle of evil, soon the floodgates!"

"I thought you couldn't get through the Diamond Gates without the luret," said Solas.

"That's true," replied Uffa. "Still many are tempted, and accidents do happen. The Diamond Crossing is quite unforgiving; I can tell you. Most fail in their attempts to pass through. It's not a pretty sight. Of course, breaches do occur from time to time. You know … anomalies!"

"Like the one we have right now, for example," said Dorian.

"Yes, although this one was quite an unnatural one, right Fergus?" The old sage grinned at the leprechaun who frowned back and brooded some more.

"What do you mean *anomalies*?" asked Solas.

"Beyond the Diamond Crossing the universe is filled with anomalies, strange events and random occurrences. The Lord Creator only knows. Countless vagrant souls have found their way here from distant shores; I can attest to that. Come with me now," he told his guests. "The time has come to show you."

Solas, Dorian and Xiao Ren's eyes lit up and the group jumped back to life. A sudden excitement took hold of them at the thought of seeing the Diamond Crossing at last. Uffa turned away and started to walk right past his pocketsize drugstore to the open terrace beyond.

13

As the group reached the platform, they observed an open cave, average in size but unlike any other. A strange natural light pulsated in waves and illuminated every wall and nook of the cavern, and a profound silence added a mysterious aura to the surroundings. Solas looked first over the ledge of the perched belvedere on which he and his companions stood. Apart from the suspicious flicker of the daylight, he did not see anything important of note, until he glanced over to his left and saw it.

"Whoa!" he said. "That's the Diamond Crossing?"

"It is," answered the old Sage of the Grotto.

"Amazing!" said Xiao Ren as she first laid eyes on the object.

Dorian stood speechless for once, and the Millikeen folks gripped onto the edge of the rock railing to catch a glimpse of the marvel, transfixed by the spectacle. Fergus crouched into a corner to pout.

The enigmatic Crossing was a near duplicate of a pure diamond crystal, only the size of a small cabin. The object projected an intrinsic light from within and hovered two feet above the ground while spinning and rotating upon itself in a most peculiar way. Its many facets would pulsate outward from its inner core and surface in sequence to turn the object inside and out. Each new emerging cell created would burst out and then swallow the whole matrix in turn before retracting back into its inner core in a perpetual flowing motion.

"It's alive!" Dorian said at last, after a long period of silence.

"It looks like a mini star, emerging and collapsing all at once," observed Solas.

"Very nice!" said Uffa, impressed by the analytical ability of the boy. "You must have been a wiz in physics at school."

"Not really," replied Solas, scoffing at the thought. "It just gives me this odd impression."

"Well," began the sage, "you're getting close indeed, my good Solas, except that the Diamond Crossing is not a star at all, but nothing more than a complex tesseract."

"What in the heck is a trisact?" asked Dorian.

"A tesseract!" Uffa corrected. "It's a sort of hypercube, a portal leading to other dimensions."

"Other dimensions?" repeated Xiao Ren.

"That's right," continued Uffa. "No one really knows how many there are. What we do know, however, is that the Diamond Tesseract will act like a wormhole and take you beyond time and space, with the help of the Will-master's luret of course; right, my dear Fergus?"

The little leprechaun stayed put and hardly blinked an eye.

"You said it was a wormhole that could take you across time and space?" asked Solas.

"Yes," replied Uffa. "You can reach back or forward through time, and travel to far-off places over the immense sea of the universe."

"Wow!" said Dorian. "That blows me away."

"But how do you control where you are going?" asked Solas.

"That's a very good question," replied Uffa. "The Diamond Tesseract is where mind meets matter. Life and the universe are composed of this quintessential dichotomy. Therefore, you can control your destination through focus, concentration and through sheer will power, and by using that little gadget attached to your sword."

"And that's why they call it the Will-master's luret," said Dorian.

"I told ye that!" cried Fergus.

Lord Uffa chuckled.

"Yes, it's true. And my little leprechaun friend will soon do us a demonstration."

"I object!" said the Millikeen leader Artin, custodian of Fergus. "The leprechaun weasel will escape beyond the doorway, never to be seen again. I cannot let this happen."

"Artin is right," said Solas. "We gave our word to the Millikeen folks that Fergus would be returned to face Millikeen justice once we had reached the Diamond Crossing. Now that we are here, he will not be needed. I think I can manage this next challenge on my own, by Lux Veritas!"

"Thank you," replied Artin. "You are indeed honorable men, and it is easy to see why the mighty Lord Creator should entrust you with his most divine missions. We Millikeen choose to accompany you to the end. We will leave once you have made a safe departure beyond the great Crossing."

Solas nodded.

"Well," said Uffa, "if that is your solemn wishes, so be it."

Fergus grumbled some more while the attention of the group returned to the Diamond Crossing.

14

For the next hour, Solas, Dorian and Xiao Ren asked many questions, which the old sage attempted to answer as best he could. Uffa explained all he knew about the mythic legend of the tesseract and its origins. Fable has it that the tesseract, tracing back close to the origins of creation, is at the centre of the universe. Each reality, wherever it may be located in time and space, has access to it. Yet, there exists only the one tesseract. Each dimension observes it from a different facet, from a different perspective. The Diamond Tesseract thus unites all tangible worlds, faraway stars, intricate realities and multiple dimensions existing in the obscure depths of the fathomless universe. The Crossing also unfolds parallel universes of bipolar realities – some positive, some negative. The depths of the Lord Creator are hence impervious to the understanding, and shall remain forevermore the object of inquiry and discovery to the most adventurous explorers.

"You see, my good Solas," concluded the old sage, "life and free-will are the Lord Creator's ultimate gifts. For he is free-will! And we are like him, free to follow our own path. In the end, right or wrong, good or bad, all paths lead back to him. As such, karma is either your friend or your enemy; you decide!"

"So what you are saying is that we make our own heaven and hell, based on the choices we make," concluded Dorian.

"Yes indeed," replied Uffa. "And the end result of bad choices is Tartarus, and of good choices Elysium, as you already know."

"Yeah," said Dorian. "That's what Master Senex had explained to us."

"So that's how the luret functions then, through faith and free-will?" asked Solas.

"That's it!" confirmed Lord Uffa, shrugging his shoulders as though there was really nothing to it. "Anyone can operate the luret, even Fergus here. That's the secret. Everything comes down to faith and will-power."

"So, if I understand well," said Solas, looking to set things right in his mind once and for all, "the luret operates much the same way as Lux Veritas does, no?"

"In principle, yes," answered Uffa, "but with one notable exception: Lux Veritas is reactive. It reacts according to the Lord creator's will, as you already know. But the Will-master's luret relies on your input. Therefore, it is proactive. It is closer to the heart; closer to *your* heart, Solas!"

"Okay," said Solas, "I think I got it now."

15

With that said, Dorian was still pondering the precept of karma, a concept he seemed unable to digest in full.

"It still makes no sense to me Uffa, why the rotten people of the world are awarded such blessings, like money, riches, success and happiness. They don't deserve a bit of it."

Lord Uffa began to laugh out loud at Dorian's remark, to the astonishment of everyone, and could hardly catch his breath to get in a response. The old sage reasoned he needed to instil more insurance and more confidence in his young guests before they could even manage to navigate the delicate temper of the Diamond Crossing. Faith and trust were of the essence. But so was the understanding.

"Well, what be so funny?" asked Dorian. "Where is justice in all of this, huh?"

Uffa dried the tears of laughter blurring his eyesight.

"Is it not obvious, my good Dorian?" he replied at last. "Do you mean to suggest that the celebrities and the fortunate people of the world have better karma than the regular folks like us?" The old sage smiled and sighed before continuing. "Perish the thought! You have heard it said before I am sure, that the Lord Creator works in mysterious ways. Some rich people are deserving of their privileged karma; they have earned it, while others not so much. For them, it is only a parting gift."

"I am sorry Lord Uffa, but I still don't understand what you mean," said a puzzled Dorian.

"Put it this way: if you were a parent with a dying child who had a terminal illness, and let's assume that the child's fate was sealed and that he only had a few months to live. What in the world would you offer him with the limited time you had left?"

"Well, I could never do enough, I suppose," answered Dorian. "But I would sure try to give him anything and everything his little heart desired. I would try to make his every wish come true, knowing that I loved him so very much and that I would never see him again."

"Great answer, Dorian!" acknowledged the old sage. "And so it is with the Lord Creator too. He does reward with good karma those who deserve it and have earned it, but also those who are forsaken, those who have forever lost their way and ruined their souls. It is a parting gift of sort, for Tartarus now awaits them."

"Wow, I never really thought of it that way. And how do these 'fortunate' people know which karma they inherited?"

"They don't. They hardly give it a thought, do they? But if you look closely at the way they carry on with their lives and the way they behave, you will no doubt be able to tell them apart."

"And what about that poor dying child with the terminal condition, what happens to him?" asked Xiao Ren, who loved children most of all.

"That was only an example, my dear," replied Uffa. "But in this case, that would be left up to the Lord Creator to decide. It is presumed that most children end up in Elysium. And as you have noticed, there are no children in Purgator. And I have never met anyone here who could ever remember being just a child back on Earth. Paradise belongs to the children, and to those of us who are like the child at heart, true and innocent."

The old sage's answer comforted Xiao Ren somewhat but left the remainder of the band feeling drab, and their gaze fixated once more on the mesmerizing fire of the Diamond Crossing.

16

Uffa felt the moment had come to put words into practice, before the good spirits of his young companions waned entirely.

"Well," he said out loud, clapping both hands together, "cheer up my young friends. Are you ready to take the plunge through the Diamond Gates?"

"I am not so sure that I am up to the task, to tell you the truth, but I have no choice," replied Solas. "I just know I have to find Amy again or my heart will forever be void like a black hole."

"That's it, Solas!" said Uffa. "Draw your inspiration from what means the most to you in your life. If it is meant to be, you will succeed." The old sage then turned his attention to the wily leprechaun still crouched in his corner, chin resting on his knee caps, sulking. "Render us a small service, won't you Fergus? Redeem yourself and do tell us what model inspired you to reach beyond the Diamond Crossing."

Fergus barely lifted his droopy eyes, but not his chin, and mumbled a half-hearted answer.

"I thought about money and more money. I saw a sea of gold, of silver and gems, and priceless treasures too …" The leprechaun's mood lifted with every mention of riches and wealth. Soon he was smiling again, up on his feet and hopping about, eyes lit up with the inner fires of passion, caught up in a deep state of phantasm and reverie.

"Thank you, thank you!" repeated Uffa. "That will do just fine, Fergus."

But once started the leprechaun could hardly stop and rambled on at length so that the old Sage of the Grotto had to raise his voice over his in order to be heard.

"You see," Uffa said with a loud but obvious cheer. "Even while praying to that God of Wealth Mammon, our passionate little green swindler managed to activate the luret and reach the outer realities to romance and hornswoggle a bevy of unsuspecting little old ladies. And so there is your proof. Anything is possible if you put your heart into it!" he concluded.

But this was not what worried Solas most. Passion, purpose and drive were one thing; tackling dimensions and unknown realities were quite another. As for Fergus, he was animated to the point of lunacy.

"I had it in me hands, I tell ye!" he screamed, eyes bulging out of their sockets.

Artin got quite annoyed at this, and in one swift motion whipped out his short blade to hold it flush against the leprechaun's throat.

"Be quiet already you fumbling buffoon or I'll feed your carcass to the Orboz mongrels."

Following this outburst, the silence was palpable. The old sage glanced at Solas and guessed his concerns.

"Look my boy," he said. "If you can find your way in, you can find your way out. But before entering the Diamond Crossing, I must warn you about the consequences of your actions once you reach the other realities."

"Okay, here we go …" sputtered Dorian.

"As you enter through the Diamond Gates, time will grab you by the wrist and will direct you wherever you wish to go. Keep focused."

"How do I know where to go?" asked Solas.

"Follow your heart, as we discussed," he replied. "And remember this – it is very important – do not change the events of the present. This could have dire consequences to your karma and to the success of your mission."

"Are we going back in time?" asked Dorian.

"There are many dimensions you can reach: the past, the future, other worlds, other realities, and some we don't even understand exist," explained Uffa. "But wherever you are, you are always in the present of the moment. You must not change it. Do your business and get out!"

"How can you be in the past and the present at the same time?" asked Dorian, "That's impossible."

"The truth is, my dear boy, the past does not exist," said Uffa. "And neither does the future."

"Now I'm lost," Dorian admitted while rubbing his eyes.

"Think about it," explained the old sage, "you don't know the past or the future. You have only ever lived in the present. That is all you know. The Lord Creator is nothing else but the present. He is eternal."

"You mean the past and the future are an illusion," said Solas.

"They are all happening at the same time," replied Uffa. "Hence we have many dimensions and countless possibilities!"

"So while in the Diamond Gates, I must pick my reality," said Solas.

"Yes, you must *feel* your reality."

"I know: follow your heart!" rehashed Solas.

"That's it," said Uffa. "And when you get to that chosen time and place, do not change anything that matters, other than your order of business, of course. Will you all remember that?"

"And why can't we change the present anyway?" asked Dorian. "What, the world will stop spinning?"

"Well, that's because of the Chaos theory," answered the sage.

"Chaos again?" said Dorian. "Well what a surprise!"

Lord Uffa seized the opportunity to teach his young travelers all that he could, knowing that the precious moment they shared together was all too brief.

"Have you ever heard of the butterfly effect?" asked the old sage in rhetorical fashion.

"You will tell us, won't you?" replied Dorian.

"In other words," Uffa continued, "can the flap of a butterfly's wings in Asphodel Meadows set off a tornado in the flats of Oneiros?"

"That's crazy talk," said Dorian. "What, a little butterfly a world away?"

"Why yes!" replied Uffa. "Chaos can begin anywhere and with the most subtle of movement, like the flapping of a butterfly's wings. The slightest change or disturbance in the atmosphere can trigger a continual series of events leading to a full blown cataclysm."

"And how does that affect us here and now?"

"In the other dimensions, your actions can trigger a butterfly effect with cataclysmic consequences in our reality. Look, see and observe but do not alter the major events of the past. That's determinism. That's the Chaos theory. It is meant to be this way."

"Well, that's all fine and dandy, but I doubt I will have time to keep track of it all in the heat of the moment, if you know what I mean," replied the ever pragmatic Dorian. "I mean if I chop some freak's head off, I should stop to worry which way its head will roll now?"

"All I am saying, my good Dorian, is that you should keep your actions down to the bare essentials," stressed Uffa. "Do not get carried away. Stick to the business at hand."

"Look, I'll do my best," said Dorian. "But if heads are going to roll, then heads are going to roll, and that's that. I do not believe my enemies are worried about *butterflies* while they are trying to slice me up into pieces. That's what I'm saying. Besides, if we must step into the past, perhaps we are meant to be there too."

Listening in, Solas reentered the conversation to put the old sage at ease.

"Do not worry, Lord Uffa," said Solas, "We will avoid the past at much as possible, and if we must go there, we will keep our dealings to the strict minimum."

Lord Uffa shook his head at Dorian's perspectives on the Chaos theory and in the end the pair shared a good hearty laugh about the whole conundrum it presented.

17

Solas prepared his traveling companions for the pending journey ahead. Only Dorian and Xiao Ren would accompany him on the voyage through the Diamond Crossing. The three Millikeen guards Artin, Broc and Dak would return to their home village of Millok with Fergus.

"Please take us down to the tesseract," Solas asked Uffa, "we're ready."

Dorian headed for the exit assuming the door through which he entered the grotto was also the one leading back out.

"Not so fast my good Dorian," said Uffa. "Do not presume that the way out is through the front door; the way to the Diamond Tesseract is discreet."

The travelers exchanged a few blank looks and were feeling quite perplexed.

"There is no other doorway that I can see," said Dorian. "Should we jump three stories over the balcony ledge or will you perform some magic trick for us?"

"Well, a magic trick of the practical kind perhaps," he replied. "All of you, come over this way," ordered Uffa, "and watch."

Once the entire group was standing idle on the platform of the terrace, the old sage stepped on a heavy corner tile which triggered open a stone trap door, a slab of rock twelve inches thick set flush against the left side wall. The trapdoor – large and wide enough to accommodate a thickset loathar – swung open to reveal a slick and polished narrow slide, winding and leading its way straight down to the floor where the Diamond Tesseract stood.

"Wow!" said Dorian.

"Who's first?" asked Uffa.

"What is the exact purpose of this passage?" asked Solas.

"You see, when trouble arises, I need quick access to the Diamond Gates," answered the old sage. "This exit provides it."

"There *is* an open door waiting at the bottom, I hope," said Dorian.

"Of course there is," answered Uffa, "unless the door jammed again."

"Oh that's funny," said Dorian.

Lord Uffa gestured for Dorian to go first.

Dorian politely declined, only because Solas wished to take the lead. He stepped forward, secured Lux Veritas by his side and slid on his back all the way down to the bottom. The exit outlet was smooth and Solas reached solid ground without a hitch. The others soon followed. No one uttered a sound during the descent, save for Dorian who thought it too much fun, and Fergus who feared for his life.

Now each member stood face to face with the Diamond Crossing. Up close, the chiselled tesseract took on a bright, serene and majestic aura, hovering, rotating and pulsating inside and out about itself like a giant diamond in perpetual motion. A deafening silence engrossed the whole matrix, which burst out a sea of temporal waves from its inner core like a series of gelatinous cells of translucent magma. The spectacle captivated the onlookers.

"How do we enter?" asked Solas.

"You take the Will-master's luret in your hands. You hold it up, and make a wish," explained the old sage. "The Diamond Crossing will respond by acting like a wormhole and opening a passage through the void. This will take you on a speedway through time and space."

"What about that bubble sphere I saw enclose around the Stealth Demon?"

"Yes," answered Uffa, "it will form and protect you too. And remember, you can use the luret to travel to and fro about the foreign lands wherever you are."

Solas Sighed.

"To think I had the luret with me all this time. I could have used it to get us here much sooner. Only I didn't know," said Solas.

"Well, now you know," replied Uffa. "Are you ready then, my boy?"

"Let's do it," replied Solas.

Dorian and Xiao Ren squeezed closer to Solas so as not to miss their lift. The Millikeen guards and Fergus stood back to observe the spectacle, as did the old Sage of the Grotto. Solas pulled out Lux Veritas from its sheath and held his weapon at arm's length before him. With both hands, he clasped the Will-master's luret fused to the sword. Solas closed his eyes and remembered Guru Roshni's *"Truth alone triumphs"* as Dorian and Xiao Ren clung to him. After a moment of pure concentration, a sphere engulfed the standing trio like a cocoon, and a singular event occurred on the surface of the Diamond Tesseract. One of the hexagonal cells split open before them like the parting of the Red Sea.

"Godspeed!" said Solas, feeling the tension and the energy increase around him.

Uffa returned the blessing as the droning sound from the pull of the void intensified. In the depth of the underground tunnels, however, another noise raised to the fore: it was the clashing of metal and the shouts of war. A battle raged on. Daemonia and its nasty ally the Torlund dwarves were engaging the newly liberated leprechauns and the Millikeen war machine. Dorian became anxious and perked his ears to the distant rumble while Uffa ignored all the commotion and kept encouraging Solas.

"Well done Solas and Godspeed to you," he yelled, just as rabid units of the Torlund dwarves rounded the corner at full speed. The surprised Millikeen guards reacted and fired poison darts at the enemy while backing up toward the Diamond Tesseract as they did so. Fergus panicked and rushed to join the sides of Solas, managing to sneak inside the bubble before the window of opportunity closed. The cocoon of the Will-master's luret began to falter.

"Keep concentrating Solas!" yelled the old sage.

Solas fidgeted but tried hard to keep focused. Meanwhile, Xiao Ren nocked her bow and Dorian pull out his katana for battle. Now all parties were inside the cocoon save for the old Sage of the Grotto. Lord Uffa was up to some old trick. By some ancient magic spell, he summoned a powerful dust storm to create a wall and stall the confused enemy.

"Now hurry Solas!" yelled the old sage. "Enter Destiny!"

Chapter VI

Enter Destiny

*"All that is gold does not glitter; not all those who
wander are lost."*

—J.R.R. Tolkien

I

A great whoosh engulfed the band and whisked them away into
the depth of the Tesseract. This was a new experience, unlike the
Wheel of Souls, where one bathed in a pool of some embryonic
type fluid while enduring violent physical changes; losing
consciousness in the process. No, this was not the same. For one,
the cocoon of the Will-master's luret protected the travelers. Solas,
Dorian and Xiao Ren remained fully conscious and experienced
no ill effect, no sense of vertigo, not even the slightest motion
sickness let alone whiplash, which one might be expecting when
being yanked as such transcendental speeds across time and space.

Inside the swirl of his protective shell, Solas held on tight
to the luret, afraid to break the magic spell should he decide
otherwise. He stayed focused on the task but even so dared open

his eyes to take in the mysterious events unfolding around him. Nothing could deprive him of this spectacle. The shelter of the luret's cloaking had a calming influence on the group, allowing them to take in the full spectrum of sights that few humans had ever seen before. At first, these consisted mainly of bursting flashes of moving lights – fast approaching dots of starlights gradually stretching into thin streamers before vanishing past the cocoon like the whipping snap of an elastic band.

And so, this went on that the three earthlings and their companions whizzed about space at interstellar speeds. Well, if this was space indeed, no one inside the cocoon could tell with any accuracy. For the general feeling was that they were standing still, suspended in limbo somewhere in the darkness of the void. Solas's concentration intensified. Soon, singularities began to appear. Time and space slowed down to the point where Solas, Dorian and Jiji could make out the particularities in each streak of light. One such light turned out to be some sort of nebulae, the likeness of a massive galaxy exhibiting the most mindboggling colorful displays of shapes and forms, fire bright hues of vermilion and purple, and exploding amber yellows. It came their way; or was it the cocoon? No time to think, at once the band was swallowed whole and entered into the giant pool of cosmic dust.

Solas thought about all sorts of things and teetered through the full gamut of emotions. He wished to find the Stealth Demon and rip him to shreds with his very last breath if need be, and in matters of the heart, he dreamt of his lovely Amy, until his ticker thumped so hard and fast in his chest that it nearly jumped out of his ribcage. His eyes started to water to think about her, and a tear softly rolled away into the crease of his battle scar, the one he had won for Amy so many moons ago. Or was it only yesterday? He remembered his Grandma Jeanie of course. She was at home and well, but he longed most to see the talented Fidem Aenas again and old Master Senex too. Oh, how he could use the help and wisdom of these two brave spirits who were once, in some not so distant reality, his own dad and beloved grandfather.

Inside the galaxy, time and space kept spitting out infinities. These phenomena did not consist of solar systems, planets and moons or even black holes, red dwarves and supernovas as some astronomers should expect. No, Solas and company had ventured into some other realm of time and space, stepping over into a dimension akin to the twilight zone. Did the Lord Creator stock here the eternal present? As the flashing images unfolded into vivid realities, that question crossed each traveler's mind. Fergus and the Millikeen guards were star-struck. Some of the holograms neared and began to take shape as visible doorways casting reflections of known places, and glimpses of people and events within the physical world. Safe inside the bubble of the Will-master's luret, Dorian and Xiao Ren were transfixed beyond words. Solas continued to concentrate and as he did so, the windows to these foreign lands transformed into the makings of Solas's wishes and personal realities.

"Over there Solas!" Dorian whispered hard.

Amongst a slew of strange options, Solas's buddy picked out images from his own world, moving pictures of land and sea from that pale blue dot tucked away on the outer fringes of the Milky Way, the fragile home to all mankind. Solas sensed it too.

"Keep it up; keep it up," continued Dorian, one hand pointing to the snapshots, the other resting on Solas's shoulder. "Get us through that doorway!"

2

Solas steered his solitary vessel as best a novice time traveler could and setting foot on terra firma now became his main objective. *Can I land this ship?* Solas wondered. After all, he had never manoeuvred the Will-master's luret before and he hoped to negotiate a much softer landing than when exiting the Wheel of Souls. So far so good; the luret responded well to the commands of its captain and there was plenty of room for optimism. All Solas's hopes and wishes must have worked wonders because, before the space voyagers knew it, the images concretized and the cocoon broke through the upper atmosphere of the planet and, upon reaching the troposphere, burst into a silent, red-hot flaming meteorite shooting through the clear blue skies.

The landing was without consequence. The shell of the luret quickly evaporated away into thin air like a mirage.

"Is everyone okay?" asked Solas, checking on the status of his partners.

Dorian and Xiao Ren verified that all was in place and in order, and that nothing was missing.

"Yes, I think so," reported Xiao Ren, smiling. "You did it Solas!"

"Yes, we made it," added Dorian, ecstatic. "We're here!"

"Good," replied Solas on a more pragmatic tone, "but where is *here* exactly?"

"I don't really know, but what a mind-blowing ride that was!" said Dorian.

"We are back in Purgator," interjected Fergus, feeling he could offer some help, "just not in our time, I don't think."

"What are you talking about Fergus?" said Dorian.

The leprechaun took a moment longer to inspect their new, yet familiar surroundings.

"Well, no doubt we're home," he went on explaining. "As ye can all see fer yerselves, we have exited the Diamond Crossing and landed smack-dab in the middle of the farmers' fields of Morphos. The city of Lalas Pur is right over there, ye see." Fergus, still handcuffed, pointed in the distance with his chin to the outline of the fortress, whose image was wavering under the heat of the mid-afternoon sun.

The band members, who had not yet looked beyond close quarters, turned around to behold the obvious.

"Damn, Carrot-top is right!" said Dorian. "But what the heck are we doing in Lalas Pur? Don't you tell me the Stealth Demon is hiding here now!"

"I doubt it," replied the leprechaun. "What ye can see here of Lalas Pur is the old fortification; the way it was before the forces of Daemonia destroyed it during the last incursion by Lord Chaos. It's all fixed up and improved nowadays."

"You mean to say that we are back in the past ..." said Xiao Ren, "back to the way it was when I lived here?"

Fergus grinned and nodded at the joyous girl.

"Yes!" she screamed, jumping at Dorian's neck. "I will see Master Senex again ... and Fidem ... and my girlfriend Linoa at the old Valhalla tavern. This is wonderful."

Dorian gave a funny look to his friend Solas.

"You did this on purpose, didn't you?" he said. "What are you hoping to accomplish? We are not supposed to change the events of the past, remember?"

"I know," replied Solas. "I just need to ask Master Senex a few questions."

"Like what?" pressed Dorian, who seemed the sensible one this time.

"I am hoping Master Senex can tell me how to defeat the Stealth Demon," answered Solas. "The beast knows about the power of Lux Veritas. The Stealth Demon doesn't budge one inch before her. I need to coax him somehow. Perhaps Senex knows the way."

"Brilliant!" said Dorian, smiling. "And you just wanted to see him again, didn't you?"

"Well, that too!" admitted Solas.

"You sly dog you!"

Xiao Ren and the two childhood buddies high-fived each other and began laughing out loud at Solas's apparent stroke of genius.

3

The group wasted little time. They hurried toward the old citadel, shunning the main dirt road in favor a stealthy advance through the tall fields of wheat and corn, thus avoiding detection from the farmhands out tending the crops and their fierce escorts, the lamentar guards, Lalas Pur's elite warriors. And indeed, a few of them were spotted here and there. They moved along and when the front gates of the fortress appeared clear within sight, the band stopped at the hedge of the last plantation to consider their options.

"I do not recommend knocking on the door," said Fergus. "The sentinels may not be so friendly, I should warn."

"Yeah Solas!" added Dorian. "Remember Bulbar?"

"How could I forget?" replied Solas. "The funny thing is … if we have returned to the past as planned, Bulbar should still be alive."

"Yeah, and he will want to get his hands on Lux Veritas again."

"Right you are!" agreed Solas. "I don't want to go through that circus again. Besides, if we are in the past, we could jeopardize our first mission in the future. Bulbar and the rest of the citizens will recognize us. They must not see us at all."

Fergus began to chuckle under his breath, which he could not hide.

"What are you laughing at, freckle-face?" said Dorian, always irritated by the mischievous gremlin. "Is something funny?"

"Everything is funny," answered the leprechaun. "Master Senex will see ye. That could change the future too."

"I'll deal with that," replied Solas.

"I have an idea!" said Xiao Ren. "The guards know me. Why don't I just walk up to the front gate? I am a citizen. They will let me in."

"Yes, that's a great idea," agreed Solas. "And then you can go tell Master Senex and Fidem that we are here. They will listen to you."

"Okay then," she said, "I will go. But I think it will be better if you could meet us behind the city walls. His house looks out over the seashore. Wait for me there. I will come out with him or send you a signal, okay?"

"Excellent!" said Solas. "Once the guards let you in, we will make our way to the rear of the ramparts by the seaside. We will await your signal."

"Wait a minute!" said Dorian. "What if you should bump into yourself? I mean, technically, there are two Xiao Rens now. You are already inside."

"That would be freaky," she replied. "I will stay low-key. According to my daily routine, I should be at Valhalla tavern right now. That's where I spend most of my day. I doubt I will see myself."

"Just be careful," said Solas.

Xiao Ren exited the tall grass and walked casually toward the front gates of the city under the watchful eyes of her friends.

One rookie sentinel, a loathar guard with a keen eye, was first to observe the girl approaching the complex from afar and advancing onto the drawbridge suspended over the moat. Xiao Ren recognized him.

"And how are you today, Tondrak?"

"Is that you Xiao Ren?" he asked while stepping in front of her to block her way.

"Why yes!" she answered with a cheer. "You seem surprised."

"I don't recall you leaving this morning, that's all."

"Well, I guess it must have been during your break," she replied.

He looked her over slowly with a suspicious eye.

"Officer Bulbar!" he yelled. "Could you come over here Sir?"

Bulbar – a stocky lamentar guard with a foul attitude – was leaning back on a chair while dozing off in the shade. He got up with a growl to have a look at what his loathar recruit could not handle this time.

"Well what is it?" he grumbled.

Under the shelter of the tall crops, Dorian began to fidget.

"Damn, it's Bulbar!"

"Sir, did you grant Xiao Ren permission to leave this morning?" asked Tondrak.

"Huh …" uttered Bulbar, clearly puzzled. "What are you bringing back with you girl?"

"Nothing," replied Xiao Ren, "I was just out for target practice."

"Don't you know it's dangerous to head out into the fields by yourself? I told you that last night at the tavern, no?"

"And I told you not to drink so much. It makes you forget things."

"Well, a smart girl like you should know better. Daemonia units are on the prowl everywhere these days. So are those nasty Torlund pests. Where's your partner anyway, that old geezer Senex?"

"Uh, I don't know. I was about to ask you the same question."

Officer Bulbar grunted, and then allowed the girl to enter the city.

"Get in!" he said. "The old man is probably home concocting another one of his potions. Ask him to make something useful to cure my hangover this time, will you?"

"You got it Bulbar!"

As Xiao Ren walked on through, she glanced behind her and gave a subtle thumbs-up to her friends hiding out in the fields.

"You're welcome," said Bulbar.

4

Xiao Ren hurried 'incognito' through the streets of her old town for fear of being accosted and getting caught up in some idle conversation from which she may not be able to extricate herself. She was the imposter after all. Still, she could not resist throwing the odd glance-up as she went by to catch the daily activities of the peasants and merchants she knew so well. Her heart palpitated from mixed emotions as she cleared the danger zones and reached the front door of her beloved mentor Senex of Morphos.

Knock, knock, knock ...

Xiao Ren was much too impatient to wait for an answer. She tried the handle. The door was open. She barged in.

"Senex!" she called out anxiously. "Senex!"

Sure enough, the master was already half-way to the front door, and standing to her side, by the fireplace, only a few feet away from her.

"Yes child," he replied. "What is the ..."

But before he could finish his sentence, the young girl rushed to embrace the wise old druid, her father-figure, the man she had held in her arms as he exhaled his last breath out on the banks of the River Lethe, oh not so long ago. Senex was caught by surprise and almost had the wind knocked out of him on impact. Xiao Ren burst into tears.

"Easy now Jiji," he said in his raspy voice, "what has happened to you my child?"

Xiao Ren's emotions were too strong and she could not bring herself to take a breath, let alone answer his question. Seeing her in such a state, Senex let her be and consoled her. After all, he had always been her shoulder to cry on.

"Are you okay Jiji?" he asked once more. "You're acting as though you haven't seen me in years."

She backed away to look at him, standing there as he was in his white cotton tunic, smiling, eyes sparkling, with his long flowing hair and shaggy white beard.

"I don't believe it," she said. "It really is you!"

"Everyday!" replied the old man.

The two began laughing and the old master offered the girl a chair by the fireplace where she proceeded to tell him all that she could about the present situation in the briefest of delays.

"Well that's a story for the ages!" said Senex.

Xiao Ren was much more relaxed and composed now. That's when she realized someone was missing.

"Where is Fidem?"

"Fidem is not here, I'm afraid. He's out running errands in the hills of Morphos."

Xiao Ren sighed.

"Well then," said the Master, "Solas should be waiting for us right behind the rear fence as we speak, right?"

"Yes, yes he is."

"Let's go check!" said the old man. "There is a beautiful view of the beaches from the upper bedroom."

Senex swung open the old wooden shutters, leaned over the edge of the window with Jiji by his side, and attempted to locate Solas and his troops. Looking beyond the city fence and past the moat, a half-furlong of swelling sand dunes still separated fort from beach. The local anglers' cogs and boats were moored a little further to the north, but it was among the sand dunes' numerous clumps of tall grasses swaying in harmony to the gusts of the warm sea breeze that Solas and friends had found refuge and kept low profile. Overhead, the squawking of the seagulls gliding on the wind added a near deafening sound.

"There they are!" yelled Solas, as he spotted the pair peeking out the window. "Stay low!" he ordered his companions as he stood up ever so carefully in hope to be spotted, but not by the sentries making their rounds about the ramparts.

"That's Solas over there," said Jiji, pointing to him in the distance.

"Yes, I see him," said Senex. "Tell him to come forward to the edge of the moat. There is a secret opening through one of the wooden logs of the ramparts. Do you remember? He can swim to it across the moat. Then we will lower him a rope."

"Great idea!" said Jiji. "But how do I send him the message, Master?"

"Fire an arrow to the edge of the moat," said the old druid. "As he comes to retrieve it, we will meet him at the opening."

As Solas hid back down into the cover of the tall grass, his group wondered just what to do next. Then, they saw Xiao Ren fire an arrow over the fence and into the sand dune at the edge of the moat.

"That's our cue!" said Solas.

5

Solas ordered the Millikeen guards and Fergus to stay put and to keep an eye on any odd movements by the locals or sentinels. They were to whistle in guise of warning, and otherwise await their return. Solas and Dorian would advance and retrieve the arrow and its message. Guided by the glint of the fallen missile, the pair progressed in spurts and reached the edge of the waterline without any trouble. Only, any casual glance of the guards could now spot them with relative ease. Solas pulled out the arrowhead from the sand.

"Nothing!" said Dorian. "There is no message at all here, Solas."

Meanwhile, Jiji and Master Senex had made their way to the foot of the palisade. They pushed open the concealed aperture to reveal the narrow passageway into the fortification.

"Come on, come on," repeated the old man with the raspy voice as he stuck his head out the rabbit hole. "Swim, swim, let's go!" he said waving them on.

Solas and Dorian had barely enough time to get over this latest surprise before scrambling into the moat. They swam a quick thirty feet through murky waters without stirring so much as a ripple. Now there was little to cling onto and still a sharp climb of ten feet or more to reach the opening. Senex lowered a knotted rope to help the young fellows make it to the top. Soon, the drenched pair of Outlanders had squeaked their way inside the city walls. But there was hardly a moment for greetings.

"Throw this on your back," said Senex as he tossed them a loose garb, "and follow me, quick!"

The four hurried through a well-kept exotic garden of esoteric plants and herbs and of fruit trees and plants leading straight through the back of the druid's house. Once inside the old man's abode, the happy foursome let loose.

"Senex!" said Solas, reaching out to embrace him.

"Solas, my dear boy!" replied the Master.

They hugged as only long-lost relatives can.

"I might have been expecting you Solas, only not under such hasty circumstances. Xiao Ren spoke of a Stealth Demon and, oh … and what a fine boy you turned out to be." he said with an immense grin of joy on his face. "If Fidem could only see you now!"

"Thanks Grand-pa," replied Solas. "Fidem is not here?"

"Not today I'm afraid."

Solas sighed in disappointment.

"There was so much I wanted to tell him."

"Me too!" added Dorian, who certainly wanted to thank him for saving his life on that fateful day deep in the nymph marshes of Rosewhynd.

"This is my buddy Dorian," said Solas.

"Hello young man!" said Senex, slapping his hand on Dorian's shoulder in an obvious show of delight. "And is this the mighty Lux Veritas sticking out from … uh, *my* sheath? That is *my* sheath, is it not?"

"Well it is, yes, absolutely!" confirmed Solas. "You gave it to me the last time I came to Purgator."

"The last time you came to Purgator, huh? This is so crazy. We sent Lux Veritas down to shaman Orenda years ago. And now you have it. You are the chosen one, Solas?"

"Well, I never had a *choice* really … but yeah, that's me!"

"Do not tell me of the future, Solas; that is, of the mission which is to come. You know, the first one," said the Master. "Only perhaps you could tell me how to find you once you get to Purgator. I reckon this time will be upon us quite soon."

"Yes," replied Solas. "By my estimation, I should be here within the next week or two, at the most. My friends and I landed scattered somewhere in the middle of Asphodel Meadows and then after wandering for a while, we reached the oasis. That's where we met Fidem."

"Perfect, the oasis!" repeated Senex. "Still, a fortnight isn't very long at all. I will send Fidem in the next few days to intercept you there. After, he will bring you here to me."

"That's it," said Solas.

"But tell me why have you come about this time, in the past, before it all begins? What kind of help do you need from me now?"

"There is a new problem, perhaps greater than before," explained Solas. "I cannot go into details but I must defeat the Stealth Demon, the king of beasts. He seems to have this impenetrable armor and he knows about the power of Lux Veritas. He is clever. How do I lure him? I must set a trap. Help me Senex!"

"Well I have not at all ever heard of this beast you speak of, Solas," answered Senex. "You must provoke him."

"Yes, but how?"

"Solas," said the Master, as he looked straight into his eyes. "You have met with victory once before. I am sure you doubted yourself countless times. Yet, you found a way. Look inside yourself, perhaps a little deeper, and the answer will come. And I will always be there with you, right by your side, whenever you need me!"

Knock, knock, knock …

6

All heads turned toward the front door as all went quiet in the room. At the most inopportune time, someone had come to interrupt this short but critical encounter. In a jiffy, Xiao Ren hopped to the front window and inconspicuously peeked through the foliage of Master Senex's colorful display of hanging baskets. It was none other than Bulbar, the chief lamentar guard accompanied by a few of his men.

"Bulbar?" whispered Senex.

Xiao Ren nodded affirmative and hurried to rejoin the group near the back door of the residence.

"You must hurry," said Senex as he quickly reopened the door leading out to the garden. "Find the Stealth Demon, follow your heart and trust yourself."

The sound of Bulbar's pounding fists intensified and echoed throughout the house.

"Come with us, Master!" said Solas.

This proposition stunned Senex.

"This is your chance to leave Purgator and to see places you never dreamed," explained Solas.

"But this is my home. What will happen to it?"

"Do not worry," said Solas, I will bring you back in due time. It will be as though nothing ever happened. Bulbar will still be pounding on that door."

"Yes Master, come!" added Xiao Ren.

Senex began to smile and chuckle. The prospect of adventure loomed irresistible to this ageless child. *I may learn a lot more from Lux Veritas,* he thought, *and I could pass this knowledge on to Solas in a fortnight.* In a New York minute, the druid had found his fountain of youth again.

"Let's go!" he said, as he jetted past the trio to lead the way.

Elated, the time-travelers exited the premises, darted across the garden overgrowths, bolted through the gap in the fence and plopped into the waiting moat waters of the guarded compound. Reaching the sand dunes, they stood up and began to run full speed toward their waiting friends the Millikeen guards and Fergus, but not before a volley of arrows began to shower down upon them.

"They're shooting at us," said Dorian, "the sentries!"

A general commotion stirred from behind as the guards scrambled to point and fire at the fleeing renegades. Lalas Pur had been on a state of high alert for quite some time. Units of Daemonia, the Torlund dwarves and other unknowns often roamed these restricted parts and the elite guards dealt with any suspicious movement with brute force. Lux Veritas had reactivated now and Solas pulled out his glinting weapon to shield the lot from the hard metal rain.

"Fergus!" said Solas upon arrival, and grabbing the leprechaun by the scruff of the neck. "Take Lux Veritas and the luret and guide us to that world where the Stealth Demon hides. You've been there before. Do it now!"

Fergus, who had been nothing more than a downcast spectator to date, appeared rather calm and perplexed under this sudden pressure, but soon jumped back to life and felt somewhat re-empowered with the new opportunity presenting itself.

"Ye may first wish to cut me loose from me shackles, ye may," he replied with a grin, "if ye hope to have yer wish granted that is. I cannot work with me hands tied like this, ye know."

"Do it, Artin!" ordered Solas, out of breath and dripping wet.

"Have you suffered some sunstroke, my young Solas, under this constant heat or perhaps are you running a fever from the bite of some foreign insect? What you ask of me is pure madness. The leprechaun is an expert trickster, and now you wish to relinquish control of our destiny to this raving lunatic?"

"Just do it, Artin!" yelled Solas. "I've got my eye on him already!"

"Solas!" said Dorian. "The elite guards are approaching round the corners."

Artin's eyes rummaged back and forth, before reaching the decision to untie the leprechaun's restraints.

"I shall keep my dagger lodged right behind your ribs, Fergus. Do not tempt me!"

"Oh, me poor hands!" said Fergus as he kinked out his wrists to get the blood fast flowing again.

As Lalas Pur's soldiers neared, an increasing number of missiles pinged off the shield provided by Lux Veritas. The charging troops yelled out direct orders to surrender in no uncertain terms.

"Let's go Solas!" said Xiao Ren.

"Come on, man!" added Dorian.

"Hold your fire!" Solas ordered the Millikeen guards, who seemed eager more than ever to release their poison darts. The group had now crouched down together as low as possible below a large tuft of dried grass under the cover of a sand dune. Senex, still soaking wet, blended in as well as possible, nodding and smiling to his new Millikeen friends in lieu of formal presentations.

Solas turned all his attention to Fergus.

"Now join your hands together with mine!" he told the leprechaun. Fergus did so hastily. Solas held on tight to the hilt of his weapon and raised it high above the group, which was now clumping to each other and forming one solid unit. "Now make a wish upon the luret and get us out of here," he ordered.

Fergus concentrated with all his might, despite the nudge of Artin's cold blade against his back. Before long, the incredulous eyes of the elite troops watched a rising swirl of purple haze encompass the members of the group. Soon an impervious spinning cocoon followed, lifting its passengers ten feet above the sands. Without as much as a whisper, the luret forthwith catapulted into oblivion and right clear out of sight.

7

Fergus steered the ship at will like a true captain. His personal motivation was unclear – fear perhaps, the prospect of freedom, riches, who knew for sure? – but he had the knack for the luret. This much was clear. Under his guidance, the vessel whizzed through Purgator in an instant, burst through the core of Holy Mountain as though it were made of some porous matter and at once entered the portal of the Diamond Tesseract to reach the multi-faceted realities of the outer dimensions. Solas took careful notes. Mastering the luret accelerated all procedures and allowed ready access to most anywhere in time and space. Physical and ethereal boundaries simply did not exist. They were crushed. Nothing could impede progress. Travel happened at lightning speeds and faster, but only if one understood the essence of the Will-master's luret. And that darn leprechaun had it down to near perfection.

"Entering Orboz Purgator!" he announced.

"Orboz?"

"Yes, Orboz," repeated Fergus.

"Is that where the Stealth Demon is, Orboz?" asked Solas.

"He was the last time I saw him."

Solas and Dorian looked at each other and took a deep breath.

"Ye must be careful what ye wish fer, yes?" added an amused Fergus.

"Laugh it up Fergus, but remember you're in this too," said Dorian.

"Just land us away from trouble, Fergus," ordered Solas. "I would like to get my bearings straight before being thrown into the midst of some mindless battle, if you know what I mean."

"Aye, aye Captain!"

The landing was smooth. The cocoon evaporated and the group now contemplated the surroundings. Solas retrieved his sword and slotted it back into its sheath.

"So where are we Fergus?" he asked.

At first glance, Orboz Purgator was much like Earth Purgator. Wide-open spaces occupied the land in all directions, lush vegetations thrived everywhere and the snow-covered peaks of some extensive mountain chain chiselled the landscape far into the distance. Yet the weather was stifling hot, and humid, like in the tropics. Moreover, an eerie cacophony of cries and odd sounds reached deep into the flatlands.

"We're at the edge of the jungle of Dupar," explained the leprechaun, "in the northern territories. That is where the Noordjins live."

"The Noordjins ..." repeated Solas, "better be friendly."

"Yes they are, fer the most part," replied Fergus, "although they don't always take kindly to visitors. But better them than Daemonia!" he chuckled.

Xiao Ren noticed that Master Senex seemed a little shook-up.

"Are you okay Master?"

"Yes, yes I'm fine," he answered. "I'm just trying to adjust to that topsy-turvy ride from that spinning luret, that's all. What a mind blowing experience that was!"

"Who inhabits the rest of this Purgator?" continued Solas. "Who lives here?"

"Out here, the Noordjins are the only ones still resisting Daemonia and the Orboz invaders from the south. As fer the rest of Orboz Purgator, it all belongs to the Stealth Demon, Daemonia and the rest of them."

"The rest of them?" said Dorian. "Can you be a little more specific?"

"Not much," answered the leprechaun, "freaks and all, ye know."

"So the Stealth Demon is down over there then?" asked Solas as he gazed straight into the distance.

"Yes."

"And Amy too ..." added Solas.

"Yes, I believe so," replied Fergus.

A warm breeze soon lifted and ruffled everyone to attention.

"Crap, I am soaked again," said Dorian. "This heat is drenching me worse than the moat waters."

"Where do we go from here?" asked Solas.

"Into the heart of the jungle," replied Fergus, "I think the Noordjins can help us."

And so the group picked up and was back on the move again, with the leprechaun leading the way, Artin still by his side and Solas following close behind. The jungle called out to them. And she awaited them.

8

The wild sounds of the forest increased as the band drew closer to the dark and dense jungle of Dupar. The members of the group advanced in silence and were awestruck by the imposing rainforest that towered before them. Solas's thoughts, however, were lost in the distance. With every step, he looked back over his shoulder and dreamed of rescuing Amy from the chains of the demon, of holding her in his arms and of going home again. They would both be free. The nightmare would be over. But fiction was better than reality and Solas was filled with mixed emotions. As it turned out, so were the trekkers who came to a halt at the brink of the wilderness.

"This looks even worse than the Forsaken Forest," observed Dorian. "These woods are thicker than the walls of Tartarus."

"Do not worry," said Fergus. "Under the canopy, it's not bad at all."

"You got to be kidding me," replied Dorian. "And what the heck are all these screaming creatures about, huh?"

"You better not be leading us astray, my little green fellow," added Artin, "or I will pump every last one of my poison darts into your sorry hide, you hear?"

Fergus frowned at the thought.

"Ye Millikeen folks need to loosen up a little. Always on me ass, ye are. Do ye never let up fer a moment?"

"Just offering you a kind reminder, that's all," replied Artin.

"Save yer energy fer the thickets, me dear friend," explained the leprechaun. "These woods are scattered with varmints, scavengers and giant insects. Best be on the lookout fer vipers too! Crazy I may be, but not so much to run off on me own. In this land, that is pure madness, I tell ye."

"Let's get a move on," ordered Solas. "You go first, Fergus. And bring us straight to see your friends the Noordjins, and fast. I'm not too crazy about this place."

"Fer the record," Fergus clarified, "the Noordjins are not me friends."

"That figures!" scoffed Dorian.

The topsoil of this strange and alien rainforest was damp, spongy and cluttered with moss-covered deadwoods, giant exotic ferns and leafy tropical plants. Walking was slow and cumbersome. The group blazed a trail by slashing through the wild undergrowth with a promise from the leprechaun that the bug infestation would soon stop. Indeed, huge parasites the size of dragonflies honed in on the trekkers for a taste of fresh blood. Unsightly critters abounded. They ran amok throughout the leafage and scattered from their refuge with each step taken. This meant the group spent as much time stomping and whacking at the insect invaders as it did slashing down the bastard weeds impeding its progress.

Colossal jungle blossoms hissed at the passing members. These flowers – carnivores that they were - rotated their cups at will, like sunflowers do, to face the newcomers. These floral predators lured birds, rodents and reptiles to a certain death by spitting a cloudy mist of spores and enticing fragrances about their surroundings in order to attract their unsuspecting victims. And so these pivoting monsters hissed and coughed up their mixture into the air like clockwork, which made breathing troublesome, especially for old Master Senex who suffered from a lung condition. Still the group pushed on. The mocking sounds coming from the canopy continued without reprieve, even increasing in intensity and frequency. Solas and his troops were intent on putting a face to the ruckus. At last, they uncovered the culprits: a gang of unruly primates, a bunch of squawking macaws and toucans, and a slew of nameless yapping birds. The incessant noise was deafening at times and Solas wondered if Orboz Purgator wasn't some sort of an odd, prehistoric place, lost somewhere in the abyss of time.

A couple of hours elapsed before the jolly explorers arrived upon some sturdier grounds. Space opened up before them. A beaten road laid down its tracks. And rays of sunshine baked the travellers once again, a hard but welcome relief for most of them.

"Finally, I can stretch my arms and legs without risking a limb. I can breathe," said Dorian.

"Don't let up now," said Fergus. "We're almost there. The Noordjins are just beyond this hill."

"Who in their right mind would want to live under these conditions anyway?" said Dorian. "There are mosquitoes as big as birds that you can punch with your fists!"

"The Noordjins do," answered Fergus. "The jungle acts as a natural barrier against Daemonia."

"Could we not have avoided this ordeal by landing the luret closer to where the Noordjins are?" asked Dorian.

"The luret won't stop in cramped areas," replied the leprechaun. "It requires a clean landing, it does."

Xiao Ren and Senex were resting on the ground and begging for fresh water. The Millikeen warriors hardly flinched.

"How far are we still?" asked Solas, concerned about his friends.

But before Fergus could answer, he heard some rustling in the distance and spotted some bodies moving.

"Look!" he said. "Here come the Noordjins, ye see!"

9

All eyes were fixated on the strange hubbub at the far end of the trail. The group looked forward to seeing the vaunted Noordjins arrive to greet them. Fergus had spoken highly of them. Still, Solas remained cautious and apprehensive, and his fears materialized once he noticed his mighty Lux Veritas glint back to life.

"Are you certain these Noordjins are friendly?" Solas asked in a harsh tone.

If the Noordjins were indeed coming, then they were coming a-running and a-jumping like a herd of springboks, like a swarm of hopping locusts. These warrior-people were nimble and fleet-footed, to be sure. Solas readied his weapon.

"What is happening to them?" asked the leprechaun. "Something is wrong."

"What do they want from us, Fergus?" asked Solas.

"I don't know."

"Go hide yourself, traitor!" Artin ordered the leprechaun. "I will deal with you after the battle. And no funny business, you hear. I am keeping this beauty right here just for you, my little hobgoblin." And the Millikeen guard flaunted his most precious and venomous dart to the baffled leprechaun.

Dorian took his position ten paces to the right of Solas. Xiao Ren and the Millikeen soldiers knelt down between them and loaded their weapons, ready to fire as soon as the charging Noordjins should come within striking distance. Fergus and Master Senex stepped back and took immediate cover behind a fallen log.

The Noordjins approached fast, skipping around in every direction to avoid bushes, logs and obstacles in their way, while paying little heed to Solas and his friends awaiting them. Solas thought this most peculiar. The Noordjins appeared to be running away from something. They were not attacking at all.

"Hold your fire!" yelled Solas. The Millikeen soldiers already had their targets in sight and Solas's reaction puzzled them. "It isn't us they're after."

"Then why is Lux Veritas lighting up like a Christmas tree?" asked Dorian.

"Look who's coming behind the Noordjins!"

"Daemonia!" yelled Dorian, after catching a glimpse of the eternal foe.

"Hold your position," said Solas. "And await my command."

The group waited it out, as ordered, and did not move an inch. The Noordjins ignored their presence altogether and whizzed past them as though they were still statues, before disappearing behind the first line of bushes of the deep, dark jungle of Dupar. Following, a slew of arrows came whistling down from the sky. One of the projectiles only missed Fergus by a nose as the missile struck the trunk of the log behind which he had taken refuge. The leprechaun forthwith got up and ran, high-tailing it to the safety of the nearby rainforest while mumbling away his prayers and cursing in some pixie language.

"Fergus … Fergus!" shouted Senex. "Where are you going? Get back here!"

Artin noticed this cowardice from the corner of his eyes, but thought better of unleashing a dart. There was nowhere to go after all, and the enemy was a much bigger concern. *Pathetic* was the only thought that crossed Artin's mind.

"Fire!" ordered Solas, much to the delight of Jiji and the Millikeen soldiers.

The demon archers were a primary target and soon started to drop like flies, convulsing into bubbling heaps of putrefying flesh whenever struck by the poison darts. It was a most morbid spectacle. Daemonia sped up its advance and charged ahead in great numbers, hissing, yelling and brandishing their swords, battleaxes, clubs and morning stars with tenacious resolve. Solas and Lux Veritas engaged the enemy, putting on another masterful display of swordsmanship, slashing, skewering, zapping and otherwise dismissing line after line of the hapless onrushing foes. Dorian's size, strength and skill with his weapon allowed him to stand his ground and overpower his adversaries with his superior reach and the sharp cutting edges of his katana sword.

Daemonia was soon left with depleted troops and the narrow land clearing where the carnage took place was now strewn and littered with the corpses of demons, imps and other indiscernible freaks, endemic to Orboz Purgator. The Noordjins – who had been observing the fighting from the edge of the forest – re-entered the battle and helped rout Daemonia once and for all.

10

Once the bloodbath was over, with only the victors standing, the Noordjins turned their attention to the weird but brave Outlanders who had saved them from their troubles. Solas and his group gathered as a unit, standing back to back, facing the four dozen remaining Noordjin warriors who were encircling them. Lux Veritas had quieted down now and Solas, satisfied that the danger had passed, lowered his weapon. Dorian and the others followed suit. After an awkward moment of inquisitive contemplation, a colorful individual stepped up, presenting himself as the active leader of the Noordjins, and approached Solas to address him.

"Who are you Outlander, and what is your business in this land?"

The Noordjins had a humanlike appearance. They were average in size but somewhat disproportionate: their legs were long, thick and sturdy; their bodies short and compressed. They were unusually trim, and devoid of any body fat, which helped define their muscle tissue in such a way that one could make out every muscle strand in every muscle group. Their faces were nothing more than skin on bones with white glossy eyes set deep into their sockets. There was no pupil or iris. They had no hair, no evidence of ears, and a dark complexion – the kind you might expect to see on aboriginal people of equatorial origin – and were scantily clad. They wore just enough to cover essentials. They needed no shoes, for the sole of their feet was like thick rubber, which no doubt helped them run and spring about the jungle lands worry-free. Of course, these warriors carried weapons: bows and arrows, knives, spears and shields too. Some wore head covers, bandanas, nose rings, gold bracelets and leather pendants with ivory and semi-precious stones. Yes, the Noordjins were a different type of humanoid, but what most set them apart were their markings: tattoos, flesh scars and multi-colored streaks of paint, tar, ash and chalk. And as Solas would soon discover, the more colorful the individual, the higher he stood in the hierarchy.

"My name is Solas. My friends and I have come from a land far, far away to take up the quarrel against the common foe: Daemonia."

The warrior said nothing more. He was puzzled by the sword Solas held in his hand. So were his kindred. Then he spoke up while pointing to the mighty weapon.

"What is this sword of lightning you carry?"

"Oh, this is Lux Veritas," explained Solas. "It's a special kind of sword."

Solas lifted the weapon from the ground to show off the item and quench the warriors' curiosity. The startled Noordjins took a step back.

"Are you a sorcerer then … like the Great Demon?"

This comment came as a surprise to the group and made Solas raise an eyebrow.

"No, I am not," continued Solas. "But whenever evil is near, like Daemonia for instance, Lux Veritas begins to shine. She has divine powers."

Again there was a period of prolonged silence among the Noordjins who scrutinized the weapon with an obvious sense of dread.

"There is no evil now. She is quiet," concluded the warrior.

"That's correct," replied Solas.

"That's because Solas and the Outlanders destroyed Daemonia!" exclaimed the Noordjin leader. Right then, the tribe began to cheer, raising their weapons over their heads in unison and sharing some sort of victory cry in perfect synchronicity while thumping the ground under their feet: *Oochalah, oochalah, hoo-hoo-hoo!* "And the enemy of our enemy is our friend!" he stated with clear delight.

After this remark, Solas and his crew began to smile and to loosen up a little before the Noordjin warriors. The tension dissipated, but only for the briefest of moments.

"So how do you explain this?" yelled the leader who did a sudden about-face.

Tsi-tsi he hissed as he sent a hand signal toward the bushes.

Crawling out of the jungle came three young warriors dragging along their latest catch: a despondent, hand-tied leprechaun whose tightly wrapped scarf, neatly stuffed into his mouth, prevented him from blathering and moaning at all.

"Fergus!" uttered the members of the group as they saw him approach.

"Is the leprechaun with you?"

Solas remained as calm as possible.

"Yes, his name is Fergus. What has he done to you?"

"We have been searching for this scoundrel for ages," answered the Noordjin leader. "He stole our gold, and brought the wrath of the Great Demon upon our people. And now he shall die a slow death at tonight's gathering."

The Noordjin warriors broke out into yet another chant, similar to the previous one. Fergus shook his head in denial and nearly collapsed to the floor in despair were it not for the two hardy braves holding him up. Dorian, Xiao Ren and Senex heard this proclamation and became quite concerned about the fate of the wee leprechaun, even if the accusations against him were in all likelihood valid. The Millikeen guards, however, became justly irritated, seeing that their cherished prisoner should get away with an easy death.

"How can a valiant warrior like Solas be the enemy of Daemonia and still befriend a treacherous leprechaun?" asked the Noordjin leader. "Well tonight, I say to you, my people will rid you of this spineless leech," he declared, "and to celebrate today's victorious battle over Daemonia, the Noordjin people invite Solas and his friends to be our guests of honor at tonight's village banquet. Do you accept?"

After a slight hesitation, and without a second option, Solas duly accepted the offer.

"Yes, we accept with pleasure," he said. "But you didn't tell me your name ..."

"My name is Arounas," he answered, smiling. "Welcome to the jungle!"

The proud Arounas spread his arms skyward to show off the exotic locality, which he called his home. Then he leaned over the distraught leprechaun dangling between the two warriors and spoke to him from just inches away.

"Do you remember where you are now?" he slurred.

Fergus's eyes lit up with fright.

"You're in the jungle. You're going to die!"

Fergus's eyes rolled back and he fainted.

I I

The torrid sun was now setting fast upon the jungle of Dupar. The celestial dish began to display patches of its red afterglow. Before long, the great collective of Noordjin warriors and the heroic Outlanders headed deeper into the heart of the jungle. Solas and his cohorts stepped over the numerous corpses of the slain foe, studying its new visage with a fair dose of nervous disdain. Arounas had gone quiet, but the jungle sounds did not. After a long walk down the trails, weaving here and there through thick foliage and across open clearings, they reached the crest of a large depression; a canyon from which the rushing waters of some wild river plummeted in steps down to the valley below.

"This is home," declared Arounas.

Solas's eyes lifted and followed the current downstream. There he saw an open vale where indeed the Noordjin village stood. Communal housings linked together by wooden spans occupied the land on both shores of the river. Above the rough waters were a couple of suspension bridges connecting the opposite sides of the steep rock faces where an intricate web of bamboo walkways gave access to a network of otherwise unreachable caves.

Arounas borrowed a path leading the group on a narrow descent toward the valley floor some thousand feet below. The slope was certainly not for those queasy individuals like Xiao Ren who suffered from the plights of vertigo or for those faint of heart like Master Senex. The druid's advanced age and lung condition forced him to reach into his waste pouch often to grab a concoction of his own medicine to combat the ill effects of his ailment. Still, the pair kept on trudging along like fine soldiers. Dorian looked forward to a good meal and perhaps a beverage of some fine spirit. Solas kept one eye on Arounas, one eye on Lux Veritas, and his mind occupied with thoughts of Amy. Solas's imagination did take him to some faraway land. Or perhaps was it all real?

Indeed, in some foreign realm, the Stealth Demon approached Amy and crouched to caress her soft silky face, cupping her chin gently into his cold scaly hands.

"Don't touch me, you creep!" she yelled, before bitting hard his finger.

The beast grimaced and growled but never budged, as he calmly forced Amy to release her bite.

"The boy is late," he said.

"Don't you worry, viper, your hours are numbered!"

The Stealth Demon grumbled at Amy, showing her his teeth from only inches away.

Now at the bottom of the trail, a welcoming party of warriors greeted Arounas and his men upon arrival. The sentries had already relayed the message that Arounas was returning victorious from the latest battle. There was cheering, jesting and laughing amongst the villagers and the warriors, and for a while, no one seemed to notice the Outlanders at all. Only once Arounas grabbed Fergus by the scruff of the neck and tossed him like a ragdoll in the midst of the lot did all go dead quiet.

"Look what I brought back," he said, "our little fortune teller!"

Solas, Dorian, Senex and Jiji looked at each other puzzled by the remark and intrigued by the sudden development. Fergus squirmed and hyperventilated as he sat up, his head swivelling in all direction, eyes bulging, his mouth still stuffed full with the bandana strap. One Noordjin villager began to laugh out loud in a mocking way while pointing at the wretched leprechaun. More followed suit. They began to circle him and started up a dance. Another yelled at him saying *you couldn't foretell this one, could you, fortune teller!* Then, one of the men began to kick at him and soon, the whole lot joined him as Arounas looked on and laughed hardest.

Solas had seen enough. He drew Lux Veritas and barged into the middle of the pack to end the senseless punishment inflicted on Fergus.

"Stop!" he shouted, as Fergus laid motionless at his feet. The Noordjin archers nocked and tensed their bowstrings in record time. Solas stared down three dozens arrows point blank, not counting knives and hatchets. Of course, Lux Veritas activated and sparkled like fiery silver. This kind of voodoo magic startled the warriors and they took a slow but cautious step back.

"Lower your weapons!" ordered Arounas. "The Outlander Solas is our friend. His magical sword saved us from the evil foe. He and his companions fought Daemonia like the fearless Og'Dar and crushed the ruthless enemy. Put down your weapons I say!"

The warriors and villagers appeared more than perplexed but trusted their leader and acted as told.

"And take away the leprechaun!" he ordered. "Cage him and display him for all to see beneath the great oak of the elders at the banquet square."

Lux Veritas quieted again and Solas, reassured the trouble was over, slotted his sword back into its sheath.

12

The Noordjin locals gathered and stared at Solas and his crew as they entered the village. They lined the trodden dirt roads of the settlement or watched from the high cliff walls' suspended platforms. A handful of eager warriors confined Fergus to a bamboo cage and whisked him away ahead of the group's entrance, which created much excitement amongst the villagers. Artin, Broc and Dak were miffed about this and wanted Fergus to stay under their watch. But little could they do now, and already they mumbled to Solas and Dorian about a plan to free the leprechaun. The boys would have nothing of it and, preaching patience, advised the three Millikeen guards to keep their tempers in check.

As the amber sun began to set over the jungle hills, the streets lit up with the soft glow of torches. As the group reached the far side of the village, they met up, at last, with the great leader of the Noordjins. Arounas saluted the chieftain before addressing him.

"I bring you great news, oh Yobora: we crushed the viper Daemonia," he said. "We had help from the Outlander Solas here, and his sword of lightning Lux Veritas. I also captured the leprechaun thief, oh Yobora."

"I saw," replied the chieftain with the unyielding gaze.

He took a moment to check out the foreigners, in particular Solas and his impressive weapon of which he could only see its golden hilt standing out from the sheath.

"I salute you Solas. Welcome to our village," he said, before turning to his leading warrior. "You did a great job, oh Arounas. But you are late getting back and dinner is almost served. Perhaps you will tell me more about your adventure at the banquet table ... and a little more about these Outlanders and their magical sword."

Yobora was the most colorful individual yet. He was the undeniable ruling chief of the Noordjin tribe. Tattoos and depictions of figures, icons and symbols, which had been branded deep into his skin and tinted with dyes, covered every inch of his body. And whenever he turned his head, the villagers could hear the jingling sound of his metal crown. It was made of golden rings linked together, each loop punctured through his scalp. From them dangled hollow tube carvings of metal or ivory about three to four inches long that chimed softly whenever he walked or turned his head. Thus, every Noordjin knew when the chieftain was present.

At least two hundred Noordjins gathered around the banquet tables when the chieftain and his company arrived. His usual entourage numbered about 50 and there was already a prominent area reserved and set to receive them. Long lines of tables were arranged at right angles to form three-quarters of a large square. On the open side of this square, across from the main table and in plain view of the chieftain, was the great oak of the elders from which the cage reserved for Fergus hung five feet off the ground from the sturdiest limb. The leprechaun sat there, grouchy, his face peeking through two bamboo bars. However, his mood improved when he saw Solas and friends arrive. They saw him too but kept quiet.

Arounas sat to the right of chief Yobora along with a few notables; Solas, Dorian and the crew of Outlanders to his left, while four Noordjin warriors stood guard behind the chieftain at all times. In the center of the square, right in front of Fergus, a half dozen Noordjin entertainers broke into a celebration dance, stomping on the ground, beating on drum skins and imploring the favors of the Lord Creator. This ritual went on for a few minutes while all of the tables watched. The grand finale was a communal cry in which all parties joined in – save for the unprepared guests – *oochalah, oochalah, hoo-hoo-hoo!* Now the feast was ready to be served.

13

Female servers brought the food to the tables on large silver platters. Game was on the menu: deer, boar, fowl but also monkeys and other tropical oddities. They were skinned, skewered and roasted whole over one of the four fire pits smoldering and crackling only a short way behind the banquet tables. The food trays were heavy and several robust girls were needed to lift them. The Noordjins were carnivores and not a single green was seen anywhere. The women did, however, bring appetizing finger foods such as fried tarantulas, giant ants and some of those charming cockroaches the group had seen earlier while travelling through the jungle underbrush. The women also brought drinks in wooden pitchers and filled the guests' goblets right to the brim.

The chieftain helped himself first by slicing off a large chunk of deer meat which he devoured straight off the end of his knife.

Solas and the others proceeded next, choosing to eat the more familiar items. And since dinner etiquette was non-existent in these parts, Dorian and the famished Millikeen guards pigged out to their hearts' content. The conversation swayed back and forth. In the beginning, Arounas did most of the talking, explaining all that occurred on the battlefield and all that he witnessed. Solas reiterated to the chieftain the nature of his purpose in Orboz Purgator in the simplest terms possible. And he made sure to bring up the Stealth Demon. Yobora acknowledged that he had seen the beast before, yet the subject triggered little emotion. Instead, his attention diverted to the leprechaun. He tore off one last chunk of meat with his teeth and pelted the caged prisoner with the leftover bone. Startled, Fergus took half-cover. The Noordjins burst out laughing. Yobora's gesture was the great catalyst that prompted one wave of Noordjins after another to chuck and toss dozens more bones at the leprechaun. The party livened up fast. Even the Millikeen guards joined in the act. Tonight, under the triple moon lit skies, all the fun was at Fergus's expense.

"How long have you been friends with the leprechaun?" Yobora asked Solas to satisfy his curiosity.

"Friend is a strong word," answered Solas. "Fergus served as our guide. He brought us here."

"Leprechauns are scum," he replied. "I see little use for them."

"Actually, Fergus was quite helpful. He tried to make amends for his wrongdoings, and brought us here to find the Stealth Demon and make restitutions to your people too. You should give him a chance to prove it."

Yobora and Arounas looked at each other and never laughed so hard.

After catching his breath, the chieftain continued on a more serious tone, with a hint of fire churning behind his chalky stare.

"The leprechaun swindled ten times his weight in gold and gems. That wretched carcass wouldn't have a *leper* on him to save his life. Look at him! He probably came back to steal some more and you, my good Outlander, have been duped."

Solas looked back at his friends only to see the Millikeen guards grinning and nodding in agreement with the words of the chieftain.

"Well, he got us here, didn't he?" said Solas. "However did he manage to steal so much gold from you anyway?"

"Things were different before," Yobora explained. "Our people also occupied the flatlands. And when the leprechaun first came, we liked him. We had no reason to doubt him at all. The mighty legend of his people preceded him."

"What legend?"

"Many moons ago, long before my time, the leprechauns arrived here in great numbers. They waged war on our enemy and nemesis the Orboz people. They tricked them, they trapped them, they captured them and shackled them, and took them away to some distant Purgator. The leprechauns also had many Orboz work deep in the mines of the local mountains to extricate the gold. This was a great and peaceful time for the Noordjins. We thought the leprechauns were our friends, but they are only self-serving thieves, the scum of the earth."

"Okay," said Solas, "but I still don't understand how Fergus could manage to trick you."

Now Arounas took over the conversation again.

"Fergus came to us claiming to be a fortune teller. We were thrilled to see a leprechaun again. We trusted him. Soon, he had stolen from everyone, especially the elders who were easily swayed by his words of comfort and the promise of rewards and redemption. He was no fortuneteller; he was a fortune thief. Then one morning he had vanished. But that wasn't all. Through his shady dealings, he had also bought with him the wrath of the Great Demon and the beast came looking for the leprechaun here. We have been at war with Daemonia and the Orboz ever since. And we are losing, Solas. We are the few left still resisting. But for how long?"

"I am sorry to hear this, Yobora," said Solas. "In the morning, I will head south and go searching for the Stealth Demon. I have a score to settle with him too, as I have told you. Can you help me find him?"

"Sure, I know where you can find him," answered Yobora, "by the great Gate of Sefira."

"The great Gate of Sefira?" asked Solas. "What is that?"

"It's the passageway to the other worlds."

"Oh, the Diamond Crossing!" said Solas.

"The Great Demon guards it," Yobora continued. "You should know about it; you have a luret just like his."

"I will show you the way to Sefira," said Arounas, "if Yobora agrees."

"I suppose you may go with him, oh Arounas," the chieftain replied. "Perhaps the sword of lightning the brave Solas wields will be able to vanquish the Great Demon. What is there to lose?"

Solas's face beamed like the sun, as did those of Dorian, Xiao Ren and Senex. Securing the services of Arounas was a great start. The Millikeen guards, however, were not so pleased. They had their minds on another matter.

14

The pelting of poor Fergus continued in sporadic spurts throughout the evening. For Artin, Broc and Dak, the fun had now worn off, and so they approached Solas and Yobora regarding the fate of the leprechaun.

"We believe the leprechaun Fergus has fulfilled his duty to you, Solas," said Artin. "First he brought you to the Diamond Tesseract and then he guided you to the world of the Stealth Demon. You must release him at once and put him back in our care, lest we break the promise made to our leader Kiltop. We must bring the leprechaun back alive and in one piece, if at all possible."

Yobora vehemently objected to the demand of the Millikeen guards and made clear his views before Solas could even respond to Artin.

"Impossible I say," shouted the chieftain as he stood up. "The leprechaun has a longstanding debt to repay the Noordjins. And pay it in full, he shall."

"But he has not yet finish paying off his debt to the Millikeen people!" insisted Artin.

"It does not matter. The leprechaun belongs to the Noordjins now," continued the chieftain. "He is on our land, in our city. His punishment is long overdue. But as a gesture of goodwill and sympathy toward the Millikeen people, I shall grant you, Artin, the satisfaction of administering the first blow."

"That is not the point!" shouted the Millikeen guard, blowing his cool.

"Do not raise your voice at Yobora, impudent," replied the chieftain, "or you will soon find yourself joining your leprechaun friend in the cage."

"He is not our friend," Solas insisted once more.

"It is settled then," concluded the Noordjin chief, before pounding his fist on the table. "The penalty is death!"

During Yobora's tirade, the whole banquet had gone quiet. But upon hearing the final verdict, the Noordjins came back to life, cheering their chieftain's decision and rendering one more unified *oochalah, oochalah, hoo-hoo-hoo* in his honor. Yobora, whose blood ran thick and patience ran thin, ordered his warriors to fetch the leprechaun. At once, two sturdy braves brought over the cage and posited the object and its prisoner at the feet of the head table. Yobora grabbed his mug full of spirits and splashed the leprechaun with it, since it appeared Fergus had lost consciousness somewhere along the way.

"Wake up you crooked stormy petrel!" he blasted.

Fergus sat up and attempted to catch his breath while wiping off the sting from his eyes.

"Do you have anything to say in your defence before we stretch you on the rack and stone you to death?" asked the chieftain, more as a rhetorical formality than in lieu of a fair trial.

The excited crowd cheered at the prospect of being thus entertained. Already, villagers ran off to collect rocks, pebbles and stones, piling them up thirty feet behind an imaginary line from the spot of execution. Others brought ready-filled buckets. Meanwhile the warriors were fast setting up the framework. Solas became concerned, as did the others in the group, and he could see that the Millikeen guards were plotting some sort of intervention which would severely jeopardize his efforts to secure more help from Arounas and the Noordjin chief. Solas needed to come up with a solution, and fast.

Fergus spoke up.

"Stone me to death?" he replied, half-sobbing. "Why would ye do such a thing? I have come to make amends, don't ye see? Look! I have brought here Solas, his divine sword and his friends to free ye from Daemonia and the Great Demon. Isn't yer peace and yer freedom worth more than a few petty bars of gold?"

"Petty bars of gold, huh? If only that was all they were to you in the first place! You bringing the Outlanders here is only interest on capital," Yobora answered. "We still want our gold."

"I will repay ye in full, I swear," cried Fergus. "Just give me a chance to prove it."

"Do you take us for fools, leprechaun?" yelled Arounas. "You arrived here as prisoner to the Millikeen guards, scoundrel. You never came here of your own free will, did you?"

"I beg ye fer mercy," implored Fergus. "Can ye not find it in yer heart to burry the hatchet?"

"Of course we can," replied Yobora, "deep into your skull!"

Fergus froze speechless. Upon their leader's command, two Noordjin warriors opened the door to the cage and dragged Fergus out and away to hang him and stretch him on the rack.

15

Yobora, Arounas and their guests of honor stood front and center at the event. The crowd secured plenty of torches and the

Noordjins took position thirty feet from the target and waited for the chieftain's orders before casting the first stone at the outstretched leprechaun. Suspended in the air, four feet off the ground, was Fergus. Long leather straps reaching to the four corners of the scaffold tied his limbs so that his body formed an X in the middle of the woodwork. These ties pulled hard on his arms causing him much pain and discomfort. He moaned and whined more than he begged, and when blood began to flow from his wrists, it became clear to everyone that this time he was not faking it. The hangmen had stripped Fergus of all his clothes, save for his trousers, which they had allowed him to keep. No one had ever seen him in such a sorry state and even the Millikeen guards thought this treatment barbarous. To Xiao Ren and Senex, the group had kept quiet long enough. They threw heavy glances of concern and disbelief at Solas, urging him to speak up and put an end to this mistreatment. Solas acknowledged their messages by nodding his head. Fergus was an ugly troublemaker, a swindler and many other things, to be sure, but none of these crimes deserved such a horrible sentence as a slow and cruel death. Not to the members of the group anyway. Besides, Solas had made a promise to Artin and the Millikeen leader Kiltop, and he was intent on keeping it.

"Artin, to you goes the honor of throwing the first stone!" said a joyous, playful Yobora. "And if you can hit the head, I will let you have another shot."

"I'll pass," answered the crabby Millikeen guard.

"As you wish," replied the chieftain who seemed to be looking forward to the spectacle. "Arounas, you are next. Show them how it's done!"

As Arounas prepared to throw, Yobora turned to Solas and said 'Arounas is a star at this game.'

Solas and the rest of the group held their collective breath as they waited for Arounas to unleash his strike. He hurled the stone like a major league pitcher throws a baseball, with the same technique, intensity and speed. The rock found its target but skidded off the side of Fergus's head as he turned to avoid the object in the nick of time. Still, Fergus was shaken. He moaned and squirmed to get loose as a cut appeared where he was struck and drops of blood started to drip. The Noordjins cheered at Arounas's prowess and laughed at the leprechaun. Xiao Ren gasped, turning away to find some comfort in Dorian's arms. Meanwhile, the Millikeen guards backed away from the hoopla and snuck away unnoticed.

"Fire away!" shouted the chieftain, thus triggering the aerial blitzkrieg.

Rocks and stones flew at the leprechaun from all angles. Resigned to his fate, the hapless Fergus stopped struggling. He could only grin and brace for impact.

Solas had seen enough, however, and he marched straight toward the leprechaun, steadfast, to shield him from harm. Inside its sheath, Lux Veritas activated to protect Solas and the Noordjins were able to witness the glowing sheen emanating from the hilt of the sword. Whatever rock neared Solas on its way to hit Fergus vaporized into dust, burning up in a nanosecond like a meteorite disintegrates when entering the atmosphere of blue planet Earth. The shower of stones ceased. Yobora, Arounas and the Noordjins were stunned into complete silence. Standing before Fergus who had once again lost consciousness, Solas spread out his arms and addressed the chieftain and all who were present.

"I know the leprechaun has done you much wrong and that he should be made to suffer, but there must be a fairer way to do it than this," he said. "This treatment is unworthy of the great Noordjin people. At least give Fergus a chance to defend himself!"

The chieftain thought about this for a brief moment.

"You want to give the leprechaun the chance to defend himself?" said Yobora. "Then so be it. He can defend himself against the mighty Og'Dar. If he lives, he will be free to go." And the chieftain began to chuckle.

The idea had merit and the Noordjin crowd wasted no time seconding the motion.

"Og'Dar ... Og'Dar ... Og'Dar!" they chanted out loud, before adding their trademark stamp of approval *oochalah, oochalah, hoo-hoo-hoo!*

And so Solas succeeded; he succeeded in getting Fergus thrown from the pan straight into the fire.

16

Fergus was forthwith untied from his bindings. They splashed him with more alcohol to bring him back to life. His body bruised up, he slowly put his clothes back on before they locked him up again in his portable prison, then carried high on the shoulders of four warriors, and redirected toward the Og'Dar pit. Yobora led the group behind the makeshift procession. The cortege of Noordjins followed close behind, carrying numerous torches and humming incantations as though the leprechaun was their latest offering to the Lord Creator. The Millikeen guards rejoined the group for fear of getting lost and were thrilled to see that Solas had not given up on the leprechaun. But the struggle was not won yet.

They followed a path into the darkness well away from the village. As they got closer to the pit where the beast roamed, they heard it grunt, bellow and bark at the moon. Fergus was perhaps too tired to shudder with fear, but the cries of the creature were enough to stall a heartbeat and raise the hair on the scalp of a bald Noordjin. Once they arrived, the chanting stopped and the growling intensified. No doubt the Og'Dar could smell a fresh victim. A late night snack was about to be served.

"Give the leprechaun a sword!" ordered Arounas. "That might keep him alive for a minute longer."

The carriers set the cage down on the ground, and without letting Fergus out, they handed him a long thin blade, a nimble double-edged rapier of sort, which was a rare item in Noordjin land. The bow and arrow was the weapon of choice here but it was too impractical and the dagger way too short to battle the great Og'Dar.

The crowd hurried and gathered all along the edge of the abrupt, rocky pit. The beast lurked somewhere below in the darkness and could not be seen, and so the Noordjins tossed several flaming torches a good forty feet down to the bottom of the hole to have a better look at the monster. And there it was, the great big beast looking up at them, its dour expression distorted in the shadows. It growled and waved its muscular arms demanding its food. The Og'Dar stood at least 12 feet tall on its hind legs and was nothing more than a giant hairless sloth with sharp fangs, long claws and a bad attitude. But unlike the sloth, it was quick and agile like a gorilla, although its paws did not allow it to grab onto any tree limb or rocky ledge. Seeing the creature for the first time, Solas and his crew despaired again.

"Fergus has no hope at all against this beast, Yobora!" he said. "This isn't a fair fight at all."

"I do prefer to watch the spectacle of death by stoning. It lasts longer and it is a lot more fun for my people. But the leprechaun has a sword now," stated the chieftain. "He knows how to use it."

"Has anyone ever survived against Og'Dar?" asked Solas.

"Many have," answered Yobora, "for about a minute or so. Then he devours them."

"He will love the leprechaun," added Arounas. "Og'Dar must be tired of eating Orboz meat by now, and all those tasteless imps."

The warriors lowered the cage by way of a pulley hanging off the high branch of a tree suspended over the pit. The beast began to agitate as its meal got closer, and the Noordjins began to spur it on by chanting *"Og'Dar … Og'Dar … Og'Dar!"*

17

Fergus hung on tight to his sword as he scrambled inside his box hoping somehow to avoid the inevitable. Artin did not much like the beast or the treatment given his prisoner Fergus. The Millikeen guards were determined to bring him back home alive so he could spend the rest of his days rotting in a dark cellar. That was only fair. The three guards retreated from sight and prepared their poison darts, waiting for the right moment to act.

Og'Dar jumped and slammed the cage with his fist sending it swinging like a playground toy, to the complete delight of the Noordjin audience. Three of the bamboo bars broke off on impact and Fergus near fell right out of the cage, barely hanging on with one hand, the sword in the other. On the sway back, Fergus let go and dropped down to the pit floor at the feet of the great Og'Dar who shattered the rest of the prison to pieces with both fists. Yobora and Arounas laughed out loud and thoroughly enjoyed the show. Meanwhile, the Noordjins started up their Og'Dar chants yet again.

Fergus picked himself up in a hurry, grabbing his sword in one hand and a torch in the other while backing away from the beast. When Og'Dar saw the leprechaun, he belched out a huge guttural bellow powerful enough to rejig the green elf's coif. Fergus waved the torch in front of him trying to keep the ogre at bay. But Og'Dar knocked it away with one swift move of the hand. Fergus seized this opportunity to strike the passing limb with his rapier causing the beast to howl in pain.

Now the beast was riled. Og'Dar gave chase to Fergus who ran for his life like never before. With the exception of a dark tunnel, which he failed to see, the enclosure was a dead-end. Fergus tired and lost his sword while running circles around the pit. The Noordjins never laughed so hard at this comical display. At last, Fergus tripped. He turned to face the beast. He thought for sure his time was up and prayed for some miracle. How surprised was he when he saw Lux Veritas land next to him. He picked it up and the item lit up at once. Fergus took courage, stood up to face the beast once more. Og'Dar cried out and swung to administer the final blow; an overhead double-fisted slam to crush the leprechaun into a tasty crepe. Fergus closed his eyes trusting to fate and the higher powers of Lux Veritas. The weapon countered the ogre by shielding the leprechaun and thrusting the blade through its abdomen, freezing the beast into a solid block of ice. With a slight delay, the great Og'Dar toppled over and shattered into a million pieces as it hit the ground, to the utter dismay of Yobora, Arounas and the Noordjin crowd.

18

The Great Og'Dar was no more. Yobora looked at the scene, speechless, and could not comprehend which of the events he had just witnessed was the most incredible. Was it the death of the great Og'Dar at the hands of the leprechaun or the dazzling display of the mighty Lux Veritas? A complete hush had fallen over the Noordjins now. Old Master Senex was first to break the silence as he started laughing out loud. Dorian and Xiao Ren soon joined him, their laughter echoing far into the night. The funniest thing was that somewhere, somehow, there was still some good in Fergus after all. The trio was well aware that you needed a lot of trust and a lot of faith to get the most out of the mighty Lux Veritas. And the leprechaun had pulled it off, in style.

"Well I guess that means Fergus is free to go now," said a smiling Solas. "He vanquished the great Og'Dar, did he not?"

Yobora shook his head and hesitated for a moment before answering with a nod.

"Is that a yes?" asked Solas, seeking absolute confirmation.

The chieftain nodded some more.

"I am sorry Yobora, I can't hear you," said Solas. "I will need an official yes on this one."

"Yes, yes, yes!" replied an exasperated Yobora, still in disbelief but coming around to his senses.

Satisfied, Solas looked down into the pit at the leprechaun. He began to clap his hands and yelled "Bravo Fergus!" Soon the whole crowd began to clap too, imitating the Outlander, and cheering the victor. Fergus was now a hero.

Down in the pit, the frazzled Fergus got up and dusted himself off. Confused, he looked up at the crowd, which was now applauding him.

"Could ye send me down a rope please?" he said. "I've had enough ogre fer one day."

They lowered him the rope from the pulley as he requested and pulled him up from the hole. "Fer-gus ... Fer-gus ... Fergus!" the Noordjins chanted all the while. On the surface, the leprechaun held Lux Veritas close to him, not knowing whether to trust the schizophrenic Noordjins at all. The Millikeen guards had rejoined the group once again, never having fired their poison darts at the giant; the angles, the movements, the darkness and the distance had made it all too challenging. They now wanted to reclaim their prisoner.

"Back off!" said Fergus, who had grown wary and paranoid.

Yobora, Arounas and the Noordjins drew back several steps.

"Give me the sword Fergus!" ordered Solas.

"I do want to thank ye fer saving me life Solas," replied the leprechaun. "Without the sword, I was as good as dead. But I cannot let go of Lux Veritas now, ye understand. Ye will all torture me again."

"We will not do that Fergus, I promise," said Solas. "Yobora gave me his word. You are free now."

The chieftain nodded at the leprechaun while still backing away.

"What about Artin, Broc and Dak? Do ye think I want to be shackled again and brought back to the mines to spend me life in some dark prison? Never, I tell ye!"

"Give me the sword Fergus," Solas repeated. "I trusted you with Lux Veritas. She saved your life. Now you will have to trust me. No one will put shackles on you, right Artin?"

Artin looked at Solas as though he had lost his mind.

"Right Artin?" Solas insisted.

"All right!" replied Artin clearly peeved at having to concede. "Now give me the sword Fergus!"

"Back off, I say!" shouted Fergus, brandishing Lux Veritas and waving the blade back and forth. "Back off! I am the master now."

Fergus transformed into a mad man, his round eyes aglow, confident in the knowledge that he possessed the sword and that any would-be assailant would suffer a swift retaliatory deathblow.

And everyone did back away indeed; all except Solas.

"Be reasonable Fergus!" he said. "Where will you go now? What will you do with the sword?"

"I have Lux Veritas. I have the Will-master's luret. I can do anything. I can go anywhere. I will bring glory to me people. I will destroy Daemonia and the Stealth Demon ..."

"Easy now Fergus!" said Solas, cutting him off in full speech while approaching him one small step at a time. "Don't get carried away."

"When all is over, I will lay down the sword at the foot of the Crystal Gates. The Lord Creator will welcome me into Elysium and I will be the greatest of all the heroes, the King of the angels, I tell ye!"

As he finished his sentence, Solas had moved in closer yet.

"Back off, Solas!" Fergus warned, "Don't make me use it on ye! I will ye know. Ye saw what happened to the beast."

But before Fergus knew what to do, Solas took one swift step forward and snatched Lux Veritas away from him. The leprechaun gasped in surprise and collapsed to his knees in sobs.

"He's all yours!" said Solas to the Millikeen guards, who rushed to put handcuffs on him.

"No handcuffs!" ordered Solas. "Let him be."

Following the dramatic events of the evening, Yobora, Arounas and the Noordjins escorted Solas and his group back to the village for a well-deserved night's sleep.

"Just how did you manage to steal the mighty sword from the leprechaun?" asked Arounas, most impressed by this feat of bravery.

"I know all its secrets," answered Solas, smiling.

Dorian, who was walking next to his buddy, whispered to him.

"That's because you didn't really want to harm Fergus. And Lux Veritas stayed inactive."

"Hush!"

On the way back to the village, Yobora pushed Solas for more answers concerning Lux Veritas and its magical powers. Solas complied and told the chieftain about its most amazing accomplishments, including the battle against the great Cerberus at the entrance to the abode of Chaos. These stories had the desired effect and Solas's plan to seek more support from the Noordjins worked. At last, Yobora offered to take up the quest against Daemonia and the Great Demon. In the morning, he would bring his army and accompany Solas and the Outlanders to the Diamond Tesseract, otherwise known in this land as the Gate of Sefira. For Yobora and his tribe, now was the perfect time to act. With the help of Lux Veritas, the Noordjins were now invincible. There would no more hiding in the jungle forests. Orboz Purgator would be free from the great evil at last.

CHAPTER VII

LOST AND FOUND

*"The first and greatest victory is to conquer yourself;
to be conquered in mind and spirit is of all things
most shameful and vile."*

—Plato

I

Come sunrise, Solas was already awake. He sat alone, high up on a platform, his legs dangling over the void beneath, eyes transfixed on the fading twilight. Inside the living quarters dug right into the hard cliff walls, his buddies slept. They were busy catching up on some much needed shut-eye. But not him; his mind was too preoccupied with thoughts of Amy. Today was the day he would discover the truth. Was she alive? Was she well? Was she even there? She had to be. He recalled some of the Stealth Demon's last words to him: *Beyond the Diamond Crossing. That is where you will find us ... Come boy if you dare to the demon haunted world ... your love will await you there.* He ached to see Amy again. Still, guilt ridden, he worried about her well-being. And this rollercoaster of emotions would not allow him to sleep.

"Morning Solas!" said the raspy voice. "What are you doing there by your lonesome self?"

"Oh hello Master," Solas replied, turning his head. "I can't sleep. And you?"

"I always wake up at this hour," he answered. "You know ... yoga!"

"Right, I almost forgot."

"What a fresh and beautiful dawn, yes?" said Senex.

He took a deep breath of the crisp morning air and noticed a look of concern on the boy's face.

"So tell me then, what's troubling you? Are you worried about the Stealth Demon?"

"No," replied Solas, "I'll fix him. Don't worry. I have fire in my veins."

"Do be careful my boy, that the fire does not consume you instead."

"Yes I know."

"It is nice to see that you have listened well to what I taught you," said Senex.

"You have not taught me anything yet," replied Solas.

"Well not now, but I will. You have said so yourself. And I am glad to see that you have mastered Lux Veritas so well. I needed to see it for myself. Now I know my efforts will not be in vain and that you will succeed in your first mission, as I am sure you will in this one too."

"Is there anything else you know about the Stealth Demon that I don't know?" asked Solas.

"Nothing else I'm afraid. But it's funny to see how things go in circle when you enter the web of destiny."

"What do you mean?"

"Don't you see?" answered the Master. "Much of what I learn here from observing you and Lux Veritas I will teach you when you arrive in Lalas Pur for your first mission in about two weeks time. If I were not here now, I might not be able to teach you so well. For every action, there is an equal and complementary reaction, all the more so in the spiritual world."

"Oh I get it. Yeah, I suppose you're right. Still you best not tell me of the outcome of this mission or I may not have enough strength to complete the first one, or both."

"I agree," said Senex. "And you must not tell me of my fate either. This way we will keep karma in balance. This is the only way to make these missions possible at all."

"It's a deal," Solas replied as he stood up.

"But tell me Solas, out of curiosity, however did you defeat Chaos?" Senex chuckled before continuing. "This much you can tell me. Perhaps I should know."

"I wish I knew how I did it, Master. After I defeated Cerberus, I entered Chaos's abode, suspended somewhere between darkness and nothingness. It was a war of will, of principles. In the end, I tangled him in his own web of lies I guess. The light of Lux Veritas grew ever brighter until it reigned over the whole darkness. Chaos was reduced to nothing more than a spot of gloom, a sphere of evil. Then he vanished."

Solas paused a moment to weigh his thoughts as the Master listened.

"I restored order, perhaps, but somehow I doubt I managed to destroy Chaos. I don't know that you can. But thanks to you Senex, you did inspire me to believe in the darkest hour."

"Well I am glad I was of some use to you," replied a pensive Senex, squinting his eyes while rubbing his scraggly white beard.

"Help me figure out the Stealth Demon, won't you Senex? I could use some help," said Solas. "He will not commit to Lux Veritas in battle. It's a stalemate."

"As I understand it, he wants to exchange the sword for Amy," said Senex.

"I won't do it. I can't do it!"

"I know that, Solas," replied the Master. "But everyone has a weakness. You must find his Achilles heel, like you did for Chaos. Trust yourself; and do not worry, the answer will come. It always does."

"I hope you're right."

"And do not stress about the girl," added Senex, "she is fine. She believes in you."

Solas nodded as he glanced away to look at the daylight breaking on the horizon.

"You should see her, Master," he said in a low voice. "She is even more beautiful than the morning sun."

Senex approached Solas, wrapping his arm around his shoulders to comfort him. Solas turned to face the Master and the two embraced.

"You make me proud," Senex whispered to him. "Remember, I love you son."

"Ditto Grand-pa," replied Solas, "ditto."

Now the sound of stomping feet echoed up the cliff wall. Solas and Senex leaned over the railing and glanced below to see Yobora, Arounas and a handful of his men come marching toward them and climb up the stairs of the scaffolds leading to the sleeping quarters of the Outlanders.

2

The Noordjin leaders arrived all decked out in war paints and carrying their favorite weapons: long, light spears and knives for close combat.

"A new dawn is breaking. Today is the day," said Yobora, straight to the point. "Are you ready Outlanders? We must be leaving now. Gather your troops."

"Mornin' Chief!" replied Solas, unwilling to forsake common greetings. "Where are all your warriors?"

"They are ready and waiting for us up on the ridge leading to the forest."

"Already!" said Solas. "I was up all night and never noticed a thing."

"After escorting you to your quarters, my warriors were eager to get ready," said Yobora. "They consider Lux Veritas and your presence among us a divine sign from the Lord Creator. They feel invincible now."

"I will go and wake up our friends," said Senex.

But before the old master could act on his words, Dorian and Xiao Ren exited the lodging followed close behind by the Millikeen guards and Fergus.

"Do you Noordjins sleep at all?" asked Dorian, trying to rub off the cobwebs. "You folks may be light-footed in the jungle but you sure have a heavy foot on those scaffolds."

"The time has come, young Dorian" said Yobora. "Prepare yourself. We shall leave this minute."

Dorian looked around, stretched and yawned as he admired the sunrise.

"As nice a day to die as any I guess," he said, looking behind him and smiling at the downcast leprechaun sandwiched between Broc and Dak.

Fergus grimaced at Dorian's poke but seized the moment to make a small request. "I do enjoy me hands being free, oh great Yobora, but I sure would appreciate me own sword too. I can help in battle. Ye saw it yerself."

"Not a chance!" objected Artin. "The leprechaun will turn on us or run away. We saw that too."

"But there's nowhere to run to," replied Fergus.

"You were running away when we found you, weren't you?" said Arounas.

"That's different. I was running fer me life, ye understand. Please Chief," begged Fergus, "I was a hero to yer people last night. They chanted me name after I vanquished the great Og'Dar."

Yobora uttered a 'tsi-tsi' and signalled to one of his warriors who rushed to fulfill the leprechaun's wishes by handing him a spear.

"We don't have any swords to spare," said Yobora. "It matters little. When we reach the battlefield, you will go on the front line and be first to die, like a true hero."

"Oh … right," replied Fergus, "thank ye!"

And without another word said, Yobora turned about and the group followed. They descended to firmer ground before heading toward the garrison of warriors waiting up on the canyon crest.

3

Chieftain Yobora quickly took control of his army, numbering near two thousand Noordjin men and women, and led the advance through the familiar jungle terrain. The forest became denser as they reached its outer limits. While trudging along in the damp jungle muck beneath the forest canopy, Master Senex noticed a persistent hint of concern cast on the face of his beloved Solas.

"Victory is almost upon us," said the old man, in an attempt to cheer the boy. "Isn't this a most wonderful day?"

Solas paid little heed to the words spoken to him and was lost somewhere in some faraway daydream.

"Solas! I am speaking to you my boy."

"Oh sorry Master, I wasn't paying attention. I have a lot on my mind today."

"What could the matter be? In a few short hours, we shall be victors. Your worries will soon fade away. Trust in Lux Veritas. You did before, yes?"

"She is no guarantee against this foe, Master. But that is not the problem."

"Well then, what is the problem?"

"Well …"

"I'm listening …"

The cries of the rainforest inhabitants eased up just long enough to allow Solas to state his concerns in a clear and sober voice.

"Tell me Master, will this game ever end? I mean, if I triumph today, will I need to do it again tomorrow? This is a vicious cycle with no end in sight, isn't it?"

"That's Chaos talking," replied the Master, wincing. "Don't let him get to you. You are stronger. You must be stronger."

"Yes, but what difference does it make if I cannot change destiny? All is already written. Whether I win or lose, I have no control. It has already been decided. Nothing matters."

"Not so my young lad," answered the Master, raising the tone of his raspy voice. "Everything matters. I do think you are missing one vital and crucial link here. And now I will teach you your first and perhaps most important lesson."

Walking close behind the pair, Dorian and Xiao Ren perked their ears to catch a morsel of the master's wisdom. They had anticipated this moment for quite some time now and this rare occasion was too priceless to dismiss.

Senex cleared his throat.

"Listen here my boy: you are and always will be the master of your own destiny. You are free as the Lord Creator is free, but you must choose which path to take. You must choose *your* destiny. The Lord Creator trusts you. Therefore, believe in yourself and make the right choices."

"Really Master; what choices do I have?"

Senex began to chuckle, finding the question rather naive and innocent.

"Do you realise, my boy, that the Lord Creator already knows the outcome of all possibilities and all options from the infinite set of destinies presented before each soul? Nothing is concealed to the Lord Creator. He is eternal. What the Lord Creator *does not know*, however, is which option an individual will choose; in this instance, the one *you* will choose, Solas! You see, the Lord Creator is free-will, and his gift to each one of us is free-will too. We and we alone choose the path to follow in this life and beyond. You have free-will, Solas. Use it as you see fit. But choose wisely: karma is ruthless. You have seen her at work in Purgator. Otherwise, it is no secret: all of the options have already been played out in the Lord Creator's infinite mind, in the eternity of his being and immensity of the universe. The truth cannot escape him."

"So the Lord Creator already knows if I will fail or succeed," said Solas.

"In a way, yes; but in the end, it is all up to you," replied Senex. "In essence, you have already failed and you have already succeeded. You create your own heaven and hell, Solas! Therefore, improve your fate through this understanding, and follow your intuition until you become, at last, *Master of Destiny*."

Pensive, the boy nodded.

"You just need to make the right choices. That is why I tell you to stop worrying. Trust yourself!" continued the Master.

"And trust Lux Veritas!"

"Naturally! Rely on her, as you did before. She will see you through."

"I think I understand," replied Solas. Then he smiled before continuing. "Thanks, Master ... or should I say, thanks Master of Destiny!"

Senex chuckled.

"It's just Grand-pa to you, Son!"

And the two hugged and laughed as they forged along, like brothers-in-arms, down the miry path toward destiny.

4

As the Noordjin army approached the wide-open flatlands, two warrior scouts rushed back to deliver important news to chieftain Yobora and his right-hand man Arounas.

"Enemy units are patrolling the fringes of the forests, oh Yobora," said one of the scouts.

"How many of them are there?" asked the Noordjin leader.

"Many groups of five or more," answered the scout.

"Arounas!" said the chieftain. "Tell the men to take cover and wait by the edge of the clearings until I give further orders."

"Yes, oh Yobora!" replied Arounas.

"What is the plan now?" asked Solas.

"Tell me Solas; did you kill all of Daemonia's units during the battle yesterday?"

"I can't be sure," answered Solas, hesitating. "We did inflict some serious damage on their troops and destroyed all those who opposed us, but some members may have gotten away. Who knows?"

"That explains it," replied Yobora. "If an imp or two managed to get away, they would have alerted Daemonia and the Great Demon of your presence here."

"You mean to say the Stealth Demon knows I am here," said Solas.

"There is only one Lux Veritas, and the Great Demon now knows you are here," replied Yobora. "He is planning something of his own. His troops are scouring the edge of the jungle to locate your position. He knows you will come for him sooner or later."

"So much for our sneak attack!" said Dorian, somewhat dejected.

"What should we do now?" asked Solas.

"The Great Demon wants a fight on the open plains, where there is nowhere to hide and he has superior numbers," answered the chieftain. "And we shall give it to him."

"We have no advantage on the open plains," said Solas. "The element of surprise is gone. This is pure suicide for you and your warriors."

"But we *do* have an advantage," said Yobora. "Lux Veritas!"

"Yes Yobora, Lux Veritas is powerful, but I cannot be everywhere at once and protect 2000 men!" explained Solas. "I am only human. We will be much too exposed and spread out."

"Do not worry about the Noordjins, Solas," replied the chieftain. "We have fought many battles and have been anticipating this day for quite some time. Here and now is where we make our stand. This is our best chance for success. Therefore, we shall live or die by the side of the brave Solas and the mighty Lux Veritas. That is all."

Solas, Dorian, Senex and Xiao Ren exchanged a few perplexed glances before Yobora turned and walked away to rejoin Arounas and his waiting army.

For Yobora, turning back was not an option and the Noordjins were fully committed to expunge their demons, come hell or high water. Solas and his group followed the Noordjin leader. Now, the morning sun ascended above the plains and a few rays of sunlight pierced here and there through the jungle canopy to reach the thick underbrush. The day ahead promised to be another dry, torrid one, with the only sign of possible relief being a cluster of ominous rain clouds brewing on the horizon. Yobora, Arounas and his whole army remained motionless, cleverly hidden under the blanket of the dark forest greens while observing their unsuspecting foes pass before them only a short distance away.

5

The boisterous beasts of doom made their periodic rounds on the periphery where jungle meets grassland. True to their vile nature, these potpourris of unruly demons, imps, Orboz mercenaries and other lowlifes and freaks patrolled the area, grumbling, snarling and jostling one another. Intense, several Noordjin sharpshooters waited for the crucial order to pounce on the beasts. When Yobora finally sputtered through his teeth the fricative *tsi-tsi* – that trademark Noordjin call to action – the warriors stormed out of the bushes like leaping gazelles and hurled their weapons at the hapless beasts, goring the lot dead through and through a half-dozen times over. The rest of the army then hopped out of the jungle thickets quiet as a mouse in a grain mill.

As the warriors retrieved their spears from the fallen enemy's corpses, hovering high above the plains, a murder of gryphons and hellbirds spotted the gathering of Noordjin fighters along the edge of the forest. They approached from afar and circled high over the crowd, squealing and squawking at the Noordjins while holding their position, thus sending a warning to all of Daemonia's foot-soldiers patrolling near the area.

"Correct me if I'm wrong," said Master Senex, looking up to the skies, "but if my old eyes don't betray me, Orboz Purgator seems to be blessed with the same hellbirds we have on Earth Purgator."

"You are right!" said Solas. "These are gryphons and spitfires. I would recognize them anywhere."

"And gargoyles!" added Xiao Ren. "Plus, they are just out of my range," she said, sizing up the flying beasts with her bow.

"Perhaps we could reach them with our blowguns," said Artin. "It's worth a try, isn't it?"

"Don't waste your breath," said Solas. "They will come down sooner or later."

"That is true, but they can stay up and circle round for a long while yet," said Yobora.

Once more, the chieftain called upon Arounas to organize the warriors in triangular phalanges of 30 men, and in advancing double-columns of about 50 men each. Exposed out in the open fields, success depended on a strong, organized defense. The Noordjins knew the drill well and were prepared.

Yobora, Arounas, Solas and his gang stayed ahead of the troops and led the army of Noordjin warriors, keeping a casual pace straight south across the plains. Before long, trouble approached from all sides. Many of Daemonia's scouting units honed in on the formations with an impatient and ravenous appetite for death and destruction. The Noordjins kept a careful eye on their foes but did not slow down. Daemonia grew stronger as the scattered units now pooled together. They edged closer and closer, snarling, growling, drivelling and tossing vernacular gibberish at the Noordjins with venom.

Yet, none of Daemonia's troops blocked the road ahead and the Noordjins were free to progress unhindered. A few hours passed under the constant mocking and pestering from the demon pursuers. At times, the most feverish ones would sneak up to the marching phalanges to attempt a cowardly strike at the warriors, as though playing a game. Now and then, others would throw the odd object or weapon at the Noordjins too. A warm southerly wind picked up, and the flying demons used it to glide about effortlessly. Often, the hellbirds would leave the area only to be replaced by others or would rejoin the flock once rested. But their numbers seemed to increase with time. The stark plume of a sinister shadow swirled overhead and Dorian began to grow restless.

"Why are they not attacking us already?" he asked. "I don't get it. It's obvious we have nowhere to take cover around here. This is just the sort of situation they thrive on. We're all sticking out like roaches in a Noordjin rice bowl!"

"They are only waiting for their friends," answered Yobora. "Be patient."

"Be patient? … Good one, chief!"

"Your question will soon be answered, Dorian," said the chieftain. "Look far into the distance, and tell me, what do you see?"

Dorian, Solas and Xiao Ren screened their eyes from the sunrays and squinted toward the horizon, focusing as best they could.

"Well, it looks like a nasty storm is headed our way," answered Dorian. "That should blow the hellbirds away and wet their wings a little, I imagine."

"Look again," ordered a composed Yobora.

After a more accurate observation, Solas yelled.

"Daemonia … by the thousands!"

Indeed, the twin nature of the dark clouds rumbling in the distance was none other than the great mob of Daemonia approaching the Noordjins like a storm of locusts, accompanied by wind, thunder, lightning and a few drops of rain.

6

The Noordjin troops were now fully exposed in the middle of the great Orboz expanse, just as Daemonia preferred it, and Yobora planed it. Anxious to meet the Stealth Demon on his own turf at long last, Solas pulled Lux Veritas from her sheath, and at once she began to glint a soft white.

"I still fail to understand why you would jeopardize your warriors like this, Yobora!" said Solas. "There are better options, no?"

"Well, the reason is quite simple, my brave Solas," answered the chieftain. "By luring the Daemonian army out into the open, you and Lux Veritas will be free to traverse through the enemy lines as easily as a knife cuts through swine offal, and then you will only be left to face the Great Demon, one on one."

"Thank you Yobora, but what about your army? You risk being crushed!"

"Solas, it is a great honor for us to fight alongside the great sword of Genesis, Lux Veritas," replied the Noordjin chief. "At last, redemption is at hand for my people. We are not afraid to die for this cause, you understand. We trust in you Solas, to slay the beast and bring us victory!"

Solas looked at Senex for guidance, or else to provide some sort of magic answer. The burden of a certain Noordjin slaughter was more than Solas could bear. This was not the sort of help Solas had been seeking in the first place, not in this way, not in this manner.

"Perhaps Yobora is right," replied the Master, reading the boy's mind. "His people are tired of running and hiding. In my village of Lalas Pur, on Earth Purgator, we have chosen to barricade ourselves behind tall walls. So we do share common sentiments with the Noordjins. Running away or hiding away can take a toll on the most resilient spirits, to be sure. But In the end you only need to remember one thing, my boy: do not worry about the dark clouds ahead, for behind every shadow the sun shines."

The first windblown raindrops reached the troops and refreshed the warriors from the heat as they advanced ever closer to their fateful rendezvous with the great Daemonian horde. Around them, members of the demon pools grew bolder, redoubling their taunts and tugs at the Noordjins. When Yobora signalled his men to stop, the warriors turned to face the enemy and adopted a cohesive defensive posture. Above, the hellbirds struggled to ride the wind but augmented their screeches and shrills in anticipation of the imminent clash. Ahead, standing only the length a football field away, Daemonia had slowed to a halt too. Yobora, Arounas, Solas, his companions and the Noordjin warriors all stood in silence, motionless, admiring the evil war machine before them. Known and unknown beasts of all sorts made up the enemy ranks, many on the front line straddling their mounts. Present among them, with that steady, contemptuous, smouldering gaze was the undisputed Prince of Darkness.

7

Solas sensed his presence and was first to notice him.

"The Stealth Demon," he said in the most usual manner. "He's here."

As he uttered those words, all his fears, all his apprehensions, all his anxieties floated away with the squall, and his confidence returned.

"I see him too!" said Dorian. "He looks like he's riding on Man o' War or something?"

"That's a goglop," answered Arounas, loud enough to be heard above the increasing gusts of wind. "These beasts are fast and strong and dangerous. And they never tire. Stay clear of them if you can; they will rip you apart."

"Right!" replied Dorian, smiling. "They can also be quite friendly."

Arounas frowned and he must have thought Dorian had lost his mind after making such a comment.

"So that's what they're called, goglops! I don't really want to shoot the poor things," added Xiao Ren. "I loved Ruffian. Besides, it's not their fault. They do as they're told."

"Do not pity the enemy, humans," said Yobora. "Rest assured that they will show you no mercy." As Dorian and Jiji reflected upon this piece of advice, he raised his voice once more.

"Arounas … bring the leprechaun to the front line; a promise is a promise. And prepare the men. We are ready!"

"Yes, oh Yobora!"

Arounas did as ordered. He grabbed Fergus by one arm, split through the three grumpy Millikeen guards and brought him to the front line, squeezing him between two tall, strappy warriors. The leprechaun half-grumbled and whined about his earned treatment, but the present situation was so dire that no one paid any heed. Arounas then stepped up ten lengths in front of the first column and facing his troops, he raised his weapon high in the air. The warriors reciprocated the motion and a sea of spears lifted in unison toward the heavens. Yobora, Solas and his group observed the proceedings, lodged between the first and second line of warriors.

"Noordjins!" Arounas screamed with passion.

Satisfied all souls were at attention, he thumped the ground with his foot and brandishing his spear over his head he yelled: "*Oochalah, oochalah, hoo-hoo-hoo!*" The warriors followed the example of their leader and repeated the war cry three more times. Then they advanced toward the enemy.

This classic Noordjin ritual – well known to Daemonia – riled up the beasts, and the Stealth Demon wasted no more time sounding the charge. Daemonia rushed en masse toward the Noordjins without any semblance of an organized battalion, in an absolute free-for-all rampage. The mob of enraged demons hissed and screamed as they charged ahead with reckless abandon. The hellbirds soon joined the fray and began to swoop down over the Noordjin troops, while the remaining scouting units attacked from the rear and the flanks. The Noordjins were now encircled and trapped.

Arounas prompted his men to action by yelling out another "*Oochalah, oochalah, hoo-hoo-hoo!*" to which his warriors once again responded in kind. Forthwith, the Noordjins jumped into a higher gear and began to jog at half speed. Then, at the decisive moment, they split apart and scattered in every direction at full speed like leaping impalas. The warriors surprised Daemonia by chucking their spears from all angles and impaling a large number of the charging enemy. The quick-footed warriors became difficult to target. Nimble on their feet, the Noordjins sprung and leapt here, there and everywhere, even bouncing off the chests and limbs of their foes to change direction. They retrieved their spears from the corpses of their fallen victims on the fly and used their weapons like a staff to strike down the nearby foes, or artfully skewering them whenever possible. Never did they stand still.

Now the mayhem was complete. Numerous victims dropped on both sides. The driving rain rendered the fields a sloppy mess and the sheer throng of demons soon overwhelmed the Noordjins warriors. The gryphons ploughed and tore into the mob without prejudice and the spitfires unleashed their flames as they skimmed over the crowd. All the while, Solas and his band of companions were stranded in the midst of the battle to face the onrush of the powerful goglops and their grim riders. Solas stood at the front of the line, shielding his friends with Lux Veritas; including Fergus who had rushed back to take cover as soon as hell broke loose and the leaping warriors deserted him.

Dorian trailed at the back while the Millikeen guards fired dart after dart at the approaching enemies in quick succession and with uncanny accuracy. Lux Veritas repelled the raging goglops with its impenetrable crystalline shield and sent the creatures bouncing off to the sides unaware. Artin, Dak and Broc used this opportunity to pump their poison darts into the dismounted imp riders, sending them into violent and deadly convulsions. Dorian, Xiao Ren and Fergus acted as rearguards and joined the battle whenever Daemonia broke through from the back but Master Senex, unarmed, took shelter square behind Solas, giving him an extra pair of eyes.

8

The rumbles of thunder and the bursts of lightning increased and the skies darkened all the more. In the distance, up on the crest of a rolling knoll, the Stealth Demon and his henchmen observed the carnage. Solas took notice and although he and his crew were now soaked to the bones from the rain, their spirits never dampened. Resilient and confident behind Lux Veritas, the group had now barged its way through the last lines of Daemonia. Behind them, however, the Noordjins warriors were all but routed. Solas looked back to the mêlée and searched for chieftain Yobora and the brave Arounas, to no avail.

Then, Solas spotted some loud warrior brandishing a spear in the air while riding a goglop. It was Yobora. The chieftain yelled his last orders trying to rally his valiant warriors for one final run of glory: "*Oochalah, oochalah, hoo-hoo-hoo!*" As always, the remaining Noordjin fighters repeated the command before being overrun by Daemonia.

"Bastards!" shouted Dorian, venting a general feeling of frustration and malaise on behalf of the group.

Soon, the tide of demons turned toward Solas and closed in on him from the rear. Throughout the battle, the hellbirds had remained unscathed and now they focused solely on the few remaining fools who had broken through the lines and were attempting a getaway.

The trampled battlefield was a sorry sight to contemplate. The blood of the Noordjin warriors flowed freely in the fields and everywhere filled the grooves and puddles created by the passage of the storm and Daemonia. The area took on a pinkish hue as the tempest subsided and the occasional sunbeam pierced through the cloud cover.

Solas, however, awaited the enemy on firm footing with the blade of the mighty Lux Veritas shining white-hot.

Daemonia still numbered in the thousands and as they closed in. The members of Solas's group quickly retreated to safety behind the umbrella provided by Lux Veritas. What's more, the Millikeen guards and Xiao Ren had precious little ammunition to squander, and daggers were now their only personal means of defence. Daemonia's next strikes came from above as the screeching hellbirds dive-bombed in pairs from different angles and in quick succession in order to divide and conquer the group. With each pass overhead, the band members ducked as low to the ground as possible, and it was on one such occasion that the hellbirds successfully separated the three Millikeen guards from the lot.

Several scavenging gargoyles swooped down from behind like gliding eagles to clutch Broc and Dak by their frocks, scooping them high up into the air before dropping them back down to the ground in the heart of the demon pack where the beasts forthwith mauled them to death. Much like his brethren, Artin would have surely suffered a similar fate were it not for the courageous and instant reaction of Fergus who, seeing the passing gargoyle approach, thrust his spear in extremis into the flying demon's chest, thus saving the diminutive Millikeen guard's life.

Meanwhile, Solas and Lux Veritas continued to fend off the enemy and countered the gryphons' attempts to snatch and grab by slashing and severing the hellbirds' outstretched limbs and claws or by discharging a flash of current into the flying beasts, felling them to the ground at once. In turn, the spitfires tasted the heat of their own fire as Lux Veritas deflected their scorching flames, returning the blaze tenfold and instantly roasting the fire-eaters into a smoky pile of burnt skin. Soon thereafter, their thick stench pervaded the area and lingered in the air for some time.

The hellbirds' raw strategy backfired; and so they flocked together, landing a safe 50 paces away, behind Solas and his posse, in the hope of cutting off their exit path.

9

The fields now bathed in sunshine once again and the sun came back out in full force. But so did Daemonia's foot-soldiers. They charged ahead at Solas with renewed vigor, fuelled by the thrill of victory, and excited by the taste of fresh-spilt Noordjin blood. The first wave of demons arrived only to be dismissed by the powerful Lux Veritas whose blade crackled like a live wire through the enemy lines, sapping the life-essence from dozens of beasts at once.

A momentary lull in the action provided Solas a little time to reassess the situation. With the second wave of demons approaching, he noticed in the mix a half-dozen galloping goglops.

"Dorian, Jiji!" he yelled. "I want you to jump on top of these goglops after I take care of the riders."

"What … those crazy goglops?" said Dorian. "Are you nuts?"

"Well, that's what Daemonia does!" Solas replied. "These creatures may be our best chance to get out of this mess. And bring me one too!"

"Come on, let's do it," said Xiao Ren, looking at Dorian. "Solas is right."

Dorian sighed, took a deep breath and slotted his katana back into its sheath.

Senex, Artin and Fergus stayed close behind Solas as Daemonia showed their teeth and trampled over their own dead to lunge at the group. Solas went with the flow, letting Lux Veritas guide him, countering and slashing the enemy one after the other. At the precise moment, he struck the ground with the blade of his weapon, which shook the earth beneath and tumbled the enemy, including the goglops. The creatures rolled on the ground before getting back up, idle, and free of their riders.

"Now!" yelled Xiao Ren.

Dorian and Jiji rushed toward the creatures and hopped on the back of the animals with one stride. Grabbing the reins, Xiao Ren quickly steered her goglop and shooed another toward Solas.

Dorian drew his katana, slashing and chopping at Daemonia while rejoining the group.

Solas jumped on his ride as soon as the creature passed near him.

"Come on, Master," he said. "It's your turn!"

Solas manoeuvred the animal into position and helped Master Senex climb up on the saddle behind him. Xiao Ren did the same for Artin while Dorian scooped up Fergus. Daemonia roared mad as they saw the six riders turn and get away from them. Under their new command, the goglops picked up speed and barged through the waiting line of gargoyles, gryphons and fire-breathing spitfires who unleashed more of their scorching blaze at the group. This time, the tip of Lux Veritas split the fire stream down the middle like the parting of the Red Sea, before trouncing the heads off the spitfires to allow quick passage through the last line of hellbirds.

Now, nothing stood before the group save for the great expanse of Orboz Purgator. Galloping through the open fields on the back of the goglops, the Outlanders enjoyed a newfound, exhilarating sense of freedom, joy and liberty. Yet, far ahead in the distance, Solas followed the spectre of the Stealth Demon and his two henchmen withdrawing and vanishing beyond the crest of the rolling hill.

10

After several hours of travelling through the undulating countryside, the group slowed down, satisfied that Daemonia was now many miles out of sight and that the wounded hellbirds did not take to the air again. Each time, upon reaching newer grasslands, the Stealth Demon waited, only to disappear over the horizon like a mirage. This game continued until the group finally reached the edge of a wooded area basking in the shadow of a nearby mountain, with a cooler climate, and vegetation altogether different from the jungle lands.

The group dismounted the goglops and led the thirsty animals to a brooklet of fresh water passing through the forest only a short distance away. As men and creatures quenched their thirst, the band noticed across the creek a modest hamlet comprised of a few primitive huts built of hard mud and straw. The habitations seemed abandoned. Metal pots, pans and utensils laid about the ground by the side of a communal firepit, and a few clucking chickens running about the area were the only signs of life.

"This place is deserted," said Dorian.

"Yes it is," added Master Senex, "and the state of the dwellings tells me it has been so for quite some time."

"What a mess!" said Xiao Ren. "There are clothes and broken items strewn all over the place."

"I suppose Daemonia rampaged through here," added the Master.

"Speaking of Daemonia," said Solas, "I should get back to the Stealth Demon. He is probably waiting, wondering what's happened to me."

"Right!" said Dorian, chuckling.

"You mean to say *what's happened to us*," corrected Xiao Ren.

"No I don't," replied Solas. "I really think you should all stay here until my return. Who knows what awaits us out there? We have already lost the Noordjins, plus Dak and Broc, and I do not want to be responsible for anymore deaths."

"Have you gone mad?" objected Artin. "I did not come all this way for nothing. Dak and Broc would have chosen to fight on, and so do I."

"Being here is a personal choice I made, Solas," said Dorian. "No one forced me."

"That's correct. Besides, we cannot stop now, so close to victory, can we?" said Senex. "Have faith in us!"

"I do have faith in you, Master. But from here on, this is a matter between me and the Stealth Demon, and no one else," replied Solas. "I will go by myself to meet the Stealth Demon. I will defeat him and free Amy, but if I cannot do so alone, I will come back to seek your help. Now I just need you to stay low, and this place is as good as any. I won't be long."

Growing distant and phlegmatic, Solas grabbed the bridle of his animal and jumped on the back of his goglop before turning away from the group.

"I need to ramble on," he continued. "I need to find the queen of all my dreams."

Silent and sullen, his friends watched him stroll away out of the woods.

"What if Daemonia shows up?" Dorian yelled before Solas got too far.

Yet, his buddy never looked back or said another word.

"That's what I thought," mumbled Dorian, before shouting, "Godspeed Solas!"

"Godspeed!" repeated Senex and Xiao Ren.

Solas raised his right hand and waved.

11

When Solas reached the flatlands, the Stealth Demon was indeed waiting for him, alone, like a dark knight, sitting high and proud on top of his grim, minacious goglop. Solas stopped an instant to acknowledge the presence of the evil one, before nudging his creature to continue on its course. 'Eclipse' – as Solas now resumed calling his mount – began to trot at a steady gait toward the hell-sent, whose own goglop moaned and steamed before turning away and vanishing over the hill once again.

Solas loyally followed the Stealth Demon's lead, confident this would soon bring him to his final destination. As he crested the gentle slope of the last ridge, he saw, in the heart of the valley below, exactly what he had been hoping: the Diamond Tesseract.

The mythical portal stood unobstructed in the middle of the open field, gyrating and rotating in endless cycles, a perfect duplicate of the Tesseract of Earth Purgator. But as Solas now better understood, the object was one and the same, only seen from another one of its innumerable facets.

The legendary gateway was unique, but it was not alone. The magnificent Tesseract was the centerpiece of a stepped pyramid carved out of stone blocks, the glorious chef-d'oeuvre of some ancient Orboz civilization. Several other smaller structures surrounded the temple. And, as Solas expected, a number of Daemonia's fiercest warriors guarded the portal. Undeterred, Solas advanced. The beasts waited patiently for the outlander to arrive. Cautious, Solas approached and prepared Lux Veritas for battle but, to his surprise, the blade of his weapon did not activate.

Instead, Solas witnessed Daemonia retreating up the steps of the pyramid toward the Tesseract. Puzzled, Solas looked closer only to see the Stealth Demon jamming the Diamond Gates open, and sending dozens of his minions out through the portal, along with a number of other beasts, Orboz and imp riders on goglops. Solas jumped off Eclipse and climbed up the stairway until he stood a mere 20 feet away from his nemesis. The Stealth Demon welcomed him with a wry grin and a snarl.

Solas crept up closer yet, brandishing his still inert sword before him. He observed an abnormal gap in the Tesseract. By some masterful stroke, the Stealth Demon held the gateway open with the help of the dark Will-master's luret, and this anomaly allowed Daemonia ready access through the portal. The conquest of the universe had thus begun and the invasion of Earth Purgator was sure to be its ultimate pièce de résistance.

With all his minions having now crossed over to the other side of the portal, the Stealth Demon yanked on the luret and released his grip on the Diamond Gates. At once, the Tesseract resumed its usual forms and motions, reoccupying the space abandoned by the anomaly as though nothing had happened. As Solas negotiated the last step of the pyramid, he reached the platform and now stood alone and eye to eye with his bête noire.

12

It was late afternoon now. The heat of the red-hot sun waned while the one between the sworn enemies intensified. The two cautious foes stared at each other while circling about in little steps, waiting for some initial reaction or movement from the other.

"You wanted me to come," said Solas. "Well I came. Now where's Amy?"

The dark demon delayed his answer, half-snarling and half-chuckling under his viscous breath, before offering a measured, gargled response.

"Give the sword first."

"Well, this is quite simple now," said Solas. "No Amy, no sword!"

Seething with anger, the Stealth Demon frowned, but tried his best to keep his cool.

"Never!" he sputtered out, his blue blood racing just beneath his slick skin.

"Right, why don't you come and get it yourself then?" replied Solas. "That's why you brought me here, isn't it? Now get on with your plan already. Show me your guts!"

The beast laughed off the boy's dare.

"Your sword has no power against me."

"Come and take it then!" urged Solas. "Don't be such a coward!"

"You will not win," replied the Stealth Demon, before stuttering on. "The sword is useless to you. Just give up the weapon, and I will return to you … the girl."

"If Lux Veritas is so worthless, then why do you want her so bad, huh?" asked Solas, mocking the beast in turn.

The Stealth Demon settled down and assumed a more confident posture as he went on to explain.

"You are a naive and foolish boy," said he, chuckling. "You serve ... the wrong Master."

"You mean to tell me you enjoy this hell you live in!" interjected Solas.

"Your ignorance ... is pathetic," continued the dark beast, grinning. "You do not understand. Lord Chaos is kind and forgiving. He rewards all his faithful. Now give up the sword and you shall have the girl ... I promise."

The beast stretched out his bony hand and claws toward Solas in an open gesture of trust.

"You will never do that," replied Solas, "because you are heartless. You know neither love nor virtue. You are empty, just like Chaos is empty."

The Stealth Demon tensed up once more, grinding his teeth, while moaning and drooling gobs of slobber.

"I do not need your feelings," contested the Prince of Darkness. "It is not the Lord Creator who will heal your sufferings; it is Lord Chaos. He will destroy them all into oblivion. Then you will find only peace."

"Don't forget loneliness and despair!" replied Solas. "At least I feel alive."

"Not for much longer!" the Stealth Demon muttered through clenched teeth.

The two continued the stare-down with neither conceding an inch. With Lux Veritas still inactive, Solas realized he needed to resort to some other means in order to disarm the Stealth Demon and gain his trust, or risk never seeing Amy again. Regardless, he had no real desire to slay the beast before its time; that is, before finding his beloved one. Solas brainstormed his past encounters with the beast and recalled seeing a minute crack in the Stealth Demon's armor while tumbling through the vortex of the Wheel of Souls. No doubt, it was there that he had witnessed the glimpse of some other being beneath the evil façade, that of a human perhaps.

"I just know that somewhere deep down even you have a heart, don't you?" said Solas. "Everyone has a conscience. Perhaps there is some bad in everyone, but there is also some good in everyone. You are not just a beast. You were not always this way, so who are you really?"

These words, however, seemed to have no effect on the Stealth Demon, who kept pacing in small circles.

The stalemate endured for a while longer before Solas pushed the issue further.

"You visited my home, beautiful planet Earth," said Solas, "blue oceans, rugged mountains, lush lands. Where is your home? You were not born in Hell. Nobody is. So where do you come from?"

"Give me the sword," the restless beast insisted. "Then you can go free."

Solas ignored the attempt at bargaining and pressed on.

"Well you must have a name. What did your Mom call you? Me, I did not know my Mom. I had a loving grandmother instead. She was amazing." Solas smiled. "What about you, huh, who loved you? Who do you love?"

Solas soon concluded that he had found the magic formula when he noticed a peculiar and subtle change in the Stealth Demon.

13

The cracks in his mantle reappeared; sudden flashes of the soul buried deep beneath the layers of evil. The images were brief, but distinct enough to offer clues as to the identity of the Stealth Demon. An imprisoned soul cried out to be released. And it was more than Solas had hoped to discover. The boy dropped Lux Veritas to the ground and turned as pale as the ghost within the beast when he saw, during this spell of inner fireworks, that the soul in question was … him.

"It is us," said the demon, grinning. "I am Solas Gambit."

Solas was speechless.

"I am dead," the beast continued, "and you are alive. What is better? You were right about me; I am empty. I feel no pain. But you were also wrong; for I am free. *You* … are the slave."

Feeling nauseated, Solas picked up the sword at his feet and used her as a crutch. Then, he leaned over and emptied the contents of his bile.

Solas stood straight up again and struggled to regain his composure as the beast resumed being itself.

"No, it's not true," said Solas. "I am me, and you are you. We are different. It cannot be otherwise."

Amused, the Stealth Demon chuckled in spurts.

"Yes, I am you," insisted the beast. "You underestimate the powers of the infinite, of the Diamond Gates. I come from Earth too, in a parallel dimension, your perfect opposite."

"Lies!" yelled Solas, clearly unsettled by these revelations.

"It is true," said the Prince of Darkness, bearing on his face the most glorious grin of vindication.

"But how can you be so evil?" Solas shouted. "This is impossible."

"Black or white, which poison is better?" said the beast.

Distraught, Solas brandished Lux Veritas in front of him as though he expected an imminent attack from the beast. Still the sword remained inactive.

"What happened to you?" asked Solas, as he slowly gathered his wits.

"To us, you mean," corrected the Stealth Demon, before continuing in his coarse voice. "I do not remember. Lord Chaos said I am from Earth. He said I was depressed. When Grandma Jeanie died, I ended my life."

Odd glimpses of the young Solas zapped to the surface as the demon carried on speaking. Still gripping tight Lux Veritas, Solas listened attentively, his face whitened by the words he was hearing and the images he was seeing.

"You committed suicide?" he said, disgusted by the thought.

"I went to Tartarus," explained the Stealth Demon. "Your noble Lord Creator abandoned me, of course. But Daemonia and the ever-gracious Lord Chaos welcomed me. He offered me redemption. He told me about Lux Veritas, and blessed me with powers beyond words. He showed me ... eternal glory. I am his servant and the rightful keeper of the mighty Lux Veritas. It is my destiny. Give me the sword, Solas. Join us! We can be ... as one. We *are* one!"

Solas shook his head in utter disbelief.

"Well, it seems to me like you made the wrong choices!" said he. "You did have another option, you know."

"I had no options," the Stealth Demon explained. "We were lonely, Solas. You know about loneliness."

"And now?" asked Solas.

"No longer lonely," answered the beast, eyes aglow. "I am forever free."

Solas felt pity and regret about his own turn of fate in the alternate universe, and a tear began to roll down his cheek, following the crease of his scar to the corner of his mouth. The voice of the demon steadied.

"Stop this endless game Solas, and give me the sword," he urged calmly.

Solas's pain was visible almost as much as it was tangible.

"You're right!" he concluded, trembling and shaking his head. Seeing himself as the Stealth Demon, he now felt betrayed by the Lord creator too. "Bring me to Amy, and I will give you the sword. I just want to go home."

The Stealth Demon welcomed this decision, and one last image of Solas as a happy 10-year old boy waved at him from deep within the beast.

14

Now the dark Prince signalled Solas to follow him. He led him inside the corridors of the stone temple where a series of pathways led to several small, multipurpose chambers. Solas was cautious; still his heart began to palpitate faster in expectation of seeing Amy again. At last, they approached a room guarded by a couple of wingless gargoyles. Lux Veritas continued to remain inactive as the Stealth Demon burst into the chamber with Solas behind him.

A pair of Orboz sentinels kept vigil inside the damp quarters where, sitting in the middle of the room and bound with rope to a cedar pole, was the blond girl of Solas's dreams.

"Solas!" she screamed.

"Amy!" he replied in like fashion. "Are you all right?"

"Yes! Yes I am," she answered. "Please be careful Solas!"

Indeed, Solas found Amy to be in good spirits and quite lively for a girl who had spent – be it only a few days – compromising moments in the heart of a dungeon among mindless brutes and beasts, and the evil one.

"Now release Amy!" ordered Solas.

"The sword first!" replied the Stealth Demon.

"Not yet!" objected Solas. "I will give you the sword once Amy and I have reached safety, outside of this rat hole."

Growing at once impatient and suspicious, the Stealth Demon grinned at the boy, flashing his pearly-white razor-sharp teeth.

"Beware!" said the beast. "I know you well, Solas … too well."

One look at his Orboz sentries and the duo hurried to cut Amy loose, and brought her fast to their master.

"Bastards!" she said as she landed in the demon's arms.

"Let's go," said the Stealth Demon. "Let's get some fresh air. I will set Amy free and you will give me the sword … as promised."

The Stealth Demon rushed out of the room, manhandling a reluctant Amy who grunted all the while. The two Orboz Sentries and the two wingless gargoyles followed in step right behind their boss, with Solas keeping pace at the back.

Night was falling, but the natural glow of the Gate of Sefira – as the Orboz and Noordjins called the Diamond Gates – lit up the summit of the stone pyramid, just as the reddish solar dish lowered over the distant horizon. Bats now began their sorties, sending out shrilling notes as they swooped back and forth between the parties.

"No more games!" said the Stealth Demon, in his usual gargling tone. "Hand over the sword, and I will release the girl."

Solas hesitated as the beast now applied more pressure onto Amy's arm. The stalemate continued.

"The girl!" insisted Solas.

"Okay," said the Stealth Demon. He tossed Amy to the ground halfway to Solas, just as the two Orboz guards armed their bows and aimed their arrows at Amy. "Now toss the sword," ordered the demon, "or the girl dies."

Amy, still on the ground, looked up to see two steel arrows aimed at her point-blank.

"Fine," said Solas.

The young man presented his static weapon at arm's length, as though he was about to throw it to the ground. Solas lifted his eyes and, unfazed, stared deep into the hollow of his evil counterpart's soul and began to mumble a few inaudible words, which made the Stealth Demon squint in wonderment. Solas was awaking the Will-master's luret. Forthwith, the mystic curio created a cocoon, and just before the relic completed the task, Solas dove toward Amy to allow her under its protective shell. The Orboz archers fired their missiles at the couple, but as they did so, Lux Veritas reactivated and crumpled the arrows on impact.

This trickery and bold act of defiance enraged the Stealth Demon to the brink of madness. Nonetheless, Lux Veritas was too great a foe, and the beast agonized over its burning desire to strike. Indeed, the Stealth Demon was back in full form. Solas and Amy stood up inside the cocoon, and despite the circumstances and the presence of pure evil, they embraced like never before.

"I knew you would make it, Solas," said Amy. "I never doubted."

Solas smiled.

"Life without you ... was never an option," he replied.

Still, the matter at hand was pressing and the Stealth Demon held little sympathy for open displays of heart-warming moments.

"Pathetic you are," said the beast.

"Jealous are we?" replied Solas.

The beast chuckled.

"You just made Lord Chaos proud, foolish boy," retorted the snarly demon, "going back on your word like this. What a fine disciple you make!"

"In your dreams!" said Solas.

A light melodious chime accompanied the luret, which was now in full force, and behind the couple, a facet of the Diamond Gates parted and held still.

"Well, it's time to go now," said Solas.

Amused, the Prince of Darkness chuckled some more while his whole demeanor changed. Oddly, he had regained confidence and seemed calm and appeased.

"See you soon!" he said, in a deriding voice.

Solas had the sudden impression that the Stealth Demon was up to something. He had given up Amy much too easily. *Am I falling for his ploy?* He thought. *If so, what could it be?* Concerned but resolute, Solas waved goodbye to the beast while Amy sent him a mock kiss just as the couple exited through the Diamond Tesseract.

Over in the abandoned village set on the edge of the temperate forest of Orboz, Solas's friends had gathered inside a hut and sat by the light of a single torch. As they prepared for the night, Master Senex held his small audience captive and expressed his views about the state of things that are, things that were and things that shall be.

"This is something Solas must do," said the Master, "alone!"

"And what if he fails and he doesn't come back?" asked Dorian.

"Has the light of faith entirely vanished from your heart, my boy?" asked Senex. "Of course he will be back!"

"I wish it were that easy, Master," replied Dorian. "That Stealth Demon looks some kind of nasty, let me tell you! Plus, he's got that dark luret too. Lord knows what the beast is able to do with that thing. Why does a dark luret even exist anyhow? Isn't one enough?"

The Master hesitated while pondering this issue.

"Well, you've heard it said before my good Dorian," he replied, "*the Lord works in mysterious ways*, and there's your proof. But methinks there's more to it than that," he continued. "It would appear that the same principles governing the laws of universal physics also govern the laws of universal karma."

"Whatever are you talking about, Master?" said Dorian, grimacing at the thought he was about to get more of an answer than he bargained for.

"How well do you remember the lessons in your physics class, my boy?" asked Senex.

"Not much really, I'm happy to say," replied Solas. "I'd say receiving a slap shot to the head would be more fun. What a sweatshop that class was!"

"Well, never mind then," replied the Master, frowning. "All you really need to consider is that the physical universe and spiritual existence are a dichotomy; we are matter and spirit at once, a dual reality. We cannot be only matter or we would not know we exist, and we cannot be only spirit because our thoughts would have no form."

"Whose thoughts ... our thoughts?" asked Dorian.

"The Lord Creator's thoughts, of course! He is the only true essence," replied the Master. "Hence, the physical universe is in principle nothing but a projection of all the Lord Creator's thought manifestations, past, present and future, all at once. Anyway, in order to exist there must be – to give you an example – an up for every down …"

"And for every over, there must be an under …" added Dorian.

"You got it!" said the Master. "And for every positive …"

"A negative!"

"That's it! And for every proton …"

"You lost me now!" Dorian conceded.

"… an electron," continued the Master, "for every matter, an antimatter; for every light, a dark; for every life, a death. That is just the way it is, my boy. It is a karmic necessity."

"Well, that's an interesting way to look at things, Master. That would explain why we have two Will-master's lurets. But what about a dark Lux Veritas then?" asked Dorian.

Dorian's statement had Senex perplexed.

"Well, if it exists, it has never been found," the Master concluded, "or at least not yet. Perhaps someone will find it someday or perhaps Lux Veritas is so unique that it has no equal. It is, after all, the Sword of Genesis."

The conversation continued as such for a while, and all the musing small talk about good and bad, justice and injustice; all had a certain effect on the lone Millikeen guard left in the midst. Artin experienced some flash epiphany, a reckoning of sort, to be sure. He awakened from deep thought and turned to address his leprechaun prisoner.

"And you, my friend, are free," he said. "Free as the wind! I tell you no lie."

Fergus could not believe his ears and looked all around him to see if all those present were hearing this overt confession, coming straight out of blue yonder.

"All this time, I truly thought you a coward," continued Artin. "I believed that your victory against the great Og'Dar was a fluke … but not anymore. You were bold and brave, and in the heat of battle, you risked your life to save mine. I know not why, but this I cannot ever forget. I am the one indebted to you now. Therefore, you are free. We are even."

Not often did Fergus lose his tongue, but for a short moment, he did.

"Do ye mean it?" replied the jovial leprechaun. "Are ye sure?"

"I am," answered Artin.

"Ye will not go about changing yer mind after it, will ye?" continued Fergus. "I don't know, perhaps ye suffered some kind of sunstroke or whatnot. I need to be sure. Give me yer word before mine witnesses here, will ye?"

"Just accept it before I change my mind," replied the vexed Millikeen guard.

"All right, all right!" said Fergus. "Ye're a fine fellow indeed. I do thank ye!"

The leprechaun stood up, grabbed Artin with both hands, planted a kiss on his forehead – to the Millikeen guard's disgust – and began to chant *for he's a jolly good fellow* and weave about the floor in some obscure folklorish elf dance of old.

"Be quiet already, you silly gnome!" ordered Artin, "your ruckus will set off Daemonia."

Upon this warning, the disappointed leprechaun stopped dead in his tracks, long enough for the startled group to hear the nearby sounds of branches and twigs snapping underfoot.

16

The leprechaun took cover and joined his four other mates already leaning against the inside wall of the wooden shack. Master Senex snuffed out the torch. Quietly, Artin and Xiao Ren readied their weapons as Dorian peeked out over the ledge of the open window to inspect the true nature of the intruders. The darkness had set upon the forest and – were it not for the streaks of natural light penetrating through the canopy from the ascending triple moons of Orboz – visibility was nil. He did see, however, someone's small guiding light bobbing by the brook. Then, abruptly, Dorian stood up.

"Solas!" he exclaimed, "Amy!" And he darted out the front door.

Surprised by Dorian's words, the group hurried right behind him as Master Senex rekindled, with a flash of druid magic, their only source of light.

Dorian greeted his friends just as the couple finished crossing the calm, shallow creek of the unearthly village.

"Amy!" said a cheerful Dorian. "Thank God you're alive. Come here and give your big bro a hug!"

Amy smiled and jumped into her friend's arms. Dorian all but swallowed her whole with his large muscular arms. He squeezed her tight and sent her on a wild whirligig with unrestrained joy and laughter. He set her back down so that Xiao Ren could have her moment too. Then he high-fived his buddy Solas.

"You did it, O Captain! My Captain!" he said as he hugged his pal like some giant teddy bear. "Well then, how did you slay the Stealth Demon? Tell us!"

At that moment, the short celebration stopped and the world held its breath while awaiting the response.

"Well, you slew the beast, right?" Dorian asked again in much more solemn fashion.

But Solas's hesitation and silence gave away the answer no one wanted to hear.

Solas took in a deep breath and sighed.

"I managed to get Amy out," he said. "That was half the battle. As for the other half, well … the Stealth Demon is much too clever."

"Well, what will you do about it now?" asked Dorian.

"It is not what *I* will do about it," replied Solas, "it is what *you* will do about it."

"You know what, if you and Senex could just stop speaking in tongues for once, the world would be a better place, for sure!" replied Dorian, clearly frustrated with the situation and fed up with the Gambit family charades.

"Well it isn't just you, Dorian," clarified Solas. "It is really up to Master Senex."

"What is it now my boy?" asked the old druid. "I am not the man I used to be – nor the druid. I cannot take on the Stealth Demon, I am afraid. That is your cross to bear Solas!"

"That is not what I had in mind," replied Solas, as he scanned the area, fearing a resurgence of Daemonia at any given moment. "I have a much better idea. Let's get inside the hut and I will tell you all about it."

The members of the group nodded and retreated to the shelter.

Once in safer quarters, Solas began to explain in detail his tête-à-tête with the Stealth Demon on top of the great pyramid where the Diamond Tesseract stands. He held his friends mesmerized by telling how the beast was gifted enough to keep the Diamond Gates open and let through countless of Chaos's minions, thereby sending much evil to the four corners of the universe. Then his friends were even more appalled to learn about the apparent identity of the Prince of Darkness.

"The Stealth Demon was you!" said Dorian, in utter disbelief. "I mean … he is you!"

"There are two of you, Solas!" said Xiao Ren. "How can this be?"

"Me guess there are two Senex, two Dorians, two Xiao Rens, two Artins and even two Fergus as well," added the leprechaun who was thoroughly amused by this proposition. "I would love to meet me counterpart," he continued. "How fun, yes?"

"You forgot two Amys!" added Dorian, who seemed to be keeping count.

"Well that is just absurd," replied Amy. "We are all unique, no?"

Solas, however, knew better and locked eyes with his high school sweetheart. Solas had seen within the beast, and evil does take many forms indeed.

"I am not at all surprised," said the Master. "That is precisely what I attempted to explain to you earlier, my good Dorian."

"Oh yeah," replied Dorian, "all that duality talk!"

"And you thought me mad!"

"All I can say is that I saw only a beast," said Amy. "There was no sign of Solas in there. The Stealth Demon is pure fire and ice, and nothing else."

"Well, I am sure glad you survived this ordeal, Amy," said Xiao Ren. "Even your injuries have disappeared."

"What injuries?" said Amy.

"The ones Solas told us about … you know the ones you received from the Stealth Demon just before he kidnapped you."

"That's true!" remarked Dorian. "You were bleeding, and there are no traces left on your neck or face at all."

"Oh those ones!" replied Amy. "The Stealth Demon healed my wounds by applying some special salve on them."

"Why would he do that?" asked Solas. "He has feelings now?"

"Are you jealous, Solas?" she replied with a smile. "He just wanted to keep me alive, I guess. I am not worth anything dead, am I?"

Solas remained perplexed, as were his friends.

"Please tell us about your plan, Solas," she continued. "I'm dying to know how you will destroy the Stealth Demon."

"Yes, do go on Solas," concurred the Master, eager to discover his role in this matter.

"Okay," said Solas, "here's the plan. I need Master Senex to go back in time to parallel planet Earth and intercept young Master Senex, Georges Gambit, before he meets his wife to be, Grandma Jeanie. You must stop this event from happening. In doing so, you will prevent my father from being born and ultimately me, Solas Gambit, for in that alternate reality I will become the future Stealth Demon."

"So you are thinking about altering destiny Solas?" asked Dorian.

"What do you hope to accomplish by doing this?" asked Amy.

"Well, since I cannot engage the Stealth Demon into a fight with Lux Veritas, I can eliminate him from existence altogether."

"I still don't get it," said Amy.

"I get it!" said the Master. "The Stealth Demon will simply vanish into nothingness. He will be no more since he never was."

"Our problem will be solved without ever engaging him into battle," concluded Dorian.

"Bingo! But that's only if we succeed," clarified Solas.

"Why don't you do it Solas? Why Master Senex?" asked Dorian.

"That's because I know precisely how I met Jeanie and at what exact moment," answered Senex, already daydreaming and smiling at the possibility. "The idea has merit. This old man just needs to stall his little angel Jeanie, the love of my life, for a little while."

"Well then tell us how ye met her, ye big silly, the suspense is killing me," said Fergus. "Even the two goglops are getting excited about it."

Indeed, the usually quiet-as-a-mouse goglops resting in the adjacent shelter began to moan and stir from their sleep.

"The goglops?" said Xiao Ren, surprised.

But before the group understood the reason for the commotion, the blade of Lux Veritas exuded light through the hilt of the sword.

"It's Daemonia!" said Solas who whipped out his weapon. "Gather around me," he ordered, "I will get us out of here."

Solas commanded the luret and the mystical item formed a cocoon all around the group, just as the demons beat down on the walls and surged through the doors and windows of their refuge. Then, like a flash, the luret whisked away the voyagers, leaving behind nothing but a sparkling trail on its exit path through the trees and beyond into the darkness of the starlit sky.

Chapter VIII

Exit Destiny

"It is not in the stars to hold our destiny but in ourselves."

—William Shakespeare (1564 – 1616)

I

Solas weaved his space pod through the fields of mystic dimensions with increasing mastery and with the uncanny insight of a tested veteran of a thousand psychic wars. The next landing was quick and smooth and came about sooner than later.

"Well you sure got the knack of that thing now!" said Dorian to his pal.

"This place looks familiar," said Xiao Ren.

"It should," replied Solas, "we're back where we began our voyage, at the Diamond Tesseract beneath Holy Mountain."

"We're home!" shouted Fergus, clearly overjoyed.

"And here comes the Sage of the Grotto, Lord Uffa himself!" said Solas.

The old and lanky druid approached the travelers with open arms.

"Solas, welcome back! I see you have mastered the luret," he said. "And you are back so soon. Please give me the good news!"

"I am afraid the job is not done yet," replied Solas, "but I freed Amy and I know where to find the Stealth Demon. The purpose of my short visit here is to bring back Fergus and Artin, as I promised. We have had enough bloodshed with the loss of Broc and Dak, and besides, these two cannot follow us to where we are headed next without jeopardizing our mission."

"Broc and Dak!" replied Uffa. "What fine little souls they were. May their bravery find favor with the Lord Creator!"

"Tell me Uffa, how are things since we left Purgator?" asked Solas.

"Well, right after you left, there was a series of battles throughout the tunnels of Holy Mountain, from top to bottom and from far and wide," answered the sage. "By necessity, the Millikeen folks and the leprechauns joined forces in order to repel the common foe, Daemonia. They succeeded ... at least for now. But I must tell you, the influx of beasts barging through the Diamond Gates continues. How long can Holy Mountain resist? Be quick and be thorough my good Solas, the whole of Purgator has already suffered much devastation."

Fergus and Artin, however, looked at each other and smiled upon hearing the news of the merger of their two nations. Indeed, they concluded, miracles do happen when folks – even those who were once enemies – face a common threat and come under great duress.

For Solas, Lord Uffa's status report was bittersweet. At least there was still hope and time to turn back the tide of evil.

"Fergus and Artin!" said Solas. "I want to thank you both for all of your help. You are free to return home now. Find your people and help in the fight against Daemonia. Victory will be ours soon."

"And I want to thank ye too Solas," said Fergus. "Ye saved me life more than a few times, and none more so than when ye dropped Luxie in the Og'Dar pit. I owe ye. Godspeed, Solas Gambit!"

Solas smiled.

"Thank you as well," said Artin in a most humble way, "it was a great honor to serve by your side, by Lux Veritas!"

Solas tapped the Millikeen guard on the shoulder and soon the brave Artin and Fergus hurried on their way to rejoin their kindred, and vanished by the closest tunnel exit leading up Holy Mountain.

Now only the high school quartet remained, plus Master Senex, whose presence tickled his fellow druid, the watchman of the Gates, Lord Uffa.

"Ha! If it isn't my old confrere Senex, the Mirandia crystal wizard," said Uffa. "Who would have thought we would meet again under such dire circumstances? How are you my friend?"

The two magicians faced each other, and in many respects – notably regarding their attire and their frazzled greyish hair – the two were much alike.

"Good to see you, Uffa!" replied Senex. "So this is where you make your stand, is it?"

"This is home!" answered Uffa. "Say, I could sure use some of that crystal dust of yours, if you should have any to spare at all. I would be much obliged."

"I'm afraid that sort of magic is in scarce supply these days," replied Senex. "I am all out."

"We must lead an expedition to that majestic tree someday, Senex," said Uffa, "and fill our needs once and for all. We can never have enough."

"Easier said than done!" admitted the Master. "Come the day, I will see to it that my good little elkin Fidem brings you a pouch full."

"That would be so kind, thank you," replied Uffa, before continuing. "And in return, I will…"

Solas understood the importance of reconnecting with acquaintances of old. These were always special times, but right now, time was also pressing.

"We must be going!" he said, interrupting the conversation. "We have unfinished business to attend to, as you are well aware Lord Uffa. We will catch up later."

"Yes indeed," the Sage of the Grotto acknowledged, "yes indeed! Be fast on your way then, and at our next encounter, I shall expect great news."

"Oh, do not worry!" replied Solas. "You will be the first to know."

"Yes and what's more," added Senex, "we shall celebrate the occasion by filling our chalice to the brim with the spirit of that crimson fruit that grows so well back home in the fields of Morphos!"

"I love it!" replied Uffa, as he waved farewell to the group. "I shall be expecting you right soon then. Now Godspeed, my friends!"

Solas summoned the luret posthaste, and before too long, the group transited through the open facets of the Diamond Tesseract: destination yesteryear, parallel planet Earth.

2

Solas continued to display his growing talent by steering his ship through an esoteric medley of interstellar nebulae and ethereal realities, none of which any of the pod passengers were able to tell apart with certainty. What first lieutenant Dorian could clearly discern, however, was hesitance in Captain Solas's navigating.

"Hey matey, where you be taking us now?" asked Dorian.

"To alter the past, of course," replied Solas, "in order to rid us of that pest the Stealth Demon. I know how to reach his home planet because I got an awesome vibe from him regarding his origins. What I do need is a precise period in time to take us there. I need Master Senex to remember and pinpoint the exact moment and place where he met Grandma Jeanie the first time. And this has to be spot on."

"Did you hear that Master Senex?" asked Dorian. "Where did you meet Mrs. Gambit after all?"

"Well it was ages ago, but it still feels like yesterday," answered the smiling old man, starting an ascent into reverie. "It was Union Station in New Haven, Connecticut, back in May of 1963. Jeanie stole my heart the moment I laid eyes on her."

Now, Xiao Ren was smiling too.

"What was the date, Master Senex?" Solas demanded abruptly.

"It was May 10th," replied Senex. "I will never forget."

"What time was it?" continued Solas. "We need to narrow this time frame down. We can't be off."

"Well let me see now," said the Master, engaging into full pensive mode, "you're asking a lot of an old man, you know."

"Concentrate, and please be accurate," said Solas, "we need to hit the bull's eye."

"Well, it was a sunny Friday morning, as I recall," explained the Master. "Jeanie and I met just before boarding the 8 o'clock morning train. Yes, it was 8 o'clock."

"Are you sure about this, 8 o'clock?" asked Solas. "Focus Master! I will pick up on your vibes."

"Well let me see now," Senex replied. "I was catching the train back home to Sherbrooke, and so was Jeanie. I had been studying philosophy at Yale at the time and Jeanie was studying law there. Our exams were over and the student riots had begun overnight. So in the morning we took the first train out of town. Yes, it was at 8 o'clock!"

"Student riots?" said Dorian, shocked.

"Yes, the riots spread from Princeton to Harvard and then to Yale!"

"What were they rioting for?" asked Dorian.

"The boys wanted sex!"

"Sex?"

"Yes," continued Senex, "during the night, thousands of young men left Vanderbilt Hall and marched toward Hadley Hall, which was the women's dormitory where Jeanie was staying. They were shouting *"We want sex! We want sex!"* but when they arrived, the police was already waiting for them."

"Wow!" said Dorian. "You guys had your hormones set on overdrive back then. And I thought you guys were all just dull nerds."

"I beg your pardon!" said the Master. "We were alive and well, thank you! We were demonstrating our freedom of expression … *and our burning passion for the fairer sex, I suppose.* It was the birth of Rock'n Roll, you know."

"Can you please just stay focused Master?" begged Solas. "And get to it!"

"Yes of course," replied Senex. "To make a long story short, we caught the 8 o'clock train back home. By coincidence or by divine providence, I met Jeanie on the dock that morning. I helped her lift her suitcase; she was struggling with it. And that's how our romance began."

"So that's how you met?" said Dorian. "You and Mrs. Gambit were running away from riots!"

"Well, young man," replied the Master, "I am quite grateful for those riots indeed. We could not stay on campus anymore, and while running away from chaos, disorder and sex demands, we both found love."

"That's kind of cool," added Dorian, "but I'm afraid you are not finished dealing with Chaos just yet."

"Quite right!" replied Senex just before Solas made an announcement.

"Parallel planet Earth, 7:45 A.M., May 10, 1963, Union Station docks, New Haven, Connecticut, here we come!"

No sooner said than done, Solas soft-landed his vessel and its occupants out of sight of the general public, square on the tracks, behind the last wagon of the first train to Sherbrooke.

3

The cocoon fast fizzled away upon landing and the group visually explored their surroundings to confirm their position. The posted signs read *New Haven Station*, and the standing whistle clock indicated the precise hour of day: 7:46 A.M.

"Home sweet home!" declared Senex, delighted to be back in the world of the living.

"Good job Solas!" said Dorian. "Now let's just hope this is May 10th."

Peeking over the edge of the docks from the far end of the terminal, the group noticed the quay bustling with people, many of them boarding the train.

"It is May 10th," said a confident Senex. "I remember this vagrant over here fumbling about the docks crying to behold, that the end times were upon us and that Jesus had landed in a spaceship."

Indeed, sitting alone on a bench, a drunken hobo, bottle in hand, watched the luret scene unfold before him. Bedazzled, he guzzled down more of his elixir and wobbled to his feet.

"Hallelujah!" he proclaimed, pointing at Senex with his bottle. "Jesus is here! Jesus is here! Praise the Lord!"

The group quickly jumped up on the docks as the tramp made half-hearted attempts at getting the attention of the crowd.

"Master, the drunkard seems to think you're Jesus," said Dorian, laughing.

The vagabond then stumbled away in the general direction of the public lining up to board the train. Many people were now heading toward the end wagons too.

"He is confused. I guess it must be my appearance," said Senex.

"Perhaps," added Solas, "but he probably saw us landing too."

"Do you think anyone else saw us, Solas?" asked Dorian, "I mean, when we entered the atmosphere."

"If they did, they won't find us anyway," replied Solas. "They'll think we were a comet, just like they did back in 2014."

| CHRISTOPHER DIGNAN

"We are kind of dressed in funny clothes though, aren't we?" said Xiao Ren.

"Well if someone asks, just say you're going to a hippy convention in California," answered Solas. "This is the sixties after all."

"Okay Solas," replied Jiji, "but Dorian and I carry weapons, and you have Lux Veritas!"

"Well, I am leaving now anyway," said Solas, "because while you guys are busy stopping young Master Senex from meeting Grandma Jeanie, Amy and I will head back to Orboz Purgator to face the Stealth Demon. This whole operation should only take 10 or 15 minutes at most, if we succeed! You do remember where you were and what you were doing that morning Master Senex?"

"Sure I do!" he answered. "I met your grandma by the third car, right over there." He pointed to the spot in the distance.

"Give me all your weapons," said Solas, "you won't need them here. Now I am counting on you Master; our success depends on it. Now hurry and I will come back to get you once we have vanquished the Stealth Demon. Godspeed my friends!"

Amy slotted away Dorian's katana and strapped Xiao Ren's bow and arrows on her back. The couple rushed off down the tracks and away from the station. In full stride, the cocoon appeared and the pair shot up straight into the open blue sky.

The return trip to Orboz Purgator was short. Solas and Amy passed through the Diamond Gates, landing just in front of the Tesseract – the towering centerpiece of this ancient and mysterious pyramid.

"Quick!" Solas said to Amy. "Find the Stealth Demon. You probably know these corridors better than I do."

"I do know where my cell was," replied Amy. "And if I remember well, the Stealth Demon's chamber was next to it. Follow me!"

The couple wound their way down the galleries as quietly as possible until they reached Amy's detention quarters. The room was empty. The pair reached the back door, where they listened for any sound of activity on the other side. Nothing.

"This is it!" Amy articulated silently, pointing to the door.

Solas readied his sword and Amy jerked the door open. Still, no one was around. The confines of the pyramid seemed deserted.

"I don't believe this," said Solas. "Relatively speaking, we were here only a short time ago, mere minutes really. The torches are still burning bright; the rope that bound you to the pole is still there. The Stealth Demon must be close. I smell something rotten here. Do you have any ideas, Amy?"

The couple remained still and pensive. Once more, time was of the essence. Solas needed to destroy the Stealth Demon and retrieve the dark luret – the primary objective – without setting the wrath of Daemonia upon him, which could allow the dark Prince to get away. Meanwhile, as the pair pressed to find a solution to their current dilemma, Dorian, Xiao Ren and Master Senex worked hard on resolving theirs.

4

Back on the Union Station docks of New Haven, Senex and his two helpers mingled in the crowd, and casually made their way toward the third coach where assuredly young Jeanie Sounders – the future Mrs. Gambit – would soon make her appearance. Vested in their loose outlander garb, Dorian and Xiao Ren thought to play the part of peacemongers, clapping their hands and singing in tune *Hare Krishna* and *Give Peace A Chance*.

"No, no, no," said the Master. "You cannot sing that song."

"Why not?" asked Dorian. "We're protesting the Vietnam war. It's perfect."

"Yes, but John Lennon did not compose the song just yet. It does not exist."

"So what?" Dorian replied. "Who will know the difference? We'll jump-start the little ditty right here, right now. Cool, huh?"

"Master," said Xiao Ren, "how do we know what Mrs. Gambit looks like? Which way is she arriving from?"

"Oh, Jeanie will be the beautiful young lady with the red velvet minidress, the white go-go boots and gloves, and the floral print headscarf. You can't miss her!"

"She sounds cute and classy," said Xiao Ren.

"Yes, she had style!" said a smiling Senex, temporarily off to dreamland again and quite happy to refocus on the task. "I remember coming up behind her from the station. She must have been a minute before me I guess. She struggled with her luggage; she had packed everything into it, you know. So I offered to help."

"Well aren't you the perfect gentlemen, Master Senex!" said Xiao Ren.

The clock now read 7:52. The crowd bustled on every part of the docks as several trains were leaving near the same hour in different directions.

Dorian came up with an idea.

"I tell you what," he said. "Jiji and I will go to the doors of the terminal to intercept *you*, Master. We must delay your arrival at the coach; even make *you* miss the train, if possible. We need to eliminate all possibilities of *you* meeting up with Jeanie at all. And you, Master, will go help Jeanie with her luggage. Do make sure she gets on that train and sitting where *you* would not notice her – in a different car perhaps – just in case *you* still managed to sneak on that train somehow. How does that sound?"

"And to think I doubted your creativity!" replied Senex. "I love it!"

"So what does a young Master Senex look like in 1963?" asked Xiao Ren.

"Oh yes of course," said the Master. "In those days I think I wore black slacks and a pale blue Yale cardigan."

"You think?" asked Dorian.

"Why yes!" replied Senex. "It's funny, isn't it? I can sure remember Jeanie, but I don't remember me so well."

"Okay, a blue Yale University cardigan it is!" said Dorian. "Anything else?"

"Yes," answered Senex with a grin, "if you have any doubts, look for the handsome kid!"

Dorian shook his head.

"Now I know where Solas gets his sense of humor! Let's go Jiji!"

Xiao Ren smiled and gave the Master a kiss on the forehead, wishing him good luck. The pair hurried off toward the front doors of the terminal, leaving the old man alone on his mission. The Master refocused on the task and sighed as he heard the drunkard slurring and preaching to deaf ears *"The savior has landed … Hic … Repent!"* Senex turned away and walked steadfast toward the third coach to await the arrival of his belle of yesteryear.

5

A sentiment of frustration gripped Solas over his futile search for the Stealth Demon.

"He was here a minute ago, I swear. Where could he be now? He knew I would come back for him!"

Since Amy could offer no worthy suggestions of note, Solas began to yell his lungs out "Show yourself you bastard! I am right here, right now, right where you wanted me! You won't chicken out now, will you?"

Still nothing.

Solas slotted his weapon in its sheath, as Amy attempted to cajole him. She seized him around the waist, drawing him snug so she could pierce into his deep blue eyes.

"Patience, my love," she said. "It will all work out in the end."

Solas forced a smile as he stared back into the depth of her soul.

"Yes, it will work out, but for good or for evil?"

"Do you doubt?"

"Yes, you're right," he replied. "I should never doubt, least of all your wisdom. You are my last and true beacon of hope in this tumultuous sea of despair."

"I am glad!" she whispered, smiling and content.

"And besides," he continued, "there was only truth in the beginning, and there will only be truth in the end, right? Good *always* triumphs over Evil."

Caught in this momentary vacuum of passion, Amy nodded her head gently in agreement. Her eyes sparkled as she edged up ever closer to kiss her man.

"Are you sure now?" she murmured softly, scarce millimetres away from locking lips with Solas.

"Yes," answered a confident Solas, "I am sure."

Just then, with his eyes nearly blinded by love, Solas caught in the reflection of Amy's pupils the brilliant spark of Lux Veritas, and behind it, the stark specter of evil.

Solas stalled cold the embrace.
"Oh Amy," he said, "Why, oh why?"
She frowned, as though she did not understand.

Guided by pure instinct, Solas rolled to his left in extremis to avoid a mortal strike from the Stealth Demon. The end of the blade intended for Solas found Amy instead, plunging straight through her abdomen right below the rib cage. Amy heaved nary a moan as her eyes swelled in shock and disbelief. Blood gushed from her lips as she stared into the hollows of the Stealth Demon's eyes. The beast grimaced and yanked the blade out from her body, and watched Amy collapse to the cold, hard floor. The Wheel of Souls appeared at once and whirled like a typhoon to snatch Amy's essence away.

The beast unleashed a wail to the heavens that shook the foundations of Tartarus. Unsettled, Solas stumbled away to a safe distance while seizing Lux Veritas. When the Stealth Demon came around at last, he calmly turned his face toward Solas and, with a look of absolute dejection, swore to get revenge.

"Now it's your turn to pay."

The demon walked straight past Solas – spewing gobs of drool at him like poison that sizzled away near Lux Veritas – and burst through the door into the next chamber. There, muted, blindfolded and bound to another cedar pole was – much to the shock and relief of Solas – Amy.

The Stealth Demon released the girl from bondage and held her by the throat flush against his chest to face Solas.

"Solas!" she said, half-sobbing with delight. "Be careful, there is another Amy!"

"Thank you my love!" he replied. "I know. Don't panic; everything will be alright now."

"Drop the sword!" ordered the beast. "Or Amy dies!"

"You won't do that," replied Solas. "Killing one Amy was enough already, wasn't it? I saw you out there. You had feelings, emotions, passion. There is still hope for you after all. Perhaps there is still time for you to join the Lord Creator. He forgives, you know. Now let go Amy!"

"Join the Lord Creator!" said the Stealth Demon, amused. "You pathetic little runt, don't you understand? The battle will never end. It will continue until Lord Chaos becomes Lord of the whole universe again. He will never stop. The universe is chaos, and Chaos is the universe. Don't you see? Your existence is nothing but a quirk, a mishap, a hiccup, a petty reflux in the vast cosmic sea of darkness. You pretentious little minnows give yourselves too much importance. You are a mistake. You will never last. You don't matter. Nothing matters."

"On the contrary," replied Solas, "we are all that matters. The rest is only cosmic noise, pure nonsense and self-denial. And here is your proof: even *you* cannot ignore us! Now accept it and join us instead. Let go Amy!"

"Give me the sword!" warned the Stealth Demon, clearly angered, as he pressed harder on Amy's throat. "I won't even count to three."

As Solas tried to find a quick answer, his deepest thoughts and strongest hopes turned to Master Senex. He prayed for success ... and this right soon.

6

Meantime, as Senex nervously waited over by the third car door for the arrival of Jeanie, while trying to recall the events of that fateful day so many moons ago, Dorian and Xiao Ren entered inside the station hall. Throngs of people still cued the long lines hoping to buy last minute tickets to catch the early trains out of town.

"Young Master must be in there somewhere," said Jiji.

"Look for the blue Yale cardigans," said Dorian.

"There are so many though!" noted Jiji.

"We'll go one by one, by process of elimination," Dorian proposed. "No doubt a lot of these young fellows were up to no good last night. I guess many are attempting to skip town, before the police catch up to them and lay misdemeanor charges on a few of the troublemakers responsible. Someone always has to take the fall somehow!"

"And speak of the devil," added Jiji, "here come the police!"

Indeed, a number of officers patrolled the station observing movements in the crowd and casually eye searching for a few particular individuals of interest. Dorian and Jiji – pretending to be anti-war hippy activists – methodically moved through the lines of waiting people, studying every possible match for a young Senex, while proclaiming *"Peace to all mankind,"* and *"Stop the killing in Vietnam – Stop the war machine!"*

"Look Dorian!" said Jiji, as she pointed to a man fifth in line over on the third row. "It's him! I found him."

Dorian took a closer look at the individual.

"Good job, Jiji!" he said, convinced the man in question was young Senex. "This one is a carbon copy."

The couple hurried towards him – as though he might get away – cutting through the lines, bumping into people while begging their forgiveness.

Young Senex appeared at a loss to understand why there were now two smiling hippies standing right at his side.

"Godspeed Georges!" said Dorian quite loud in order to garner attention. "Are you leaving Yale already?"

"Do I know you?" retorted young Senex, perplexed.

"It isn't because of last night, is it?" continued Dorian. "Man, you were like a wild animal out there. Way to stand up for our rights, man! I love you, brother. Peace!"

Dorian raised his arms in the air and made the peace sign, expecting a forthcoming brotherly embrace from young Georges Gambit.

"What in the hell are you talking about?" asked young Senex. "Who are you?"

"What … you don't remember me?"

"No, not at all!"

"Oh come on Georgie! You were so drunk last night; I can still smell the booze on you."

"Go away punk!" said young Georges turning to face the other way.

Now the crowd of people were listening in and the commotion did catch the attention of three nearby police officers. Dorian got more and more animated.

"Oh yeah, you were screaming like this: *We want sex! We want sex!* and *Down with the pigs!* And you and the boys stomping your feet on that overturned cop car … that was the best part, brother! Come to California with us, brother; we could sure use a man like you!"

Young Georges had all but lost his patience and grabbed Dorian by the shirt.

"Brother this, hippy boy, I will end your karma right here and now if you don't clam up and fast, kapisch?"

"Feisty, aren't we?" said Dorian, smiling back all the while. "I love it, Master Senex!"

"Say what?"

Young Georges could hardly understand Dorian, let alone make sense of his remarks. He did realize, however, that all this attention could soon get him into a pile of trouble, guilty or not of any wrongdoing. Inevitably, the police approached and stopped the three: *'Papers please!'* And the time-consuming routine check Dorian hoped for was underway.

7

Out on the docks, Master Senex waited patiently for Jeanie. He studied those old familiar student faces passing through the crowd. They brought many a memory rushing back. Over and over again, old Georges rehearsed a few kind words to say to Jeanie. Each time, his poor old ticker skipped a beat at the sight of a red outfit rounding the corner and heading his way. What could a weathered old man possibly say to the most wonderful woman in the world, to the one who became – unbeknownst to him then – his one and only, the love of his life? He thought about it through and through but never felt quite satisfied. *You old fumbling fool,* he thought, chuckling to himself. *You may be a wise old crackpot, but you sure are no poet. Whenever will you learn?*

A suitcase plopped at his feet followed by a huge sigh of relief. Startled, Senex turned around and, lo and behold, there was Jeanie.

"Hello Sir," she said, slightly out of breath, "do you know if this is coach B?"

The old master processed the question but was unable to answer. In one singular act, Jeanie had robbed him of his vocal chords, and of his wits. The surreal event struck home and Senex remained standing there like a frozen ghost before the stunning lady in red.

"Sir?" she repeated. "Are you okay? Is this coach B?"

"Oh yes!" replied the Master. "Yes it is. I remember."

Jeanie returned a perplexed look. Senex flashed a broad smile, his petillant blue eyes sparkling like those of a young child finding his special gift on Christmas morning. Of course, Jeanie couldn't help but notice.

"May I carry your luggage on board for you, milady?" he asked like the true gentleman he was. "It looks rather cumbersome."

"Oh thank you Sir," she answered, "but this won't be necessary. I wouldn't want you to overexert yourself on my behalf."

"Not at all!" insisted Senex.

They both reached for the handle of the large rectangular suitcase and lifted it together.

"Please Sir, I'll be fine," she said, as they both struggled to gain control of the luggage. "Thank you!"

"It will give me great pleasure Jeanie, truly!" replied the Master.

Jeanie released the handle immediately and backed away.

"You know my name?" she asked. "Did I just tell you?"

Senex now huffed alone as he heaved on the bulky baggage, as per his wishes.

"Why yes," answered the Master, with a little hesitation. "You did."

Jeanie frowned, more perplexed than before.

"I mean, you must have, no?" continued the Master. "By the way, my name is Georges. And now that our introductions are done, I shall bring this suitcase on board."

Jeanie shrugged her shoulders and followed right behind the Master as he lugged the travel case onto the coach.

The Master placed the luggage with the others, in the space allotted for them at the front of the car. This was an economy coach and the alleyway was narrow, with two rows of seating on either side. He helped Jeanie aboard and guided her toward her seat.

"I am in seat 21, Mr. Georges," she said. "Where are you sitting?"

Master Senex's mind raced ahead as he tried to recall his seat number, and seeing that he had forgotten it, he made one up.

"Huh, 24!" he said. "I am right across from you, by the window."

"You didn't bring any luggage with you?" she asked.

"No!" the Master answered. "I travel light."

"Why are you not sitting down?' she asked, seeing that he stood idle in the middle of the alleyway. "The train is about to leave."

"I prefer to stand up, at least for now. It's better for my legs." The Master replied.

Jeanie seemed amused by the gentle old man. She tilted her head to the side and squinted her eyes as she took a more carefully look at him.

"Do I know you from somewhere?" she asked. "You seem oddly familiar."

"No, I can't say we've ever met," answered the Master, wearing the sting of nostalgia on his face as he stared straight into Jeanie's eyes. "Perhaps in some other life, milady," he added, forcing a grin. "Or perhaps have we crossed paths in some other karma, in some distant realm beyond the gates of our wildest dreams!"

Jeanie burst out into laughter. Her face lit up as bright as the sun, enough to melt the old man's heart.

"Mr. Georges," she said, "you are such a poet!"

The coach began to fill up fast. The Master scanned the docks, keeping an eye out for his younger self, in case the boy should find his way onto the train after all, despite Dorian and Xiao Ren's efforts to stall him. The clock whistled 8 o'clock. At last, the conductor announced the immediate departure of the train and did his last minute checks. The Master snuck toward the exit, satisfied that Jeanie was on the train and that young Georges was not. The old druid concluded that his colleagues had succeeded in holding the boy back. Then, just as the doors were closing, Master Senex jumped off the coach. He smiled, content of a job well done, and looked up to see a young man rushing out of the terminal, weaving his way through the crowd and screaming for the train to wait. It was young Georges indeed.

8

Master Senex could not believe his eyes. The train had not yet started to roll and the old man now worried that the boy would derail their plans after all.

"Stop the train!" yelled young Georges, insisting. "Keep the door open, please, Sir! I have to get on that train."

Senex understood that the boy had intended his words for him, and although the Master still had it in his power to keep the door jammed open until the boy arrived, he pretended not to hear the request.

"Damn!" cried young Georges. "It's shut!"

He pounded on the door of the wagon, hoping the conductor or the passengers would notice. Someone did. Of all the people inside coach number three, Jeanie answered the call of distress. She got up from her seat and, to her surprise, noticed that old Georges and a young man were standing outside on the dock. She rushed to the door and yelled to get the attention of the conductor.

"Please, open the door!" begged young Georges as he locked eyes with the beauty in red who had come to his rescue.

"It's locked!" she replied, as she struggled to pry the door open. "Someone help!"

The conductor arrived just as the train moved forward. Young Georges pounded on the door again, begging the controller to do something, while Jeanie pleaded her case on behalf of old Georges.

"I can't do anything," said the controller. "There is another train leaving at 10 o'clock," he continued, signaling the time with the help of his fingers.

The train then picked up speed and the two young people – who might have otherwise shared a full life together under more favorable circumstances – stared at each other while watching karma roll away, unawares.

The Stealth Demon was only a fraction away from cutting Amy's throat open as he started his countdown. Amy's eyes started to roll skyward under the pressure of the demon's claws. Solas's eyes mimicked those of Amy, as he looked up to the heavens too, praying for divine intervention. Then he witnessed the most singular event unfold before him. The Stealth Demon began to vanish into nothingness, slowly, at the rate of the train at the Union Station docks pulling apart young Georges and Jeanie. In this parallel reality, the couple would never meet. Hence, the Stealth Demon could never exist. The beast's claws retracted, his dark scaly skin fizzled away, while his body and limbs transited into a more distinguishable and familiar form: young Solas Gambit. Amy stumbled away to the ground, released from the demon's grip. The beast was no more, yet for the briefest of moment, eyes aghast, the lingering spirit of the Stealth Demon witnessed its truer self. Incredulous, the boy lifted his eyes only to vaporize, by the manifestation of some ghostly vapor, straight into the realm of Neverwas. Forthwith, an object plopped onto the cold tile floor, gently bouncing and pinging as it settled down. It was the dark luret, the negatron of the Will-master's luret. Its opposite force, the positron – or white luret – had already melded onto the hilt of Lux Veritas.

Amy stood up, shaken but otherwise unscathed. She walked slowly toward Solas and hugged him without saying a word, as though they had never been apart. Both stared at the vacant space once occupied by the Stealth Demon.

"They did it!" said Solas.

He slotted Lux Veritas and picked up the dark luret with a profound measure of respect. Solas held the mystical object in the palm of his hands and observed its intricacies before entrusting the relic to Amy.

"Hold on to it!" said Solas. "I am getting us out of here."

Solas drew Lux Veritas once again and after conjuring up the white luret, the cocoon appeared and the couple made a fast exit out of Orboz Purgator.

9

Solas rushed his vessel back toward parallel planet Earth to pick up his trio of friends. He explained the situation to his travel companion Amy, giving her the quick version of the events. Solas guided the luret out of public sight, landing behind a hedgerow at the Union Station freight yard. The couple then ran toward the docks of the passenger trains where they tried to locate Master Senex, Dorian and Xiao Ren. Solas did his best to keep a low profile since he still carried with him the mighty Lux Veritas. The whistle clock indicated 8:08.

"They should be around here somewhere," said Solas.

The docks still swarmed with people and cluttered with sounds, one of them the loud cries of a drunken vagrant swearing that he saw Jesus land in a spaceship.

"I see Master Senex," said Solas, "right over there, near that drifter!"

"And isn't that Dorian and Xiao Ren too?" added Amy.

"You're right!" replied Solas. "Let's go get them."

Now, Solas and Amy threw caution to the wind. It did not matter any longer if there was public concern over Lux Veritas. They had a visual on their friends and soon they would all be gone in a flash. Still the couple picked up the pace through the crowd.

"Master!" called Solas, as he got closer.

"Solas!" the trio yelled back. "Amy!"

The friends cheered, embraced and rejoiced over their reunion and overwhelming success.

"Hallelujah! Hallelujah!" screamed the nearby drunk as he witnessed the new gathering.

This public disturbance caught the attention of the police officers still scouring the station in search of the handful of culprits of yesternight, and their presence doused the party's high spirits.

"Hey you!" said one of the officers. There were the two familiar policemen, just 20 feet away.

"Damn!" said Dorian. "It's those same cops again. They almost arrested us; we had no papers."

"Let's run!" said Solas. "Follow me!"

The band was indeed on the run again and a clear order to stop proved useless. Now the police were fast after them as Dorian helped the Master to trot along and keep up the pace. The group no sooner rounded the corner of the next building that the luret activated propelling the band away and over blue yonder. The officers, who arrived mere seconds behind, now stared into a void and felt about as empty.

10

Solas returned to Earth Purgator looking for Lord Uffa, the wily old Sage of the Grotto, the watchman of the Diamond Crossing. And when Solas landed his friends this side of the Tesseract, the tall bearded druid was waiting there, as stalwart as a Greek statue.

"Welcome back!" declared Lord Uffa.

"Hello again old friend!" said Master Senex.

"Hello Lord Uffa," replied Solas. "You were expecting us?"

"Well of course I was," the druid answered. "You were right, Solas: good news travels fast. Your victory had an immediate impact in Purgator. There was a massive exodus of the unwanted, a cataclysmic whoosh that sucked much of the evil straight off our land and out through the Diamond Gates. I knew then that you had won, and of course, that you would soon be returning."

"Well that's great news!" replied a joyous Solas. "And here we are in the flesh!"

"Not only did you vanquish the Stealth Demon, but you also freed the lovely Amy, I see," added Lord Uffa. He turned to her and offered his greetings, and Amy was eager to return hers. "I should presume that you also have in your possession the dark luret, my dear boy."

"Yes I do!" replied Solas with pride. "Well, Amy does actually."

The girl pulled out the object from her pocket to show it off to everyone.

"Ha!" exclaimed the old druid. "What a lovely piece indeed! Well, that should complete the puzzle then, doesn't it?"

"Well, not really," replied Solas. "I still don't know how to pry off the white luret from Lux Veritas." Solas presented the sword again so that the Sage and the Master could study the object once more. "Do you guys have any more worthy suggestions?"

"Well, as I told you before," said Lord Uffa. "*Mighty is the man who can tear asunder what the Lord Creator has joined together.* However, I do have an idea. Bring me the dark luret please."

Everyone gathered around the sword as Amy delivered the dark luret to Lord Uffa, all under the watchful eye of the living, breathing Diamond Gates.

"I just wonder," said the old Sage, "if I bring the two opposite lurets closer together …"

Before Uffa finished his sentence, the white luret began to lift from the sword, as though under the effect of some powerful magnetic pull. Lord Uffa held on tight to the dark luret, grunting all the while, and Solas gripped Lux Veritas with both hands to resist the force. Then, both lurets spun loose at once and landed on the dusty ground, spiralling out of control just two feet apart from each other, before settling on a continuous spinning pattern, while being suspended five inches off the ground.

"Wow, you did it!" said Solas. "Lux Veritas is whole again. Bravo, Lord Uffa!"

"That was a lucky shot," replied Uffa, shrugging his shoulders. "I was just playing a hunch. Positive and negative forces always seem to repel each other, yet they attract each other too. What do I know?"

"Well, it worked!" said Solas. "Now what will we do with the two lurets, and Lux Veritas?" he continued. "We have accomplished our mission. My friends and I must return home, as does Master Senex; only he belongs to Purgator one fortnight removed!"

"After all that, you are still a worrywart," replied Lord Uffa. "What if I told you that I too can navigate the white luret?"

"You can?"

"Of course I can!" answered the old Sage. "I just never had the chance to prove my skills. Still, I have learned most of the luret's secrets over time. Moreover, I have seen a lot too, in my time posted here before the Diamond Gates. Just follow your intuition and the whims of the heart, isn't that right Solas? And surely you will agree, if Fergus the leprechaun can use it, then so can I!"

The members of the group began to laugh. Lord Uffa had a talent for putting words into perspective, as well as delicate situations.

"Here is what I propose," he said. "I shall take you, Solas, along with the lovely Amy, the brave Dorian and the splendid Xiao Ren back to Earth, and we all shall see how well I fare."

"What about the Diamond Crossing?" Solas asked.

"What of it? I shall be back in a flash, won't I?" answered Uffa. "Besides, I do leave it unattended from time to time. I am only human after all."

"And what about Master Senex?" asked Xiao Ren.

"He will be the next one home!"

"Great, that's one thing," said Solas. "But what will become of the lurets and the mighty Lux Veritas now?"

"I have a plan," answered Lord Uffa. "I will go with the twin lurets to the temple of Kashi and bring them back to Guru Roshni, to be placed in the care of his monks. That's where they belong."

"I hope they do a better job of keeping an eye on them this time!" said Dorian.

"We live and learn," replied the old druid. "As for Lux Veritas," he continued, "I shall become its custodian, for now; I have just the perfect place for her," he said with a wink. "At first opportunity, I will send a messenger to find shaman Chepi in Lalas Pur. He will come for the sword, I am sure."

After further consideration, Solas and his friends agreed with the plan proposed by druid Uffa. Eager to get back home, the group prepared for the next launching of the luret, Lord Uffa style.

I I

The voyage went off without a hitch. The old Sage landed the cocoon right on the slope of the Iroquois fields across from Solas's house.

"Home!" screamed Amy and Xiao Ren.

"Well done, Lord Uffa," said Solas. "You got some skills for a novice!"

"Thank you very much!" replied the druid. "I only hope I landed us in the right time frame too."

"I think you did," replied Solas. "I can see a police helicopter hovering over the Iroquois complex on top of the hill. They must be looking for the killer of shaman Orenda. This event occurred only a short time ago, in relative terms. So that could only mean that we are in the right time and place. Let's get to my house and see Grandma Jeanie now."

The group arrived and burst through the front door. Jeanie was waiting.

"Solas!" she said, as she hugged her boy and stared straight at the hilt of Lux Veritas.

"Oh my goodness!" she said as she stepped back.

"That's Lux Veritas, Grandma!" explained Solas.

"She's ... beautiful!"

She looked around at his company and noticed two unusual characters standing at the rear. Grandma Jeanie soon concluded Solas had rid them of the Stealth Demon.

"You did it, didn't you?"

"I sure did," answered Solas, "with a little help from my friends here."

"Oh thank you, thank you all very much!" she said, as she saluted the two strangers.

"This is Lord Uffa," said Solas as he presented the tall druid. "He comes from the heart of Holy Mountain, in Purgator. He is the keeper of the Diamond Gates."

"Oh!" said Grandma.

"I'll explain later."

"Nice to meet you," said Jeanie.

"My pleasure Madam," replied the old Sage of the Grotto.

"And this is ..."

"Georges!" she uttered, recognizing at that instant the man beneath the white shaggy hair and scruffy beard.

Master Senex smiled.

"Hello sweetheart!" he said, his eyes sparkling brighter than Lux Veritas on a good day. "It is I."

Jeanie put her hands over her face and began to tremble as she approached him in little steps. Georges welcomed her with opened arms.

"Words will never be enough to let you know just how much I miss you, Jeanie!"

"Ditto!" she replied, ditto being a longstanding Gambit family trademark.

Jeanie stumbled into his arms and began to squeeze him as the couple shared a warm embrace. Solas and Dorian smiled while Amy and Xiao Ren stood on the verge of tears.

The police sirens went off in the distance, in another one of life's cruel twists. The cruisers were heading up the hill toward Grandma's house, and fast approaching.

"Damn!" Dorian said, summing up in one word everyone's feelings. "What do they want now?"

"Don't panic!" said Solas. "It may not be for us. They're probably looking for a killer in a Halloween costume, remember?"

"Time is up already, I'm afraid," said Lord Uffa. "We should leave now."

"I shall wait for you beyond the Crystal Gates, my love!" said Georges. "Don't you be late now!" he added, wearing a mischievous smile.

Solas quickly handed Lux Veritas and the sheath to the Master. Jeanie stepped back and stood amazed as she watched Lord Uffa work the magic of the white luret.

"Bye Solas!" said Senex. "I shall see you again soon, my boy. Godspeed my friends!"

Solas returned a thumbs-up.

"I love you!" Jeanie cried out at the last instant.

"Ditto, my love!" replied the Master, as he blew her a kiss farewell the moment the luret burst away in a flash.

She waved and smiled. Her eyes welled up with tears, and then she collapsed in the arms of Solas.